Rub X
Rubino, Jane.
Plot twist : a Cat
  Austen/Victor Card$ 24.95
1st ed.

 W9-DIJ-589

PLOT TWIST

A Cat Austen/Victor Cardenas Mystery
by
Jane Rubino

A Write Way Publishing Book

The series:
Death of a DJ
Fruitcake
Cheat the Devil

This book is a work of fiction. The characters, incidents and dialogue are products of the author's imagination and are not to be construed as real. Any resemblance to actual events, organizations or to persons living or dead is entirely coincidental.

Copyright © 2000, by Jane Rubino

Write Way Publishing
PO Box 441278
Aurora, CO 80044

First Edition; 2000

All rights reserved. No part of this book may be reproduced in any form, except by a newspaper or magazine reviewer who wishes to quote brief passages in connection with a review.

Queries regarding rights and permissions should be addressed to Write Way Publishing, PO Box 441278, Aurora, CO 80044
email: staff@writewaypub.com

ISBN 1-885173-80-6

1 2 3 4 5 6 7 8 9 10

For My Family
Bronwyn, Caitlen, Nicholas
Bill

One man—like this—but only so much longer
As life is longer than a summer's day,
Believed himself a king upon his throne,
And play'd at hazard with his fellows' lives,
Who cheaply dream'd away their lives to him.
The sailor dream'd of tossing on the flood:
The soldier of his laurels grown in blood:
The lover of the beauty that he knew
Must yet dissolve to dusty residue:
The merchant and the miser of his bags
Of finger'd gold; the beggar of his rags:
And all this stage of earth on which we seem
Such busy actors, and the parts we play'd,
Substantial as the shadow of a shade,
And Dreaming but a dream within a dream!
Life is a Dream
—Pedro Calderon de la Barca

PROLOGUE

EXT: BEACHFRONT PARKING LOT: NIGHT
GERRY grabs KATE'S arms, shoves her against the side of the car.

GERRY (Spitefully)
I don't need you! I know plenty reporters'd pay me for what I got up here—

GERRY taps his forehead. Camera pulls back to reveal a gloved hand gripping a revolver in the foreground, unseen by GERRY and KATE.

GERRY
—all's I gotta do to cut you outta the loop is drop a dime!

KATE yanks herself free, backs off.

KATE
Drop dead.

The gun is fired twice. GERRY lunges forward,

hit. He falls against KATE, throwing her
to the ground.

Cat Austen flipped to the few faxed call sheets tucked inside the front cover of the script.

COPWATCH PRODUCTIONS PRESENTS
Death of a Shock Jock
Date: Monday, March 25; Sunset: 6:15 PM
Day: 1 out of 6; Weather: Clear/hi 30s
Crew Call: 7 AM Location TBA; 6 PM, Site One
Paragon Studios/CopWatch Productions
Director: Eduardo Melendez
Producer: April Steinmetz
Executive Producer: Lou Tellegen
Associate Producer: June Mathis
Screenplay: Harold Anderson

Cat let the cover close with a soft vinyl slap, took a sip of her cappuccino, checked her watch. It was the sort of crisp, sunny Saturday morning she didn't want to give over to work. *CopWatch* had commanded her wits, her recollections, her patient ear for the past month. Their frenzied preparations consumed real time, yet she refused to be taken in. *Death of a Shock Jock* would fall into pre-production limbo. It would never be.

"Jeez, Cat," her brother Freddy had declared, "whaddaya mean, you don't believe it? Why wouldn't they shoot here? Tell me, where in the US were they makin' movies before they cut to the Coast?"

"New Jersey," she said.

"New Jersey." As if that settled it. Freddy was star-struck. They all were. Only Victor was untouched by the adrenaline.

Cat was sitting in the back room of the North End Café, a coffee shop a few blocks from her home. It was a favorite hangout of the local newspaper people, writers, artists. Two rooms, wooden floors, local artwork on the pastel walls, soft jazz or reggae from the speakers mounted in a corner, the local papers stacked on a shelf by the door.

A mural, daffodils and hyacinths, had been tempera painted onto the large unshaded windows, muting the strong eastern light. Through the green stalks, Cat saw Ron Spivak's slender form sprint along the sidewalk, waved.

Cat heard the cowbell clang at the door; after a moment Ron appeared with a cup of coffee in one hand, a plate of poppy-seed scones in the other.

Ron Spivak was a reporter, the colleague to whom Cat owed her involvement in the Jerry Dudek murder, her consequent involvement with *CopWatch*. He had been good-looking before the accident that had compelled him to drop the Dudek piece, just nondescript enough to lull suspicion, just handsome enough to charm confessions from the reluctant. The accident, the reconstructive surgeries had given his features a revealing asymmetry. Compelling still, but with the subtlety stripped away; now, Cat thought, he wore his soul.

Cat would be the first to concede that the Dudek piece had been a fluke. She had been—was—"Entertainment Girl" for *South Jersey Magazine*, the logical successor to the Dudek profile when Ron had to back out. Then, the TV series *CopWatch* seized on the script potential of the shock jock's murder, announced their intention to shoot some of the principal photography in Atlantic City where the murder had occurred and signed this year's strongest Oscar contender to star as Kate (Cat).

Competition for proximity to the shoot was fierce among local journalists and Ron was not willing to cede the inside track to Cat or anyone else. He had actually gotten himself cast in the small, pivotal role of Gerry Donner (Dudek), on the strength of his bit part in some TV movie shot in Philly the previous spring, was plotting a ruthless course to the star at the center of the shoot.

"Got anything lined up with Her?" he asked.

Cat could not think of Her in lower case. "Nothing definite. I've got to set it up through Her PR person."

"The formidable Dianne King." Ron's restless fingers wandered to the bridge of his nose; it was his third and best prosthesis, a keeper. "She's got this Garbo shtick down cold." Shtick came out 'shdig'; other than that, the consonants had cleared up considerably since last fall. "You dig up any of Her backstory?"

Cat shook her head. "What everyone has. *Illyria*, the marriage, the make-over, the career, the filmography. I'm just starting off with 'A Day on the Set' for Ritchie."

"I'm done with 'A Day on the Set.' Small time."

Cat shrugged, a bit nettled. "*I'm* small time."

"You are what you settle for." He paused. "I mean, don't you ever wonder where she came from, what she was doin' before *Illyria*, back in the day?"

"She was a nobody back in the day. Good heavens, Ron, if nobodies were worth knowing about, *I'd* be a celebrity."

"Nobody's born famous."

"I know. Some achieve fame and some have fame thrust upon them," Cat paraphrased from *Twelfth Night*.

"And some grab it by the balls."

"I must have missed that line. But I'm thinking you didn't ask me to meet you so that we could misquote Shakespeare."

Ron's grin went lopsided. "Nope, I wanna ask you to keep an eye on my place, I gotta go out of town."

"When are you leaving?"

"I have to shoot the insert with Cici Bonaker this afternoon, I'm flying out tonight. Be back Tuesday."

"Tuesday!" Cat flipped open the script, pulled out Monday's call sheet. "You're supposed to be on the set Monday for the funeral scene."

"So, April plops a wig on some bozo who's five eleven, forty regular."

Cat lifted her dark brows. "Ron, I don't get it. *The* celebrity interview is in town for a week and you're giving the rest of us nearly three days of a head start?"

"Churning out 'A Day on the Set'? Takes more than that to make me nervous." Ron shook his head. "Or you got 'Local Extras in *CopWatch* Cast,' too?"

"'Background,'" she said. "They don't say 'extras,' they say 'background.'"

Ron winked. "And background's what I'm after." He pushed his plate to the center of the table, nodded at the sprinkling of crumbs. "That all you're willing to go after?"

Cat shuddered. There was a callousness in the remark that was so like Jerry Dudek's. Dudek, homely and vicious, exuded a sort of weasely charm, died with three women wearing his ring(s). Ron could be charming, too, in a wily fashion, and he was attractive and glib, a chameleon. Casting him in the minor role of "Gerry Donner" had been inspired.

"What sort of background?" she asked.

Ron poked at the stray poppy seeds with an index finger. "You know anything about her husband, ever check out his client list?"

Cat nodded. "Gloria Ramirez, Teresa D., the rapper who calls himself Bigg Phat—with-a-PH—P.I.G. Eric Obermeyer before he died, the actress you mentioned, Cici Bonaker? Ritchie told me the two of you were dating for awhile."

Ron shrugged. "She's with Hal, now. Whaddaya think of him as a writer?"

Cat rolled her eyes. She had endured a dozen frantic phone conversations with Harold Anderson, who had scored a double coup: third billing as "Tim Harper," and, after Ted Cusack's arrest, the episode's screenwriter. "I thought he would just want the background,

and he'd flesh it out from there, but we keep getting mired in minu-
tiae: 'Should I say weapon or piece? Should I stick with Kate or maybe
go with Kit? Did Jerry grab me and *whirl* me around or grab me and
spin me around? Or *seize* me and spin me around?' He has got to be the
most insecure person I've ever talked to. I hope he's a better actor."

"Didn't you check us out in *South Street Stakeout?*"

Cat shook her head.

"I'm crushed. You can borrow my copy. It's how the three of us
hooked up, me, Cici and Harold." Ron dug into his pockets and
tossed his keys on the table. "Top lock, bottom lock, mailbox. Just
dump the mail on my desk. Oh, and recyclables, paper in the bedroom, cans and bottles in the kitchen, can you put them out?"

"No problem."

"The movie's on the bookshelf in the living room. Don't blink
or you'll miss my two lines. Oh, and I got a folder with the articles I
did on the Philly shoot in my file cabinet. Says 'Spivak' and *South
Street Stakeout*, I think there's some copy on Hal." He shifted to his
"Gerry" voice, "Gerry" mode. "There's plenty reporters'd pay me for
what I got in there. All I gotta do is drop a dime."

Cat smiled, weakly.

"It's your line, Cat-Kate-Kit," he prompted.

"I haven't gotten that far in the script yet," she lied.

"It's 'drop dead.'" He did his Gerry Donner cackle.

Cat felt a shudder scuttle up her ribs.

"Drop dead," he repeated, pointed his index finger at his temple
and said, "Ka-pow."

CHAPTER ONE

INT: KATE'S BEDROOM: NIGHT
*Camera tracks KATE'S leg as she slowly draws
on a black stocking, pulls back as she stands
and faces her reflection in the mirror.*

KATE (to her reflection)
Just this one. As a favor to Ricky. And then no
more damn celebrity profiles.

Kate. That was *Her*. Cat looked over the cast sheet, the copy of
the deal memo that pledged *Her* participation in *CopWatch*, still could
not believe that *CopWatch* had achieved the unimaginable, had lured
the last great goddess of the screen, four-time Academy Award nominee, Best Actress shoo-in for *Redemption*, away from her pre-Oscar
junket to star in their *Death of a Shock Jock* episode. To play Cat. Not
Cat Austen, of course. It was Kate, now, Kate Auletta, rogue reporter/
amateur sleuth. Cat's name, kids, best friend, brothers, late husband
had not made the cut.

Green-lighted (green lit?) and fast-tracked to make a May sweeps
air date. When April Steinmetz, the episode's line producer/location
scout told Cat that She had been signed, Cat sighed. Hollywood
hype. When June Mathis, the producer's associate/assistant script
supervisor phoned Cat to ask where she wanted the script notes, the

call sheets, her set pass sent and said, yes, She had started shooting the principal photography, Cat smiled. Hollywood hoax. When co-star/screenwriter Harold "I-know-you-don't-know-me" Anderson had initiated the series of telephoned, e-mailed script conferences ("Should the cop say 'scum*bag*' or 'scum*wad*'? 'Roust' or 'brace'? 'Doer' or 'perp'?"), and maintained that he had gotten the job because he knew someone who knew Her, Cat shook her head. Hollywood hopes.

Then Ron Spivak buffed up his SAG card, tested for (won!) the role of DJ "Gerry Donner," and Cat began to suspect that there might be something to the rumor, because if there was anything Ron knew how to do, it was how to weasel himself into a hot story.

The last spark of skepticism was snuffed when Butler Talent Management's publicist, Mrs. King, phoned to suggest that Cat join April Steinmetz when April met Her at the airport. The limo would come for her at three-thirty, Sunday afternoon. Unless, of course, it was not convenient for Mrs. Austen to meet Her at that time.

Not *convenient*! Cat cringed as she recalled her tongue-tied, "Uh, no, three-thirty's fine," vacillated in a silk teddy, upswept hair, third best earrings, *makeup* for heaven's sake, with a *limo* coming in five minutes *And The Nominees Were ...*

Jeans, white shirt, black blazer, black boots? No.

Gray ankle-length dress with matching cardigan? No.

Navy slacks, white cotton/poly shirt, wool vest? No.

Plaid skirt, ribbed turtleneck? Maybe. Cat scrutinized her hips. No.

Brown silk slacks, white silk shirt, paisley scarf. No.

From below, Jane screamed, "The *limo's* out*side*!"

And The Winner Is ...

Her family, gathered for a Sunday meal, fell into a death-row silence as she came down the stairs, an awe that Lorraine punctured with, "Is *that* what you're wearing?"

Cat began to pivot, but Ellice lunged, grabbed her shoulders and shoved her toward the door. "C'mon, kid, the audience is waiting," she hissed, "Now get out there and shine!"

April Steinmetz shoved aside her sheaf of papers to make room for
Cat, glared at the mantle of opaque glass. "Is this typical? Is this typical
Jersey?" April Steinmetz had worn the jeans, the white sweater, the
low-heeled black boots, but the blazer was cherry red like the tendrils
of hair she poked back into the delinquent chignon. "This is June." She
nodded to the wan figure to her left. "What's with the fog?"

Cat realized that she was supposed to say something. "Perhaps
it's the visitation of the gods. Wasn't Danaë covered with mist? Of
course, that was gold, not silver."

"Danny? That local got hired on the security crew?"

Cat sighed.

"I did not budget fog. The call sheet for Monday says 'clear,
slightly overcast.' June, get the Weather Channel."

June's head bobbed. She was quite devoid of melanin, hips; she
favored oversized jeans, black high-top sneakers.

"Listen," April went on, "This here's just your meet-and-greet,
how much actual face time you log is up to her and goes through
Dianne King. Or him, Butler. The Pig, I think I can hook you up,
and Red, he'd kill for some copy. And then there's Harold and Cici
Bonaker."

Cat mentally plucked the names from short-term memory: Talent czar Ben Butler was *Her* husband of twenty-one years. The Pig
was the rap star Bigg Phat P.I.G., from whom Jane had instructed
Cat to obtain a signed 8x10 glossy, personalized, *or else she would die.*
Red was Red Melendez, actor-director-activist whose star had risen
and waned with the long-since-canceled television series, *The Advocates;*
directing, co-starring (as "Lieutenant Victor Calderone"), in *Death of
a Shock Jock*, was what Ron Spivak referred to as a "Lazarus gig." Cat
wondered what had motivated his resurrection. "A hungry director is
an accommodating director," Ron Spivak had told her. "They're not
budgeted for artistic differences." Perhaps a hungry actor/writer was
an accommodating actor/writer, Cat concluded, for Harold Ander-

son had snagged the screenplay, the co-starring role on a lackluster résumé that consisted of a one-act play, Ted Cusack's arrest, WGA dues paid in full and seventeen years of commercials, bit parts and regional theatre. "Cici Bonaker?" she asked.

"She's the fast track to Her. That's how come your pal Spivak knows her. You see his test, by the way? Terrific. Slime, but with a certain charm. What I'm thinking the real Dudek musta been like. You see *South Street Stakeout?*"

"No." A TV movie. Ron, angling for copy, had coaxed a talent agent to pitch him to the casting director, not only made the cut but snagged a pair of lines, "He's got a gun!" and "He's got a *gun!*"

"Yeah, well he knows Cici from there. She's been Her stand-in for, what, six years, but she wants to act and Butler's priming her. You saw *Redemption*, right?"

Cat nodded.

"She's the gal who played Selena in the flashbacks."

Cat called up a frame from memory. "That's an amazing resemblance."

"Nice kid. Talented, too. *Shock Jock*'s a backdoor pilot. It goes series? Cici's Kate. June get you your rundown sheets?"

"Yes." *Series?*

"It'll be called *Auletta!*"

Cat heard the exclamation point, winced. "And she's ... this Cici Bonaker ..?" *Another* me?

"Yup. Skinny is that's the real reason *She*'s doing *CopWatch.* Butler's got a verbal handshake from the network. He produces Her and The Pig, a week from now She hooks up with Uncle Oscar, I deliver for the May sweeps, and Cici'll ink a guaranteed forty episodes. I heard she's pretty tight with Harold, got Butler to okay him for development."

Cat wondered if she should read anything into June's sigh. "What happened to her and Ron?"

April's shrug set off a downward undulation along her plump form. "They were tight on the set of *South Street Stakeout,* then he had the nose thing, she went to England for *Redemption*'s London premiere."

"That's the coverage; what's the backstory?" Cat had been studying the lingo.

April snorted. "Spivak came on to Cici to get close to *Her*, Cici got wise, Harold caught her on the bounce." April shook her head. "You shoulda seen his test. Slime. Great."

The limo had coasted so smoothly to a stop that it took a moment for Cat to realize they were no longer moving. The fog was separating into spirals, revealing fragments of pavement. Flashes of light cut through the fog. Cat thought that it was lightning, thunder; but the flashes were bulbs, the vibrations were the human voices chanting the three syllables of Her name.

"Here She comes." April's voice had dropped to a hush.

The flashing bulbs peeled away at the fog and a form materialized in fragments; a loose indigo dress billowing with the graceful gait, waves of red-brown hair, a tan, slender arm. Now Cat saw indigo eyes, now the high, symmetrical cheekbones, now the smooth, unlined forehead, now the enigmatic smile, then all of it together, the radiant, unearthly beauty of the most beautiful woman in the world, floating closer, closer. Closer, she glowed brighter, revealing a perfection that was not a gimmick of the screen, a trick of lighting, a cosmetically-induced camouflage.

I only caught a glimpse of her at the moment, but she was a lovely woman with a face that a man might die for. The line was from *A Scandal in Bohemia*, Sherlock Holmes' description of *The* Woman, Irene Adler. *She* had played Adler in a BBC version of the adventure, her only other television credit. Until now. Until she consented to the inconceivable, to a guest appearance on *CopWatch. Death of a Shock Jock.* Playing *me*, Cat thought.

She felt her lips moving silently, picking up the cadence of the cries outside the airport. Tommi Ann, Tommi *ANN, TOMMI ANN.*

She heard herself whisper, "Tommi Ann Butler." And it became real.

CHAPTER TWO

INT: NIGHTCLUB LOBBY: NIGHT

*KATE AULETTA slips into the club's lobby. A
few people are hanging around. They are all
younger, flashier. For a moment KATE looks
like she wants to back out, then decides to
hold her ground.*

KATE (to herself)
This is going to turn out to be a mistake, I
know it. These are not my kind of people.

Cat found herself sitting opposite the tall, broad-shouldered man
wearing a shearling jacket that had cost money over the-hell-with-
how-I-dress jeans, blue chambray shirt. Ben Butler, Tommi Ann Butler's
husband and manager. Butler was about fifty with a rugged virility
that seemed more backwoods than Hollywood, very handsome, with
brown hair graying at the temples, broad shoulders, several inches
taller than Tommi Ann, who had to be about five eleven. He was the
lord of Butler Talent Management, a boutique agency that guided a
handful of careers to megastar status. "His rejects," Ron had told her,
"are everybody else's A list." The slight woman with the tinted spectacles, so light-skinned that Cat knew she was black only because Ron
had told her, was Dianne King, Butler's publicist, who doubled as

Tommi Ann's right hand, the only other constant in Tommi Ann's surprisingly spare galaxy.

And then there was Tommi Ann Butler. Four feet away, under scrutiny, which Cat hoped came off as polite interest and not goggle-eyed awe, no fault lines emerged, no shadows, no blot on the perfection.

"It's lovely to meet you at last, Mrs. Austen," Tommi Ann said. She had a refined, fluid contralto. The eyes were chameleon hazel; her indigo dress made them sparkle like sapphires.

She spoke to me. Tommi Ann Butler, the most beautiful woman on the screen, four-time Oscar nominee, spoke to ME. DON'T SAY ANYTHING DUMB. "Uh, thanks."

A blue-jacketed form materialized at the open door; Cat caught a glimpse of COPWATCH SECURITY on a nylon windbreaker. He leaned down, and Cat was surprised to see a familiar face. "Mrs. Butler, I'll be riding in front. Is there anything else you need?"

"No, thank you."

"Cat."

Cat raised her chin. "Danny."

He closed the door, soundlessly, got in the front.

"You know him?" April asked.

Cat nodded.

"He's a card."

"Wild card," Cat muttered.

April turned to Tommi Ann. "I'm telling Cat here that she'll have to go through Dianne to get some face time, timewise, we're tight. I told her maybe she'll wanna get some copy on Cici while we're here."

Tommi Ann smiled. She had a smile that emerged, her face a serene mask one moment, the next the eyes were glistening, the lips curved, the transition seamless. "I believe Cici and Harold will be waiting for us at the hotel. Have you met Harold Anderson, Mrs. Austen?"

"We spoke on the phone several times. About the script, the characters. He seems very"—*insecure*—"nice." *Good Lord.*

"He's quite a talented actor."

"I haven't seen him in anything."

"I hope you didn't tell him so," Tommi Ann said. "Actors have gossamer egos."

"Yeah, but writers are dense as redwoods," April added. She looked at Cat. "No offense."

"None taken," Cat replied, stowed the phrase *Gossamer Egos* as a working title for one of the half dozen pieces she hoped to wring out of the *CopWatch* shoot.

"That boy needs better representation," Ben Butler observed. "Time he made his mark."

Cat saw June's head bob unconsciously in accord, felt the tickle of laughter threatening to undo what little composure she had. No use, the laugh emerged, and the others looked at her, curiously. "I'm sorry, I'm sorry." She felt a ripple of movement as April shifted away from her, afraid, perhaps, that Cat had insulted the Butlers, trying to establish distance between herself and this small-time reporter who was Not One Of Them.

"It's just that," Cat explained, "I can't imagine what it must be like to work as long as Harold Anderson worked—he told me he'd been at this for about seventeen years—and finally make your mark as psycho-killer-of-the-week on *CopWatch.*"

Tommi Ann's laugh was as lovely as everything else about her.

"I toldja she was a hoot," April assured them. "I toldja talking to her was something else."

Cat couldn't remember ever saying anything amusing in her few phone conversations with April.

"Our pinnacles can't always be traced to our beginnings, Mrs. Austen. Nor conform to our expectations. I'm sure Harold is grateful that his break came when he's got time to make something of it." The gemstone eyes were not cold, but they were penetrating, targeting that chord of empathy that a small-time actor who caught a break ought to inspire in a small-time reporter who had done the same.

"You don't believe in luck, then?"

"I believe in a delicate balance of talent and wanton desperation." Tommi Ann leaned forward, patted Cat's hand. "I imagine you must be somewhat apprehensive, Mrs. Austen. Watching actors recreate these particular incidents must be almost as bad as having lived through them."

"Worse." Cat ordered her inner censor to shape up.

But Butler laughed, and even Dianne King smiled. Cat thought that Mrs. King had completely tuned them out. The moment she seated herself in the car, she had taken a crossword puzzle from her tote bag, adjusted her tinted spectacles and begun working her way through it. Cat had glanced into the tote, seen several soft-bound books, MENSA this and MENSA that. Apparently, the Butlers did not suffer fools.

"Did I tell you?" April gave Cat a proprietary nudge, closed the couple inches she had put between them. "Did I tell you how she talks?"

Cat felt like she was on stage, being prompted to say something clever. "Of course, this time, nobody's really going to get shot." *Did I really say that?*

"No?" Tommi Ann affected a pampered star's whine. "But I was *promised.*"

"Well, hell, sugar, anyone doesn't suit you, just point him out, I'll open fire."

"Ben, my love, what will Mrs. Austen think?"

"I'll think that 'there are always some lunatics about. It would be a dull world without them.' Sherlock Holmes."

Dianne King laid down her pen. "You read Conan Doyle, Mrs. Austen?"

"My, um ..." How should she refer to Victor? Boyfriend? "Lieutenant Cardenas does. He believes that the principles of investigation are pretty much contained in the Canon."

"Wise." Dianne had an agelessness about her, a face where the planes angled smoothly from high cheekbones, arched black brows, dark hair that had a reddish aura.

"That's Calderone," April interpreted. "The one Red's playing. The guy who's been stonewalling us."

Tommi Ann dropped her voice to a conspiratorial whisper. "Perhaps we can ingratiate ourselves if we confess that we're readers, too."

Cat smiled. "I was thinking of Conan Doyle when you got into the car. His description of Irene Adler. 'A face that a man might die for.'"

"I loved the story, of course. I even played her. But the idea, to die for a beautiful face?" Tommi Ann shrugged. Her shrug had the composure, the exquisite indifference of immutable beauty.

The fog had cocooned them, insulated them from peripheral distraction, though Cat didn't think that anything could divert attention from Tommi Ann's mesmerizing presence, not until April shrieked, "Is that an elephant's *butt?*"

The driver had taken the leisurely route to Absecon Island, driven down the boulevard, the bridge into Margate, and turned left on Atlantic Avenue, bringing Margate's claim to kitsch into view.

"That's Lucy the Elephant," Cat explained, blushed a bit, as if she were responsible for this sixty-five-foot oddity. "It's sort of a tourist attraction. You can go inside, there's a little museum. Outside there's a gift shop." She felt a little silly, as though she were attempting to rationalize a pachyderm in her parlor.

April was transfixed, her round eyes taking in the object's dimensions, speculating on the possibility of a crane shot into the howdah. "Maybe we could move the Kate and Tim slugfest up there, you think? And then Tim could, maybe, go over the side and—" she smacked her palms together. She looked at Cat accusingly. "When we were scouting locations, why didn't you tell me about this?"

"I guess it slipped my mind."

"You got a sixty-foot elephant in your backyard, how can it slip your mind? June, get Hal out here, see if he can do another rewrite."

Tommi Ann began to laugh, turned her attention to the route into Atlantic City, her eyes scanning the terrain like a general surveying the field of combat. The limo coasted down Atlantic City, past a blazing marquee that said ATLANTIC CITY WELCOMES TOMMI ANN BUTLER AND COPWATCH. The limo turned into a neon-lit garage; Cat had a sense of missed communication. April had said the cast was staying at the Marinea Towers; they didn't have a parking garage.

A sturdy figure wearing the regulation Phoenix blazer, green with a gold crest, appeared at the open door; his employee ID read STERLING PHOENIX SECURITY.

Oh, no. Cat turned to April. "I thought the cast was staying at the Marinea Towers."

Butler got out and held out his hand to Tommi Ann.

April leaned toward Cat, whispered. "The plebes. The inner circle's at the Phoenix. June mentioned that." She gave Cat a nudge and Cat lurched out of the limo.

Cat caught a flash of panic from June, took pity on the kid, who had *not* mentioned that the Butlers were staying at the Phoenix, of all places. She exchanged a glance with Danny Furina, whose handsome face was alight with mischief.

The green jacket was reciting his perfunctory greeting. "Welcome to the Sterling Phoenix, Mrs. Butler, Mr. Butler. We'll be taking you in through the executive entrance. Mrs. Sterling has sent the dress down from New York and said to tell you the fittings can be scheduled at your convenience."

Fittings? Oh, Lord, The Gown. The Oscar Gown. *Fawn Sterling's designed Tommi Ann's gown.*

"This is Mr. Furina. He's with the production security," Tommi Ann said, smoothly.

The green jackets glowered; they knew who he was. Their gazes shifted in sync, settled on Cat.

"Has Gary Biggs arrived yet?"

"Yes, Mrs. Butler."

Danny's dark brows were raised in amusement, daring Cat to challenge Sterling's people. Cat wasn't going to give him the satisfaction, turned to the group. "I'm sorry, I'll have to excuse myself."

"I thought you would come up to the suite for a few minutes, Mrs. Austen. Dianne could take you through the pre-interview."

"Thank you. But what these gentlemen are diplomatically not saying is that I'm sort of banned from the Phoenix."

"Banned!" April was fascinated. "What for, like you have a system? You're one of those card counters?"

"Well, I think it would be accurate to say that I was a bit too adept at keeping track of the players in a very high-stakes game."

Danny ducked his head, the thin fabric of his windbreaker shuddering.

"The hell." Butler took his wife's arm, turned to the hotel security team. "Tommi Ann decides who she'll see and who she won't see. Mrs. Austen, you come on with us."

Cat glanced around, realized that they were on the fifth level of the parking garage, outside the executive entrance, *twenty feet from the elevator.* "No, not now, thank you. I think it would be better if I went on, I have a few calls to make, and I'm sure you all want to unwind. I'll call tomorrow and see if you can set aside some time for me."

... where she had turned up the dead Santa Claus that had thrown her Christmas into chaos.

"Mrs. Austen." Tommi Ann disengaged Ben's arm, drew Cat out of earshot. "It must have taken a great deal to have alienated Mr. and Mrs. Sterling to the point of exile from the Phoenix."

"I don't think it's limited to the Phoenix. I'm probably banned from all of the Sterling properties. Worldwide."

"I'd love to hear the story."

You tell me your story, I'll tell you mine. "Which would you prefer, their fiction or my reality?"

Tommi Ann smiled. "Is there a difference? In the end, reality's whatever we have to do to survive the day. Reality's what we make it."

CHAPTER THREE

EXT. KATE'S HOUSE: NIGHT
Camera tracks KATE as she walks to her car,
turns to look at her house. Camera closes
slowly on KATE'S expression, one of affection.

KATE (to house)
You're not much. But you're all mine.

They had dropped April and June at the Marinea Towers, headed back to Ocean City. Cat gave in to giddiness at the thought of poor Harold Anderson being told he had to work a sixty-five-foot-high elephant into the script. Why not? The tiers of frenzied rewrites had pretty much obliterated the reality of the Dudek case, Cat's involvement in it.

Reality's what we make it.

Cat shoved her copy of the script in her canvas tote, took out her Tommi Ann Butler folder, combed the scant background once more. Not much; no celebrity bios, no flash, no scandal, just scraps, well picked over: born in Kingman, Kansas, only child of fundamentalist parents, home-schooled, orphaned, foster care until the age of majority, left for New York when still a teenager. Then the fable converted from David Copperfield to Cinderella, charming, inspiring and unencumbered by mundane detail. It was the tale of a skinny, red-haired, nineteen-year-old who had appeared in a twenty-thousand-dollar modern-dress, indie version of *Twelfth Night* called *Illyria;* of a filmmaker who had carted his film to New York, Cannes, Toronto, hunting for a distributor; of a far-sighted, bottom-rung talent agency minion named Ben Butler who had huddled in the dark in some SoHo art house and fell in love; how Butler had quit his job, tracked down the director, got the last known address of "the red-headed gal who played Viola," made his way to the seventh floor of a Ninth Avenue walk-up, walked those seven flights with the scent of soy sauce and oil and compact heat from the street-level Chinese take-out below clinging to him every step of the way. Knocked. She answered and he fell in love again, for good.

Cat took out her copy of a *New York Magazine* profile, eight years old, written at the time of Tommi Ann's third Oscar nomination. She and Butler had consented to an interview that was little more than a filmography, and some good-natured anecdotes from Butler that amended the tale: like everyone else, he had capitulated to the girl on the screen; it had taken a heartbeat or two longer to fall in love with the flesh, for what had answered his knock was a too-pale, too-tall wraith in baggy jeans, a man's T-shirt clinging to the bony frame. And yes, there had been a moment of "What the hell did I do to my career?"

But just a moment. Something happened. That something, the writer speculated, may have been a word of welcome spoken in Tommi Ann's signature contralto, or perhaps Butler's near-prescient instincts had sized up the embryonic beauty, as well as the budding talent. Perhaps kindred souls recognize each other at first sight, however ragged the disguise. The writer had concluded with a "whatever" and the Act One finale: Two days after the meeting, Ben Butler took Tommi Ann to the Caribbean, and six days after that, they returned wearing matching gold bands, matching surnames.

IndieNews, Cat had trolled through the Web for an hour for the next installment. Ben Butler had taken out a loan, and begun to create Tommi Ann Butler. He had bought the existing prints of *Illyria* and had the credits reshot to read "Tommi Ann Butler." He took her out of the country to lie low, rest, put on a few pounds while he set about getting a distributor who would move the film while he kept her just unavailable enough to get a good buzz going.

Six months later, Tommi Ann Butler was nominated for her first Oscar. Tommi Ann and Ben remained out of sight, waited, accepted scripts, but turned down interviews, a move, it was thought, to cultivate the image of Tommi Ann as her generation's Garbo. Butler hired Dianne King; the remainder of the retinue were per diems: the voice coach who eased out the hint of a twang; the doctors who tended to her long-neglected health; the out-of-work Pratt grad, her Ninth Avenue neighbor, who created the look. By the time Tommi Ann and Ben made their first walk down Oscar's red carpet, the frail chrysalis had dissolved and a tall, slender young woman with an arresting, almost haunting beauty had emerged, a radiance that evoked the great faces: Garbo, Dietrich or striking little-knowns like Dorothy Mackaill. The latter comparison was inevitable when Butler chose *Abandoned* for his bride's follow-up, the film a more thoughtful, less histrionic remake of Mackaill's *Safe in Hell.* Archive photos of Mackaill's remote, seductive features next to Tommi Ann's stills, everyone wondering how Butler had seen the affinity. Second Oscar nomination.

The filmography: *Illyria, Abandoned, Northanger Abbey, Tangled Web, The Merchant of Venice, Second Coming, Booked For Murder, Cloak and Dagger, A Poisoned Pen, Mariposa, Spellbinder, A Scandal in Bohemia, Black Orchid, Queen's Ransom, George Sand* (third Oscar nomination), *The Devil to Pay, Dark Before Dawn, Double Jeopardy, Isabella, Macbeth,* all the way to her stunning performance in *Redemption.*

Cat closed the folder, leaned back on the lino's glove leather, hoping that, if the driver should glance through the rearview mirror, she would not come off like someone who had only ridden in a limo four times in her life: once when she had married Chris, once when she had buried him, last month when the pimp James Easter had abducted her, and today. *What must it be like to be used to this,* Cat wondered? What must it be like to be beautiful and rich and *chosen.* Wouldn't you like to be *glorified,* Jane had asked once, and Cat had laughed, but sailing in the limo, the scent of Tommi Ann's perfume still in the compartment she thought, *perhaps for a day. A week. A year.*

"Here we are, ma'am."

Cat looked out the tinted window, saw silhouettes clustered behind the dining room sheers, Jane on the porch. She was tempted to ask him to run her around the block a couple times, but got out. The house was three stories, a scrap of lawn in the front, porch railings in need of sanding, the mailbox rusting in the salt-laden air. An old Raggedy Ann sheet that Jane had outgrown was tacked inside the front sliding door of the ground-floor apartment. Freddy and Ellice hadn't gotten around to picking out drapes, furniture.

"Nice place, ma'am."

The driver's comment was sincere. He was young, some kid making his bills, tuition, by driving a limo. To him, she was somebody. To some plodding cabbie, the limo driver's lot would be envied. Cat wondered where the bottom was, how close to it Tommi Ann's beginnings had been, how many rungs lay between those beginnings and a penthouse.

"You're not a suite at the Phoenix," she couldn't help paraphrasing, "but you're all mine."

"*The Phoenix!*" emerged from the stream of Spanish obscenities. It would have amazed his unit, the other bureaus of the prosecutor's office, horrified his mother, to hear the rococo of profanity resonating through Victor Cardenas' small apartment, Spanish except for the three-syllable English refrain, "*The Phoenix!*"

Remy Cardenas was impervious to her brother's fury, and replied with a scornful, "*Te ahogue en un vaso de agua.*"

"*Le faltas un tornillo.*"

"I'm not the only one missing a *screw,* '*mano,*" she shot back. "Celibacy's all that's wrong with you. Stop being such a monk."

"*El habito no hace al monje.*"

"Mmm. So I see." She drew the collar of his plush velour robe around her throat. "She give you this?"

"No. Did you bring any clothes of your own?"

Remy gave him a wry frown. "What's the matter, you afraid she's going to get a whiff of my perfume when she wears it?"

"She doesn't."

"What else doesn't she wear?"

"Remedios—"

"Victor," she mimicked his level baritone. "You're my brother, not my keeper, an' whatever went down between you and the Sterlings, that's got nothing to do with me." She crossed her arms over her chest. "I don't get opportunities like this every day. *Madre mia*, you know who's staying at the Phoenix? Tommi Ann Butler! I'm lucky, she hasn't found anything yet to go with the gown, maybe she'll be wearing something of mine around her throat."

"You hold your show at the Phoenix, you'll be wearing something of mine around your throat."

Remy laughed. She wasn't afraid of his rants. It was when he didn't rant that he was dangerous. She drew his robe tightly around her whippet-thin figure, covering the fading bruises from the last affair, bruises she knew better than to let Victor see. "So, when do I get to see her?"

"When you're fit to be seen. Can I have the bathroom?"

"Go ahead."

"You're not holding your trunk show in the Phoenix."

"Am too," she replied, but not until he was out of the room.

Victor stalked into the small bathroom, yanked Remy's stockings down from the shower rail. *Dios mio.* He had forgotten what it was like to live with a woman. Territorial, and they drove you crazy. It would be like that living with Cat, perhaps, if they ever got past this damned television shoot, got their romance out of neutral. Driving him crazy, that much she had gotten down.

He turned on the water, stepped into the shower. Even his Ivory and generic shampoo had to yield ground to tubes of oatmeal-scented soap, almond-scented shampoo, pear-scented conditioner, a pink plastic razor, a loofah, a discarded foil packet that had something to do with hot oil. He closed his eyes to it, thought of Cat. Unleashed, his thoughts inevitably found their way to her. Their destination, which he had seen so clearly, had become like a mirage, a shimmering possibility that dissolved at his approach, his mind telling him that this was not material, not graspable, his heart picking up and following once more.

The *CopWatch* shoot had put another obstacle between them. It was preoccupying Cat completely. He was certain that it wasn't the television show alone, that Cat was erasing the previous month from her mind with desperate activity, erasing the prospect of intimacy along with it.

Damn *CopWatch* and everyone connected with it.

He had spoken to Dominic about it, that morning after Mass. Dominic's faith was getting him through the events of last month, but Cat hadn't come to terms, wouldn't even mention Kevin's name, overloading herself with her home, Freddy's upcoming wedding to Ellice, writing assignments she would ordinarily have given a pass, advising some lame-brain writer from *CopWatch*, establishing an amicable relationship with her new computer. "It's almost like she's testing herself, trying to see how much she can take on without breaking," he had told Dominic.

Dominic had nodded. "Perhaps. She may be testing her strength this way, trying to see if she's strong enough to accept what happened with Kevin. They were really close as kids, Victor." He removed his glasses, wiped his eyes. "Just don't start to look at her work, this television project, like a rival. You can't want the relationship to be based only on her needing you. I know—all of us know—what it feels like to want to look after Cat. To be afraid of what's gonna happen if she strikes out on her own too much. I think we've all had to confront the fact that part of that fear is the fear that she won't need us anymore."

What Cat needed. Was he really thinking about that, or only about what he wanted? Just that morning, Remy had put it quite succinctly. "Men, they're all selfish pigs."

He turned the knob to cool, rinsed away the layer of soapsuds. *Don't be selfish, be supportive, let them have as much of the bathroom as they want.* It would be easier if there was a book somewhere with all this written down.

He turned off the water, yanked the towel from a rack, rubbed it over his hair, knotted it around his waist.

Remy was in his bedroom, wriggling into a pair of jeans. "Do you mind if I get dressed?" he asked.

She flung herself back onto the bed and squirmed the zipper closed. "Like it's something I haven't seen." She pulled on a red halter top, a loose bodice that dropped over her shoulders, knotted under her breasts. "Take me over there, why don't you, I wanna meet her."

"Some other time."

The doorbell rang. Remy got up, checked her hair, finger-fluffed it, pouted at her reflection, testing the careful layer of makeup. "I'll get it."

Victor was dressed when she came back, not bothering to knock, her dark eyes glittering like jet. "It was your landlady, Victor, guess what?"

"I don't guess."

"She says the *CopWatch* crew is going to be filming on the street tomorrow! Tommi Ann Butler! Do you think she's really as hot as she looked in *Booked For Murder*?"

"Is she really as buff as in *Double Jeopardy*?"

Anticipation was almost palpable, almost comic. Cat yanked off her coat, tugged the scarf from around her neck, tossed it over a chair. The house smelled of basil, tomato. "What, did you think I was going to bring her home with me?"

"She can't look as good as she did in *Isabella*," Lorraine declared. She was the wife of Cat's second brother, Vinnie. "I bet a hundred dollars she had a face lift." She was munching on celery sticks; S&M CASTING out of Atlantic City had picked her up for background in the funeral scene, and she was determined to get into a black cocktail dress she hadn't worn in four years.

"Well, she certainly doesn't have any visible scars," Cat said. "Where's my Mats?"

"I'm cookin' with Nonna."

Cat helped herself to a carrot stick. "She is, without question, and with nothing more than a little lipstick that I could determine, the most beautiful woman I've ever seen in my life." She raised her voice, "Except for you, Mama."

"Hah." Jennie emerged from the kitchen, a bib apron wrapped around dark slacks, a white turtleneck sweater. "So, why didn't you invite her to come eat?"

"Mama, she's up for an Oscar."

"So? She's gotta eat." Ristorante Fortunati had fed Dean Martin, Burt Lancaster, Ethel Merman.

"Nectar and ambrosia, maybe," Cat murmured. "Stop *glaring* at me Jane, I'll get you a picture. In fact, I'll take orders. Anybody who wants Bigg Phat P.I.G.'s autograph raise your hand." Hands went up: Vinnie's three teenage boys; Marco's MJ and Andrea; Sherrie's daughter, Meryl; Jane. Mark, the street kid the courts had handed over to Carlo last month stared at her sullenly.

"What if you *never* get to see him?" Jane declared.

"He's almost as big as Lucy the Elephant," Cat replied. "How could I miss him?"

"What if he won't give it to you?"

Cat curled her fingers into claws, crept on Jane. "Then I'll huff, and I'll puff, and I'll blow his ninety-thousand-dollar customized trailer with TV, VCR, PC, fax, refrigerator, stove, tile-bath down!" She took a deep breath, tickled Jane's ribcage.

"Mom!"

"Who's afraid of the Bigg Phat P.I.G.?"

"You really think you're gonna get to see him?"

The words were followed by silence as though the question was profoundly meaningful. Mark seldom spoke.

Cat nodded. "They're shooting some exteriors tomorrow afternoon and the funeral scene at St. Agnes tomorrow night. I know he's in that. Tuesday, I think they're doing the brawl at CV's; Wednesday, back to CV's for the nightclub scene and the parking lot scene with Tommi Ann and Ron; the crowd scene at the parking lot Thursday night; Friday's the interviews and the roundtable; Saturday for whatever they don't get done; and Sunday, they're outta here."

Lorraine frowned, as though the linguine Jennie placed on the table was scheming to keep her out of that dress.

"Why at night?" Freddy griped. He began passing plates. "I'm workin' four to midnight this week."

Cat shrugged. "It depends on when they can get the permits, and some of the shots involve gunpowder, so they try to do it when there are fewer bystanders around."

Jennie produced *rigatoni al forno*, fried eggplant. "You keep your hands off the food until Victor gets here," she told Carlo. Mark almost smiled. It amused him that this big retired cop still had to listen to his mother.

"She looked really thin in *Redemption*. Is she?" Sherrie handed baby Gio to Joey.

"She's gotta be at least forty-one, forty-two," Lorraine remarked, grimly.

"Joey's forty-two," Sherrie said. She was thirty.

"You think she'll get the Oscar this time, or what?" Joey laid a napkin over the shoulder of his designer shirt, coaxed a burp out of the baby.

Jennie put two baskets of *foccacia* on the table, one at each end. "Hold his head," she told Joey. "So, they work all night, who fixes something for them to eat?"

Cat looked at her.

"I'm just askin'.." Jennie retreated to the kitchen.

The phone rang. Cat picked it up in the kitchen. "Mama, don't wait for Victor, the kids are hungry." She put the phone to her ear. Ritchie Landis, her editor, demanded, "And? *And?*"

Cat slid into the kitchen booth. "And yes."

"Yes, what?"

"Yes, I got to meet her and Tommi Ann Butler is just as beautiful as she looks in fill-in-the-movie-title. What do you know about Tommi Ann's stand-in?"

"That gal Spivak hooked up with in Philly last year?"

"I'm thinking she might be someone you'd want copy on."

"Why?"

"April? The producer? She called this Cici Bonaker the fast track to Tommi Ann."

"Then make tracks, but don't forget to bag the rhino. And speaking of rhinoplasty, what's in LA?"

"Smog and overpaid talent, why?"

"I mean, what's Spivak got cookin' in the City of Angels? Cherry said that's where he went. I think. Jets for the coast and leaves Tommi Ann Butler to the likes of Channel Five, Channel Six *and* Channel Seven, not to mention *NewsLine90*, Friedlander, Allessandro, Wszybyk. He must be off his rocker. You know why he went?"

"You know him better than I." Cat heard the doorbell.

"So when's your interview with Tommi Ann?"

"There's a snag. The USDA prime is booked into the Phoenix where I'm sort of *persona non grata,* in case you've forgotten."

"Jeez, Austen, it's not like they got your wanted poster up. Just tart yourself up, sneak in undercover, like a hooker or something. Get some pointers from your pal Jimmy Easter."

"Ritchie, for the love of God, would you ask Ron Spivak to do something like that?"

"No way. You ever seen him in a garter belt and pumps?"

"Have you?" Cat blurted.

"Halloween party, a couple years ago—"

"Ritchie. I am not going to"—she lowered her voice—"tart myself up in a rhinestone bustier, lamé skirt, spike heels, fishnet stockings and fuschia eye shadow so that—"

There was a rap on the archway. Cat looked up.

Victor stood listening attentively to her conversation. Cat closed her eyes. "Ritchie, I have to go. I'll call you after I talk to Tommi Ann's publicist tomorrow, and I'll be seeing her on the set tomorrow night."

"Don't let Karen Friedlander get the drop on you. And hang onto the fishnets and the spikes."

"You must be confusing me with Kate Auletta." Kate Auletta would probably do that undercover hooker thing four, five times a season. "I don't do undercover."

"I meant, maybe we could go out sometime."

Cat hung up.

Victor slid into the booth, looked at her.

"Lieutenant, I would think long and hard before I risked any light-hearted banter."

"I do think long and hard. Particularly when I envision you in— what was that?—spike heels and a rhinestone bustier."

"Victor, my mother is standing ten feet outside this room."

"Your mother's crazy about me."

Jennie called out, "Victor, come get something before it gets cold."

He grinned.

Cat took her place at the dining room table, Victor stood beside her, waiting until Jennie sat.

Conversation ricocheted around the table, "Tommi Ann Butler," the verbal refrain: "Is she really? Is she really? Is she really?" Cat allowed her thoughts to drift, picked up scraps of the conversation at the pushed-together card tables in the center hall, where the kids were sharing, savoring gossip about Bigg Phat P.I.G., Jane's, "I *read* it. I read it in *Teen Talk*," lifting above the buzz.

What could Ron be after that beat angling for "face time" with Tommi Ann Butler? Wasn't that why he had wormed his way into the production in the first place?

"*Hay problema?*" Victor murmured in her ear.

Cat smiled, shook her head. "Are you going to be dropping by the set? Everyone is crazy to meet the real Victor Calderone."

"I hadn't planned on it."

Cat's family exclaimed at this blasphemy.

"How can you not want to watch them film a *TV* show?" Sherrie demanded. She, too, had secured work as an extra.

"I suspect the actual process is much like police work," he said. "Sounds exciting, plays dull."

"Perhaps they could arrange for a murder. Make it worth your while."

"Promises, promises," he said.

After dinner, Cat and Victor went for a walk on the boardwalk. Late March was fickle at the shore; the daylight promised warmth, lured people from their homes, then vanished quickly by early evening, abandoning them to wintry cold. It was not yet six, the waning sun threw a mantle of smoke-blue over the whispering sea; the mantle was threaded with scarlet, undulated like silk.

"What's bothering you, *querida?*"

"Nothing."

"'Nothing will come of nothing, speak again.'"

"Ron Spivak asked me to meet him for coffee yesterday. I thought he wanted to talk about the shoot, maybe brainstorm a little. But what he wanted was to ask me to check on his place, take in his mail for a couple days while he took off for the west coast."

Victor leaned against the boardwalk railing, held Cat's hands in his. The wind blew strands of hair across her face. "I thought he'd gotten a role in this thing."

Cat nodded. "The part of Gerry. It's really only a couple scenes, because of course Gerry gets killed early in the show, but you don't find yourself in the same zip code as Tommi Ann Butler and jet to the coast."

"His health? He's not having more plastic surgery, is he?"

Cat shrugged. "His nose looked fine yesterday, and his speech is just about back to normal."

"It's the nose for news, then?"

Cat leaned against Victor. He opened his coat, drew it around her. He felt the threads of hair teasing his chin. "I asked Ritchie, he doesn't know either, so it's not something he's doing for *South Jersey* or the *Chronicle*."

"And your curiosity is getting the better of you?"

"Sometimes I think it's got the worst of me." She arched her neck, looked up at him. "I'm thinking it may have something to do with Butler; maybe Tommi Ann is part of a bigger story on the clients of Butler Talent Management."

"Are they worth knowing?"

Cat nodded. "The A-plus list." She ticked them off on the buttons of his shirt. "Gloria Ramirez, she was local cable in the Dallas area, now she's the queen of afternoon talk; Teresa D.—the D stands for Diaz—the Tejana princess, Butler's got her crossed over to pop, jazz. Three Grammys so far, plus she recorded *Trespass*, the theme song from *Redemption*? She'll be singing it at the Oscars. Gary Biggs picked up his weight in Grammys last year, and Butler's seeing some screen potential in him. Eric Obermeyer until he died. The girl who stands in for Tommi Ann, she's headed for the screen, too."

"And his wife, of course."

Cat looked up at him. "And Tommi Ann. And a writer, the guy who wrote the book they based *Redemption* on."

"A talk show hostess, a director, a couple popular singers, a budding actress, a writer? Pretty eclectic group."

"They say the writer got two million for his book contract and the screenplay rights," Cat said, a little wistfully.

"Why isn't he writing the *CopWatch* script?" Cat looked puzzled. "What I mean is," Victor continued, "Butler's wife is starring, her stand-in and the rapper have roles. You told me they were even using the kid's latest single in the nightclub scene." He felt her shudder at the mention of that scene. He didn't want her to be on the set, watching the screen Jerry pursue the screen Cat, watching him get shot all over again.

"They are."

"He's got so much of the talent locked in, he's got a writer in his pocket and they were desperate for a pinch hitter—or pinch writer— why not draft the two-million-dollar man?"

"I don't know."

They were silent for a few minutes. At last, Cat said, "You're really not going to ask, are you?"

"Ask what?"

"If Tommi Ann Butler is really as beautiful as she looked in fill-in-the-movie-title?"

"Is she beautiful enough to play you?"

"She has a face that a man might die for."

"Just as long as he doesn't do it on my watch."

CHAPTER FOUR

INT: HOMICIDE BUREAU: DAY

*LIEUTENANT VICTOR CALDERONE, head of the
Homicide Squad, is a man of mystery even
to the efficient team of investigators
who have worked with him for years. He
enters his office—*

Victor snatched the script from Remy's hands, threw it on top of his unread paper.

"Is that the script?"

Victor scowled. They had sent it over for him to vet, and he had tossed it aside, promptly forgotten it, managed to avoid the phone calls from the writer, Anderson, and the director who was playing him, some guy named Melendez.

Remy was standing in her slip in his living room, scrutinizing the arrangements of earrings, clips, pins, pendants adorning his couch, half-listening to *Philly5Live!* interviewing "Hometown actor-writer Harold Anderson, who will be co-starring in that *CopWatch* episode being filmed this week at the Jersey Shore. Tell us, Harold ..."

What's Tommi Ann Butler really like? Victor filled a Thermos with coffee.

"What's Tommi Ann Butler really like?"

"Put some clothes on," he told Remy and walked out.

He eased the Jag between the cones that a team of overalled work-
ers were setting up at the intersection of Atlantic and Delancy, gave a
passing glance to the van, the equipment, figured it was about time
the city patched up three winters' worth of potholes, snapped on his
car radio, caught a bit of the Sonny At Sunrise morning talk. Sonny
was interviewing Red Melendez, who was stating "—because to be a
cop and to be an actor, they're not so different after all. You're handed
a story and you've got to look at it from all the angles, you have to
figure out which one you feel carries the most validation, and of course
from a humanistic perspective—"

Sonny cut him off, said they had a caller. Red wished the caller,
"*Buenos días.*"

"Mr. Menendez?"

"Melendez," Sonny corrected.

What's Tommi Ann Butler like to work with? Victor predicted.

"What's Tommi Ann Butler like to work with?"

He snapped the radio off.

The conservative dark suit and green-and-gray tie, the calm good
morning, the implacable expression betrayed nothing of: A) the six
AM phone call from his mother demanding to know if he had seen
Tommi Ann Butler in person, she had been so wonderful in *Mariposa*, her Spanish had been so perfect and was his sister giving him
any trouble? B) the battle with Remy for bathroom priority, all the
time Remy telling him if he pushed her around, she'd do to him what
Tommi Ann Butler had done to J.P. Faulkner in *Booked for Murder,* C)
his landlady's phone call reminding him that the city had issued permits for *CopWatch* to film on Delancy, and they might even be shooting the exterior of her house. "Do you think ..." she had asked him,
tremulously, "she might ..?"

Victor reverted to Holmes. "'Life is infinitely more strange than
anything which the mind of man can invent,'" he said, which she
took for absolute confirmation. Victor wished her good morning.

He shook loose thoughts of *CopWatch*, parked in his usual slot beside the large rambling structure in Northfield where Major Crimes was housed, intercepted the photographer who had been hiding between a pair of parked cars. In their accidental collision, Victor inadvertently tripped him up, managed to catch the kid's camera, though the film popped out, was exposed.

He found his three detectives in a day room huddle over the morning paper, held up five fingers, indicating they were to report to his office in five minutes. He set his Thermos on his desk, hung his coat on the battered oak rack in the corner and unrolled the newspaper. RETURNING TO THE SCENE, read the headline. ACTORS TO VISIT COUNTERPARTS ON COPWATCH LOCATION, with a picture of him that had been taken three years ago following his testimony in a sensational trial next to a ten-year-old photo of Red Melendez, taken in his *Advocates* days.

Stan Rice, Phil Long, Jean Adane entered. Victor waited for Adane to sit before he took his seat. "Okay, what have we got?"

Long's eyes were fixed on the files on his lap. "Bevilacqua's got the Adkins' girl's death tied up in pretrial whatever. The conspiracy against Sterling is going nowhere fast, especially now that the mister and missus are on the mend."

"Or putting on a good act," Victor concluded.

Long handed over the Sterling file, opened it to an article at the top of the papers. It was from the fashion section of a New York paper, *Garb OH!* Long had highlighted the line: *decided to forgo the established couturiers in favor of hot newcomer Fawn Caprio-Sterling, whose spring CapriOH! line was a smash. Ms. Caprio-Sterling and Tommi Ann Butler are both mum on the details, but speculation on The Gown certainly has overshadowed those ugly rumors of the Sterlings' marital and business woes. Redemption, indeed!*

Victor closed the file. "Thank you."

"So it looks like the first trial's gonna be Cape May county, the assault on Stan." He hesitated.

"Was there something else, Detective?"

"I talked to their county DA, he says it's a weak case, that some of the witness statements"—the look clearly said "Mrs. Austen's state-ment"—"are bound to get shakier the longer they delay, and they're not rock solid now."

Victor's expression never altered. "Go on."

"Missing persons. They catch about ten, fifteen a day, but there're two we may wanna look into. One was Denise Santos. I interviewed her, the Dudek investigation, she knew the sister. She's been working a revue, got herself some work on the *CopWatch* shoot. Roommate says she's been gone a couple days; she sounded a little worked up." Long shrugged. "It may be nothing, but the roommate says Santos was crazy to be on TV, she'd never drop out before the shoot."

Victor nodded. "Who's the other one?"

"Woman won't give her name, she says her friend Inez Gabriel's been missing almost a week. Name rings a bell for some reason. Anyway, this woman's been callin' the locals, the DA, ODOR, she's callin' from a pay phone, won't give her name, but she won't give up, either."

"She say she has any reason to suspect foul play?"

Long shook his head. "Nothin' else, except city vice called, they said they got a head."

"Ahead of what?"

"No, a head. A head." Long snapped his flattened palm under his chin.

"Identifiable?"

"ME says it's not 'Hey, that's Bob,' but it ain't the Cro-Magnon man, either." Long went back to his notes. "Hit and run out Tilton Road, vic's critical. Guy tried to crack the cash-for-gold near Pennsyl-vania and Pacific, the owner's dog took a chunk outta the doer's thigh, he bleeds out and the doer's next of kin wants we should arrest—"

Victor took the folder Adane handed across. "—the store owner," he concluded.

"Nope. Fido."

"He wants us to arrest the dog?"

"Yeah."

"What else?"

"Over Somers Point? A guy kills his wife and her sister."

"Domestic dispute?" Victor pushed his chair away from the desk, crossed one leg over the other.

Phil cleared his throat, made a conscious effort not to look at Stan. "Not exactly. He says he had to do it on accounta he was saving them from getting abducted by the space aliens."

Victor stroked his mustache, thoughtfully. "Had he engaged in some sort of extraterrestrial communication that led him to believe this was an imminent possibility?"

"Not so far as we've been able to establish. But, I mean, you gotta admit ..."

Stan crossed his arms tightly over his shaking ribs.

"—there's not much chance of them being abducted by aliens now, is there, so in a way—"

"Detective."

"Well, like you're always saying how Sherlock Holmes said sometimes circumstantial evidence points straight to one thing, but you shift your point of view, you find it's pointing to something different?"

"Yeah." Stan's expression was earnest, but his dimples were showing. "You gotta look at stuff from all the angles, see which one's got validation, from a humanistic—"

"I'll have it incorporated into the Academy's training manual. Anything else?"

"No, except," Long added, "we got the op to work OT on the *CopWatch* payroll; they figure they'll need some extra muscle for crowd control. C'mon, Lieutenant. Captain Loeper says it's okay with him."

"I don't have the authority to override Captain Loeper," Victor replied, evenly. "But I think this unit can find a better use of its abilities than to work overtime on the *CopWatch* shoot. Anything else?"

"That guy Melendez called, he wants to drop by."

"For what purpose?"

"He said he wants to hang with you a little, get a feel for your operational style, absorb the ambiance."

Victor tugged at the corner of his mustache. "If Mr. Melendez calls again, please inform him that my operational style does not permit me to indulge the curiosity of celebrities regarding the state of my ambiance. Is there anything else?"

"That about covers it."

Victor rose and dismissed them, settled behind his desk, checked his calendar, went through his messages. A note from Manny Alvaro, notifying him of Gino Forschetti's removal from active duty due to his medical condition, putting "medical condition" in quotes. Victor understood. Gino had been hitting the booze pretty heavily since Sheila's murder last month, a thought that deepened his contempt for *CopWatch*, its allegation to be based on fact. The truth of what he did couldn't be wrapped in ninety minutes with commercial breaks. The effects were long lasting; the resolution of the crime did not guarantee that lives would be restored. Often, the destructive effects dragged on for months. Forever. He thought of Cat, laying the flowers on her husband's grave the day of Kevin Keller's funeral, her fingers tracing the letters of his name. How she was trying to wrestle memories of Kevin into some corner of her brain that would make sense of what he had done.

His phone rang and he reached for it, hoping it was Cat, heard his sister's frantic voice. "Victor! Victor, there're people breaking down the door!"

In the background, he could hear pounding. He rose from his desk, hammered the two-way window between his office and the day room with his fist. His three detectives hurried in. "Rice, go get a unit over to my place, asap." He spoke into the phone. "Remy, go into the bedroom and lock the door, pick up the extension, I'm on my way." He tossed the receiver to Adane. "My sister, Remedios, keep her talking."

Victor was unlocking his car when Adane came dashing from the building, calling his name. "What is it?" He did not want to have to tell his mother that something had happened to Remy while she was in his care.

"It's all right, Lieutenant, it's just ..." Adane hesitated. "Apparently your landlady didn't realize your sister was in the apartment before they started dismantling your front door."

"I beg your pardon?"

"They're replacing your door so that they can film some exterior shots of your house. They didn't think your front door was ... photogenic, I suppose."

Victor leaned against his car door, looked at Adane. "Adane, give me your opinion. That extraterrestrial defense, the aliens made me do it? You think it might be exculpatory?"

"Do you mean, if you eliminated the members of a film crew, would you be able to convince the court that your actions had been influenced by extraterrestrials?"

"Hypothetically speaking."

Adane spoke seriously, as always, but her blue eyes were alight with rare mischief. "I think it depends, sir. If your position was that the extraterrestrials had induced you to shoot the crew because television programming presented a serious threat to the well-being of the universe, you might have a case. On the other hand, if your position was that of the man from Somers Point, that you were attempting to prevent the crew from alien abduction," she shook her head, "you would have to convince the court that the extraterrestrials considered the victims desirable enough to warrant abduction, and that might be beyond even your abilities, sir."

"It was just a thought."

CHAPTER FIVE

INT: NIGHTCLUB: NIGHT
KATE AULETTA steps into the nightclub, takes
in the crowd, the pounding music, the flashing
lights.

                          KATE
This takes more than an hour, I'm gonna want
to kill someone.

"Should I change that line, do you think? I mean, Kate's pretty
low-key up to this point, is it too, you know, what's the word ..."
    What do you mean "what's the word"? Cat thought. *You're the writer,*
for heaven's sake.
    "Ballsy," April grunted. "It's fine Harold. Kate's supposed to have
balls."
    Cat looked down at the blank page of the notebook open on her
lap. She was having the Hollywood equivalent of the ride-around,
touring the locations the second unit was going to shoot. Harold
drove, June Mathis sat in the passenger seat, Cat was in the back with
April. Cat listened to April describe what a second unit did and
maintain that the second unit was the backbone of the production.
After this assertion, there was a pause. April shot Cat a meaningful
look and Cat took the hint, got out her pen and dutifully wrote, *The*
second unit is the backbone of the production.

"They're unions, so I gotta ride their keesters," April explained. "Today, they're shooting exteriors, some principal photography over Calderone's street. There was a little flap about replacing a door or something. June, you square that?"

Cat saw June's head bob.

They're unions, so I gotta "ride their keesters," maintains producer April Steinmetz, Cat wrote, put "ride their keesters" in brackets, her personal notation to come up with a euphemism for the phrase when she wrote her copy.

"They're shooting day for night. It'll go quick, since it's Tommi Ann, Red and Hal, they're all pros."

Cat offered a smile that did not reveal that her overwhelming impression of Harold Anderson had been one of extreme paranoia. But perhaps that was just his writer persona, he might well be a Barrymore in front of the lens.

They coasted to a stop on Atlantic. Delancy had been blocked off at the intersection. A long trailer had been parked along the curb opposite the house where Victor lived and a crew had staked out the small, dead-end street, was mounting lights and gels that would simulate night. There were about two hundred people on Atlantic praying for a glimpse of Tommi Ann Butler.

Harold parked the car, disappeared in the trailer, emerged as Tim Harper. The crew set up for a quick take of Harold/Tim parking a dark sedan in front of Victor's house, getting out, looking up at the lighted window, drawing out a gun, firing at the door. Cut, and coverage, adding the close-ups of the gun in Harold's gloved hand. Cat noticed that the prop man—April called him Wally—had custody of the firearm until it was handed over to Harold for the take, that all was done in view of a cop she thought she recognized. When the shot was finished, Wally took the gun back, locked it in a rolling metal cabinet. Interesting procedure, she thought. Might be something she could work into a piece.

Next take: Master shot of Tommi Ann/Kate and Red/Victor mounting the steps of the three-story house where Victor lived. They stopped on his second-floor landing, looked at each other. Cut, coverage; Tommi Ann giving a little nod, just the faint inclination of her head to indicate that she didn't object to going into his apartment. Cat was allowed to take a peek through the video monitor, saw that Tommi Ann was getting it all, that first-date tremulousness merging with the determination not to let his gauntlet lie unchallenged. Cat remembered that shaky first date with Victor, thought, *She's got me. She's inside my head.*

Cat let her eyes pan the scene; the second unit director, carrying out Red's instructions; the guy perched on the crane above the gelled lights; Harold Anderson, standing off to the side; the cops manning the blocked-off intersection; Danny Furina, his dark eyes both watchful and amused as he scanned the onlookers. Cat looked at them, the earnestness of their veneration, had a sense of the weight of that worship, the burden it must be to live by the eyes of the world.

April leaned close to Cat. "This is what makes it worth it," she murmured. "This is what makes me real."

A five-minute break sent them shuffling off to the craft service cart, which provided a scant assortment of sandwiches, doughnuts, fruit juice, coffee. Tommi Ann accepted a cup of tea from an intern who all but genuflected when she handed it to the star; Cat noticed that Tommi Ann exchanged a few words with the girl, seemed to draw her out with a couple questions. Harold began flipping through the script; April locked into a conference with the second unit director; Red Melendez migrated toward the onlookers.

Cat watched him show himself off until at last someone called out "Roberto Aguilar!" Roberto Aguilar was the darkly brooding, Cervantes-quoting, martial arts master guru to a team of renegade public defenders that he had played in *The Advocates.* Ten years ago. He kept himself visible with guest shots, PSAs, personal appearances that traded on the Roberto Aguilar persona. An old friendship with Ted Cusack, who had written the treatment of the Dudek story, pitched it to *CopWatch*, had brought Red's name to the table. Butler okayed him and Cusack's arrest for the killing of a prostitute hadn't induced a sense of indignation or shame by association that might have prompted Melendez to resign from the shoot. Loyalty was all well and good, but a juicy part and the director's gig, that was something else altogether.

"Tommi Ann! *Tommi Ann! TOMMI ANN! We love you Tommi Ann!*"

Flashbulbs fired off. Cat watched Danny Furina move into position, shadowing the star as she set down her cup, moved toward the line. Arms stretched out, Danny guided her into position, keeping her outside of their reach, handing her the notepads, scraps, photos to sign, his eyes panning the line of bodies.

"Must be heaven."

Cat turned and saw Harold Anderson standing at her shoulder, watching Tommi Ann work the crowd.

Harold was a tall, slender young man. Middle-aged man, she corrected, for he was probably thirty-four, thirty-five, although the mild, slightly baffled blue eyes, the blonde waves and innocuous face made him appear younger.

Harold smiled, nodded toward the beach at the end of the block. "I used to come down here when I was a kid," Harold said.

"So did I."

"I, uh, hear you're a friend of Ron Spivak's."

"We're not really friends. We live about five minutes from each other. I've seen him maybe three or four times. We've talked on the phone quite a bit, especially lately."

"What's the deal with this trip of his? April said he took off, left a note for her, she finds it waiting when she checked in." He glanced up to make sure April couldn't overhear. "You could hear her hollering all the way to Gardiner's Basin."

Cat smiled, "Well, I think Gardiner's Basin's getting a bit too lackluster, they need some livening up."

Harold looked at her through steel-rimmed spectacles, part of "Tim's" costume. "It's gotten Cici a little antsy, too. I worked with Spivak before. He didn't seem like the kind of flake who would throw us off schedule."

"Will it? I mean they don't absolutely need him tonight, they could get someone to double for the coffin and he said he'd be back for the nightclub scenes."

Harold nodded. "I hope. If something throws a wrench into this project, it'll never get back on track. The whole thing'll just get shelved."

"Is that why Cici Bonaker's antsy? Because it might derail the series?" Cat asked. "I mean, suppose something happened that the show fell through, or didn't make the air date—April does have her heart set on sweeps month—would the series go down with it?"

Harold shrugged. "I hope not. Cici's terrific."

"So I've heard."

"From Spivak?"

Cat shook her head. "He never mentioned her, really, except to say that she was a good double for Tommi Ann. I didn't realize she played Selena in *Redemption*. What's Tommi Ann going to do for a double if Cici gets spun off?"

"I don't think she cares. Cici wants to act, and Tommi Ann seems really anxious to help her lock in her dream."

Cat looked at him. "From what I hear, Cici's not the only rising star. Ben Butler thinks you're very talented."

Harold looked at her, eagerly. "Did he say so?"

Cat nodded. "And I don't suppose it hurts that you and Cici are close."

The blue eyes flashed. "You think I'm using her to get close to Tommi Ann and Ben?"

The ocean breeze caught a few of the words, carried them toward the crew; they glanced toward Harold and Cat.

Cat sighed, patiently. "I didn't say that, Harold."

He shook his head. "Yeah, well, I don't wanna come off like a saint, we're all hustlers. You see how it is. Hell, the damn interns all got scripts they carry around with them just in case they get close to Butler. I bet the bit players've been handing you their bios and publicity stills and press packets."

"A few." *Dozen.*

Harold looked toward the street, the theatre of self-importance that had mounted in the process of filming a simple exterior shot. "In this business, everything's for sale. Sell yourself, sell out. Who can help you, who you know. Who's in, who's out. I want it to be normal, between Cici and me, but I know what everyone's thinking. 'What's he getting out of it?' 'What's she gonna do for him?'"

"You seem to be doing okay. The script, the part." Cat concentrated on her sense of pity; it was nobler, she thought, than the particle of envy that chafed whenever she recalled what Harold was getting paid for the screenplay.

"I hope. It's a damn good part. It's the best part I've had in ... ever. Writing the script? That's gravy."

No taste, no texture, watered down, Cat thought. "I never saw *South Street Stakeout.* I'm watching it this week. And Ron said I could read his copy from the shoot. If I get to it in the next couple days, can we set something up, maybe for the end of the week?"

"A feature? On me?"

She hadn't said a feature. *Oh, well.* "Sure. They don't have to shoot the roundtable interviews until late Friday afternoon, maybe we could meet earlier in the day."

Harold nodded, brightened. "That'd be great." He saw one of the crew yanking the tarp from the car. "I'd better get back. Red needs a lot of coverage because we've only got this site for today."

Cat nodded, walked up the ramp to the Boardwalk. It was narrow at this end, non-commercial, a simple promenade. She sank onto a wooden bench, watched as they set up for a shot of Tommi Ann and Melendez getting out of the car.

"Hey, Alley Cat, you interviewing Prince Hal, heir apparent?" Danny Furina strode up the ramp, wearing his nylon blazer; beneath it, Cat could see the buttoned collar, knot of a tie that could not subdue the roguishness, the light of mischief in his dark gaze.

"Heir to what?"

The sweep of his arm encompassed the set, lights, crowd.

"Is he?"

Danny shrugged. "He's tight with Cici, and Cici's tight with Her Majesty. But you know what they say, heir today, gone tomorrow."

"And how's life at court, Danny? Doesn't it get a little awkward, in and out of the Phoenix? You might run into Fawn. Or Sterling. And I hear they're a couple again."

"Yeah, they're a pair, all right. Just between two kids from the neighborhood, Fawn doesn't mind me comin' in and out. Oh, I know they're puttin' on the face, but they both know the Amis woman took the fall for him and they both know he blew the hit on his better half."

"And she would rather stick around and twist the knife than call it quits?" Cat shook her head at the woman's coldness, thanked God again that Fawn Caprio had walked out on Freddy, married Sterling.

"Well, he figures he's gotta keep on the good side of anyone makes the kinda dough Fawn pulls in, in case the Sterling Org goes into a slump. Not to mention she thinks living under the same roof with a guy set her up to be hit is a kick. And it is just 'living.' They're not sleeping together."

"And which one are you in bed with?"

"Ow!" Danny punched his chest, laughed, his dark eyes dancing. "I been hit! That sounds more like it, Alley Cat. I'm not on their pay-roll, I'm *CopWatch* property, for the week at least."

"How'd you get the job?"

"How d'you think I got it? Knew somebody. I woulda thought

you woulda had some of the boys pick up work on security detail. It beats the street, and the stuff you pick up, I could write a book."

"Who've you been picking up?"

"Jeez, you've got it in for me."

Cat propped her elbow on the back of the wooden bench, looked him over. Still the renegade. "Or perhaps I should ask who's been picking you up."

"What's that supposed to mean?"

"I haven't seen you since Christmastime, Danny."

"Except at Kevin's funeral," he reminded her.

Cat nodded, studied the rhythm of the waves, low, undulating rollers, like watching the ocean breathe. "You look solvent; you've been working."

"I have. Not the glam, high-paying stuff like this, but the Sterling business got my name in the papers, that got me a client here and there."

"What client got you this glam, high-paying stuff?"

"Mutual friend, actually. Your buddy Spivak."

"Where do you know Ron from?"

"He did a piece on local PIs a while back, we did lunch. He didn't use any of my quotes as it turned out, but he picked up the check."

"And got you this job to compensate for not using your quotes? I'm not buying that, Danny. I'm thinking that you either have something on Ron, which is unlikely, or you did something important for him that calls for payback."

Danny grinned. "You're sharp, Alley Cat. Yeah, I did a little work for him."

"Guard his body, like you did for Fawn?"

"Nope, scut work, records check, that kinda stuff."

"And what sort of records-checking earned you a stint on the *CopWatch* payroll?"

"The Bonaker girl. You know they were girlfriend, boyfriend last year."

"He hired a PI to check up on his girlfriend?"

Danny shrugged.

"I haven't met her yet. What's she like?"

"A beauty. Dead ringer for Tommi Ann. Talented, too. You seen any of her dailies?"

"Dailies?"

"Sometimes they call 'em ru—"

"I know what dailies are. On Tommi Ann's stand-in?"

"Yeah, most of her scenes are done. She's playing the sister, Nadine."

"Jerry's sister was named Noreen."

"Whatever. She's good."

"Ron had her followed? I didn't know he was that serious about her."

"He's serious about something." Baiting her.

Cat shrugged. She had acquired her shrug from Jennie, who could simulate aggravating indifference.

"What happened to the old curiosity, Alley Cat? Stars in your eyes burn it off?"

"'The stars move, time runs, the clock will strike, The Devil will come,'" Cat murmured softly.

"What's that, something from the script?"

Cat's dark eyebrows rose, amused. "I hardly think that's in Harold Anderson's vein, Danny. It's Marlowe. We read it in high school."

"I forgot almost everything they tried to teach me in high school." He looked up, saw that they were taking another break. "Gotta go guard bodies. You ever need someone to cover yours, Alley Cat, you got my number."

"I've always had your number, Danny."

CHAPTER SIX

INT: KATE'S CAR: NIGHT

KATE glides down Pacific Avenue, naked shadows
thrown over the tawdry vista by the blaze of
lights ahead. The brittle illumination at the
maw of this tunnel of despair seduces like a
neon Circe; casino row looming to her right,
like a neon predator's neon bait, as full of
false promise as the sequined figures who
haunt the corners ...

Harold's prose was like a bad accident; Cat didn't want to think about it, couldn't keep her eyes off it. All through dinner, she sat at the table, the script in one hand, reading the scenes to Ellice.

"It reminds me of that line from Pope," Ellice commented. "'He whose fustian's so sublimely bad, It is not poetry, but prose run mad.'"

"Well," Cat conceded. "He's had to churn out a hundred pages of this in under a month, not to mention the daily rewrites."

She put the kids to bed early and headed into Atlantic City. The first glimpse of neon brought the phrase "tunnel of despair" into her head and started a fit of giggles that lasted halfway up New York Avenue.

New York bisected Atlantic City at the waist. St. Agnes Church was at the seedier end that caught just enough leftover light from the casinos along the beach to expose its shabbiness. Two blocks in every direction, the square block that contained St. Agnes Church, the primary school and the rectory, was barricaded, closed to traffic.

Cat nosed her Maxima up to the line of gray sawhorses. A uniformed officer stepped forward, held up a flashlight as Cat braked. She rolled down the window, showed her set pass and driver's license. He leaned down, recognizing her. "Hey, Mrs. Austen, you can go through, just you'll have to park it right on the street, they're using the church lot."

She felt a blast of icy air. "You're certainly earning your overtime."

"Hell, I'd do it free for a look at her."

Cat looked past the cordoned-off perimeter, saw a small army of uniformed officers; private security wearing navy windbreakers with CopWatch Security on the back; the green blazers of Phoenix private security.

The officer lifted away one of the sawhorses and Cat negotiated her car behind a tan sedan that had a *CopWatch Productions* logo clipped to a lowered visor. She made her way along the sidewalk, skirted a small generator, squeezed through the clusters of PAs and techies; they gave her the Is-she-anybody? once-over, went back to muttering over clipboards, stepping over cables, hauling equipment.

The intersection of New York and Barents was blocked to traffic; Barents, with the church and rectory on one side, a few modest homes, the convent on the other, had been appropriated by the customized trailer that took up the width, almost all of the length of the short block. Cat followed the caravan of cameras, lighting equipment, sound carts, metal lockers along Barents and around the corner to the small church parking lot on Kentucky. A ramp had been propped up to the double doors that accessed the broad corridor linking the church proper to the rectory (same door, same ramp by which coffins made their exit,

Cat noted) and the equipment was queued, ready to be wheeled into the sanctuary. *The shooting set*, Cat amended.

She winnowed between a pair of massive metal trunks and bounded onto the ramp, turned toward the sanctuary where they planned to shoot Jerry Dudek's/Gerry Donner's funeral scene. A familiar scent teased Cat's nostrils; it emanated from the open stairwell between the ramp and the nave, originated in the second-floor kitchen/recreation/dining area. There were double doors to close off the stairwell, but these had been propped open, and the aroma filtering down from above had begun making its way into the corridor, the nave, triumphing over the less appetizing scent emanating from the double doors at the other side of the hall, the passage that branched toward the primary school where the production company's caterer was setting out the food for the evening dinner break.

Cat walked up the stairs to the large rectangular room used for church suppers, receptions. Several long folding tables had been laid out. Behind the counter that separated the dining area from the kitchen, Cat could see her mother, Rose Cicciolini, Mrs. Muffoletu, old Mrs. Zuccaro, ranking officers of the St. Agnes Daughters of Sicily.

Cat caught her mother's eye, shook her head.

"What?" Jennie demanded. "What?"

Cat crossed her arms over her chest.

"We gotta get the *pasqua* made for the Easter baskets," Jennie said, innocently.

Cat looked around the kitchen. There were two vats of boiling water on back burners, a third with sausages simmering in tomato sauce. Foil-wrapped loaves of garlic bread were oven-ready, trays of *pepperonata* and melon with prosciutto. On a table in the dining room, a coffee urn was ready to be plugged in, surrounded by trays of cookies.

"Where's the *pasqua*?" Cat asked.

"Oh, that's been done hours ago, we got it in the freezer. You take one home to the kids."

"Mama, this has got to be the most underhanded thing you've

done since you got me to eat *cunigghiu cu passul* and told me it was chicken."

"It tasted just like chicken."

"For years, whenever I watched *Bambi*, I had to close my eyes when Thumper came on the screen," Cat told the others.

"The kids, they watch *Sesame Street*," Jennie maintained.

"What's that got to do with anything?"

"They look at Big Bird, they still eat chicken."

Cat gave up. "As I recall, baking *pasqua* doesn't usually call for Sunday best and a visit to Louie's Cut-N-Curl."

"Is she down there, Cat?" Rose asked. Cat and Rose had gone to school together. It was Mazza now, not Cicciolini, she was on pregnancy number six. "I saw *Redemption* eight times, I never cried so hard in my life."

Cat threw up her hands in surrender. "Okay, I'll make sure the downstairs door stays open, but that's as far as I go." She hunted up a small paper bag, filled it with cookies, gave her mother a kiss on the cheek and headed down the stairs, giving the rubber wedge under the stairwell door a good kick. She heard a raised voice, saw the light on in the church office, slipped across the corridor. The door was ajar, someone was saying, "No, he didn't show, he really did take off." Then, "Cici, just tell me what you think he's up to that would"–Harold Anderson lowered his voice–"that would mess up the shoot? C'mon, honey, I know he's a ferret, but there's nothing to ferret out. You like that? I think I can use that line somewhere." Another pause. "No, don't go there, wait awhile, I'll try his place again later, maybe he's back in town."

Cat backed off, headed for the church. What *was* Ron up to, she wondered for the hundredth time that day.

The fact that Dudek's funeral service had not taken place in a church hadn't fazed *CopWatch*, or Harold. April had told Cat that a church would crank up the funeral scene, asked if there was a local church that had a little zip to it. What St. Agnes was lacking in zip, it made up for with its set of beautiful stained-glass windows (minus the one that had been boarded up), an imposing stone exterior, oak pews that took to the artificial light, acoustics that didn't drive the sound man nuts, and an honest-to-God bell tower. Ted Cusack had penned his melodramatic finale there, the one where Kate and Tim wrestled it out, and Tim went out the window. Cat reminded April that the "real Tim" was not dead, had in fact made bail and was mounting a costly defense. April's reply had been, "What's that got to do with anything?" After that, Cat held her tongue and CopWatch Productions had fronted for the repair of the bell tower flooring and replacement of its door, as well as the reconstruction of the stained-glass window and the recarpeting of the sanctuary. She had been impressed that the work had been accomplished in a month despite the wrangling over who would perform the construction, union or non-union, *CopWatch* crews or city crews, whether a portion of the work would be assigned to minority contractors. April knew how to get things done.

Still, Cat hoped something would happen to alter their plans for a bell tower death struggle. That, she couldn't watch. Not after what had happened last month. Watching a Lucy the Elephant death struggle, her only quandary would be how to keep a straight face, how to keep from laughing after Red called for sound off.

Cat saw the coffin laid perpendicular to the altar railing. Dominic and Monsignor Greg had agreed that there would be no traffic on the altar, that the purple-swathed statues would not be uncovered. A pert makeup girl was daubing something onto the face of the corpse, giggling. Cat saw only the crown of a brown mop, a gray-suited figure that was about Ron's height. A knot of people sat in a circle at the rear of the nave, Tommi Ann and Ben Butler, Dianne King, Harold Anderson, Red Melendez, a couple of the supporting players.

"Come join us, Mrs. Austen." Tommi Ann gestured to the vacant chair beside her. The crew, PAs wearing their I'm-used-to-the-company-of-gods nonchalance, took note. That Cat was "the real Kate Auletta" had meant nothing—reality and illusion were inconsequential distinctions as far as they were concerned—but the possibility that Cat had that most precious of commodities, the favor of Tommi Ann Butler, removed her mantle of invisibility, made her someone they might have to want to know.

Cat sat, unobtrusively slipped her notebook onto her lap. The chair began to vibrate under her, and for a brief moment, she thought they were having an earthquake. Except the cries from the street preceded the tremor, the PAs, interns, crew were excited, not fearful. Bigg Phat P.I.G., for whom the role of station manager Barry Fried had undergone considerable renovation, had left the customized trailer and been escorted to the premises.

Cat shielded the page with her hand, wrote, *They circle as though held in his orbit by the gravitational pull of his considerable mass.* Cat looked him over. He was immense, over six feet tall and three hundred pounds, with a part sheared down the center of his short hair, and round, fun-loving eyes. The eyes took in the lights, the cameras, the trappings with undisguised awe; Cat would have thought him too accustomed to this paraphernalia to feel amazement, too conscientious of the homeboy persona to betray it.

Four personal satellites, Cat noted: two plainclothes, two of the Phoenix green jackets. She had an image of remora tracking the whale shark, living off its scraps. She wrote, *The stars are the beasts, the underlings, scavengers piloting for a bigger share of carrion,* figured she would decide which analogy—mountain, planet, whale shark—she would use later. A shadow fell over the page and Cat looked up. Bigg Phat P.I.G. was standing over her, looking down.

Tommi Ann made the introduction. "Gary, this is Mrs. Austen. Harold's script is based on her reporting."

"The one Tommi Ann's playin'?" He held out his hand.

"That's right." Cat felt the current of interest rush toward her, couldn't determine if it blew hot or cold.

"What'cha writin' there?"

Busted, as Jane would have said. But when Cat held up the pad,

Biggs only grinned. "That's real good. Wish I could write. You know, knew how to do it? Like Harold?"

No, I don't know how to do it like Harold. "You write some of your own lyrics," Cat replied. Her peripheral vision caught one of the massive guards shifting as if to intercede. *Trying to hustle him away from the lowly press?*

"Yeah. That's not, you know, the same."

"You don't impress me as someone who wants to be the *same* as anyone else," Cat was relieved that he hadn't been insulted at the comparison to a whale.

"Only jus' where it counts."

"Where what counts?" Cat sensed that not only Biggs' handlers, but also Tommi Ann, Ben Butler, and Dianne King were monitoring her conversation carefully, poised to intervene.

"To be the same as other folks. You gotta be 'nough like them to, you know, get where they at so you connect. You get what I'm sayin'?" He smiled, broadly. "Like how Tommi Ann does. Tommi Ann plays a part, don' nobody say, 'I don' get it,' everyone always get it. Get what I'm sayin'?"

Cat was feeling mischievous. She offered the open bag to Biggs. "Cookie?"

The Pig shot Tommi Ann a sly look. "I'm s'posed to be watching my weight." His massive hand plunged into the bag, nonetheless. "But I could eat something."

Cat smiled. "That's how my brother puts it."

"You watch out there, Mrs. Austen," Butler called. "You feed him, you're never gonna get rid of him."

An uncertain pause; then laugher from Biggs, Tommi Ann, which licensed laughter from everyone else. *Dear Lord,* Cat thought, *do these people need to have their sense of humor validated by the gods?*

Tommi Ann smiled, patted Biggs' sleeve. "Red, I think we ought to try to run it, don't you?"

Melendez jumped up, assumed his directorial posture. He wore a baseball cap backward, the short ponytail sprouting from beneath the brim. He backed up to the center of the aisle, pitched his voice to cover the crew manning the lights mounted on an overhead scaffold. "We're Tommi Ann to her mark, Pig, Harold, Anita, Kelli, my background, lines, lines, eulogy, eulogy, pan back, the cop, old man Donner and cut. Tommi Ann checks out Donner, gets up, follows him to the door, cut. Wind up the eulogy, Harold get up, do the stumble, cut. We'll break and Mae, you'll be setting up pick-ups of Tommi Ann, Harold, the cop, Donner, maybe our priest while we set up for the Kate-Tim-Wanda. Mae, you can get the background outta the corral."

That sounded efficient, Cat thought. If everything ran as smoothly as the afternoon shoot, she would be in bed by eleven.

The first scene was a relatively simple one. Tommi Ann would slip into a rear pew. Biggs would enter, escorting a bit player named Anita Garvin, who was playing Gerry's devoted girlfriend, Candi. A series of entrances: Tim Harper, Wanda the Weathergirl; a few takes of the background; the guy playing the priest would move to the front and give a short eulogy; the camera would glide to Kate, who would observe Donner, Gerry's estranged father, slipping out the back, would follow, tail him. Pickups, then a set-up for Kate exiting the church, intercepted by a drunken Wanda, saved by Tim, a shot of the old man pulling out of the lot, close-up of Tommi Ann mouthing his license number. Cat took a chair against the back wall, sat beside Dianne King, who was calmly doing crosswords with the slow deliberation of someone who had a lot of time on her hands. Okay, Cat decided, a couple retakes, a couple fluffed lines, maybe. Eleven-*thirty*. She looked up, saw Lorraine, Jackie Wing in the clutch of extras, gave a quick wave.

Tommi Ann stood motionless while a makeup girl—the one who did everyone, not a personal attendant, Cat noticed—gave the star's hair a final touch-up with trembling hands, a camera assistant held a light meter to her nose, her breast, backed off.

Mae called for sound off and quiet locked in. Red growled, "Aaaaaaaaaandddd ACTION!"

Tommi Ann's move is effortless. Biggs and Anita walk down the aisle, hit their marks, Biggs says the first of his two lines, "Yo, Ms. Auletta."

Cut.

Red summoned April, Harold, the script supervisor, Mae and Biggs into a huddle. Several of the PAs orbited like gnats around fruit. Cat leaned forward, heard enough to understand that the script called for Biggs to follow up his "Yo, Ms. Auletta," with a "Yo, Timmy, over here," when Harold made his entrance. Red, upon earnest deliberation, had speculated whether this might be one "Yo" too many. What did April think? What did Mae think? What did Biggs think?

Cat observed that no one asked Harold, who had penned the lines, what he thought.

Twenty minutes of discussion ensued, whereupon it was decided that one of the "Yo's" would have to change to "Hey." Another twenty minutes to decide whether it should be "Yo, Ms. Auletta," and then, "Hey, Timmy, over here," or perhaps, "Hey, Ms. Auletta," and then "Yo, Timmy, over here." It was proposed that "Yo" might be just a tad too casual an address even for Barry, the hip, GenX station manager, to direct toward the streetwise, yet elegant, sassy yet reserved, Kate Auletta, and therefore the lines would change to "Hey, Ms. Auletta," and "Yo, Timmy, over here." Another twenty to drum the change into Biggs' head.

Action! Biggs, Anita, "Yo, Ms. Auletta." Cut.

Take Three: Biggs, Anita, "Hey, Ms. Auletta"; they move to the third row and Biggs is unable to jam himself into the narrow pew.

Cut.

"Didn't we re*hearse* this!" April cried. "Didn't we run *through* this once to make sure everyone could do the moves? Get me two unions to rip out those first three pews—"

Cat gasped, saw two massive young men stroll toward the first row. "April, wait a minute," she suggested. "Why don't you just put a row of folding chairs in the front? Let The Pi—Barry—Mr. Biggs—sit in the front row?"

"Why didn't any of you come up with that! Why do I have to look to a *writer* to come up with an idea around here? Where can I get myself some folding chairs?"

"April, this is a church," someone said. "What church don't got folding chairs?"

"June, go knock on the priest's door, ask him how much to lease a dozen folding chairs for the night. Todd, you go with. Do it yesterday."

For the night, Cat thought, with a discreet look at her watch. Folding chairs. "April?" she called out. "You can get them upstairs in the kitchen, they've got plenty." *Mama, don't ever say I didn't do anything for you.*

"Todd, June, get the chairs."

June Jejune attempted to protest. "April, Todd's not supposed to run errands like that, he's IATSE—"

"Then he'd better get those chairs to where I at, *see?* I'm not budgeted for union whinemeisters. Harold, where the *hell* do you think you're going?"

"I'm just gonna run make a phone call—"

"If calls were balls, I'd be Errol Flynn. Phone home when you're unemployed. Any you schmucks try a disappearing act, they'll be serving your liver on the lunch line."

"They already are, April," someone muttered.

"Who said that? *Who said that?*"

Todd and June came back with folding chairs; Todd whispered something to one of the other techies, nodded upward toward the second floor and Cat predicted an imminent *coup d'etat* in catering.

Action. Biggs, Anita, "Hey, Ms. Auletta," up to the front row; Anita stalls, mid-aisle. "Red, when you told Piggy to move to the front, does that mean that I'm supposed to move to the front, too, or should I still sit in the third row?"

Cut.

FRONT ROW. Cat willed her thoughts into Red's brain. Impenetrable. Ten minutes of let's-try-it-this-way/let's-try-it-that-way.

Take Four: Tommi Ann (Kate) in her seat, Biggs (Barry) and Anita (Candi), "Hey, Ms. Auletta," move to the front row, Biggs takes the first chair, sits. Cat saw the narrow metal legs do a *demi plie*, winced. Anita moves in from the aisle, descends, her blonde bouffant sinks like—Cat opted for the mountain metaphor—the sun behind the Tetons.

Cut.

"Can't you put me on the aisle?" Anita pleaded. "If you put me upstage of Piggy, *nobody will be able to see me.*"

Ten minutes to revise the blocking, get Biggs to move one chair down, so that Anita could take the aisle seat. Biggs' "I'll sit on the floor you want, just so's we get through this," looking toward the bag of cookies he had left on a chair in the back of the nave.

Take Five: Biggs, Anita enter, "Yo, Ms. Auletta."

Take Six: Biggs, Anita, "Hey, Ms. Auletta," move to the front, second chair in, Anita sits on Biggs' left, whips out a hankie and lets fly. Enter Harold. Biggs half rises in his chair, "Yo, Harold, over here."

Cut.

Biggs: "What? What?"

Tommi Ann: (patiently, and with some amusement) "You called him 'Harold,' Gary."

Biggs: "Sorry, Red. Sorry, everybody."

Take Seven: Biggs, Anita, "Hey, Ms. Auletta," move to the front, and despite the coaching, Biggs' derriere descends toward the aisle seat as Anita docks in the same port. The resulting collision propels Anita toward the coffin, which causes the lid to slam shut.

Cut.

Cat heard a familiar "Hey! Jeez!" Four unions hustled over to yank the lid. Stan Rice sat up, his Gerry wig askew. "Somebody wanna shove a wedge or something in this thing?"

Red did his Roberto Aguilar/Victor Calderone amalgam, addressed the unions with "You know the drill, get a handle on it." Six unions executed the arduous and highly skilled task of removing the rubber wedge from beneath the corridor door and shoving it next to one of the hinges in the coffin lid.

Take Eight: Tommi Ann, Biggs, Anita, "Hey, Ms. Auletta," sit, Harold enters, "Yo, Timmy, over here," Harold walks to the front, sits, recedes into invisibility behind Biggs' girth and Anita's bouffant.

A fifteen-minute musical chairs with Biggs, Anita and Harold shifting positions so that every possible combination could be carefully evaluated. "My agent said this was gonna boost my career, he never said it was gonna *be* my career."

Cat turned, saw the girl who played Wanda, Kelli Something, jumpily tapping her spike heels. Cat checked her watch. Had two hours gone by already? To film a six-minute scene!

Take Nine: "Yo, Ms. Auletta."

Cut.

Cat gave a furtive glance toward Dianne King, halfway through her crosswords. She slipped her notebook out of her tote and tried to come up with something, some witty, pithy insights on the intricacy of shooting a television show for the fly-on-the-set piece she had half promised to get to Ritchie by tomorrow, deadline for Thursday's *Chronicle. Nothing's happening.* Run through, set up, cue lights and sound, position actors, roll film, screw it up, do it again. *The glamour of making a television program is a myth,* she wrote. *In reality, watching a TV show shoot is several notches below watching wallpaper peel on the glee meter.*

Cat felt a current of interest forming somewhere behind her. She turned and saw Victor emerge from the corridor, step into the rear of the nave.

CHAPTER SEVEN

EXT: PARKING LOT: NIGHT
LIEUTENANT VICTOR CALDERONE strides through
the crowd and the crowd parts. Their stares
suggest that he is an enigma, that nobody
really knows him nor ever will.

Cat noticed even Dianne King looked up from her book, that the calculated nonchalance of the PAs evaporated.

Red Melendez began to inflate with relevance, dredged up the grim authority he had worked as Roberto Aguilar and ordered, "C'mon, now, let's make this one a keeper, Mae, sound off." Show the lieutenant how things operated on his turf.

Sound off. Action.

Take Ten.

Victor looked at Cat, tapped his watch, flashed all ten fingers.

Cat smiled weakly, nodded.

Biggs, Anita, "Hey," sit, Harold, "Yo," sit, Kelli takes her first step and an overhead light blows with an audible Pop!, everyone hits the carpet. Harold takes a lateral dive under the bier, Biggs shunts Anita to the floor, Danny Furina leaps on Tommi Ann, hired muscle surrounds her, hustles her toward the exit.

Silence. A few heads lift, observe that Victor and Cat remained standing calmly at the back of the nave.

Red bounded to his feet, donned his Aguilar/Calderone authority. He informed them that everything was cool, that nothing was hinkey. Cat, leaning close to Victor, felt the slight expansion, contraction of his chest, a sigh withheld.

"Is Tommi Ann all right?" Mrs. King, genuinely alarmed.

Butler nodded, "She's okay, Dianne."

April squirmed to her feet. "Who's my bulb jockey?" She turned to Victor. "Who're you?"

"Victor Cardenas."

She looked at Cat. "You didn't tell me this was what he looked like."

"This is what he looks like," Cat informed her.

"You knew that wasn't a gunshot?" April approached Victor, her canny gaze making a rapid assessment.

"Of course."

Cat saw Red nodding, verifying that of course it wasn't a gunshot, of course he, too, knew as much.

"You ever do any acting?"

"In high school, I played the murderer in *Macbeth*, and Mercutio in *Romeo and Juliet*."

"I mean real acting, like commercials, TV, voice-overs, anything, like, significant?"

Victor thought of his three years undercover, identity submerged beneath a scripted persona, when missing a mark, a line, a cue meant it was over. "No," he replied, politely. "Nothing significant."

"You wanna make a quick seventy-six fifty, I can use you in my background."

"Thank you, but I think a border of professionalism needs to be preserved."

"Oh, yeah? Tell it to the dick in the coffin. Okay," April yelled, "Riddle of the day, folks: How many unions does it take to screw in a lightbulb?"

It took a mere six, who with remarkable dexterity and mechanical skill had the light replaced in half an hour. Another two, in an impressive display of efficiency and manual aptitude swept up the glass, having first determined that April wanted *all* of the glass removed. None of which took place immediately, however, as the unions reminded April that it was time for their mandatory dinner break.

"If breaks were snakes, I'd be Cleopatra! Red, we'll give 'em thirty, then it's start to finish, so somebody brace The Pig on his lines."

Victor leaned down to Cat, murmured, "'The pox of such antic, lisping affecting fantasticoes.'"

Dianne King overheard, looked him over with a suggestion of a smile.

Victor cut through the actors exiting the pews, made his way to the front of the nave, looked into the coffin. Stan Rice was lying prone, smoothing down the vest of his gray, three-piece suit.

Stan tugged at the lapels of the jacket. "You like the threads? Spivak's. Wardrobe loaned 'em to me, tailor-made stuff. Perfect fit, you think?"

"Let's see." Victor reached across the open coffin, yanked the wedge free. The lid fell shut. "Perfect fit." Victor walked up the aisle, his dark eyes panning the scene.

"A couple of you unions wanna get the Sarge outta the box?" April yelled.

"I had assumed they would be finished by now. I'd hoped to lure you away for a drink," Victor told Cat.

"Never assume. They haven't even gotten the first scene down and I have to hang around. I've got to get something together I can deliver to Ritchie. But we can have some coffee upstairs." Cat led him toward the stairwell, a bit conscious that they were being watched, the real Kate Auletta, the real Victor Calderone.

"I smell more than coffee."

"The Daughters of Sicily just *happened* to be cooking."

About forty people, crew, PAs, supporting cast, had accidentally found their way to the source of the wonderful aromas, were drifting into the room. Cat felt the vibration of the cumulative tread of Biggs and his posse, watched as he entered the room, inhaled. "Man," he whispered, ecstatically. "Man." He spotted Cat. "Hey, there, Ms. Auletta. I mean, Austen. I can't keep those lines straight to save my skin." He was grinning, the dimples sinking deep into the plump cheeks.

Cat could feel the Daughters of Sicily staring. *Okay.* "Mr. Biggs, this is my mother, Jennie Fortunati." She introduced the other women. "Mom, this is the singer the boys were telling you about." "The boys" were Jennie's teenage grandsons. She couldn't bring herself to say "Bigg Phat P.I.G."

Jennie opened with the Sicilian gambit. "Mr. Biggs, you look like a boy could use something to eat."

"You just call me The Pig, like they all do."

Rose Cicciolini's oldest two were teenagers; Cat could see her starting to go stupid behind the kitchen counter.

A couple of the PAs, Anita, the old guy who played Gerry's father, a half dozen of the unions drifted into the room. Someone came up with a lame, "Sorry, we thought this was craft service," but didn't leave.

Cat poured coffee into a pair of Styrofoam cups, nodded Victor toward a table away from the entrance. "You remember that New Testament passage about the loaves and fishes?" Cat whispered. "That was nothing."

Within ten minutes, the five women in the kitchen were feeding the television strays with the ease and abundance as if the seventy were seven.

"Career change?" Victor nodded toward Jennie.

"All of the Fortunati women are late bloomers," Cat said. "We wait until mid-life and then it's Jekyll into Hyde."

Victor saw her mouth curve in amusement, asked, "What's so funny?" with a simple lift of his brows.

"I was just watching you. The way you always case the joint. My brothers do it, too." She lowered her voice. "You should see Red Melendez trying to imitate it. He does this frozen-faced sort of—" she squeezed her facial muscles into place, shifted her eyes from side to side. "And he gives himself close-ups when he does it."

Victor smiled, nodded toward the room. "I suspect it would be unmannerly of me to say that I don't recognize anyone here. Fill me in."

Cat half-turned in her chair. "You know who Biggs is, the rap singer who's playing the station manager. Remember Barry Fried?"

"Didn't he have the part of the DJ originally?"

"I think it had something to do with the lines. Ron's only got a few scenes, but he has a lot of dialogue. Either that or the image. Apparently Butler controls the image, and he may not have wanted Biggs to play a sleazy shock jock." She nodded to his companions. "Those four are his personal detail. That blonde girl is the one playing Wanda—remember Whitney Rocap, the weather*person*? The old guy is playing Gerry's father. You know half the people in the background." Cat waved to Lorraine, who had gotten a plate of food, was craning her neck, looking for Tommi Ann. "The petite girl, she's Gerry's girlfriend. Test me, I've got them down cold."

"Muscular girl with the frizzy hair?"

"Boom operator."

"Bald guy in the plaid shirt?"

"He's the key grip."

"And that would be?"

"King of the gripsies." Cat turned back to Victor so that they couldn't catch her giggle. "And don't you dare do something someone else is supposed to be doing, even if they're *not* doing it or the unions all go to their union forepersons, which are all men in this case, but you still have to *say* fore*persons*, and talk about their issues of communication for an hour and that drives April crazy."

"The anorexic girl in the oversized clothes, the one who walked out without eating anything."

"June Mathis. She's April's right hand."

"Guy with the tattoos and the blond ponytail, the one who's trying to look like he's not looking at us."

"Wally Something. He's the powder man."

"As in Cover Girl?"

"As in duck-and-cover. Explosives and weapons. I don't know why he's here tonight, they're not using weapons. The rest are mostly the extras and bit players."

"How long are they scheduled to go? Do you want me to wait around?"

Cat shook her head. "It went pretty fast this afternoon, but there was a lot of hanging around the second unit and watching them rehearse the background—the extras—for the nightclub scene. All afternoon, bumping and grinding, I barely made it home for dinner."

"Run that past me again?"

"I meant watching other people bumping and grinding. The club habitués. Trying to get it to look like ... Well, remember last week when you came over and Jane turned on MTV, that music video I made her turn off, the girls in the background?"

Victor cleared his throat. "I would like to assert my fifth amendment privilege."

"All after*noon*. Because the assistant director was having a hard time getting them to—and this is a direct quote—'crank up the backfield, keesterwise.'"

"Where *is* everyone! Where are my people! What is this?" April Steinmetz stormed into the room, lifted her head, took one critical whiff. "What's this? Who's the new caterer? Did June hire a new caterer? Where's June?"

There was an equivocal silence; no one knew whether to admit to June's whereabouts or deny having seen her; the wrong answer could banish the speaker to the outer rim of the concentric configuration that had Tommi Ann at its core.

"April, you oughta try this." Biggs spoke with his mouth half full.

April turned to the kitchen crew. "Are you union?"

Jennie shot her a scornful look.

April hustled into the mix. "How much you charge?"

"Charge?" Jennie asked, innocently.

"And the Oscar goes to ..." Cat murmured.

"For food service, what're your rates?"

"Eight-hour shoot we can give you a hot meal and a cold meal, including antipasto, salads and bread, coffee and dessert service the whole time for– Whaddaya payin' those people downstairs?"

"Five-fifty a day for seventy-five people."

"You're gettin' robbed. The Daughters of Sicily can do two hot meals for three hundred a day, a hot and a cold for two and a quarter, we provide all the transportation, setup, cleanup, you got anybody's on a special diet, we need twenty-four hours advance notice."

April stuck out her hand; Jennie's disappeared into April's plump grasp. April handed her a card. "Call me tomorrow, we'll make the arrangements."

Jennie walked back to the kitchen with elaborate casualness; Cat heard a whoop from Rose Cicciolini.

Victor rose. "Walk me out."

They strolled along the back of the nave. Cat saw Jackie Wing leaning on the coffin, chatting with Stan Rice. "Tell Rice he's at his desk tomorrow at eight, no matter how exciting things get around here."

"If it gets any more exciting, it'll put me in a coma," Cat said; an open mike picked up her comment and they heard Ben Butler's chuckle from a corner.

"This is Lieutenant Cardenas, Mr. Butler."

Victor nodded. Butler snapped his cell phone shut, stepped forward to shake hands, looked him over. "You seen any of the footage of Tommi Ann and Red?" he asked Cat. She shook her head. "They don't call Tommi Ann the greatest actress in the world for nothin'. You leavin', Lieutenant? Afraid we might put you into a coma, too?"

"I'm not afraid of much, Mr. Butler."

Victor left her at the entrance, whispered, "Call me if you need CPR."

Cat checked her watch, nodded to Butler and went to hunt up Dianne King, see if she could lock in her interview. She strolled toward the parking lot to watch the crew set up for the short confrontation among Kate, Tim and Wanda.

"–I can unload 'em, no problem, it's never been a problem. I got some inside help setting up the–"

The words were being whispered urgently; Cat caught sight of a bulky blond figure, standing behind the crook of the open door, a cell phone pressed to his ear. She descended the ramp to the parking lot, noisily, heard the click of a cell phone being flipped closed, saw the powder guy, Wally, emerge from his corner.

Cat walked past him, pretended to be fascinated by the mounting of lights on a large overhead crane. She began composing her copy in her head: *If you ever have occasion to watch a television show being filmed, the most important thing to remember is to BRING A BOOK.* She checked her watch: twelve fifty-five. She wandered back into the nave, sat. Red Melendez ran them through the scene three times; Biggs missed his lines twice, got them down once.

Sound off.

ACTION!

"Yo, Ms. Auletta."

Cut.

CHAPTER EIGHT

INT: NIGHTCLUB: NIGHT
KATE closes her eyes to the hectic whirl of
lights, dancers, movement. She hears the
conversation with her editor, RICKY, in
her head.

RICKY (voice over)
Get them to talk about where they came from.
How they hooked up. Pay dirt from the past.

KATE (voice over)
What if there's no dirt in their past?

RICKY (voice over)
There's always dirt.

Cat rolled deeper into her pillow; her cheek settled on something flat and crisp that crackled in her ear like a gunshot. She catapulted upright, a convulsion of pure reflex shocking her out of sleep. She blinked, looked around her room. Hard mid-morning light cut a vertical border below the near-shut drapes. Last night's clothes lay where gravity had deposited them. She heard a ringing phone somewhere below, looked on her night table. Ellice must have unplugged her phone. The digital display on the clock read 10:39. Cat saw a square of note paper on her pillow. She must have rolled over it, the rustling of it like a shot against her ear.

She pressed one hand to her throbbing forehead; the previous night was filtering into consciousness, the spirit-crushing boredom of it. She held the paper up to the light, read, *You promised me a picture of Bigg Phat P.I.G. Did you get it? Are you going to be home when I get home from school? Kellianne Wheat doesn't believe you got to see Bigg Phat P.I.G. in person. XXXOOO, Jane.*

Cat smiled. Jane's note was meant to provoke an indignant "I did *too* get to see Bigg Phat P.I.G.," a renewed commitment to get his photograph, if only to purge the blot Kellianne Wheat had cast upon the Austen family honor.

Cat shuffled over to the mirror, looked at the tousled chestnut hair, the oversized gray sweats. She was winter pale, a trace of veining tinting the flesh under her eyes. *I haven't slept this badly since the kids were babies.* She and Chris shambling around like the undead, sharing the nurse/diapering routine, punchy and unromantic. Chris, nestling against her back, muttering, "Az zoon as I haf the energy, I vant to bite your neck," dropping into sleep like a stone through water.

Cat shuffled down to the kitchen. Whiteness, the stark predominant color, hurt her eyes and she squinted, made her way to the coffeepot by instinct. Ellice was sitting at the dining room table, Mats on her lap, reading a new book about fire trucks. She pointed out small words, Freddy's diamond sparkling on her left hand. "I put Jane on the bus. You look like the queen of the undead."

Cat poured herself a mug of coffee.

"We went to the bookstore," Mats told her.

"Isn't that the third time since last week?" Cat asked. "Ellice, you don't have to do that."

Ellice shrugged. "It could be worse. He could be wanting to go to the v-i-d-e-o store. Besides, I haven't been called for a week." Cat met

Ellice when Ellice had been fleeing a violent relationship; the offer of a haven had resulted in a deep friendship, one which had Cat blessing her Good Samaritan instincts. Ellice had set about working her way back to a normal existence, earning her keep as an underpaid and overly skilled substitute teacher, and had become engaged to Cat's brother Freddy. "I unplugged your phone. You had calls from Ritchie, I lost count, one from that Friedlander woman, one from *Front Cover*—"

"No kidding?"

"April Steinmetz. Victor, who said I shouldn't wake you."

"Jane mad?"

"Yes. You'd better produce that picture of the porcine one, or she's going to be shopping for a new mother."

"You can't buy new moms," Mats informed Ellice. "They're not on sale."

"That's right, baby." Cat slumped into a dining room chair.

"What time did you get in, anyway?"

"Three-thirty. I forgot they *had* one of those in the morning. And I went blundering into Ron's apartment at four a.m. to put out his recyclables because I forgot to do it yesterday, thank God he doesn't have neighbors, they would have thought I was a burglar. And I've got this notebook full of nothing that I've got to turn into something gossipy and fascinating for the *Chronicle*."

"When's Spivak coming back?" Ellice asked.

"Tomorrow, I think."

"What's he up to?"

"I don't know. But I have the feeling that whatever he's onto is something really blow-the-locals-out-of-the-water sensational."

"If he was after sensation, why didn't he stick around? Isn't this where the action is?"

Cat shrugged. "Did Dianne King call?"

"No. Who's Dianne King?"

"The publicist for Butler Talent. Tommi Ann's right arm. She's supposed to call about setting up an interview." Cat pushed herself up. "I've got to get dressed, check Ron's mail, put last night's shoot through the keyboard and see if it comes out of the printer sounding fascinating."

"Did somebody get shot?" Mats wanted to know.

"I wish. Anything to liven it up."

Cat went up to her room and got a quick shower, tugged her wet hair into a French braid and blow-dried her bangs. She pulled on jeans and a magenta sweater, heavy socks and retired running shoes, dropped into the chair in front of the work station set up on a library table under her bedroom window. "Settling for crumbs," she murmured.

The winter had generated a lot of excitement, but little copy. The Sterling conspiracy, pretty much as she had recited it to Blaine Sterling, had so far been unprovable. Sterling was back in a shaky alliance with Fawn, and Carlton Amis was vigorously planning a defense strategy for his wife in the Earlene Adkins murder and its aftermath. Cat would not touch the St. Agnes killings, of course, and the rest of the media were too wrapped up in the advent of *CopWatch* to spend much time speculating whether the series of murders was connected with the accident in the bell tower that had resulted in the death of St. Agnes' deacon, Kevin Keller. Real murder couldn't compete with TV murder, uncelebrated dead were nothing compared to a living goddess.

Cat picked up the phone and called Karen Friedlander, got her machine. "Yeah, it's Cat Austen checking back with you, I've got to run, I'm late for an appointment"—*liar*—"I'll try to get back to you before I have to meet with Tommi Ann." *Liar, liar.*

She hung up, dialed Ritchie's office. "Ritchie, I was up until all hours with this shooting, I'm trying to sleep in, why on earth do you keep calling me so early?"

"You can sleep after Tommi Ann blows town. You get some time with her yet?"

"I'll call Dianne King about it today."

"Take one of those pocket thirty-five millimeters, snap the Oscar duds when she's not looking. I heard she's wearing a CapriOH! original. How'd the shoot go last night? How'd they make out without Spivak?"

"They had a stand-in. And the shoot was boring. They take a half hour to shoot something that's going to be on the screen for thirty seconds and then someone yells 'Cut' and they quibble about what was wrong with it and then shoot it again and again and again."

"You got some backstage skinny I can use for the *Chronicle*?"

"I'll drop something by this afternoon."

"Look, I'm tellin' you, hook up with Tommi Ann, this is your only shot at her. Spivak gets the goods on her first, you're left eatin' cold copy."

"I can't imagine what goods he would be getting three thousand miles from where the goods are."

She hung up and dialed Victor's office extension. "Hello, love. I told Ellice not to wake you," he said.

"Why would someone go to extraordinary lengths to achieve something and then just when you're almost there, walk away from it?" she proposed.

"Is this a philosophical inquiry or a practical one?"

"Ellice says that the philosophical is generally practical."

"I've come to the conclusion that the answer to many philosophical inquiries is 'I don't know' and I imagine it will have to do here. Who walked away from what prize?"

"I've been thinking about Ron's trip."

"He may have something better. More pressing. I understand he never works fewer than a half dozen stories at a time."

Cat tugged at her bangs, absently. "But you don't put Tommi Ann Butler on hold so you can wrap your exposé on toxic waste."

"May I suggest a wonderful investigative technique I've used with considerable success?"

"What is it?"

"Call him up and ask him."

"I don't even know where he's staying." She paused. "Victor, there's something else. It's probably nothing, but if I acted like it was nothing and then it turned out to be something, you'd tell me I was holding out."

Victor cleared his throat. "There is an observation to be made here about holding out that I will be gentleman enough to refrain from putting out. Excuse me, putting forth."

"I was waiting around for them to start shooting again and I overheard this guy talking on a cell phone. You remember the blond guy I said was a powder man?"

"As in duck-and-cover. Yes."

"He was saying something about he could unload something, it was never a problem and he had inside help."

"What else?"

"That's it. It's just ... he wasn't on the crew call sheet last night, there was really no reason for him to be there. He's only on the set when they use gun props, and they're shooting blanks or using some kind of explosive, something like that."

"I'll check with Stan Rice. Meanwhile, ask around, see if anyone else has worked with him before."

"You're asking me to investigate?"

"Just enough to kill the time during those interminable shots. Ask the producer. Or Melendez."

"Ugh. Every time I talk to him, I feel like he's taking the opportunity to try out his Victor Calderone moves on the real Kate Auletta."

"Well, if you're as impervious to his as you've been to mine, I don't think I've got anything to worry about. Where will you be today?"

"Here and there. Can you come by for dinner tonight?"

"I'll try." He hesitated. "Not nervous about tomorrow night's shoot, are you?"

"A little." Tomorrow night they were scheduled to recreate the scene where Jerry Dudek had pursued Cat into a dark parking lot, gotten shot. "But I just keep telling myself, it's only a movie, it's only a movie."

Cat managed to knock off two short pieces, one on the shooting in the church, using the production company's restoration of the building as her angle, the other on the Daughters of Sicily taking on catering for *CopWatch*, faxed both pieces to Ritchie, then asked Mats if he wanted to take a ride with her.

Ron Spivak lived on the west side of Ocean City, a two-story condo complex whose bedrooms and living areas overlooked the bay. The outdoor lot was bordered in white chain-link with a small driveway entrance. There were only two cars in the painted rectangles that portioned out the parking spaces for the occupants. Cat recalled that last November, no one had been around to hear Ron's cry for help, hear the commotion that must have occurred when Hopper had dismantled his apartment. Come summer, that would change. Sunbirds would rent for a couple weeks or a season, dock their small watercraft, string up lights for the July Night In Venice parade, party on their cramped decks.

Cat picked up Ron's plastic/glass receptacle that she had dropped next to the Dumpster at four AM, locked her car and held Mats' hand as they walked up to the bank of metal mailboxes at the foot of the steps.

"Are we bein' secret agents again?" Mats wanted to know.

Cat grinned, shook her head. Last December, Cat had gained entry to Danny Furina's office with Furina's mail in hand and Mats in tow, told Mats they were playing secret agents. She groped in her pocket for the keyring Ron had given her, pushed the key into the box labeled SPIVAK, R. She pulled out a few envelopes, locked the box and headed up the painted metal steps to Ron's second-floor unit. *Déjà vu* constricted her stomach like nausea. She had been on the phone with

Ron, he had been filling her in on Dudek's background when his strangled cry for help had aborted the conversation. Cat had called nine-one-one, beaten them to Ron's apartment and found him on the floor, his face and his possessions badly worked over. Mounting these stairs the day after she had watched Jerry's funeral re-enacted yanked her back in time, walking her through her past as if she hadn't done it right the first time, hadn't gotten her lines down, moved onto the scene too slowly or too soon.

In Ted Cusack's treatment, there had been a Van-somebody, a smarmy yellow journalist, not all that different from Jerry—or from Ted himself—who had placed a phone call to Kate, the cry coming right before the commercial break. Fade-in to Kate, rushing to the apartment, using her kick-boxing skills to boot in Van-somebody's front door.

Harold had told Cat that Butler reviewed the treatment, decided that Van weakened the dramatic structure; it diminished Kate's role to have someone else come up with key information on Gerry's past. So Van had gone the way of the kids, the late husband, the savvy housemate, the brothers, but Ron had the last laugh when he won the role of Gerry.

Cat realized she was hyperventilating. "Cut," she ordered herself. "It's only a movie, it's only a movie."

"What's only a movie?"

"We're pretending we're acting in a movie."

"Who are we being?"

"I'll be Kate Auletta, gal sleuth and you can be Dinny Dinosaur."

"Uncle Vinnie says he's gay."

"I think Uncle Vinnie's mistaken."

"What's 'gay'?"

Cat slipped her key into the lock, turned to Mats. "It's when if you're a woman, you fall in love with other women and if you're a man you fall in love with men."

"And dinosaurs be in love with other dinosaurs?"

"I think."

"Dinny's in love with Maggie Mammoth."

"Then I think he's probably not gay. Of course"—she gave the door a tentative push, saw a foot of foyer, the small table against the wall reflected in the mirrored doors of the coat closet—"it could just be platonic. In which case, they both might be gay." She looked down at Mats, who was taking this in, thoughtfully.

She was half tempted to slip her arm in, shoot the mail onto the table with a snap of her wrist and retreat. *Don't be silly*, she told herself. *There's no chance you're going to find Ron lying unconscious on the floor, he was written out of the script.*

Cat gave the door a Kate-Auletta-what-the-hell fling, opening her sight line into the small foyer, the living area beyond. No blood spattered on the off-white walls, no corpse on the faux marble foyer, no suspicious creak from behind the mirrored doors of the coat closet.

"Are we allowed in here?" Mats asked.

"Yes."

The living area extended to the sliding-glass doors, the deck that overlooked the bay. Open-weave curtains, dusty green, admitted enough light to see that the room was well, if inexpensively, furnished, plump faux leather love seats face to face across a glass-topped table, a couple pole lamps with frosted globe shades. Bookshelves, half books, half videos. A wicker basket on the floor under the coffee table was overflowing with newspapers. Magazines were stacked on the low-nap carpet. On top, the latest issue of *Bellissima!* with Tommi Ann on the cover. She was wearing flesh-hugging gold, her slicked-back hair and shoulders dusted with gilt powder, her hands clasping the hilt of a golden sword held vertically in front of her, the pose a replication of the Oscar statue.

Cat took a few tentative steps into the foyer to give herself a wide-angle of the room. Empty, and very still, the vacant stillness of an unoccupied apartment in a sparsely tenanted building on the quiet section of a resort island off season. Not, Cat tried to tell herself, the sinister quiet of a lurking prowler, an abandoned corpse.

The small dining area, round maple table, four captain's chairs, the counter/wine rack that separated it from the narrow kitchen, the cabinets of pale varnished wood, the appliances, utilitarian white, were all comfortably unthreatening. Cat set the recycling container on the kitchen floor, checked out the videos on the shelves, found *South Street Stakeout*, read the jacket copy: *Vigilante ex-cops-turned-PIs take on pimps and pushers in the city of brotherly love. When Cal MacCabe (Harold Anderson) teams up with Kendra "Ken" March (Cici Bonaker) the sparks and bullets fly in this action-packed thriller from the producers of Death Drop.* Cat noticed a generic tape next to it, labeled "Outtakes," and a date, the approximate date of the Philly shoot. Cat shoved it back, put *South Street Stakeout* in her tote, followed a small passage with a closet on one side, a powder room on the other to the bedroom. The bed, night tables, dresser, portable TV were standard issue. Weighty drapes were pulled back, the sheers drawn across the sliding-glass doors admitting diffuse sunlight and an impressionist's rendition of the bay. Across from the bed was an elaborate multi-drawered workstation with PC, fax, printer/scanner flanked by a pair of two-drawer file cabinets. Cat tried one of the drawers, came upon a thickly-packed row of manila folders, articles Ron had clipped and filed. He had meticulously separated the files by topic, with copies of his own work in files prefixed "Spivak." A lot of them, thick enough to make Cat sigh with envy. Ron was a single guy, she reminded herself. He didn't have a big house, a family, a couple kids, he could devote all his time to writing. And if he wanted to drop everything and take off for LA, all he had to do was phone the travel agent, he didn't have to think about who was going to get the laundry done and get the kids fed and off to school, and who was going to shop for groceries.

Cat laid Ron's mail on the desk blotter; her eye caught a scrap of white under the desk, probably spilled out of his recycling bag when she had groped blindly for it at four AM. She picked it up, saw that it was a half envelope with some penciled notations. Ron was probably as thrifty as she when it came to paper, wrote notes, lists, phone messages on envelopes and junk mail. She held it into the light, saw King, Imogene, 180 mi. 114, 380, 82, 83, written as if taken down in haste.

Imogene King? A relation to Dianne King? The number of digits implied a long distance phone number, though the commas baffled her. The name and phone number of whomever he had run off to see in LA?

"Is that a secret code?" Mats asked.

"Yes, I think."

Cat spied a stack of phone directories tucked under the desk, lifted one onto her lap, scanned it for a 114 area code, found a 514, a 214, a 714. It was possible that Ron's seven looked like a one. Probable, since that was in the Los Angeles area. She would try it from her own phone.

Cat kneeled on the carpet and began searching the files for a folder on the *South Street Stakeout* shoot. Ron had been very meticulous, prefaced the files with his own name, then alphabetized them: Spivak, *Atlantic Arts and Media*, Spivak, *Atlantic City Magazine*, Spivak, *Belleville Times*, Spivak, *Boardwalk Beat*, Spivak, *Cape Atlantic Chronicle*, and so on.

Cat picked up the first folder, flipped through it casually. At least two dozen articles, for a small arts journal! The sheer volume of his work depressed her; Mats would have to be in high school before she would be free enough to match this sort of output.

Cat pulled the Spivak, *South Street Stakeout* articles, walked her fingers in reverse until she came to a file labeled, *Butler, Tommi Ann*. Thin; no bigger than her own. A handful of features, a batch of film reviews, interviews with directors who had worked with her, a glowing critique of her acting skills, fan pages printed out from the Web, a spread of their New York penthouse in *Architectural Digest*, Tommi Ann and Ben dwarfing their diminutive interior designer. A series of extraordinarily beautiful photos from a piece called "The Last Great Face."

A metallic scrape, the familiar sound of a key probing a lock, startled her. Ron wasn't due until tomorrow, unless he had caught an early flight. Cat set the mail down and gripped Mats' hand firmly, walked into the living room just as the door opened, and Tommi Ann Butler entered the room.

CHAPTER NINE

INT: NIGHTCLUB: NIGHT
KATE, sitting alone at the table, checks
her watch. A young woman approaches. She
looks familiar. It is NADINE.

NADINE
Excuse me ... you're Kate Auletta, aren't
you? The one who's writing a feature on
Tim and Gerry?

The muted light that filtered through the translucent drapes camouflaged the intruder for that first instant. After that instant passed, Cat was able to assess how strongly Cici Bonaker resembled Tommi Ann by how effectively Cat had been deceived, from ten feet, in person.

The girl could be no one else. Cici Bonaker was tall and slim, with chestnut hair, a shade darker than Tommi Ann's. Her skin was a shade tanner, too, although, Cat thought, that might be the effect of the dimly lit room. The hazel eyes had a more decisive tint than Tommi Ann's, held to their gray-gold hue despite the dark green sweater she wore. She was stunning, with an elegance quite unlike the vapid pertness that seemed to pass for beauty on so many of the young female clones Cat saw on television.

Cat felt a little thrill. *If* Death of a Shock Jock *goes series, she's playing* me. "Hello," she said.

The girl spoke. "I didn't ... I didn't know anyone was here."

"I'm Cat Austen. We haven't met yet. Ron's a friend of mine, he asked me to take in his mail while he's away."

Cici said nothing, her slender fingers closing over the key in her hand.

"He probably forgot that he'd given you a key. When was that? When you were seeing each other last year?"

Cici nodded.

"Or he might have asked you to look after the place. But of course, I'm only a couple blocks away and you're in Atlantic City. I guess he didn't change the locks after what happened to him last November."

"Are you going to tell him?"

"Tell him what?"

"That I broke into his place?" A note of bitterness hardened her voice, making her seem more mature, tougher, like Tommi Ann in *Double Jeopardy.*

"You didn't break nothin'," Mats said.

The girl smiled, faintly. "Is that your little boy?"

"I'm five," Mats told her. *Little!*

"Mats, I saw a TV in the bedroom; I don't think Ron would mind if you turned it on."

Jane would have held her ground, but gossip was no competition for television as far as Mats was concerned.

Cici walked over to the sofa, sat. The fake leather made a slight popping sound. "Please don't tell anyone. Especially not Tommi Ann. Please."

Cat tried to shut off the shameless *There might be a story here, a story Ron doesn't have.* "Tell them what, Cici?" she asked, gently.

The girl looked up. The face was desperate but her voice was cold. "You're like all the rest of them, aren't you? Vultures."

"Vultures feed on carrion. There are no dead bodies here."

"Do you know where he went?"

"LA, I heard."

Cici looked puzzled, a little relieved. "LA? Not ..? Do you know what took him away so suddenly?"

"He didn't say. But he's a pretty diligent researcher, and it wouldn't surprise me if he flew three thousand miles to confirm a story he was working on."

Cici looked at her. "How long have you known him?"

Cat sat on the arm of a chair, opposite Cici. "On a face-to-face basis, not long. We've talked on the phone and he's helped me out a few times when I was stuck for some background. He was particularly helpful with the Dudek story."

Cici looked puzzled.

"*Death of a Shock Jock*," Cat interpreted.

Cici nodded. "I've only known him since last year."

"*South Street Stakeout.*"

"Yeah. Ron had a bit part, he was doing it mostly for the copy he would get from the shoot."

"I know. I haven't seen the movie. Sorry."

"That's all right. It was pretty good, actually. Which, in television jargon translates as it didn't stink. It was my first starring role. Co-starring, really, with Hal. Harold Anderson? It was the first time I wasn't working with Tommi Ann." She shrugged. "Ron and I sort of started to hang out."

Cat nodded to indicate that she was listening.

"I liked him. He was smart, and funny, we had some good times. I haven't had a lot of time for a social life," she added, a bit wistfully. "It's been the career, you know? Get the career on the upswing."

At thirty-seven, Cat had barely gotten the career off the ground. The upswing was still a mirage. "I imagine that when you find yourself in a situation—like making a movie, which has to be pretty"—

boring—"exciting, and you run into someone who's reasonably compatible and the isolation from the familiar, and the intimacy and the"—*sheer boredom*—"excitement of it all can make a relationship seem like more than it is."

"Is that how it was with you and Lieutenant Cardenas? After the DJ got shot?" Cici smiled. "April had breakfast with us this morning, he's all she would talk about."

"I don't think we have a location romance, no."

Cici sighed, nodded. "It lasted a little longer than the shoot, not much. We both liked TV and movies. I say I'm an orphan, he says, 'I'm an orphan, too,' I tell him how I was adopted, he says 'I was adopted, too.' I tell him about my parents' accident—they died a year and a half ago—"

"I'm sorry."

"He's got no folks. I'm an only child, he's an only child. I'm from Texas, he's *been* to Texas. We're both alone, both trying to cut it in a tough, competitive arena."

"Except you've got Tommi Ann and Ben behind you. And all Ron has is talent. And determination."

Cici pushed herself up from the couch, paced in a slow, confident stride that suggested familiarity with the room. "And talent? Let me tell you, you act, you write, you dance, you paint, whether or not you find an audience, a market, has nothing to do with talent. Nothing. Sometimes, you just go into a slow fade, and sometimes you get desperate. You'll do just about anything to make your mark."

"And you think Ron's getting desperate?"

"He didn't want me to hook him up with Tommi Ann, land him an interview. I know that's what everyone thinks."

"What was he after, then?"

Cici's sigh conceded defeat. "He thinks Tommi Ann's my mother."

Cat was speechless.

Cici smiled, wanly. "That's what I said when he brought it up."

"Where did he get an idea like that?"

"That was my line, too. He said, 'Look in the mirror.'"

"You do look a lot like her. When you walked in the door, for a minute, I thought you were Tommi Ann."

"Yeah. I hear it all the time. But a stand-in's supposed to be a close match. I mean, a lot of times, Tommi Ann's had to make do with a guy in a wig, because of her height."

"How did you meet Tommi Ann? An audition?"

"No, college. UTex, Austin. Tommi Ann and Ben came down to judge a film festival. They saw me in one of the student films, got in touch with me, offered me work as her stand-in. It paid my tuition, which took a load off my folks, and it hooked me up with the right people."

"Because you wanted to act."

"Yeah. I thought the doubling was just going to be short-term, you know? Because I guess you've noticed that Tommi Ann doesn't have the entourage. The people who do her hair, her makeup, her lighting, it's whoever the production hired."

"She's not a prima donna?"

Cici shook her head. "Not at all. She's generous, too. She seemed to go out of her way to introduce me to directors, producers. Ben started looking for roles for me."

"The TV movie last year, the small part in *Redemption,* now a possible TV series."

"Yes. But *Redemption* came before the Philly shoot."

And the Philly shoot came right before Ron hired Danny Furina to check out some records. "Is that what made Ron think you were Tommi Ann's daughter? Not just because of the resemblance, but because she was playing fairy godmother?"

"I guess."

"You were adopted as an infant?"

Cici nodded, began to pace, the willowy to-and-fro Tommi Ann had done in *Black Orchid*. "A newborn. It was a private adoption because my parents were too old to adopt through normal channels. But they were wonderful. I never had any desire to know who my birth mother was."

"Was there an intermediary?"

"I think it was arranged directly with my birth mother."

"Did they ever meet Tommi Ann?"

"Yes, a few times. They thought she was lovely."

"But they never let on that they might have known her, that she might have been your mother?"

"No, not at all. If it were true, she would have been a kid. Tommi Ann's the rare case who's never had to shy away from her age. She's almost forty-two. I'm twenty-five."

"It happens." Jennie had been some months shy of nineteen when Carlo had been born. Victor's mother had been in her teens when he was born, too.

"My parents died in a car accident a year and a half ago. If they'd been around when Ron started bringing this up, I could have asked them. They would have told me the truth."

"Did you ever think about asking Tommi Ann?"

Cici nodded, reluctantly. "Because—I don't know—sometimes I get the feeling that there is something she wants to tell me. Something personal. I've talked to Dianne about it a couple times, she's been with Tommi Ann and Ben forever. Not about whether Tommi Ann's my mother, but just asking why Tommi Ann's done so much for me."

"What does she say?"

"She says if there ever is anything Tommi Ann wants me to know, she'll tell me in her own time."

"But Cici, suppose—most extreme scenario—Tommi Ann gave birth to you and gave you up and now she's trying to what? Make amends? Why would that be such a hot story?"

"What if Ben doesn't know? Twenty-five years ago would have

been before they met. Sometimes I wonder if Tommi Ann arranged to be at that film festival because she knew I'd be there."

"Trying to find a way to get you back into her life without Ben knowing?" Cat recalled the look in Butler's eyes when he watched his wife, the devotion close to worship. Cat could not believe that a twenty-five-year-old indiscretion could shatter that. "Was that the angle Ron was pursuing?"

"I don't know. When he had that accident back in the fall, and he had to have the surgery, I thought maybe he'd forget about Tommi Ann. But I don't think he has."

"And so you're here because you wanted to check Ron's place to see if you could turn up notes or files of what he was working on, where he'd gone."

"They've been good to me. I can't let Ron hurt them."

"Cici, look. Ron gave me free rein over his files, I've already gone through them for some material he's loaning me, I didn't see anything other than the usual fan stuff on Tommi Ann. Isn't there anyone on the set he was friendly with, someone he would have talked to about what he was working on? What about Harold?"

"No. Maybe some of the crew we knew from *South Street Stakeout.*"

"Anyone in particular?"

Cici thought for a moment. "Wally Reid. The firearms supervisor. He worked on *South Street Stakeout.*"

"Blond ponytail, tattoos?"

Cici nodded.

"Well, if he's with *CopWatch* now, and *CopWatch* is based in LA, maybe Ron is doing something on him. People behind the lens, something like that." *I'm done with A Day on the Set. Small Time.*

"Do you think so?"

"It's possible." *But not if he had a hot item on Tommi Ann Butler.* "Mats!" Cat called. "Come on, baby."

"I's watching Dinny Dinosaur."

"Tell me," Cat asked, "is 'Cici' a nickname or something? Your real name wouldn't be Imogene would it?"

Cici shook her head. "No. Off the record, please. It's Cressida. Cressida Ann Bonaker."

"What about someone named Imogene King? A relation of Dianne King's maybe? It would be by marriage, I guess. It's Mrs. King, isn't it?"

"I've never heard Dianne mention any relations. Tommi Ann told me once her marriage didn't work out."

"Already the divorced Mrs. King when she went to work for Tommi Ann and Ben?" Cat worked the chronology. "That would be more than twenty years ago, and Mrs. King doesn't look more than forty."

Cici shrugged. "It seemed like a sore subject. I never asked."

"What about someone on the crew?"

Cici shrugged. "I guess you could ask April or June."

Mats came out. "Dinny made a whole cake with stuff outta his magic bag."

Cat drew him close to her. "Cici, I can understand Ron seeing the resemblance and suspecting—or hoping—you're related to Tommi Ann. But to confirm it, he would have to get at the papers. And you said it was private."

"And I didn't find that out until I was about ten or eleven. The names on my birth certificate are Ada and Clyde Bonaker."

"All that had to cost them something."

"They were pretty well off."

"Twenty-five years ago, not much of a paper trail. Did Ron ever hint at how he would go about proving something like that?"

"Private detectives, that was my first thought, but then, even for a PI, it would seem like such an underhanded thing to do, where would he find a private investigator to do something like that?"

Cat thought, *Danny Furina.*

CHAPTER TEN

INT: NIGHTCLUB: NIGHT

> GIRL (screaming)
> Gerry! Look out! Look out!

> *GERRY shoves the girl aside as her*
> *boyfriend takes a swing at him.*
> *GERRY ducks.*

CUT TO:
> *KATE ducks under a table and begins*
> *scurrying toward the exit. Several*
> *fights break out. KATE can be seen*
> *in the background, making her way*
> *out of the club.*

Not so bad, Cat told herself. *I can watch this.* She was sitting on a canvas folding chair in a corner of CV's, watching the crew and stunt people get coached through the brawl that preceded Kate's flight to the parking lot, the encounter with Gerry, Gerry's shooting. A slender stunt man was doubling for Ron, who would not have done his own stunts in any case. Still, the absence, that scrap of paper with the name Imogene King, the list of indecipherable numbers, continued to pester her.

Cat watched Cici running Tommi Ann's moves. Watched Tommi Ann step in for the close-ups. They moved smoothly, slipping in and out of the same character fluidly; Cat wondered if that body exchange was the result of skill or genes.

"I imagine you'll be happy to get this part of the filming over with."

Cat turned; Dianne King had settled in the folding chair beside Cat's.

"This is sort of a run-through for me, too," Cat told her. "If I can watch this, I can watch the rest of the nightclub scenes and if I can watch them, I can watch the scene in the parking lot."

"Tommi Ann said if you feel at all uncomfortable, you're welcome to sit it out in the office." CV's was a club and restaurant. The offices adjacent to the restaurant had been turned over to Tommi Ann for her dressing room. The loft above the club's dance floor had been fitted for wardrobe and makeup for the supporting players.

"I'm fine."

Dianne King's smile was perfunctory, but not unkind. Her face was broadened by prominent cheekbones, the jaw descending sharply to a tiny, pointed chin. Ageless, with lineless, untroubled flesh; genes or a clear conscience, Cat thought. Dianne wasn't pretty, but there was something that suggested tenacity as well as intelligence, which conveyed beauty despite the unremarkable face.

Dianne's spectacled eyes watched as a few PAs passed their chairs, hurried toward the restaurant. She waited until they were out of earshot before she spoke. "I'd like to know if you plan to tell Mr. Spivak that Cici entered his apartment this morning."

"She didn't hurt anything. She didn't take anything," Cat parried. "Did she tell you what she was doing there?"

"Mr. Spivak hinted that he was going to do an exposé on Tommi Ann. I believe he implied that it might be unflattering."

Something—apprehension, suspicion—carried the silence out a heartbeat too long. "In what way?"

Dianne shrugged. "I can't imagine. But if Cici were charged with breaking and entering, even if the charges were dropped, well, I don't have to tell you that's the sort of publicity Cici doesn't need at this point in her career." She paused. "I realize that a story like that might be worth something to you, if not now, certainly when Cici is more established."

"Perhaps," Cat replied. "But I like to leave my soul a little elbow room."

"Commendable. But you're expected to produce a scribbled form as well, to make ends meet."

Smart. Cat had paraphrased *King John* and Dianne King had extracted a phrase from the same speech for her comeback.

"So I'd like to make the arrangements for your interview with Tommi Ann." She paused, drew a folder out of her tote bag; Cat noticed that there was a fresh stock of brain teasers, crossword books. Had she finished up yesterday's supply already? "We were thinking that tomorrow morning might be the optimum time. Tommi Ann has a round robin scheduled for Thursday morning, but we thought you might prefer some private time with her to a quick five minutes. Would you like to go through the pre-interview material now?"

"Pre-interview?"

"Just a few things we need to review. I've already faxed the release to your editor, I'm sure he'll provide you with a copy. If you don't connect before tomorrow, I'll have another ready. A pre-interview is standard with Tommi Ann. What would you say to an hour and a half?"

An entire hour and a half! "Uh, fine." She had hoped for fifteen or twenty minutes!

"You can fax your questions to me this evening, so I can run through them before you come up. There won't be a problem in the Phoenix, Ben's taken care of that."

Which meant that Ben Butler carried more weight than Blaine Sterling, Fawn. "I'm sorry if that was a problem."

"Not at all." She wrote the fax number of their suite on the back
of one of her cards, handed it to Cat.

"I've never been asked to provide questions in advance," Cat said,
tried to sound like Ron Spivak, Karen Friedlander. The truth was she
hadn't done all that many interviews, personality profiles—she dis-
liked them. When she had acquired the Jerry Dudek/Tom Hopper
profile, in the aftermath of Ron's accident, she had called Barry
Fried at KRZI, asked him what would need to be done to arrange the
time, were there any specific areas he wanted her to cover, his re-
sponse had been, "Whatever."

"With Tommi Ann, this is pretty much boilerplate," Dianne
replied. "Tommi Ann prefers to limit questions to the current project,
although I'm sure that since it was your feature, and your experience
that inspired the role of Kate Auletta, you may want a little latitude
in that direction."

"I'd like to talk about how she got into acting, was she one of
those kids who played dress-up in front of the mirror, did she do
high school plays? It's an area that hasn't really been covered, as far
as I can determine."

"I think Tommi Ann would prefer to keep the questions to the
CopWatch project. And of course, the Oscars. And we'll need a quote
check. That will be in the release agreement."

Cat nodded.

"It would be good if you could get there a half hour in advance,
so we can go over this again."

Cat nodded, again. She had forgotten what time they had agreed
upon for the interview. Red called for sound off, a take. Cat watched
the fake Jerry duck the breakaway chair, watched the fake Cat
scramble for the exit. Cat wondered if Tommi Ann was so good at
sliding into her role, into Cat's past, because she was not anchored
to a past of her own.

***

Cat ran home, dumped her clothes into the laundry hamper, did a quick sort, tossed in a load of darks; checked her phone messages: from her sisters-in-law; Jennie; Victor; a couple "no-messages"; Vinnie.

Cat called Vinnie back first; he rarely called her, never from work.

"Carlo tell you about the kid?" "The kid" being Vinnie's epithet for Mark.

Carlo had been the dominant member of the family, but now his retirement was taking its toll on them all; he was driving them crazy. The advent of Mark came when Carlo badly needed a project and the kid needed someone who gave a damn. Carlo went to family court and petitioned guardianship and the judge said yes, just like all the members of the law enforcement community in New Jersey, who didn't dare refuse Carlo "The King" Fortunati anything he asked for.

Her two oldest brothers were tight, but Carlo's philanthropy brought out all that was skeptical and clannish in Vinnie. Cat had heard about Vinnie and Carlo's verbal jousts from her mother, and smiled, remembering Carlo's indignation when she had taken Ellice into her home.

"No, what happened?"

"He's caught shillin' some pirated videos in school, it comes across my desk." Vinnie worked Burglary.

"You mean, like, X-rated?"

"Nah, it looks to be stuff was taped off *CopWatch*, stuff with that Pig guy in it. Rough cut, but the kids, they'll buy anything today."

Cat thought of the tedious retakes, poor Biggs unable to come up with his lines. "Outtakes?"

"Who knows? Rap. Kids. Jeez."

Cat heard the squeal of the school bus tires, told Vinnie she would call him later, went over to unlock the door. Jane stomped up the porch steps.

"Did you *see* him?"

"Not today, sweetie."

Jane dropped her book bag on the foyer tile. "Why not?"

"Jane, I'm lucky to get to be around these people at all. I'll see him tomorrow night and I'll get you your picture."

Cat called Carlo and invited the three of them over for pizza. Annie had to work late, but Carlo agreed to come by with Mark. She sat Mats on the counter to watch while she started making *pepperonata,* was slicing peppers when she heard a thud at the front door.

"*Mark's* here with Uncle Carlo!" Cat heard the note of infatuation, suspected Jane had a budding crush on the sullen kid.

Carlo lumbered into the kitchen, ducking his gray head under the low archway. "You come give Uncle Carlo a kiss," he said to Mats, scooped the boy up in one arm.

Mats squealed. He was awed, thrilled by Uncle Carlo's height, girth. He reached his tiny hands up and Carlo boosted him until he touched the ceiling. Mark hung in the background, watching.

"Hello, Mark," Cat said.

"Hi." He wore a black T-shirt, jeans, too baggy for his slim frame. The dark hair was straight, falling over his forehead. The eyes were alert, sullen. "Can I go sit outside?"

"Yeah," Carlo grunted. "But stick around here." He waited for the boy to stalk off. "You hear?"

"Since when are there secrets in this family?" Cat began peeling cloves of garlic. "So what happened?"

Carlo set Mats down. "Go look out front, tell me what Mark's up to."

"Carlo!"

Carlo took over the stove, waited for Mats to scamper off. "His story is he's cuttin' school, hangin' out, at the arcade, it's 'Kid, you want some tape hot off last night's *CopWatch* shoot?' Guy's got one of those recorders you can watch a tape with? He slaps in a tape looks to be the stuff they throw out, whaddathey call 'em, outtakes? Ten bucks, he says."

"Who's the guy?"

Carlo drizzled olive oil into a skillet. "He don't know. Big guy, blond, trucker-type is what he says. I'm tryin' to keep this outta the DA's office, I tell him what kinda idiot stunt does he think he's pullin', you know what he says to me?"

Cat shook her head.

"Don't tell Grammom. He don't want *Grammom* to know. 'Cause he blew the cash he was savin' up to buy a present for *Grammom*. You know who he means? Mom. *Our* Mom. He calls me Mr. Fortunati, and he calls Annie Mrs. Fortunati when he opens his mouth at all, but all of a sudden, she's his *Grammom*."

"Then he does care about someone," Cat said, gently.

"Yeah, well, it ain't me." Carlo sighed. "I can't give him a pat on the back, nothin'. Annie, she gets to give him a hug if it don't last too long. I figure, okay, I get it. Kids like that, they go through stuff, they don't want to be touched, period."

Cat got up, got into his face. "You thought taking on this kid was gonna be a piece of cake because it was so easy with Carla and Mikey, and all of a sudden you got a kid who's more streetwise at fourteen than you are at fifty-two and you can't handle the fact that there's really someone who's not overwhelmed by King Carlo, that you've met your match in a street-smart kid who doesn't want to be touched."

Carlo turned toward the stove. "Gimme somma that garlic."

Cat laid her head against his broad back. "Carlo, give him a break. We had it so good growing up, we don't have any idea what it must be like for a kid like that. A kid who doesn't know the ground rules, doesn't know how family works."

"That's kinda what I wanted to talk to you about. You know, how family's s'posed to do for you and all."

Cat rolled her eyes. "Okay, is a signature enough or do you want it personalized?"

"Do I want what personalized?"

"Since we're talking about a fourteen-year-old kid, I suspect it's an eight-by-ten of Gary Biggs. If he was a year or two older, my guess would be Tommi Ann Butler."

"So tell me, she look as good as she does in the movies, or what?"

"Don't worry, Biggs is on the call sheet tomorrow, I'll corner him between takes. This time tomorrow, Mark will think you're a hero."

"I don't wanna be a hero."

"Sure you do. We all want to be heroes to our kids."

"Right now, I'd settle for a handshake."

Cat grabbed his massive paw, gave it a shake. "You're doing a grand and noble thing."

"Vinnie thinks I went stupid." He turned back to the stove. "Victor coming over?"

"I think. I've got a movie for after dinner if you want to hang around. *South Street Stakeout.* Ron Spivak's got a bit part in it. It's about renegade cops taking on pimps and pushers in the city of brotherly love."

"Jeez," muttered Carlo.

"No, really," Cat said. "Two former cops who are now rogue PIs, Cal and Ken—"

"Whoa," said Carlo. "Whoa."

"Short for Kendra," Cat told him.

"Oh. Okay. For a minute, I thought we were talkin' Dinny Dinosaur here."

"And while we're on that subject, I would appreciate it if my brothers did not tell my son that Dinny Dinosaur is gay."

Ellice walked in. "Dinny's gay? I thought he hooked up with Maggie the Mastodon."

"Mammoth."

Carlo held up the wooden spoon. "Hey, I dated Maggie the Mammoth, it'd be enough to make me go gay."

Mats crept in and looked at his mother, his Uncle Carlo. "How come everyone's laughing in here?"

"Don't you and Jane get a little loud sometimes?" Cat asked.

"Jane does."

"It just sounds louder because we're older and we've had more practice," Cat told him.

"Uncle Carlo, did Mark get under arrested?"

"Who said he got arrested?" Carlo demanded.

"He did. He told Jane he did."

Cat rolled her eyes. "Oh, God, I can see it now. The fascination of the bad boy. It's going to be like Danny Furina all over again."

"Dumb fuck," Carlo muttered. Danny's name inevitably provoked those two syllables with Pavlovian promptness. "I see his face, I wanna Jersey smack him up good." He lifted Mats onto his hip to give him a better view of the stove. "Lemme show you how to make *puttanesca*. An' take it from me, it don't matter how good looking you are, in the end, what a woman wants is a nice guy knows how to cook. An' you get to be my age, don't go chasin' after the young stuff." Carlo handed the spoon to Mats, allowed him to poke at the sauce. "Lemme tell you, Mats, sometimes a guy thinks he really wants a hot woman, you know, but after awhile all he pretty much wants is a nap."

"I take naps," Mats told him.

"Ellice." Carlo's eyes were on the skillet. "I eat every word I said back when Cat took you in."

Cat and Ellice went to sit on the top step of the front porch while Mats peddled a wobbly course along the sidewalk, showing off his new bike to Mark. Concentration set his features in a frown, made him look so like Chris.

Mark hung at the bottom step, watching Mats with calculated disinterest. Cat leaned her back against the porch railing, described her day to Ellice.

"—and I think I've got a clean getaway when Red Melendez reminds me that we're supposed to talk. And the thing is, I don't remember setting anything up with him, but I figure, okay, it might be good for a short something I could market to a couple different places, so I set that up for the end of the week because I've half-promised to do something with Harold that day, so I can use each of them as an excuse to get rid of the other, and I figure you'll be here to play chaperone."

"Melendez trying to put the moves on you?"

Cat sighed, nodded. "It's more like he's practicing on me, working out his Victor Calderone on the real Kate Auletta. To give his performance *validation*. Because *CopWatch* teleplays are—and I quote from their television promos—'based on *actual fact.*'"

"As opposed to mythical fact," Ellice concluded. "I'm surprised he's talking to you, considering he was pals with Ted Cusack."

"Loyalty is for us, the plebes, dear. All that talk about honor and a code were lines written for Roberto Aguilar, the somber, Cervantes-quoting, darkly mysterious chief of"—she deepened her voice, gave it a melodramatic rhythm—" '*The Advocates!* These renegade public defenders put their lives on the line to be the voice of the voiceless.'" She shook her head. "It's been ten years since his last good role, he's perfectly willing to throw over a long-term friendship to cozy up to his new best friends. And he's a reasonably good TV director, which by Cici Bonaker's definition means he doesn't stink."

"Does he call you Cat or Kate?"

"Just as long as it's not 'Kiss me, Kate.'" She sighed. "He's no worse than the rest of them. They don't look you in the eye, you know. Except if you're the only one in the room. Somebody else comes in and their eyes start to pan and scan, sizing up the competition. The bit players, they don't really care that I'm the 'real Kate,' they only care that I'm press. They figure they haven't got a shot at The *Inquirer* or *Tomorrow, Today* or *Front Cover,* so a few inches of local print is better than nothing. I've already got a folder full of bios and résumés, an earful of 'did-you-see-me-in?'" Cat took a swig of her Pepsi. "Now the PAs—the production assistants? They're cold. Entertainment girl from *South Jersey* magazine for God's sake, what the hell good could five inches of her copy do for them? The only thing that keeps me from being a complete nobody in their eyes is the fact that Tommi Ann talks to me." She laughed, a little wearily. "And they're stupid! I mean, I'm no Einstein, but I was telling Red how Tommi Ann was asking what it was really like to watch my life being played out, so Red asks what it was like. And I said that it's like when people are worked over by the EMTs, and after they're revived, they talk about this extra-corporeal experience, and he says, 'What?' and I go on about like seeing a light, hearing the voices of angels and he goes, 'No, what does extra-corporeal mean?'"

Victor's Jag pulled up to the curb, he got out. Mark turned his back, pretended to be watching Mats wobble along the sidewalk.

Victor settled onto the step below Cat.

"Carlo's inside," Cat said.

"How's he doing?"

Cat shrugged. "He's cooking."

"Is that good or bad?"

"You'll know when we eat."

"So what did you say?" Ellice prodded.

Cat rolled her eyes. "I said it meant out of body, like when people who've been rushed to the ER say they experienced a sense that they were disconnected, looking down at their own bodies? And I said that's how I feel, except I'm looking down at someone else's body. And the people working me over aren't the real doctors and nurses, they're actors from that TV show, the one about the inner city emergency department. Which was the wrong thing to say, because Red immediately goes into his Did-you-know-I-was-up-for-a-part-in-that?"

"Don't tell me," Ellice said. "He told you he didn't get it because they went with a white actor."

"Well, he said Caucasian, not white, but yeah. And you know how much discrimination is out there, and how minority performers have to struggle for visibility, for representation, for dignity, for fill-in-the-blank."

"He's not represented by Butler, is he?"

Cat shook her head. "He'd kill to sign with Butler." She wondered if Ron was going to do something on the diversity of Butler's clients. Diversity was vogue. Gloria Ramirez and Teresa D. were Hispanic, Biggs was black, Eric Obermeyer had been gay. "Red Melendez said he thought Tommi Ann took the part in *CopWatch* because she was at an age when it was important to reinforce her sexual viability."

"He didn't say 'sexual viability,'" Ellice protested.

Cat crossed her heart. "I heard she's doing it to give Cici Bonaker's career a leg up. That this episode's going to be a spin-off." *Or payoff? To the daughter she gave up?*

Mats wobbled to a stop and toppled off the bike. Victor felt Cat tense behind him, stopping herself from getting up.

Mats righted his bike. "Vi'tor, could you ride a two-wheeler when you was five?"

Victor pursed his lips, thoughtfully. "Five ... no, I believe I was about six before my training wheels came off."

"Did you fall off sometimes?"

"A lot."

Mats stole a look at his mother. "Did it make you not like your bike?"

Victor considered the question. "Once, I think I said I hated my bike, but that hurt my father's feelings. Because he worked so hard to buy it for me, you see."

"You're not asposed to hurt people's feelings."

"Yes, I know, but sometimes it slips out."

"Did you have to put away your bike your own self without help?" This with a reproachful glance at his mother.

"I think my father always *wanted* to help me," Victor said. "But I decided if I was big enough to get my training wheels off, I was probably big enough to put it away myself."

"I'll help you, kid." Mark's words had a hint of triumph, as though he were getting the better of Victor. Mats had that awestruck joy little kids get when they have snared the attention of the older ones.

"That was real smooth," Ellice said to Victor, rising to her feet. "You've got a way with kids."

"Thanks. It comes from commanding a homicide unit. How's the apartment coming?"

"Okay. Just furniture and drapes and this and that."

Mats trotted toward the front of the house. "Mark says he'll put the bike in the shed for me. Victor?"

"Yes?" He held out his hand to the boy.

Mats gripped it and skipped up the steps. "Would you rather have a hot woman or a nap?"

Victor caught Cat's dangerous gaze.

Cat got to her feet. "I'm going to make sure Mark gets the shed door locked. Go give my brother a smack on the head for me," she told Ellice.

"You're not asposed to smack people," Mats told her, as she trotted down the steps, rounded the house.

Mark was struggling with the door, which was warped, another victim of the sea air. He looked up, "I wasn't taking anything."

"I didn't say you were taking anything," Cat replied. "I just thought you might have trouble getting the door to close. You have to sort of—" She shifted sideways, dropped her weight, gave it a firm butt with her hip. "Mark," she said as she pushed the padlock into place, "I heard about the videotape today."

"It was my money!"

"Mark, look, you want to blow your money like that, it's nothing to me, but I'd like to know who sold you the tape."

"Some guy."

"Describe him to me."

"I already told the cops," Mark replied, sullenly.

"Mark, look, how'd you like to have a set pass?"

"What's that?"

"It's a pass, like a name card, that allows you onto the set when they're shooting."

The sullenness dissolved. "You can't get me on the set."

"Yes, I can." I *can?*

"I guess it'd be all right."

"*Quid pro quo.*"

"What's that supposed to mean?"

"It's Latin. Something for something. Tell me who this guy was."

"I didn't know his name. Blond hair, ponytail, tats. Big guy. Said he had more where that came from."

I can unload 'em no problem, it's never been a problem.

"Thanks, Mark."

CHAPTER ELEVEN

INT: NIGHTCLUB: NIGHT
*GERRY saunters up to KATE, who is sitting
alone beside the dance floor.*

GERRY

Wanna dance?

KATE

I've used up all my good moves, thanks.

GERRY

Want a preview of tomorrow's show, Katie?
Want a family secret to end all family secrets?

Cat got Jane and Mats to bed and went to her room to compose
her list of questions to fax to Dianne King.
   What's next, after the tremendous reception of Redemption*?*
   What would the Oscar mean to you at this point in your career?
   Why would Ron Spivak think you're Cici Bonaker's mother?
What was it he expected to learn in LA?
   Call him up and ask him.
   Cat pulled a phone book from under the bed, began shuffling through
the Yellow Pages, to Travel Agencies. Maybe Ron had booked on-

line, but it was worth a shot. She rehearsed an urgent-situation-came-up-and-I-need-to-contact-him-at-his-hotel routine, thinking, *I bet even Tommi Ann Butler couldn't do as smooth a job.*

Nothing but voice mail. *I feel like Harold Anderson,* Cat thought. *I've honed the skills, but can't land a part.* She dialed her last prospect, doodled questions while the phone rang.

Did you persuade your husband to manage Cici Bonaker's career because Cici's the daughter you gave up?

A human voice startled Cat. She blurted out her intro, realized she hadn't prepared a follow-up.

"Are you a relative?"

"No, I'm a work associate. Friend. I've been checking on his apartment while he's away."

A pause, keyboard in the background clicking out the ominous rhythm of rejection. Cat upped the stakes. "We've been working on the *CopWatch* set together, and I needed to nail down a couple items regarding my Tommi Ann Butler interview."

The cadence altered, became upbeat.

Hollywood, Cat thought.

"Yeah, he booked to LA, but we didn't book the hotel, just the air with the connection. I got the idea he'd be staying with a friend or something."

Imogene? "Connection?"

"Yeah, we coulda booked him direct, but he said he wanted to be routed through DFW."

"DFW?" Cat asked.

"Dallas-Fort Worth."

"Oh, that's right," in a Now-I-remember voice.

"To hook up with some friends, he said. Said he had a dinner with some of them in Dallas, didn't know how long it would go on, then business on the way back."

"He had to connect through DFW both ways?"

"Yeah."

"Maybe I could track him down through the car rental?"

"Didn't book one, not through us, anyway. Just the air. Maybe his friends were picking him up at the airport."

Maybe Ron never intended to go to LA, maybe it was cheaper—or more evasive—to book a round-trip to Dallas indirectly, let everyone think he'd gone to LA. Why? *Because he wanted to hide the fact that he'd gone to Texas.*

Cici Bonaker was from Texas.

"Well, I guess it's not life-and-death, but I wanted to go over a few things before I sit down with Tommi Ann, since I'll probably only get this one shot at her."

"What's she like? Tommi Ann Butler. She look like she did in *Alibi?*"

"Better." Cat thanked the woman and hung up. She ran down, retrieved the torn envelope from her coat pocket, studied the sequence of numbers. Not a phone number. Not a credit card number, the order was all wrong. Too long for a flight number. Reservation number? Maybe.

Hotel or rental car?

Cat decided it would be easier to try rental agencies, starting with their one-eight-hundreds. She rewrote the script, rehearsed her My-husband-misplaced-his-credit-card-and-I-was-wondering-if-he-had-left-it-at-the-desk speech, ran through it a few times and began to dial.

She had to do three takes before she got a "I'd sure be happy to check for you, ma'am," followed by a "No ma'am, I'm real sorry, Mr. Spivak's card hasn't been turned in."

"I don't suppose he's returned the car yet?"

"No, ma'am. I see here he requested a map and we fixed him up with directions to where he'd be stayin', said he misplaced what he wrote down. It's pretty tricky, if you don't know the country."

Directions? Route numbers. Highways.

"Right," Cat agreed. "He was to take one fourteen to three eighty—"

"Yeah, head on west 'til he came to eighty-three, to eighty-two. I guess you could try calling where in King he's staying at. You wanna hang on a minute?"

Cat heard a muffled, "Bo, did that guy rented the four-door compact, wanted directions out to King County tell you where he'd be stayin' at?" Heard an inarticulate answer.

"I'm real sorry, Mrs. Spivak, Bo says you should maybe try the newspaper office, I believe it's the *Western Counties Weekly Gazette*. Bo says your husband made mention of some business over there."

"Thanks for your help, I'll just cancel the card if it doesn't turn up by tonight."

"You do that, ma'am."

Cat went back downstairs, rooted around the wall-wide bookcases, looking for the old road atlas she picked up at a yard sale to help Jane with a geography project. The atlas was divided into two sections, one with US state maps, one with detailed maps of major cities. Cat thumbed through to the image of Dallas-Fort Worth and scanned, turned up a Route 114, traced it westward with her index finger until it connected with 380. Westward again, until it was intersected by a Route 83. North, where it hooked up with 82 in a small town called Guthrie. In the center of—or, considering the locale, *smack dab* in the center of—King County, Texas. Maybe it wasn't Imogene King, maybe it was Imogene who *lived* in King.

The 180 might have been a reference to the mileage. Or, Cat considered, the population. It certainly didn't look like that black dot on the map represented more than a hundred-eighty people. Ocean City, which shrank to one-fourth of its size in seasonal population by October, only three homes on Cat's block occupied year round, was probably a throbbing metropolis by comparison. At least, she decided, there probably wouldn't be a glut of Imogenes. But what could this Imogene have to do with Cici Bonaker, who had been raised hundreds of miles to the east, in Houston? Or with Tommi Ann, whose bio claimed she was from someplace in Kansas?

Western Counties Weekly Gazette. Perhaps Imogene was a reporter with the local weekly? Cat went back upstairs, threw the map on the bed and got the paper's number from information.

"Pressroom. Lamont, here."

"My name is Mrs. Austen, I'm calling from New Jersey."

"Well, I'll be."

Cat waited a moment, expecting something more in the way of a predicate, decided, finally, it was implicit. "I'm trying to reach somebody named Imogene."

"Imogene?"

"Yes. Actually, I'm trying to contact a mutual friend, a Mr. Spivak?"

"Brown-haired fella, kinda crooked face?"

"Yes."

"He's here earlier talkin' to Davey."

"Could I speak to Davey?"

There was a pause; Cat heard a muffled, "Davey still in his office or he gone to home?" Another pause, then, "He's in his office, lemme give him a holler."

After a moment, Cat heard "Davey Wheeler here."

"Mr. Wheeler, my name is Mrs. Austen, I'm calling from Ocean City, New Jersey."

"It's where that fella Spivak is from. He didn't really get himself into a television show with Tommi Ann Butler, now did he?"

"Yes."

"Well—"

I'll be.

"—I'll be."

"Do you know her? Tommi Ann Butler?"

"You b'lieve we've never met? Just him, Ben. Hell of a nice fella. I guess I coulda hung around they made *Redemption*, but it looked to be pretty boring and I got my hands full with the paper. I mean, just because you win the lottery, don't mean you have to quit your day job, does it?"

"Of course not," Cat replied. *Absolutely.*

"And what with your e-mail and your fax machines, I didn't need to be in New York when we were working out the bidness about the script. I'd just as soon stay put, but Ben wants me to get myself to Los Angeles, so I'm trying to put my office in order here."

Click. Click. Click. *Redemption*, winning the lottery, working out the script. Wheeler was the writer whose novel had been picked up by Butler, the novel that Tommi Ann's Oscar-nominated film, *Redemption*, had been based upon. "Congratulations, Mr. Wheeler—"

"Hell, you call me Davey."

"Davey. You must feel like you really did win the lottery."

"Hell, yes. I got rejected left, right and sideways. I heard Ben Butler is always on the lookout for a good role for Tommi Ann, I figure, what the hell. Even with Gloria goin' to bat for me, it took some to get his publicist on the phone, but once I did, Butler calls me back that night, says, you send your book right around. After twenty-nine rejections."

Even with Gloria goin' to bat for me ... "Do you mean Gloria Ramirez?" The queen of afternoon talk.

"You bet."

Was Ron doing a piece on Ben Butler's clients after all? "Ron was interviewing you for an article about Mr. Butler's agency, then?"

"I reckon. He was askin' all about me an' Gloria and the rest of us came up together."

"Came up? You mean Mr. Butler's other clients?"

"No, came up through school."

"You went to school with Gloria Ramirez?"

"You bet. Graduated the same year. You tell me what're the odds, two kids from some dusty little speck on the map, turn out like we did? Hell, it was Gloria's show finally got us our cable down here."

"Are the odds that great?"

"If you go by the percentages. Two outta seven, that's what? Mor'n twenty-five percent. You show me a graduating class got one quarter of its kids making it as big as Gloria Ramirez and me. Actually, it was two outta six, TJ Sontag, he dropped out. It was him, me, Gloria, Tomas Gomez—TJ was a 'Tom', too, we had ourselves two Toms— Austin Finney, Ricky Sorensen, Glenn Luckenbaugh."

"Gloria Ramirez must have had a heck of a graduation dance."

Wheeler chuckled. "We had a right nice party, come to think of it. Six of us went over to Knox County and raised a little hell. What about yourself?"

"Graduation? Some friends and I went up to the church bell tower to ring in the celebration and one of us fell through the wooden floor, wound up in the ER having four-inch splinters removed from his ... posterior."

"Now you're just trying to make me jealous."

Cat laughed. She liked the sound of Davey Wheeler, felt her resentment against his success receding, wondered if Ron had felt so magnanimous toward a small-time writer who had hit the jackpot. Was he after an exposé on Ramirez, perhaps? "That, um, hell-raising wouldn't be anything that might publicly embarrass Gloria Ramirez, is it?"

"Hell, Gloria's told the story herself on TV just so's people wouldn't think she was as dull as dirt."

"What became of the rest of your class? The Toms and Ricky and Glenn and Austin?"

"I got myself to college, took up the paper, been writing the past twenty years. Tommy Gomez and Austin, they're on the county commission. Glenn, he was the sheriff before he took a job in San Angelo. Ricky's got himself a nice little vending machine business."

"What about the dropout? Sontag?"

"TJ." There was a sigh. "That's a sad tale." He paused as if considering whether to continue. "Got a girl pregnant, dropped out an' run away with her."

"How long ago was this?"

"Twenty-five, twenty-six years ago."

Cici Bonaker was about twenty-five.

"The girl wasn't Gloria Ramirez, was it?"

"Hell, no. It was the Cox girl, the youngest one. Neither one of 'em were of age when they run off. Some fella give 'em a lift down to Mes'co, stood up for 'em while they got themselves hitched. Big Tom, he's the sheriff back then, he hauls their raggedy butts back over the border. He's not gonna have his boy runnin' after the likes of Annie Cox. He says who's to say who's that baby's father? This was before your DNA and your paternity."

Annie? "Annie?"

"Uh-huh. They said Big Tom paid off her family to send her off to Houston to have her baby, TJ run off after her."

Houston.

"What became of them?"

"The Lord only knows. Like I told that Spivak fella, I never seen nor heard from either one again." He paused. "You wanna make it through this life, you pick your battles and you pick your mem'ries. Some stuff, you just let go of or it's gonna drive you crazy."

"What was she like? Annie Cox?"

"Skinniest human being I ever saw in my life, how she was gonna carry a baby I don't know. But, she was smart, you know? Almost too smart to be a Cox. And there was something about her, in the face, something downright unearthly. Like Nature was havin' some kinda joke, puttin' a face like that on one of those shiftless Coxes. Eyes could look clean through you."

Cat felt the chill of Tommi Ann's mutating eyes, cutting straight through to the heart of Kate Auletta.

"Hell of a scandal. Shoot, most excitement since then was when Jacob Turner got liquored up and hacked down Hazel Finney's rose bush, the one she's gonna enter in a show. Hazel went after him with a pair of hedge trimmers and we had a little dust-up." He chuckled. "You wouldn't think I coulda got a whole book outta the doings around here."

"Mr. Wheeler?"

"Davey."

"Davey. I imagine King County isn't heavily populated."

"I reckon there's about three-hundred-fifty souls, mostly here in Guthrie, out to the ranch."

"So everybody would know everybody."

"Pretty much."

"Do you know a woman named Imogene? Someone who might have been connected with you or your classmates? I found a notation Ron left about going to Imogene's, but he didn't leave her number or address with anyone."

Wheeler chuckled. "Be hard to do, Mrs. Austen, since there's no more Imogene than there is an Elvis, not now. It's where I'm from. TJ's family lived out there, too, so did Annie Cox. I told that fella Spivak, Miss Zeda might be able to dig up a few copies of the old *Advisor* over to the county library. Don't reckon the population ever did get past ninety, even in the good years, if there were any, but around the time I went off to school, it flat out dried up. Now most folks live out to the ranch, or in Guthrie or moved east to Knox County. Imogene's not a woman, Mrs. Austen, it's a ghost town. I wrote the book, I changed the name to Redemption, but Imogene, Texas is the place I had in my head." And he laughed outright, as though he had played a great joke on his past.

CHAPTER TWELVE

EXT: NIGHTCLUB/PARKING LOT: NIGHT
*KATE races across the street, vaults the
stone wall and heads for her car. She
hears a footstep behind her, hears
someone calling out her name-*

"MOMMMMMMMM!"

Jane! Cat shot out of the comforter's womblike burrow, dropped onto the floor, groping in her nightstand for her gun case; her sleep-encrusted eyes couldn't make out the combination. She was still somewhere in a tawdry dream scripted by Harold Anderson and her fingers couldn't execute the commands of her sluggish brain; besides, the weapon wasn't loaded, she kept her rounds downstairs in a canister in the kitchen.

Cat lunged into the hall with the case in both hands; it was steel-lined with protruding hinges; it made a good shield and could deliver a sound smack (*You're not asposed to smack people*). She stumbled down the stairs in the direction of Jane's scream and stopped; Jane, dressed for school, was perched at the living room window, staring down into the street, a Second Coming fire in her eyes.

Fear backed out with the force of a riptide, and Cat felt irritation trickle into the vacuum. "Jane Cassandra Austen!" She heard a heavy tread on her porch step, another. Heard a knock on the door, a timid rap that was mindful of the fact that the occupants might be sleeping.

"What's the matter with you, Jane?" Cat set her gun case down and padded to the door, gave it a yank. "What time is it?"

Bigg Phat P.I.G. stood on the threshold, his quartet of bodyguards at his flank. Cat looked past them (no simple maneuver), could see a stretch limo idling at the curbside.

Cat heard herself say, "Good morning, Mr. Pig."

"Your Ma was gon' come by, I's gonna give her the car, but she didn't wanna leave off cooking so I said I'd come by for her, she needs to borrow some stuff." He pulled a sheet of paper out of his pocket.

"You were over my mother's?"

"She's gettin' the food ready for tonight, I axed her can she show me how to make those grits like she made."

"*Polenta*." Cat shook her hair away from her head. "I'm sorry, come on in."

The five men entered, filled the tiny foyer. Cat backed up, waved them into the living room. Ellice appeared in the dining room archway. "This is Ellice Watson, my son Mats, and the girl with her lower mandible on the carpet is Jane."

Biggs held out his hand, said, "Hey, little sister."

The muscles of Jane's face began to twitch. "I gotta go to the bathroom!" She fled.

"I scare her?"

"Don't worry about it. C'mon into the kit–" She remembered his unsuccessful attempt to wedge himself into the church pews. He would never cram his three hundred pounds into her kitchen booth. "Into the dining room," she amended. "How about some coffee?"

"No, thank you, but you go on ahead." He looked up at his entourage. "You got that envelope I axed you to bring?"

One of them produced a manila envelope, with *Pig In A Poke Productions* printed on the top corner.

"You have your own production company?" Cat asked.

"Ben set me up. So I can have people review projects, television, stuff like 'at." He took a batch of 8x10 glossies out of the envelope. "Your Ma said your daughter wanted a picture."

Jane reappeared in her black jeans with the white top-stitching, appliquéd sweater, had exchanged the nylon band in her hair for a silver scrunchy.

"What you want me to put on this, little sister?"

Jane swallowed. He *talked* to her. "Jane," she whispered.

"How you spell that?"

Jane was mute.

"J-a-n-e," Mats told him.

"Well, you're a big boy, aren't you?"

"I'm five."

Biggs handed the picture to Jane, took out another, asked Mats how to spell his name.

"Don't take it to school, honey." Cat didn't have to elaborate. In the six and a half months Jane had been at the middle school, she had been relieved of her hot pink high-top sneakers, the key chain made of real rabbit fur, two scrunchies, four dollars and seventy-five cents in lunch money and the canvas hat Aunt Charlotte had sent her from Belize, with *You Just Gotta Belize* embroidered on the brim. It was unlikely she would be able to retain possession of an 8x10 of Bigg Phat P.I.G. beyond first period.

Biggs carefully penned the letters of Mats' name, added, "Be cool, Stay in School." "She's something, your Ma. I had a Ma like that ..." he shook his head. "You good to your grammmom, aren't you?"

Jane and Mats bobbed their heads, obediently.

Cat poured Mats a bowl of Cheerios while Ellice rounded up the inventory of utensils and groceries. "Jane, come get some breakfast?"

"Wh—what do you eat for breakfast, M-Mr.—"

"Aw, honey, you can call me Pig."

Cat stepped into the dining room. "No, she can't. How about 'Gary'?"

"That's fine. Tommi Ann, Ben, Cici, Dianne, that's how they call me. I just don't see that I look like a Gary."

"But you don't look like a pig, either," Mats told him. "You look like Uncle Carlo."

"My brother," Cat explained. "He's ... big. And Mr. Biggs eats whatever's put in front of him for breakfast, isn't that right?" She winked at him over Jane's shoulder.

Suspicion gave Jane's dark eyes a flinty cast. She was being played. She took her bowl from the kitchen table, carried it into the dining room.

The coffee pot began to pulse. Cat began making Jane's lunch, checked the clock. "Jane, do you or do you not want me to walk you to the bus stop?"

The No Parental Accompaniment rule had been relaxed when Cat had hooked up with *Cop Watch*.

"Are you going to wear that?" Jane's dark eyes surveyed her mother's old flannels, slouch socks, disheveled hair.

"I'll throw a coat on."

Jane's mouth twisted, cynically.

"I'll comb my hair."

Jane sighed.

"I'll put on an evening gown and perfume and spike heels and a fur coat."

"You don't *have* a fur coat." The mouth began to curve.

"I'll wear the Ufflanders' dog."

"He barks," Mats informed her.

Cat put her arms around Jane, kissed the top of her head. "It's okay, sweetie, I get it. When I was your age, one time Uncle Freddy and I were walking to school and I forgot my lunch and Nonna came out running after me in this old brown robe and curlers and a couple of the kids made fun of me, all the way to school." *Those damned Colucci twins.*

"What did you do?"

"Nothing. I was too embarrassed." *But Uncle Freddy and Uncle Joey jumped them at recess.* "I wished she could look like the moms on television."

"Don't be wishin' away your mom." Biggs reached for the bag Ellice handed over; one of his handlers intercepted it. "How 'bout we pack up this stuff for your grammmom, an' I'll give you a ride to school. That be okay wit' you, Miz Austen?"

Jane's entire form compacted in a plea, the compressed lips squirming out a whispered, "Pleasepleaseplease."

"I suppose it would be all right," Cat agreed. "I have a lot to do to get ready for my interview and the shoot tonight."

"You go get your coat, little sister. I's gotta get this stuff back to your grammmom, then they got me talkin' to the kids over St. Agnes today, 'bout how they need to stay in school, stay off the drugs."

"Are you sure it isn't any trouble?"

"They got me this limo, I can go anywhere I want. Tommi Ann's got a fittin', then later she gonna run lines with me, so I figure I'll just go back up to the kitchen when I'm done, help out your Ma." His eyes were roaming the dining room, across the center hall to the living room with its cozy dark floral upholstery, its wall of books. "You got a real nice place. A real home. You read all those?"

Cat smiled. "Most of them. I don't suppose you have any time to read, unless it's a script."

He shook his head. "Dianne, she reads all the time, does crosswords, find the missing word, Scrabble, stuff like 'at, I say 'Dianne, your brain gonna explode you read so much.'" He shook his head.

"Take one if you want," Cat offered. "I don't suppose there's much in the way of reading material in your suite." She helped zip Jane into her jacket, whispered, "Now, don't be all that and a bag of chips when you get to school."

"Mom? Does Tommi Ann Butler have any kids?"

"I don't ... think so." She smiled at her daughter. What would her life be without Jane? What would it be to know that she had a daughter somewhere, being raised by someone else? "Some people are just lucky, I guess."

Jane's small mouth concentrated in a pout.

"And the rest just get to be movie stars."

Cat watched from the dining room window as Biggs, his escort floating about him in a loose diamond formation, conveyed Jane to the waiting limo. She understood her daughter's dallying when she heard the squeal of the bus brakes, saw the bus lumber around Morningside. Biggs strode up to the driver's window, exchanged a few words of explanation. Cat saw the eruption of small, astonished faces at the row of windows, saw Jane stroll nonchalantly toward the limo as Biggs waved the bus on.

Cat turned and smiled at Ellice. "I am not seeing this kid as some hard-core rapper."

Ellice smiled. "You ever see his videos?"

Cat shook her head.

"I checked them out. *Killadilla, Booty Duty, Yo' Mama.* Make's you wanna wince when you hear it, except *Killadilla* is about the high school girl who's got brains, ambition, how the guys have to shape up to deserve her, she's the—"

"Killadilla," Cat concluded.

Ellice nodded. "*Booty Duty* is working to improve the situation of people around you. How it's your duty to put your booty—that would be in the monetary sense, not the anatomical—back into your community."

"And *Yo' Mama* is about how you should respect, well, yo' mama?" Cat surmised.

"You got it."

"Jane is not going to be fit to live with this afternoon. It's such a relief that you're not star struck." Cat poured a mug of coffee. "You should have been there when I dropped Mats at preschool on Monday.

Parents who never gave me so much as a nod, it's 'Hi, Cat' here and 'Hi, Cat' there. And regarding Tommi Ann: A, is she as beautiful as she was in *Black Orchid*; B, is she as exotic as she seemed in *Spellbinder*; C, does she really have those biceps she flexed in *Double Jeopardy*; D, did she take the part in *Alibi* because she's really bi? And those close-ups in *Redemption*, did I think she had a facelift? Was she having an affair with Eric Obermeyer when she met Butler—"

"Wasn't Obermeyer gay?" Ellice asked.

Cat nodded. "Is it true she had an affair with Ford Matthews, when they made *Mystery Loves Company*, is it true she had an affair with Geneen Terry when they made *Murder, Ink*—"

"Isn't *she* gay?"

"The only thing they didn't ask was whether Tommi Ann had an affair with Rutger, the seeing-eye dog in *Mirage.*"

"So, is it just the mystique? Or is she really the most beautiful woman in the world?"

Cat pursed her mouth. "Yes, to both questions. I always thought film stars would be sort of shriveled, you know? Drab and scrawny and stunted close up. But she is a beauty. And the mystique?" Cat tugged on a strand of hair, thinking of her conversation with Davey Wheeler. "Something about her reminds me of that passage from Dostoevsky, about beauty being a terrible thing because it cannot be fathomed. Did you ever read *Redemption, Texas*?"

"Yeah, way before the movie. I liked it. Guy's a talented writer. I hate to admit it, but I can't come up with his name right now."

"David Wheeler. Davey. I talked to him on the phone last night. He's one of Butler's clients, too, the most recent one, I think. Can I borrow your copy of the book?"

"It's in my room. Go get your act together, I'll get Mats dressed for school."

Cat found the book on a stack of paperbacks next to Ellice's makeshift bookshelves. The actual shelves had been reserved for the likes of Marcus Aurelius, Pope, Milton; modern fiction was consigned to the floor.

Cat took it into her room, tossed it on her bed to pick up her ringing phone.

"Hey, I like the piece on the catering broads."

"Ritchie, I'll thank you to remember that the president of those broads is my mother." She picked up the book, read the copy on the back: *Redemption, Texas. Death in a small town and the scattering of a community becomes the métier for the erosion of our shared values. Wheeler writes with passion, graceful simplicity and a profound sense of mourning for the dissolution of the ties that bind. A winner!* Cat checked the photo on the inside back cover. Wheeler was an attractive forty, dark hair, regular features, an everyman. Not a two-million-dollar man. "I found out where Ron went," she said.

"LA."

"No. Texas."

"Texas! What the hell's in Texas?"

"Land, cattle, oil. Texans. You know, a lot of Ben Butler's clients were from Texas."

"Yeah, Gloria Ramirez, Teresa D. I think that rapper, The Pig, too."

"I didn't know that."

"Yeah, well, they ain't there now, are they?"

"David Wheeler is."

"Who's he? Don't tell me, don't tell me, it's ringin' a bell. Jeez. It's like in that movie, a bell rings, someone gets his wings."

Cat loved movies, but her brain was sleep-deprived. "Gets his wings like a pilot?"

"No, that's the one he played Charles Lindburgh. Jimmy Stewart. The other one, where he's watching his own life? How if he doesn't get born and he's not there, everything around him goes to pot."

"If he's not there, how can there be anything *around* him?"

"He's invisible. Like he's there watching, but he's not all there, you know what I mean?"

"That you're not all there."

"I give, who's this guy Wheeler?"

"He wrote the book *Redemption* was based on."

"So?"

"Ritchie, it's indecent for an editor to be so indifferent to a writer. I'll bet you know who *starred* in *Redemption*."

"Jeez, who doesn't? By the way, I get this fax from her publicist. King? You should see this thing. It tells us where the interview can be published, it won't be circulated in unapproved publications, we won't resell the rights, no this, no that, they get a quote check, plus—get this—a fall cover for the Bonaker gal. They must really love her."

"They asked for a cover for Cici?"

"Yeah. I mean, natch I'll give her a cover. Of course, they provide the photo."

"Ritchie, what do you know about Tommi Ann before she got famous?"

"Jeez, Austen. There was no Tommi Ann before she got famous. Why?"

If nobodies were worth knowing, I'd be famous.

"No reason. I'll call you to let you know how the interview went."

She dropped to her knees, groped under her bed for the black canvas tote that had a legal pad with the questions she had scribbled down to ask Tommi Ann, tossed in a notebook, a few pens, threw together her folder on Tommi Ann, filmography, magazine articles, thought of Ron's meticulously organized desk. *Organization*, she told herself, *is the key*, began to rummage around for her house key. *If I call a cab, I can read on the way into Atlantic City.*

She showered, threw three outfits on the bed, settled on a mocha-colored linen sheath with a matching cardigan.

"You look pretty, Mom," Mats told her while she put together his lunch. Cat grinned, handed Ellice her car keys. "Translation is 'I hardly ever see you out of jeans or sweats, Mom.' Thanks for shuttling him to school."

Cat called a cab, reorganized the contents of her tote, shoved in the copy of the latest *Bellissima!*, the one with a gilded Tommi Ann on the cover.

"Is she a looker, or what?" The cabbie's rearview reflection nodded at the magazine cover. "I seen every movie she ever made. *Abandoned, Black Orchid, Alibi, Je Reviens,*" H pronounced it "Gee Ravines." "Hell, I even went to see *The Merchant of Venice. Booked for Murder,* like to've jumped outta my seat. *Double Jeopardy?*" He raised one hand off the wheel, splayed his fingers. "Five times."

They were cruising down Atlantic Avenue; he was wise to the tempo of the traffic signals, coasted from Longport to Margate to Ventnor in one smooth, uncomplicated course which allowed the driver to give Cat a detailed plot summary of *Double Jeopardy.* "—and she's undercover, see, except the guy she's pretending to be got killed? He's a, well, he's a guy, so she's gotta pretend *she's* a guy and the ab shot, she's really cut, plus she musta worked with one of those personal trainers on her biceps, and then, like, the mob's gotta hook up so they can work out how the hit's gonna go down, and the only place they can get clear of surveillance is in the john, you get me?" He chuckled. "So, like, what's she gonna do? She's gotta go in and—"

They were approaching Delancy; Cat saw Victor's Jag parked along the curb.

"—and the four guys, they go up, whip out their—"

"Could you turn left here? I need to stop at a friend's house."

"They shot somma *CopWatch* here the other day, I go outta service an hour just to try an' get a look at her." The cabbie's eyes coasted to the magazine cover, Tommi Ann's gold-sheathed figure. "My wife looked like that, lemme tell you, I'd be a better man."

She handed him the copy of *Bellissima!* "I'm done with this, you can keep it."

"You want me to wait, or what?"

"I'll be okay." Cat paid the fare and got out. Victor lived on the second floor of a three-story house. The front door, the serviceable but unphotogenic steel-reinforced one, had been restored, though Cat could see that the landing and stairs were scored by heavy boots, dropped tools.

Cat rang the bell, waited. After a moment, the door was opened by a thin brunette, her mass of brown-black hair piled on her head and held in place with chopsticks. The oversized neckline of her sweater had slipped over one shoulder, exposing a prominent collarbone faintly blue where it met the hollow of her throat. "Yeah?"

"I'm sorry ... I thought I might catch Victor in."

"Catch him in what?" The dark eyes were lively, a bit sensual. "He's gettin' dressed, you wanna come in?"

"I don't want to interrupt anything."

"C'mon, I need a woman's opinion. You the one he's with now?"

Cat stepped over the threshold. Victor's coffee table had been pushed up to the kitchen counter and a small, brass-bound trunk was sitting in front of the sofa. It was open, with sea green and gold chiffon spouting from within. Brooches, jeweled barrettes, strands of beads, pendants had been pinned to the chiffon to give the effect of a sea chest spilling its treasure into the surrounding ocean. Victor's small television had been propped on the counter that separated the living area from the small kitchen. *Philly5Live!* was on. They were doing an interview by remote with Red Melendez. He was talking about how important it was to retain the dramatic texture of truth and yet be free to experiment visually, which might alter the Dudek story structurally, but would retain the—

Humanistic perspective, Cat thought.

"—humanistic perspective—"

The girl was studying the effects of chiffon and gems. Her turned-down mouth resembled Victor's characteristic scowl. "What do you think? What does it need?"

"It's—I mean, it's beautiful. I don't think it will serve as a coffee table, though."

"I'm Remy, Victor's sister?" The girl extended her hand. The diameter of the wrist wasn't much wider than a broomstick.

"I'm Cat. Austen."

"Victor's letting me hang out here a couple days. So, I heard you get to work with Tommi Ann Butler. What's she like? She as beautiful as she looks on the screen?"

Cat nodded.

"She ever leave the penthouse? Go down to the shops?"

"I don't know."

Remy's mouth pressed into a frown. "I was hoping she would find her way down to CapriOH! My show's today, tomorrow, Friday."

"Show?"

"Trunk show. I get one window and a corner of the store. I don't know who gave Fawn Caprio my name. Here—" She grabbed a handful of glossy color postcards from a stack on the couch, handed them to Cat. The front had an image of a pair of earrings and a brooch, silver and amethyst, nestled in a mist of gray chiffon. On the back, there was an announcement of a three-day trunk show of original semi-precious stone creations by Remy Cardenas. "You can slip her one, I'd appreciate it."

Cat took the cards, dropped them into her tote.

"I was ticked when the show got postponed from last month, but now? You ever see her wear any jewelry?"

"She had a pair of beautiful earrings on yesterday. Sort of a smoky topaz inlaid in old silver. But they may have been property of the wardrobe. When she flew in on Sunday, all she wore was her wedding ring."

"Victor," Remy cocked her head, leaned down to pluck at a fold in the chiffon, "he's on my case about showing in the Phoenix. He's really got it in for the Sterlings."

Victor walked in, his tie hanging unknotted around his neck, his jacket over one arm.

"I was on my way into Atlantic City and I saw your car. Didn't they let you keep that lovely Victorian door?"

"No. Remy, what's this?"

"It's my window."

"It's in the middle of my living room floor."

"Cat says it looks nice."

Victor looked at her.

"It does look nice."

Victor walked into the kitchen, snapping off the image of Red Melendez.

"I was watching that!" Remy stalked over and turned it back on. "God, *The Advocates*, I had such a crush. Who would have thought he would turn out to be such a jerk?"

"Did you have breakfast, Cat?" Victor asked.

"Yes. I'm on my way to the Phoenix for my interview."

"Spivak back from LA yet?"

Cat shook her head. "And it's not LA, it's Texas."

"What's in Texas?"

"David Wheeler. He says to call him 'Davey.' He wrote *Redemption, Texas*, the novel they based the movie on."

"Oh, I loved that movie." Remy straightened up. Her sweater slipped over her collarbone. She snatched it up to the neckline, close to her throat.

Victor set his Thermos on the counter, walked into the living room, looked her over. With two fingers, he pulled the neckline of the sweater away from the bruise.

Remy snatched it back.

The mask seemed to emerge from muscle, fix the overlying flesh firmly in place.

"Excuse me, Cat, I gotta change and call a cab."

"Maybe we could share one. I took a cab here."

"That'd be great." She gave her brother a baleful look and stalked off to Victor's bedroom, slammed the door.

"I like her," Cat said.

"I wish she liked herself a little more. Sit down."

Cat circled the trunk, sat on the sofa.

"An interview can't fill a day. What else are you up to?"

Cat thought of the encounter in Ron's apartment. "What makes you think I'll be up to anything?"

"'Suspicion always haunts the guilty mind. The thief doth fear each bush an officer,'" Victor quoted, glibly.

"I'm averaging five hours' sleep. I'm bushed, officer."

"Well, then you haven't been getting yourself into trouble, if the principle of Sherlock Holmes holds true."

"What principle?"

"That work never tired him but idleness exhausted him completely. If you're bushed, you haven't been out on some tenuous limb."

"Only the unsubstantiated branches of an elusive family tree." She paused. "Victor ..."

"Would that be the 'Victor' that precedes 'Victor, I've inadvertently sawed said branch from beneath me'?"

"I wouldn't say that exactly."

"You're saying less and less *exactly*. Recent escapades have compromised your vocabulary to the point where I suspect, to paraphrase Holmes again, that your well of English seems to be permanently defiled."

"'Defiled' makes me sound dissolute, depraved, mildly carnal. In other words, way more interesting than I am."

"I'll reserve judgment until I've been given the opportunity to form an opinion on the subject."

"Give me an opinion on a familiar subject, then. You know about breaking and entering, how it's sort of something you sometimes report to the police? Well, what if there's no actual *breaking*? I mean, you wouldn't have a certifiable B and E, then would you? You'd just sort of have an ... E."

"In the devout hope that this is purely an academic discussion, I would say that an E, barring extenuating circumstances, would be sufficient for it to warrant a call to the police and there would be no 'sort of' about it."

Cat sighed. "Look, you said we have to trust one another. I'm trusting you now, do you want it or not?"

"Yes."

"To be trusted, I meant."

"Ah."

Cat raised her chin. "You know Ron asked me to check on his place, take in his mail."

Victor nodded.

"When I was inside, Cici Bonaker sort of came in."

"Bonaker. The actress in that *South Street Shootout*?"

"Stakeout."

"You leave the door unlocked?"

Cat shook her head. "She had a key. Ron gave it to her last year, when they were making that movie. At the time, they were ... you know."

"I can, at least, imagine. If he's been letting her use the place, why did he ask you to check on it for him?"

"I don't think he was letting her use the place. I think she was planning to see if, well, if Ron had anything in his files that had to do with Tommi Ann."

"What, specifically? Did she say?"

Cat bit her lip. "Evidence that Tommi Ann Butler's her mother."

Victor raised his dark brows, surprised. "Mrs. Butler doesn't have children, does she?"

"Not *after* her marriage to Ben Butler," she said, significantly.

"Ah. And is there a link to the trip to Texas? And to this writer Wheeler?"

"I found out—don't ask how!—that Ron booked to LA, with a connection at DFW and got off in Dallas, rented a car and headed to a small town in West Texas that happens to be the birthplace of this guy Wheeler, and also Gloria Ramirez. You know who she is, don't you?"

"My mother would have my head if I said no. She never misses the show. So that sounds like your theory was correct, that Spivak might be doing a story on Butler's A list. I don't see the connection that links the Bonaker girl to Mrs. Butler."

Cat repeated Wheeler's tale of the dropout and Annie Cox. "The upshot is that these two kids ran away. There was some talk that Annie was sent to Houston. Twenty-five years ago, Cici Bonaker was privately adopted by a Houston couple. She has no idea who her birth mother was."

"And what became of Annie Cox?"

Cat's mouth puckered, thoughtfully. "Wheeler said no one ever heard of her or her boyfriend again, but I keep thinking of that line from Congreve's *The Double Dealer:* 'No mask like open truth to cover lies, As to stand naked is the best disguise.' If you want to conceal yourself, does it matter whether your camouflage is shadow or limelight?"

CHAPTER THIRTEEN

INT: NIGHTCLUB: NIGHT
KATE is sitting at a table with TIM and
GERRY.

KATE

You've been hinting at a change in format.
What gives?

GERRY

Next week. Floozy Tuesday is gonna be Tell-All
Tuesday. Prime grime, and all local.

KATE

That sounds slanderous.

GERRY (laughing)
Slander's if it's not true, babe.

Remy chatted non-stop on the drive over to the Phoenix. "Victor,
you know, when *Papi* died, it's like, all of a sudden he's the boss and
he's bossing me ever since."

Cat thought of Carlo. "I know what you mean."

She helped Remy ease the trunk out of the back seat of the cab, watched, amused, as Remy charmed one of the bellhops into carrying the trunk up to CapriOH!

Cat followed with something like trepidation. She half expected one of the green-jacketed security to stop her, one of the eyes behind the eye-in-the-sky to blow the whistle as she crossed the crowded slot floor, ascended the escalator to the mezzanine.

"Find out what she's wearing to the Oscars," Remy whispered with an agitated glance in Clevinger's rival display that concentrated on 18K and emeralds, the Phoenix signature green and gold, colors that would compliment Tommi Ann's tawny complexion, russet hair.

Cat promised to do her best, approached the penthouse elevator, feeling the knotting in her stomach. But the green jacket never blinked, simply reached in and pushed the PE button for her. Cat emerged on the penthouse floor. Danny Furina stood outside the elevator, a Phoenix security guard at the end of the hallway, Dianne King outside the door to Tommi Ann's suite. Her smile was civil, professional. "Good morning, Mrs. Austen. Let me walk you through the routine before we go in."

Routine? "Fine."

"You can have as much of the next ninety minutes as Tommi Ann can spare. The questions you submitted were fine, and have to stay limited to her participation in *CopWatch*, and, if you wish, the Oscars, though of course, that will have concluded by the time any of your copy reaches print."

Cat nodded. "What about personal questions, her marriage, why she lives in New York instead of LA?"

"No." It was said with a gracious smile. "And we'll provide a still, there will be no pictures. Mr. Landis approved this and also that you will do a feature on Cici. And we would like *South Jersey*'s May cover for Tommi Ann and the September cover for Cici."

Cat clearly heard: "No covers, no interview." "Ritchie—Mr. Landis—told me that's fine with him." Cover, television series, certain stardom. *Payback for abandoning her child at birth twenty-five years ago?*

Dianne's smile became sincere, awakened a dormant prettiness. "Please understand, Mrs. Austen, this is for Tommi Ann's protection. Her pinnacle is a narrow one, very precarious and very susceptible to the worst elements."

And our pinnacles can't always be traced to our beginnings, Cat recalled.

"What seems excessive to you is routine precaution for someone like her."

"I don't think it's excessive," Cat conceded.

Dianne unlocked the door to the Butlers' suite. "After the preliminaries, you'll be alone with Tommi Ann; I'll be in an adjoining room if you should need me. I have the consent form here." She produced a sheet that looked like some sort of form letter. "I already faxed a copy to Mr. Landis. It's standard."

Cat took the sheet and read it over. *This agreement made with respect to an*—(a blank had the word "interview" typed in) *between* (Tommi Ann Butler) *and* (Mrs. A. Austen) *on* (date) *will be subject to the following terms. No selling her material to other sources without the written consent of Butler Talent Management, no disclosure of information to other media, no financial consideration will be offered by Butler Talent Management.* Cat had signed her share of small contracts; none of them had been as detailed or restrictive as this prerequisite to ninety minutes' worth of Tommi Ann Butler.

Dianne King took it with a smile. "I'll send it down to the business center and have a copy ready for you before you leave." Dianne led Cat into the suite, gestured for Cat to take a seat on the sofa. "I must say, I admire your courage, Mrs. Austen."

"Courage?"

"For attending the shooting tonight. It has to be the incident from your past that you're least anxious to revisit."

Cat thought of Ted Cusack, how long she had kept that secret, how it was still unknown to all of her family save Freddy, had never been revealed to Chris. "Close. I'm not sure it requires courage, though. It may just be curiosity. Foolhardiness."

Dianne King smiled, quietly. "Well, I expect there is a component to real courage that is foolhardiness. Facing up to something that you're afraid of requires that you put aside the fear, even when instinct tells you to act in your own defense. I never confuse fearlessness with courage."

"You remind me of my friend, Ellice. She studied philosophy, and she's always saying things like that."

"I never studied philosophy, Mrs. Austen. Sometimes the rigors of living are the only guiding principles you need."

"Has it been rigorous?" Cat was working on a segue that wouldn't seem too obvious. "You've been with Tommi Ann almost since the beginning. Since *Illyria*." She wondered to what extent Tommi Ann had made Dianne a confidante, how much Dianne knew of Tommi Ann's past. "A wonderful allegory, as it turns out. I mean, it does really seem that Tommi Ann was washed ashore without any traces of a past clinging to her."

The eyes behind the tinted spectacles were unreadable. "Of course you understand that you're not to broach the past with Tommi Ann."

"Yes."

"We all have some debris from our past that we would like to discard, just set on the curbside for disposal. I can't think your own history has been completely tranquil and uncomplicated."

Cat thought of the attempted rape, and how she had fled rather than bringing charges against Ted Cusack. Of her shock at meeting up with him last month. Of Chris' murder. "After my husband died, I had this plan for keeping my life on an even keel."

"Were you successful?"

Was this part of the "pre-interview"? Cat shook her head.

"What happened?"

Cat felt her lips curving, involuntarily, felt the four syllables emerge on the crest of a rueful laugh. "Jerry Dudek." She added, "I sort of backed into the fast lane. If Ron Spivak hadn't been injured at the time, I wouldn't have picked up the Dudek story. It was his piece. Which means, I suppose, that if he hadn't been injured last November, Tommi Ann wouldn't be playing my alter ego right now."

Dianne King smoothed her skirt over her lap. She was dressed in a dark blue skirt, white blouse. The skirt was tailored wool crepe, the blouse heavy silk; the Aigner pumps were black leather with gold bands at the base of the heels. There was a dull gold bangle on her left wrist and an antique gold band on the left third finger. Cat wondered why she still wore it if, as Cici had said, the marriage had ended badly. "Cici mentioned the assault. Of course, they were not still intimate by that time. I imagine that that sort of jeopardy is part of Mr. Spivak's profession."

Tommi Ann floated into the room. She was wearing loose burgundy slacks, an off-white top with a wide ballet neckline that skimmed her collarbone, displayed her beautiful shoulders. She carried tea things, iridescent cups with the Phoenix crest, a silver tray with the falling phoenix engraved on its surface. "I am sorry not to have much time to give you, Mrs. Austen, but I thought this would be better than plugging you into the round robin." She set the tray on the table, sat next to Dianne and began to pour. "You'll have to make do with my inept ministrations here, but for the life of me, I have never gotten used to being waited on."

Cat drew out her notebook, opened it, rummaged for a pen.

Tommi Ann's quick eye spied Remy's postcards, paper-clipped to the inside cover of Cat's notebook. "May I?"

Cat nodded.

Tommi Ann took one, looked it over, laid it on an end table next to a suspended game of Scrabble. "I understand, Mrs. Austen, that your mother's taken Gary under her wing."

Cat smiled. "He showed up at my door this morning, with the entourage and limo. I don't think there'll be any living with my daughter this afternoon."

Tommi Ann smiled. "What's her name?"

"My daughter?" Cat hesitated. "Jane."

"Jane Austen?"

"Well, in every disposition there is a natural defect which not even the best education can overcome," Cat paraphrased. "And mine was to name my daughter after a writer instead of a movie star."

Tommi Ann laughed. "I hope even a less literate woman would think twice before putting 'Tommi Ann' on a birth certificate."

Cat shrugged, easily. "He was saying to me—Gary Biggs—that he didn't think of himself as a 'Gary.' Do you think of yourself as a 'Tommi Ann'?"

"Do you think of yourself as a 'Cat'?"

"Do I have nine lives, you mean? I do have the propensity to land on my feet. So far."

Tommi Ann set her teacup down, tucked her slender legs under her. "But it's not your given name."

"No."

"So, my theory bears out. Reality is what we make it."

"Why doesn't your reality include an entourage?" Victor's tactic, change directions unexpectedly, watch to see how rapidly the subject adapted.

Dianne King shifted in her seat—not having left yet—prepared to intervene if Cat breached the contractual limits on the conversation.

Tommi Ann shrugged. "You don't have to take something, just because it's dangled in front of you. Many people in my business think that an entourage is a symbol of rank, but believe me, when you reach a certain level, privacy is the true gauge of one's status. And the ultimate luxury."

"But you didn't wait to get to that level to enjoy that luxury Mrs.—" She saw Dianne shift, heard her clear her throat, discreetly.

"Please call me Tommi Ann. I feel like we've— Well, I feel like we're almost the same person."

I don't. "Tommi Ann. You didn't come to value privacy as your fame increased, you valued it from the start. There never were the retainers: personal trainers, chauffeurs, hairdressers and the like. Except for Mrs. King, who seems to serve as assistant, secretary, publicist, gatekeeper—"

Tommi Ann smiled at that.

"—in other words, serves a half dozen functions to keep you from having to deal with a half dozen people."

"True."

"When you came in, we were talking about that, about how Mrs. King had been with you almost since *Illyria.* I was wondering how you came to recognize the need for a personal assistant so early in your career. I don't think you could have been more than twenty when you made *Illyria.* How did you know ..?"

"That there would be a career that would justify a gatekeeper?" Tommi Ann asked. "I don't know if I did, but Ben always had faith in me. And he's a far better manager than I am an actress. Always has been."

"So you give Mr. Butler credit for the course your career took? You don't credit your own talent? And, what was it? Wanton desperation?"

Tommi Ann threw a slender arm over the back of the couch. "There are a lot of talented people in the world, Mrs. Austen. There are actors working regional theatre who are ten times as good as you'll see on Broadway in any given season. There are writers collecting rejection slips who are head and shoulders above anyone on the best-seller list, and folks in the church choir who sing better than anyone on the Billboard chart. What did Mae West say, 'Goodness had nothing to do with it'? Well, neither does talent."

Cat recalled what Cici Bonaker had said. "So, if I review Mr. Butler's remarkable track record—Eric Obermeyer, Gary Biggs, Teresa D., Gloria Ramirez, David Wheeler, it has less to do with their talent—not that they're not talented, mind you—than with your husband's determination to make them stars."

"And his ability." Tommi Ann took a sip of her tea. "Did you read *Redemption, Texas?*"

"The novel they based the movie on? Not yet."

"I believe Mr. Wheeler got two dozen or so rejections before he got the peculiar notion to send it to an acquaintance of his whose word carried some weight with Ben."

Gloria Ramirez, Cat thought.

"And it was every bit as good when it was sitting in someone's slush pile, when it was shoved into an envelope with a rejection letter as it is between book covers."

"Yes, and it sold over a hundred thousand copies. Hardcover. Which is excellent for a novel, but a fraction of the movie tickets that were sold. If *Redemption* wins the Oscar, it will be the screenwriter who gets the statue and the glory and a miracle if Mr. Wheeler even gets mentioned in the acceptance speech."

Tommi Ann laughed. She had a generous laugh. "Spoken like a closet author, Mrs. Austen."

"Call me Cat."

"His name will get mentioned. Ben insisted."

"Insisted that the screenwriter mention his name, or insisted that he win?"

Even Dianne King laughed at that. Her laugh was sweet, almost musical.

"Don't underestimate Ben's commitment to his clients' careers. He's the best at what he does. There should be an Oscar for that."

"What's David Wheeler like?"

"We've never met."

"Really? Didn't you shoot part of *Redemption* in Texas? He's from there, isn't he?"

"Texas," Tommi Ann's silky contralto floated over the words, "is a big state."

Dianne King rose. "Tommi, I'll excuse myself now. I need to finalize our travel arrangements for Los Angeles. I'll see you this evening, Mrs. Austen."

"Los Angeles," Tommi Ann echoed. "Mr. Spivak will be flying in from there, I understand."

"No, actually he's in Texas." Cat realized she had heard Dianne's quiet tread get as far as the door, had not heard the handle turn, the door open.

"Really?"

"I believe he went to interview Mr. Wheeler."

"Indeed?"

Nothing in the face to betray her. Nothing.

Cat heard the soft footstep, vacillating. *Say it! Are you Annie Cox? Are you Cici Bonaker's mother?* "Can we go back to *Illyria* for a minute?" *Coward.*

Tommi Ann's nod was equivocal. Her off-white blouse converted her chameleon eyes to the color of champagne.

"It's just that it's such an apt metaphor. You began with *Illyria.* Personally as well as professionally, you washed up with no past. But then, if I remember the play, Viola wasn't without a past, was she? She concealed it to protect herself in alien territory. Do you feel any particular affinity for that role?"

Tommi Ann shrugged. "Acting is about hiding who you are, all disguise and dissemble, annulling your personality. To that extent I do. Tell me, have you ever seen a stand-up comic, an impersonator do an impression of me?"

Cat shook her head.

"Because I've given them nothing to impersonate. I am the vessel of the character, nothing more."

"And when the curtain falls?"

"When the play ends, I am what I am. One of tens of thousands of nobodies who got lucky. I venture any of those stories are more colorful than mine."

"Except you're the one who became Tommi Ann Butler."

Dianne King reappeared, so quietly that Cat did not realize she had re-entered the room until she resumed her seat. Tommi Ann seemed oblivious to her presence. No, Cat decided, not oblivious, not un-aware, just comfortably aware, that taking for granted that one comes to feel for a long-time companion.

"I'm the one," Tommi Ann corrected, "who made myself Tommi Ann Butler."

CHAPTER FOURTEEN

INT: KATE'S BEDROOM: NIGHT

> KATE (to her reflection)
> Just this once. As a favor to Ricky. And then no
> more damn celebrity profiles. And if he asks—

> *KATE makes a gun of her thumb and index finger,*
> *"fires" at her reflection, raises the index*
> *finger to her lips and blows on it, sensuously.*

Jane was not fit to live with. Biggs had actually gotten out of the limo and walked her up to the entrance of the school, in front of all of the Popular Girls. Jane's mother getting shot last fall (canonization by fourth grade standards) had sunk to nothing. *Jane Austen, that little nobody had been driven to school by Bigg Phat P.I.G.!*

Cat put on an attentive face, allowed her eyes to drift toward the television screen, where Whitney Rocap was reporting on another day the city hosted the *CopWatch* cast, showed footage of Biggs talking to a rapt primary school class about the evils of drugs, a snippet of a confrontation scene Ron and Cici had filmed last Saturday, tagging "—Jersey Shore's own Ronald Spivak—" onto the shot, winding up with a studio still of Tommi Ann, her russet hair falling over the white satin skimming her shoulders.

"Mom?" Mats asked. "How come you look like that?"

Cat smiled. "I was thinking, if you ever went away and came back grown up and tall and different, I could look into your eyes and still know you were my boy."

"But you're not goin' away 'til I grow up, right?"

"I would never go off and leave my little boy. Or my little girl."

"I'm *not* a little girl."

"You're *my* little girl," Cat replied.

Jane set her rosebud mouth, but she was smiling. "What about when I grow *up.*"

"It doesn't matter how big you get, you'll always be my little girl."

"Like is the big fat pig somebody's boy?" Mats asked.

"He must be."

"He was raised by his *grandfather,*" Jane declared, picking the disks of pepperoni off her pizza, blotting the cheese with her napkin. "He told Meryl's class. He didn't have any parents and his grandfather raised him until he *died.*"

Cat gave the pronouns a pass. "So how did he get famous?"

"He got found singing on the street. I read it in *Teen Talk.*"

Cat looked at Ellice. "I have never thought of *Teen Talk* as a research tool."

"Honey, you oughta talk to my teens. Only way I'm gonna get an ounce of culture into their fallow skulls is if Hamlet shows up on MTV." Ellice dropped her pizza on her plate. "You know, something like, 'He blew in from England, An' kick up a fuss, 'cause Momma do the nasty with Claudius'." She jumped up, began mimicking the hip-hop posturing, "He goes actin' schitzy, but he's no fool, 'cause the play's the thing, if he plays it cool, An' Ophelia thinks he be hot for her, but it's not to be, if it ever were—"

"Stop!" Cat cried, tears running along her jawline. "Oh, God make me get something lucrative out of this so I can get my kids out of public schools."

"Why can't you *home* school us?" Jane demanded.

Cat rolled her eyes, began piling the discarded crusts onto a plate, bussed plates into the kitchen with Ellice. "I dread going over there tonight. I'd opt out if I didn't think there was a chance to shake loose one more crumb of information from Tommi Ann." *Settling for crumbs, just like Ron said.* Cat wondered if he was home yet.

Cat bathed Mats and got him in his PJs, read him a few Aesop's fables. She checked on Jane, who had laid five outfits on her bed, was scrutinizing them. "Mom, am I pretty?"

Cat sat on Jane's bed, looked at her daughter. The face was losing its roundness, the contours were delicate, the eyes dark and long-lashed like her mother's, the hair the color of Chris'. "You're the prettiest girl in school."

"All Moms say that."

"The other ones are lying."

"When I grow up, I want to be a star."

Cat smiled. "I think all nine-year-olds want to be stars."

"Did you?"

Cat thought about it. "I don't know. I liked writing. Stories. I thought if I was going to be a star, it would be because I wrote a book. I don't think I ever wanted to be a movie star."

"Some of the kids in school say you're practically *famous.*"

Backhanded fame, because she had gotten stuck with the Dudek case, caught a killer, got to work with *CopWatch.* "I suspect the Popular Girls are treating you better because you showed up at school today with Bigg Phat P.I.G., not because your mom's *practically* famous."

Jane nodded.

"Honey, you know what I think? I think people don't want to be famous, not really. I mean, the things people in the movies have to do? All day, doing the same thing over and over just like people who work on an assembly line. And they have people fussing with their hair and their faces and they can never just run out in sloppy clothes without someone making fun of them, and they can't go out to McDonald's without people staring at them and pestering them. I think, when people say they want to be stars, they really want to be treated like stars. They want other people to treat them like they're special. Stars get treated like they're special, even when they don't deserve it."

"That's not fair."

"No, it's not. Good people should be treated like they're special, but a lot of good people never get a break in life." Cat kissed Jane's hair. "I like the red turtleneck with the khakis. I'll do a French braid with ribbon in it, okay?"

Cat went into her room and changed into black jeans and a heavy gray sweater over a white turtleneck, pinned her hair in a loose chignon. She fired up the computer and began trolling the fan pages and filmographies for information, came up with the same photos that everyone had, the same stats she had read everywhere. She turned up a grainy still, black and white, of a youthful Tommi Ann in *Illyria* side by side with the shot *NewsLine90* had used, Tommi Ann looking exotic with her luminous skin, the white satin turning her chameleon eyes to crystal, the generous mouth with a hint of a curve at the corners as if holding back a smile that might reveal her secret to the world. The younger photo conveyed some terrible determination at the core of the pale teenage waif. Talent and wanton desperation, Cat recalled. The desperation had evaporated in the later photo, and she was a vessel given form by its contents, and its contents were a million unanswered questions, a million dreams.

"*I was dust poor.*" She had granted an hour-long television interview, only once, to Gloria Ramirez.

"*You mean dirt poor,*" *Ramirez had said.*

The enigmatic smile, the hint of a sway that may have been a gentle tweak of Gloria Ramirez's lingering twang. "You can plant something in dirt. You can root yourself in it and take the form you're meant to have. I come from dust, and dust"—she put the gathered fingertips of one hand to her *lips, blew, splayed them—"scatters a long way before it settles. And when it settles, it takes on another form."*

A form so changed that Gloria Ramirez wouldn't recognize little Annie Cox?

Cat's phone rang. Like Ritchie, April began the conversation as soon as the phone was picked up. "You heard from your friend Spivak?" April demanded.

"No. I think he said he'd be going straight to the club from the airport."

"His final scene, I have half a mind to shove a live round in the gun and let that jerk take a shot to the head, the stress he's causing me. That would be something, wouldn't it, art imitating life if he got shot?" Her laugh was a husky, sexual, monosyllabic *Haw!* "Thanks for putting us wise to your mom, she's a great cook. The Pig's in hog heaven."

"April, could I get a couple set passes for tonight?"

"You kiddin' me?"

Cat wasn't sure if that was an assent until she heard a muffled aside, "June! Get two Annie Oakleys for Cat Austen!"

Cat still wasn't sure of an assent until April asked her what names June should put on the passes, told her the passes could be picked up at the club entrance, she would notify security. "So how'd the lieutenant like the shoot Monday night? Him, I'll give a pass anytime."

"I wouldn't count on it, unless someone does get shot."

"I'll work on it. Get myself a pat-down by someone looks like him, you wanna know what I'd do?"

"I don't think so, no."

April told her anyway.

Cat called Carlo and told him that he and Mark could sit in on the shoot if they liked. As long as Mark didn't rat her out to Jane.

She went downstairs, found Ellice at the dining room table, balancing her checkbook, scribbling some calculations on a sheet of paper. "I'm sorry about this. But this is the last night shoot."

"I got some busywork," Ellice shrugged, grinned. "Just get me a signed eight-by-ten for Freddy, will you? Have her put something sweet on it. 'Love, from one real trouper to another,' something like that." Freddy was a state trooper.

Cat went to the closet, pulled out a black peacoat, a white wool scarf. "Any other requests, make them now. If this is a repeat of the church shooting, I'm taking off early. I don't care how many pickups or inserts or cutaways they have to shoot. As soon as Ron hits the ground, I'm out of there."

Within an hour, Cat was too preoccupied suppressing her yawns to remember why she had been apprehensive in the first place. The only strain she sustained was in trying to freeze her Isn't-this-fascinating? expression in place. She was sitting against the back wall of CV's, cables snaking around her ankles; the PAs, who hung on the perimeter of the set, gabbing into cell phones; Red Melendez, his ponytail hanging below the brim of his backward baseball cap, watching through a monitor as Tommi Ann and Cici ran through their brief scene; the hairdresser standing behind Cici, coaxing her hair into a soft chignon; the makeup guy brushing up her pallor, the silent totem-like presence of Ben Butler leaning against the wall next to her chair, watching intently; Dianne King sitting in a chair beside Cat, calmly running her pen over a word puzzle, impervious to commotion.

Cat watched the two women together. Tommi Ann's light, beaded sweater stripped the color from her mutable iris eyes, gave them a hollow, otherworldly look. Cici's pallor seemed real, and more than once, when they broke for another run-though, she glanced in Cat's direction, pressed her palms together covertly, a plea for Cat's silence.

To her dismay, Cat had been drafted to read for Ron, sit off to the side with the current script and read, "Wanna dance?" feeling more than a little foolish.

And Tommi Ann would reply, "I've used up all my good moves, thanks," to the vacant chair at the small table.

And Cat would read, "C'mon, we'll make it a threesome, I'll get Timmy. You seen him, by the way?"

At which point April stopped them, asked Cat if she could crank it up a little.

"It's fine, April," Tommi Ann said, with a generous smile at Cat. "This is for me, anyway, so that I get it down."

As if there was any question about Tommi Ann missing a beat, flubbing a line. She played a wary Kate, gave it a prim edge, determined to ride out the unpleasant interview, yet out of her element, the incompatibles—wariness, primness, determination, unease—fused in a seamless rendition that she called up, run-through after run-through. *Had she consented to the interview in order to encode my speech patterns, posture, inflection, mood?* Cat wondered. She had them all down, smoothly incorporated them into Kate Auletta. They broke and Tommi Ann rose, thanked Cat and headed toward the office that had been designated her personal green room. Cat stood, tapped her pen against a blank page of her notebook. Too many blank pages, after her hour and a half with Tommi Ann. Had courage failed her, or had decency won out? She tried to tell herself that if the truth about Tommi Ann's past was bound to emerge, it would be better, kinder, coming from her rather than Ron Spivak. She wasn't convincing herself.

"If someone doesn't dig me up Spivak in sixty seconds, I'm gonna put a hit out on that sonofabitch and play the part myself!"

"April, it's not even six—"

"If six was kicks, I'd be a Rockette!"

"Maybe he can't get through security."

Cat spoke up. "That's a possibility, April. He told me he was driving here straight from the airport. I had to park four blocks away."

"Tell the hired muscle to keep their lids peeled back!" April ordered, checking her watch, fuming, muttering that if Spivak didn't show she was going to kill him, kill the casting director who had allowed herself to be persuaded that Ron could handle the part, kill the next person who assured her he would turn up and then kill herself, if the networks didn't see to it first. She was also going to kill June because June was probably cozying up to Harold somewhere when she should be seeing to it that Harold was running his scenes with Wally, and she was going to kill Harold because he was God-knows-where when he should be someplace else.

Closing her eyes, the comic panorama in front of Cat disappeared and the club smelled like home. The Daughters of Sicily had taken over the kitchen of CV's oceanfront restaurant, and the scent of tomato sauce, basil, garlic, parmesan drifted through the narrow corridor that connected the restaurant to the club, giving an edge to the unions who were checking their watches, counting the minutes until the one AM dinner break.

Cat slipped to the back of the club where a few of the supporting players were marking time. She remembered the postcards Remy had given her, slipped her stock of them on the corner of the bar. Red Melendez was trying on the black trench coat he would wear as Victor Calderone, trying on his Calderone scowl. One of the techies popped his head in the restaurant door, made an observation about the possibility of clouds that set April off once more.

"Have you heard from Ron?"

Cat turned, saw Cici Bonaker, tear tracks etched into her makeup. Cat shook her head.

"Dianne said you told Tommi Ann he went to Texas. You told me he was in LA."

"I told you what I was told, Cici. I only found out about Texas later. Somewhere in west Texas, King County."

"That's not anywhere near Houston." Cici looked a bit relieved, baffled.

"Cici, look. I don't know what Ron was up to. Maybe it has nothing to do with you and Tommi Ann. Maybe she's your mother, maybe she isn't. But wouldn't it be better to thwart an attempt to embarrass Tommi by having it out with her? If it's true—if she's your mother—you wouldn't want her to be blindsided by a reporter, would you?"

"I asked Harold to talk to him. To just ask him as a friend to think twice before he did anything he'd regret."

"Would Ron listen to Harold?"

"They got on pretty well last year. Ron wrote some nice things about Hal in his *South Street Stakeout* copy."

"Did you tell him what Ron suspected?"

"About her being my mother?" Cici shook her head. "I just told him that he'd been hinting about some sort of exposé on Tommi Ann, that I was worried if he did something to upset her it could have repercussions on the shoot. I mean, the only thing that sets this apart from your run-of-the-mill *CopWatch* is Tommi Ann's participation."

"And that it's being pitched as a series pilot."

"I don't care about the pilot. There will be other opportunities for me, but this shoot means a lot to everyone else in the cast, the crew. Even Dianne says—"

"You talked to Dianne about this?"

Cici nodded. "When she told me he'd gone to Texas, I asked her flat out if she thought there was any chance Tommi Ann could be my mother."

Cat tried not to disclose her shock. "What did she say?"

"She says I should at least wait until after the shoot so I don't upset Tommi Ann, and that I should take time to think about why it's important to me."

It's true. Cat felt her stomach go slack. *It is true, and Dianne knows it.*

Chris had been devoted to his firstborn, changed diapers, walked the floors, jumped when she cried. "What's the matter, you can't put that kid down?" Cat's brothers had kidded him. "I'm imprinting," Chris had responded, seriously. "I want to be able to remember this feeling when she's twenty."

"What do you think I ought to do?"

"I hate to say this Cici, but Ron's pretty aggressive. If he's unearthed some proof that Tommi Ann's your mother, he's not going to think twice. Not in today's climate. If you've got something, you run with it, or it winds up all over the Internet and you lose out." She laid a hand on the girl's arm. "Victor—Lieutenant Cardenas—is a fan of Sherlock Holmes. Quotes him a lot. Holmes said once that any truth is better than indefinite doubt."

"Do you believe that?"

Cat thought of Kevin. Was she better off for knowing who the boy she had grown up with really was, what he had done? Wouldn't she rather not know? Never have known? "I think ... we learn how to live with indefinite doubt. Sometimes, with truth? We run the risk of learning something we can't live with."

"Can you talk to Ron?"

"Cici, we're really not all that close—" She looked at the girl's pained eyes. "Okay, I'll talk to him."

Cat heard a ripple of commotion from the entrance to the club, heard April's voice arise from nowhere in particular, "You get your keester into makeup while you still got one to sit on, you shmuck—"

Cat heard Ron Spivak yell, "I hadda park all the way over on Fairmount! Where they got Makeup?"

Cici squeezed Cat's hand. "Promise?"

Cat nodded. She couldn't wedge past the crew that was pushing wheeled trunks through the narrow corridor that linked the nightclub to the restaurant so she backed up and took an alternative route, passing behind the bar to the kitchen. At the opposite side of the kitchen was a narrow staircase that linked a service entrance to the loft.

The loft had been converted to Makeup, Wardrobe. Ron Spivak was buttoning his shirt, yanking his narrow black tie into place. His dark eyes were hectic with excitement. He winked at Cat, nodded her over. "Miss me?" Cat recognized the flirtation of triumph.

"How was LA?"

"Sunny."

"And how about Imogene?"

"Defunct." Ron didn't look incensed; he was glowing. "Okay, whadja do, trace me, or did Landis do it?"

"I did."

"And?"

Cat looked around, dropped her voice. "Annie Cox."

Some of the glow faded. "You did do your homework."

"No, I just had a chat with David Wheeler. He said I could call him Davey."

"What did you and Davey chat about?" Leery now, wondering how much she knew.

"High school. He graduated with Gloria Ramirez. King County, Texas. Seven kids in his class. One dropped out, ran off with a girl he got pregnant, a girl named Annie Cox. Twenty-five years ago. How'd I do?"

"So-so." Ron's eyes flicked left and right. "Look Cat, it was just wanting to get close to Tommi Ann at first. Everyone on *South Street Stakeout* knew Cici was the shortcut. I get to see her close up, dead ringer, right? She's on her own, sort of at loose ends, we go out, we come down the shore, we're gettin' it on, Cici tells me how she's adopted, I'd be nuts not to wonder, 'Is it possible?' So I pay a few bucks to a local PI to do some legwork for me—"

"Danny Furina."

"You got it. He talks to people she went to school with. He gets a hold of someone clerked Family Services twenty-five years ago knew the Bonakers. Everything's completely under the table. The Bonakers had dough. Birth mother dropped the kid and dropped out." Cat thought about the moment Jane had been put into her arms, the pale down plastered to her head, the dark eyes fully open, already checking out her world. Cat would sooner hand over her own head than deliver her baby to strangers. "Look at Tommi Ann," Ron urged, whispering. "Listen to her voice. Think of what it musta been like shakin' dust outta those vowels. She's the most glamorous woman in the world, married to Number One in talent management. Beauty, class, money—what's the last image you would have of her as a kid?"

"Some itinerant, pregnant, dust poor—"

"I mean the very last. Dead last."

Under the table. Dough. Cat looked at him, quizzically. "Money changed hands?"

Ron's eyebrows lifted; he beckoned "Come on."

"Compensation to the birth mother for medical expenses? A little money to get back on her feet?"

"Define compensation," Ron proposed. "Gimme a figure."

Cat blinked. "Well ... twenty-five years ago, I guess that ten or fifteen thousand would be generous."

"Quadruple that. Sixty grand changed hands." He paused to let the sum sink in.

A couple of the bit players clattered up the wooden stairs, giggling. Ron lowered his voice. "That's not the doctor's bill. That's not getting-back-on-your-feet money. Cici wasn't just adopted. She was sold."

CHAPTER FIFTEEN

INT: RADIO STATION: AFTERNOON
*KATE is pacing the station manager's office,
waiting for GERRY to arrive for his interview.
GERRY leaps into the room, brandishing a toy
gun. It looks real. KATE shrieks.*

GERRY

Whadja think, it's real?

The scripted scenes were starting to merge with memory. Cat
stood inside the entrance to CV's, her eyes locked on the gun. Across
the street where the crew was dressing the parking lot, Wally was
drilling Harold Anderson in the handling of the gun under the
baleful eye of a city cop. Even from a distance, Cat could see the
relaxed grip, the attentive nods as Wally and the assistant director
coached Harold in the movements of raising the gun, pointing it
toward the dark red sports car that was Ron's mark.

"Cat, are you all right? You look like you're seeing ghosts."

Cat turned and saw her sister-in-law, Sherrie, and her friend Jackie
Wing. Their faces were carefully made up and they were dressed in
the flashy attire of a club crowd, Jackie in a glossy black skirt, a red
off-the-shoulder blouse, Sherrie in a short satin dress, the aquamarine
color darkening her blue eyes.

"I don't dare walk past the buffet," Jackie giggled. "Every time I inhale, I feel like I've gained another pound." Jackie was as thin as Remy Cardenas, petite, with short spiked hair and a voice that prompted telemarketers to ask, "Little girl, is your mother at home?"

"Cat, do you want me to get Joey?" Joey was Cat's brother, matinee-idol handsome, he had easily made the cut; this counted as their first real night out since the birth of baby Gio last December.

Cat shook her head. "I just keep telling myself, it's only a movie. I was just waiting to flag down Carlo and Mark, I got them set passes." Her eyes were fixed on Harold, who was listening attentively to Wally. She nodded to the cop behind them. "Who's that? Is that Gino Forschetti?"

Jackie nodded. "Stan says the PD has to put an observer on the set whenever they use an explosive, guns, fire bombs, anything like that. That gun he's holding is what they call a firing prop, I think. It means it fires real rounds or blanks or something." Jackie, who had already worked the St. Agnes shoot, said knowingly, "Trust me, in an hour, you'll be praying for someone to fire off a couple rounds just to relieve the boredom."

"It's *not* boring." Sherrie, like Jane, was all awe and italics. "There're all *kinds* of behind-the-scenes stuff, it's better than all the backstage soap operas when I was working in Vegas." Sherrie had been a showgirl.

Cat turned. "Yeah?"

Sherrie bobbed her head. "I went out the Boardwalk entrance to check out the crew and I heard these people talking and this woman was saying, 'I don't know what he knows, I'm just afraid it could kill this shoot.' And then one of the assistants asked me to move, because they're blocking out the background on the Boardwalk, for the scene where Victor shows up at the club? So I went inside."

Cici Bonaker, Cat thought. Pleading with Harold.

"And then after they did our makeup, I went into the ladies' room to check it out and I bumped into Cici Bonaker. She already had

her makeup done and she was crying so hard, it got all messed up. I
helped her fix it," Sherrie added. "I used to do all my own makeup for
the stage."

Jackie tugged at her neckline. "Stan said the makeup girl told him
that Cici had been dating Ron Spivak last year, and they broke up.
Maybe it has something to do with them being on the outs."

"WHERE'S MY BACKGROUND!"

Sherrie grabbed Jackie's arm. "She could be a drill sergeant."

Cat turned her eyes back to the street, saw Harold clear and
present the weapon to Wally under the eyes of the cop, head back to
the club. Security had established a firm perimeter around the shooting area. The Boardwalk ramps were cordoned off for two blocks in
either direction; a ten-block section of Pacific had been shut to traffic. Biggs' customized trailer had been laid across Belmont at the
intersection of Pacific, and the half-block of Belmont between Pacific
and the Boards had become an exterior location. Technicians were
lighting the street and the parking lot for Kate's flight from the club
and the brief, fatal exchange with Gerry. Across Pacific, a platoon of
uniforms on overtime and private security held back the crowd that
was willing to endure thirty-seven degree temperatures for a glimpse
of Tommi Ann or Bigg Phat P.I.G. Cat saw a large form make his
way through the crowd. Cat pushed the door open, flagged Carlo,
waving the two set passes. Carlo had one hand on Mark's shoulder.
Mark had dressed neatly, which meant his best jeans, had slicked
down his straight dark hair.

June was herding the background onto the dance floor for the
set-up, run-through. Cat saw Ron sitting at a table on the perimeter
of the small dance floor, a technician holding a light meter an inch
from his nose; Ron's fingers did a nervous quickstep on his lap,
ready to intervene if the techie made contact with the prosthesis. Red
called, "Take one in thirty!"

Cat heard an uproar that had the cadence of a hog call, concluded that Biggs had emerged from the customized trailer, was making his way toward the club.

"Hey, Ms. Austen," Biggs greeted. "Hey everybody, I'm not late, am I, Mae?" he addressed Red's assistant.

"You're early."

Cat put a hand on his sleeve. "Can you come meet some people, just for a minute?"

"Mae, can I say hi to a couple folks just a minute, or do you need me to be here?"

Mae was a freckled black woman with steel-rimmed glasses, steelier composure. "Gary—"

Cat had realized that she liked people who addressed Biggs as Gary more than she liked those who called him "The Pig."

Mae perched her clipboard on her hip, slipped her headphones off her ears. "Here's a riddle for you. When does a three-hundred-pound-multimillionaire-recording-star with an armload of Grammys take five?"

Biggs chuckled.

"Anytime he wants. Don't go far, okay?"

Cat could see the baggy legs of Mark's trousers vibrating. She pulled Carlo down, kissed him on the cheek, whispered, "Don't say I never did anything for you," and turned to Biggs. "Gary, this is my oldest brother, Carlo."

Biggs held out his hand. "I see why your momma cook so much, man. I tell you, she was my momma, you'd never get me away from the table."

"And this is Mark, he's living with Carlo."

"Just while I'm in foster care," Mark muttered, testing out his ability to speak to the idol.

"An' he took you in? Tha's great, man. My folks took off, it was my grandad took me in. I tell you, folks take in kids, there's gotta be a room in heaven they got all to theyselves. How old're you?"

"Fourteen."

"I's fourteen, when my grammpop took us in."

The skepticism was melting away from Mark's gaze. "Who's we?"

"I got a sister, brother. They in school. I didn't get much school; I want them to get it right." He was one of the few people who could look Carlo eye-to-eye. "When my grammpop died, I's eighteen, so I's on my own, but they took Charlene and Jonah and put them in a home. All's I wanted was to get them out. Tommi Ann and Ben, first thing they did when they took me on was get me my brother and sister, so I could raise them up myself. They grow up, they do the same for someone else. You gotta pass it on, Mark. That's what Tommi Ann always says."

"Where the hell is *HAROLD!*" April Steinmetz stalked into the club. "I'm paying a thousand dollars an hour for this dive, my unions ring the dinner bell at one a.m., I want his keester on the set *yesterday!*"

"I—I'm comin'." Harold hustled down from Makeup.

"If comin' was drummin', I'd be Ringo Starr." She turned to Red. "How many times you gotta run through it for the schmuck?" "The schmuck" being April's epithet for Ron.

"He's ready to go, April."

"Gary?" Mae took the latest rewrites Harold handed her.

"I'm comin'." He winked at Mark. "They take the shoot outside, you come by get a look at the trailer they gimme." Biggs seemed amazed that such a grand toy had been turned over to him, hadn't quite figured out what he had done to deserve it. "Go on in say 'hi' to your grammom, tell her I said save me some of that lasagna, don't let all the crew eat it."

Mark's head bobbed. Carlo guided him toward the corridor. Cat noticed that the kid didn't shrug off Carlo's hand on his shoulder.

"You just made my brother's day," she told Biggs.

"You make your day so's you can live through it, an' then you go on and make someone else's. That's what Tommi Ann says."

***

Cat took her place beside Dianne, whose eyes were scanning the page of a puzzle book, something that looked like a geometrical riddle. June approached, seeming to float inside her oversized jeans and shirt. "Mrs. King, someone handed me this, said it was for you."

Dianne held out her hand without looking up. Cat noticed that it was one of the postcards she had put on the bar, the announcements of Remy's trunk show. Dianne apparently detected an unfamiliar texture, size of the object, glanced at it, turned it over, read something. Cat saw Dianne's facial muscles tighten, concentrating the planes and hollows into a cold mask. Cat wished she could see the expression behind the tinted lenses. Dianne slipped the card into her bag, went back to her puzzle.

Ben Butler emerged from the corridor, walked over to Cat's chair, knelt down eye-level with her. Cat sensed that his attention was being analyzed; what did Butler Talent Management have to say to Mrs. Austen, was he going to sign her, perhaps? Get her a screen writing deal? Impossible. She was over thirty-five, after all. Nobody over thirty-five got so much as a commercial jingle these days.

"Are you all right?" Butler asked. "You gonna make it?"

"It's only a movie," Cat told him. "That mantra was created for just this occasion."

"There's nothing that makes you ready to take a good look at your own life. You wanna go sit in the office, out in the trailer?"

"If they can take it, so can I. Play it."

Butler chuckled, patted her arm. "You got the stuff, Mrs. Austen." He got up and gave her a wink, loped back toward the restaurant. After a moment, Tommi Ann appeared, dressed in the dark skirt, beaded sweater, dark hose, looking perfect. Perfect. *How much does perfection cost, Cat wondered. Who do you have to sell to attain it?*

Set up for the shot of a frantic Tim/Harold cutting through the dance floor, running up to the table where Kate/Tommi Ann was sitting, demanding to know where Nadine/Cici had gone, running after her. Gerry/Ron appearing in his wake, dialogue, the segue to the brawl that had already been filmed. Cut. Shoot cutaways, close-ups. Set up for the scene that preceded it, the conversation between Tim/Harold and Kate/Tommi Ann while the background bumped, ground to the rhythm of *Killadilla*, Bigg Phat P.I.G.'s latest Top Forty that Butler had gotten *CopWatch* to use.

"Lights!" Red called, hunkering behind the monitor. "Cue the music. Okay, let's get my backfield in motion."

Cat saw Mae concealing a smile with her clipboard. *At least I'm not the only one who thinks Melendez is a self-aggrandizing jackass.*

"*Death of a Shock Jock*, Scene Ten, Take One, Mae, give me a sound off aaaaaaaaaAAAAAAAND ... ACTION!"

The take went south fast. Harold ran up to Tommi Ann, missed his mark, uttered an expletive and muttered, "Sorry, sorry, sorry."

Cat sensed the surprise that rippled among the crew; Harold could get flustered when someone else screwed up, but he was rarely the first to err.

"Relax, Hal," Tommi Ann smiled, turned and positioned herself for the next take. The Kate Auletta aspect settled over her like a veil, ready to go again before anyone else. Perfect. Perfect. *What was the going rate for perfection?*

"*Death of a Shock Jock*, Scene Ten, Take Two."

Take Three, Four, Five.

Harold: "That girl you were talking to, where'd she go?"

But Cat heard: "*Where'd she go?*" "*What, you mean that girl? Ladies' room maybe–*" She gave her head a shake. *It's only a movie, it's only a movie, it's only a movie.*

Harold shook out the nerves, and the scene began to fly. Cat realized with a little shock that he was good. Not good, she corrected. Superb. The slick, formulaic *South Street Stakeout*, the attack of jitters, the indifferent writing skills hadn't prepared her for his smooth, nuanced performance. Cat nipped back a smile as she watched Gary Biggs whirl and rotate his three hundred pounds. Cat caught Sherrie's eye and gave a covert thumbs-up, saw Red shift the monitor to concentrate on Sherrie's showgirl moves.

Set up for the next scene, Ron's dialogue with Tommi Ann. Offstage, his face pancaked, his head covered with the floppy brown wig, Ron bore an eerie resemblance to Dudek. Cat's eyes panned past him to the corridor where Cici Bonaker was standing in back of a couple PAs, her eyes fixed on Ron. Even at a distance, Cat could see the careful re-layering applied to the area around her eyes.

Red adjusted his ponytail under his baseball cap, Mae called "*Death of a Shock Jock*, Scene Eleven, Take One." A camera dollied in, tracked Ron as he approached Tommi Ann, snaked his upstage arm around her waist, pulled her close, a totally confident, completely convincing Jerry. Gerry.

"*Wanna dance?*"

Cat saw herself and Jerry bickering at their table, but the words emerged in an odd syncopation and made no sense; she realized the dialogue was overlapping her own memory fragments of the encounter.

I've used up all my good moves, thanks.

C'mon, we'll make it a threesome, I'll get Timmy. You seen him by the way? He went looking for some girl. Tall.

Short dark hair. Not "dark." The line had been changed to "auburn" for Cici. Nadine.

Nadine.

Then it's you an' me.

No, it's just you.

Something was wrapping itself around her ribcage, waiting for her to exhale, tighten itself. Victor's landlady had a boa, she thought wildly; it circled its prey and slowly tightened itself with each exhalation until the poor prey suffocated. Cat realized she could feel the effort of her own breathing, hear it. Would the mikes pick it up? Would her panting ruin the take? She imagined April bellowing, "Who's BREATHING while we're trying to shoot?"

"*Want a preview of tomorrow's show, Katie? Want a family secret to end all family secrets?*"

Were they having a brownout, Cat wondered? Had the lighting technician messed up? She gripped the arms of the chair, terrified that if she fell over, the crash would ruin the take. But it didn't matter, because she heard someone yell, "Cut! Damn it, *cut!*"

CHAPTER SIXTEEN

EXT: BEACHFRONT PARKING LOT: NIGHT
KATE is running toward her car. GERRY pursues her, intercepts her.

GERRY

Hey, Kate, chill out. Whaddaya takin' off for?

KATE

I think I've got my copy.

GERRY

Kill it. I've got something hot. And you don't look to me like a gal who'd settle for A Day with a DJ.

KATE

How do you know what I'd settle for?

GERRY steps between her and the car door. KATE tries to sidestep him.

GERRY

Five minutes.

KATE

That's about six minutes too long.

Cat allowed herself to gasp, audibly, felt a chilly sweat trickling under her sweater.

"Ben, what the hell—"

Cat blinked hard, realized that it was Butler who had halted the scene, not Melendez. She saw April rapidly inflating to the point of explosion, saw Melendez vacillating, saw Butler's tall form loom in the foreground.

"Where's that security guy, Furina?"

"I'm sorry," Cat said, faintly.

"Hell. You keel over, the take's shot anyhow. Besides, Spivak blew his line."

Cat thought he was probably saying that to make her feel better about the fact that she had nearly keeled over in front of everyone.

Danny Furina hurried over, bent down. "C'mon, Cat, let's go take a walk. Stroll in the moonlight with the big 'D' is bound to get the juices flowing."

She felt his hand cup her elbow and she whispered, "Let's go through the club, I don't want Mama and Carlo to think anything's wrong."

"No prob." Danny kept his arm under her elbow. Cat felt a gentle hand on her arm, heard Tommi Ann ask, "Are you really all right, Cat?" which dislodged latent murmurs of concern from the crew.

The first hit of cold air shocked her brain back to consciousness. The coastal wind, rebounding off the narrow Atlantic City streets, the drumming of the waves, the percussion of her heart were beating in unison, but she no longer felt like she was fading. The March air was chilly, with a breeze blowing a fine mist of sand from the beach, starlit, just like the night back in November when Cat had fled CV's, been pursued into Bel-Ave Parking by Jerry, who had some dark secret he wanted to share, was gunned down ...

Cat and Danny settled on a bench on the vacated stretch of Board-walk behind Bel-Ave parking. The lot below had been cleared of all but the strategically placed set cars, the periphery crammed with cables, mounted lights, cameras. A group of techies was attempting to ma-neuver a car into position to catch the reflection of CV's purple neon marquee off the windshield of Kate's red sports car.

Uniforms, a few green jackets, plainclothes; protection everywhere, Cat thought, recalled again that night when Jerry had pursued her, when the two of them had had words, Jerry had been shot, and there had been no one around.

"For a minute there, I thought I was going to have to give you mouth to mouth."

"In your dreams, Danny."

"Hey, you oughta know. You starred in a couple of 'em." Danny shook his head. "You know, I know what I'm doin' here, but I swear I don't know how you can put yourself through this, Alley Cat. They must be payin' you a bundle."

"Not enough." Cat directed her gaze to the parking lot. "I was sitting behind the lights, in the shadows. How could Butler see from across the room that I was fading out?"

"Butler sees everything. It's what makes him a career-maker, 'cause he can see the long road, the big picture." He leaned back, eased his arm around Cat's shoulder. Cat just as smoothly took his wrist and unwrapped the arm, dropped it in his lap. Danny chuckled. "So what's it like, watching her?"

"Unnerving, I have to admit. When she plays a scene, it calls up what I was feeling back then. I mean, the script has altered every-thing, *everything* about that episode. Watching this"—she swept her arm toward the crew positioning the cars, spattering the stone wall with graffiti, redistributing the trash, so that the parking lot would look like a prime-time TV rendition of a parking lot—"and I don't have any sense of that night, no *déjà vu*. Except when I watch Tommi Ann, and I feel like she's spent some time in my head, wonder how on earth she got there. She's really me. All the rest is invention and hype." Cat's eyes soared above the uniforms, working overtime, to the onlookers packed six deep across the street, mesmerized by a team of techies raising lights, shouldering booms, wondered if they were looking back at two people sitting on the cordoned-off Boardwalk.

Danny scoped out her thoughts. "They're wondering if we're somebody, that's what you were thinking."

"I was wondering what the price tag is on fame."

"I'd pay it."

"I don't doubt it."

"Hey. At least I could read it."

Cat arched her eyebrows. "Is that some sort of hit?"

"Not you, Alley Cat. You haven't figured it out yet?"

"Figured what out?"

Danny glanced around. "I been on Pig patrol—"

"Don't call him that, he's a nice kid."

"Yeah. Anyway, it's a lot of marking time, but it's not so bad because you get to float, and nobody gives you a second look. Anyway, I'm working the twenty-fifth floor. He's got the whole twenty-fifth floor, mind you."

"You're kidding."

Danny shook his head. "And I notice the inner circle's spending a lot of time with him in his rooms. Not just Tommi Ann, but Dianne King, the Bonaker girl. Anyway, they drop in on the ... Biggs ... I make a couple passes by the room and at first I'm thinking they're running lines, but then I get it. They're helping him read. The Pig can't read."

"What do you mean he can't read? How can anyone in his position not know how to read?"

"Some people, they can write their name on a check, it's all they gotta know to get by."

"I've seen him sign autographs," Cat protested.

"Yeah, with the goons standing right over him. They're not just there to guard his carcass. I'm not sayin' he can't spell his name, read your Dick and Jane, but he ain't gonna be arm wrestling Dianne King for her *Times* crossword any time soon. I'm not kiddin'. There's a story for you."

No, he wasn't kidding. Cat recalled how Biggs had stared at her bookcase in wonder, asked Jane how to spell her name.

He says the P.I.G. stands for Peace In Justice, April had told Cat last month.

With all due respect to Mr. P.I., um G., I think justice starts with a J. Not the way he spells it.

"So," Danny moved to another topic. "What's with Cici Bonaker and Spivak? I didn't think they were speaking. 'Course, I wouldn't call it speaking, exactly, not on her part, more like bawling—"

"And that would be b-a-w-l?"

"Right. She's saying something about what did he find out, is it worth that much to him, she can get him a job on the show when it goes series, Butler would do it for her if only he'll keep his mouth shut. You think it's gotta do with those records he had me nosing around after, stuff to do with her adoption? What, were the Bonakers in the mob or something?"

"I hardly think so," Cat said, slowly. "I suspect they were just people who couldn't have a child and wanted one at any cost." She looked up, saw Dianne King walking toward them, wrapped in a light trench coat.

"How are you feeling?"

"I'm fine."

"Ben sent me out to check on you. They're breaking for dinner. Perhaps you should come inside and have some tea."

Danny helped her up, kept an arm on Cat's elbow.

"Why don't you stay inside the club, Mrs. Austen, when they shoot the parking lot scene?" Dianne suggested.

"No, I'll hold up."

"You mustn't be a devil to yourself, Mrs. Austen and tempt the frailty of your powers."

Cat recognized the phrase, from *Troilus and Cressida.* Cici was short for Cressida. Cat was certain now that Dianne King knew about Cici's past. Was she trying to provoke a reaction from Cat, prompt Cat to reveal suspicions of her own?

Cat entered the restaurant. The tables had been pushed into clusters, with the food served up at a long buffet against the wall. Cat observed how food induced parity, thought of Jennie's unofficial motto, "Whatever happens, you still gotta eat." Even the PAs, tenaciously scrambling toward a higher rung, were happy to share a table with the lowly background, the interns, their roving eyes stilled while they concentrated on their plates.

Jennie was berating Danny Furina. "Whaddaya mean, you called your mother two weeks ago? You don't talk to your mother every week?"

"Mama Jen, she says once, twice a month is all she can take. Every time I call, her blood pressure spikes."

"That's 'cause you don't behave yourself. You see Cat over there? She behaves herself."

"That's her problem, Mama Jen."

"You get something to eat?"

"Later, I'm on duty."

"Try the eggplant."

Carlo was sitting with Mark, Biggs, a few of the bodyguards. He excused himself, trudged over to Cat. "Biggs says we'll have a bite with him, then go check out his trailer. The kid's in heaven. He called me his 'foster dad.' First time he called me any kinda dad. I owe you. What were you doin' out with Furina?"

"Necking under the Boardwalk."

"Dumb fuck lays a lip on you, I'll Jersey smack him up good."

"Have you seen Ron Spivak?"

"I think he went back up to fix his face."

Cat cut through the kitchen, where Rose was piling *foccacia* in napkin-lined baskets, shouting, "Ma, they need more gravy out there," made her way up the back stairs to the loft. Ron Spivak was sitting in front of a bulb-rimmed mirror carefully pressing foundation around the bridge of his nose, flirting mildly with June, whose pale face was pink with interest.

"Hey, Cat."

June looked up, grabbed her clipboard and scurried off as if caught in an unsanctioned act. Ron's wig was askew, a few of the longer strands falling over one ear.

"Why aren't you eating?"

"Just getting myself together. What happened to you, you pass out?"

Cat shrugged. "I guess 'it's only a movie' only takes you so far."

"Then come up with something that takes you farther." He turned to her. "Can you see the seam, here?"

Cat approached, perched on the edge of the makeup table, looked close. The foundation had camouflaged the juncture of prosthesis to skin, the makeup quite professional, but Ron was probably a pro by now. She yanked his wig into place, handed him a comb. "Sorry I messed up the take."

Ron grinned at the reflection in the mirror; the grin etched mean creases into the carefully applied cosmetics. "You didn't."

A voice called from below, "Spivak, you need a hand, you got yourself back together?" One of the makeup team who had abandoned her post for food.

"Fine!"

"What happened, you shoot pickups for the brawl? I thought all of that had been shot."

"Nah, I went a couple rounds off camera." He raised his chin, rolled his head left to right, pushed his chair away from the table.

"You always know the goods are worth something when people are willing to take a shot at you for them."

Cat shuddered. That sounded like something Jerry Dudek would've said.

Ron stood. "What's the weather like outside?"

"Cold."

"Good. Lotta people are ticked at me, wanna come out and see me get shot. Let 'em frost their cookies." He yanked his coat from the back of the chair, hung it on a peg on the wall. "You got my keys, you can throw them in my pocket. You gonna come out watch me get whacked?"

Cat swallowed, nodded.

He allowed Cat to help him into the black leather bomber jacket that was his "Gerry" costume for the parking lot scene. "Thanks for takin' in my mail. Any problems?"

"No."

"I'd buy you a drink but as soon as they wrap the scene and do the cutaways, I'm gonna jet, I got some copy I gotta get down tonight. How 'bout the coffeehouse tomorrow?"

"Fine. But don't you have to stick around?" She felt a shudder pass through her, remembered asking Jerry Dudek why he was taking off, leaving Tom to handle the emcee duties that night. *I thought you had to stick around*, she had said.

"Nope. One to the head, play dead, and I'm gone."

CHAPTER SEVENTEEN

EXT: BEACHFRONT PARKING LOT: NIGHT

KATE
That's about six minutes too long.

GERRY grabs KATE'S arms, shoves her against the side of the car.

GERRY (Spitefully)
I don't need you. I know plenty reporters'd pay me for what I got up here—

GERRY taps his forehead.

Why is this taking so long? Why can't they just shoot him–shoot it—and get it over with? Cat, sitting behind the cameras, on the outer rim of the parking lot, glanced over her shoulder to the crowd across Pacific. Willing to be crushed, shoved, frozen for a glimpse of Tommi Ann Butler. She turned her attention to the scene in front of her, Cici Bonaker, dressed in the dark skirt, white sweater, mannish jacket that was Tommi Ann's costume, walked through the scene over and over, so that lights, camera angles could be adjusted for Tommi Ann's costume, coloring, height.

Is that her? Is that her? Cat wasn't certain if the question had been uttered somewhere across the street, carried on the wind, or if it was the issue of her imagination. She noticed that when Cici receded from the lights, the peripheral rays catching the height, the tint of the hair, the restless grace of the figure did tend to convert her into Tommi Ann.

The ululation that erupted behind her signaled an Appearance. Cat turned and saw Biggs' detail bulked up with added security, moving him from the club entrance to the trailer. Cat saw Carlo's iron-gray mane cruising above the knot of flesh, shook her head. If this didn't make him a hero to Mark, the kid was lost forever.

Red Melendez appeared on the crest of the excitement, wearing his Victor Calderone coat, his Roberto Aguilar glower that dissolved into an unctuous smile at the first, "That's the guy was on TV this morning," a smile that flagged with the follow-up, "What's his name again? What was he in?" He turned slowly while a wardrobe peon checked for stray threads, spoke with conspicuous authority into the cell phone Mae handed him, managing to stay well inside the crescent of light that kept him visible.

"Cici, we're good here," the lighting technician called down from his perch. "I'd like to run through it with him."

Cici nodded, crossed the parking lot, her face set in a troubled mask, looked up and tried to smile at Cat, didn't quite make it. One of the techies directed an expletive to the migration of cloud cover that made its way across the moon. The March night, clear then clouding, was playing hard to get, making the unions work for it.

Cat watched Melendez directing an exaggerated scrutiny at the sky, as if he could command the cooperation of the moon, the clouds, choreographing his movements for the crowd, the media held at bay. Cat saw Harold Anderson hustled out of the club by April, who was berating him for something. The wind sent "—wait until *after* the shoot before you cross swords with the schmuck—" in Cat's direction. She saw Harold throw up his hands in helpless apology, get in a huddle with the powder man, Wally, who was standing over a pair of revolvers on the prop table, revolvers that, Cat noted, looked disconcertingly real.

Whadja think, it's real? Who said that, Jerry or Gerry?

Red huddled with Wally and Harold, held his palms up toward the lighted area, thumbs at a ninety-degree angle, framing the center of the set, coaching Harold to step forward, raise his gun hand, index finger and thumb angled like a firearm. Red coaxed Harold's hand up another couple inches, studied the effect, nodded. Did it again, this time with Red watching through the viewfinder. Again, this time with one of the revolvers Wally took from the table, checked in view of the cop standing behind him, before he handed it to Harold. Raise, aim, fire at Ron. Jerry. Gerry.

Cat felt her stomach rotate. *You don't have to watch.*

Red dismissed Harold, huddled with Wally and the camera operator. Harold walked away, dropped into a chair beside Cat, his elbows braced on his knees. He made a movement to prop his face in his hands, stopped, remembering the makeup. "I can't wait until this is over." He glanced at Cat. "What is it, some kind of endurance test with you? Need to see how much you can take?"

"Harold. You need a vacation."

"I've had a vacation. I've had a seventeen-year career of not working at my chosen profession."

Cat smiled. "The curse of getting what you want. That's what my mother would call it."

"I guess it beats watching from the wings," Harold conceded, shook the tension from his shoulders, neck. "Watching guys with a fifth of what you got starring in movies. To have to be scared of every little two-bit review by every little two-bit critic because you haven't got past the place where he could put an end to you with one sentence." He chuckled, mirthlessly. "The death sentence."

Cat thought of Davey Wheeler, plugging away for years, suddenly the two-million-dollar man. "I know something about it. About feeling envious of people in your profession because they got lucky."

"I'm tired of living for luck."

"If you wanted certainty, you would have been a plumber." Cat patted his sleeve. "I don't think you'll have to rely on luck much longer. Inside, it was the first time I've really watched you work, Harold. You're good. I mean it. Don't forget, we've got an interview on Friday." Harold might just be the breakout performer in this mess, and she would have first crack. Thank heaven for the instincts that nudged her into agreeing to a feature.

Cat saw Cici Bonaker emerge from the club, Ron Spivak on her heels; Red motioned for them to run through the movements a few times for the camera, Cici hopping the stone wall, Ron in pursuit, the turn, the exchange beside Kate Auletta's red car.

Ron stood there while someone ran up, held a light meter an inch from his nose; Ron's hands went to the prosthesis, automatically protective.

"Take One in thirty," Red called and gestured for Harold to join him in another huddle with the powder guy, this time with Ron included. Ron looked over his shoulder at Cat, fired at his temple with his index finger, winked.

Cat's stomach constricted in a quick spasm.

"Okay," Red called, "We're just about a go. I want one run through with Tommi Ann, make sure I'm getting the sound level. Tommi Ann does her turn. Ron, really toe your mark, don't pull back. Hal, your hand's gonna come up in the foreground—" Red raised his hand to shoulder height, dramatically. "Bang, bang. Bang number two, Ron connects with Tommi Ann, as soon as he starts the fall, we cut."

Cat saw Tommi Ann slip out of the club so unobtrusively that it took Cat a minute to realize it wasn't Cici.

Dianne King followed, caught Harold's eye and gestured "Are you sitting here?" nodding to the chair next to Cat.

Harold gestured for her to take the chair and Dianne sat, wedging her book-filled tote under her seat. Cat had decided that the duration of the shoot was in direct proportion to the bulk of Dianne's tote bag, concluded that tonight's shoot was a long one. But the last one, she reminded herself.

Ben Butler strode up. "Mrs. Austen, why don't you go sit in the trailer, they're havin' quite a little party in there, your brother and his boy, it'll go a lot easier on you."

"I'm fine. I'm sorry about what happened inside."

"Hell, that wasn't you, Spivak blew his line, they woulda cut anyway. Look, this starts to drag out, promise you'll go sit inside."

Cat crossed her racing heart, smiled.

"Okay, we're gonna try one for the camera." Red pitched his voice to carry across Pacific, intensified the pomposity of his strut. "We're gonna run through once, hold off on the shots"—he directed this toward Wally—"until we do the first take. It'll be 'bang, bang' so we get the rhythm. Harold? You with me?"

Harold's head jerked up, bobbed in assent.

"We cut so that Cici can move in and take the fall. So it's lines, marks, bang, bang, cut, we get that much, we try a take. Spivak, you getting this?"

"Dead to rights."

"I'm cold," Dianne crossed her arms over her chest, chafed her sleeves. "I'm going to get some coffee before Red calls for sound off. What about you, Mrs. Austen?"

"No, thanks, I'll wait until the break."

She saw Dianne walk over to the prop table, ask Wally, Harold, Gino if they wanted coffee, head into the trailer.

Ron and Tommi Ann ran through their scene.

"Hey, Kate, whaddaya, mad?" Fluid. Perfect.

What was the price of perfection? How much did it cost to turn a dust-poor girl into a goddess?

Sixty thousand dollars.

Cat thought of the baby she had lost, one week after Chris' murder. It could not have been more than a thimbleful of protoplasm, but she had cried, "Not my baby, not my baby!" and losing it had broken what was left of her heart.

Cat felt herself breathing, realized that she was making a conscious effort to inhale, exhale, inhale, exhale to keep from hyperventilating or holding her breath. *I can hang on.*

Dianne King resumed her chair, cradled a Styrofoam cup in her palm. She took a sip and the steam fogged her glasses. Set it down, slipped off her glasses. Cat looked at her, noted that Dianne's eyes were opalescent gray, and glowed like pearls in the moonlight. She put her glasses back on, set the cup down beside her chair.

Hey, Cat, whaddaya, mad? Look, don't print that about that stuff in there, happens all the time. Look, what say we cut out together, go somewhere for a drink?

"And bang," Red cried. "And bang!" It sounded very far away.

She heard: *Hey, one lousy drink won't kill you. I guarantee the goods. Long lost kin, kinky sex, dysfunctional families, you reporters get off on that stuff, right?*

The limber, brown-wigged figure became Jerry Dudek. Promising her scandal, certain she would "get off" on the titillation, the dirt. If Ron hadn't been put out of commission, how would he have dealt with it? Would he have stayed in the club, negotiated for the goods instead of fleeing in panic? And if he had, did that mean that Jerry would still be alive?

A Tommi Ann Butler exposé, what was the price on that?

"Okay," Red yelled, "we're ready for a take. Are you okay to go, Tommi Ann?"

Tommi Ann gave him a thumbs-up that included Ben, who was leaning against the trailer.

"Harold, gimme the gun, so we can adjust for the frame."

Wally picked up one of the guns from the table, handed it to Harold.

Harold waited for Tommi Ann's line—*Drop dead*—stepped up to the periphery of the lighted area and raised his arm, the gun in his gloved hand.

"Okay, that's perfect. We're ready for a take. Let's get our positions."

Cat heard a hush settle over the crowd, saw a shimmer of gold, Sherrie's hair glowing under the lamplight. The extras and PAs huddled on Belmont, watching Tommi Ann take her place, wait calmly for the lights.

Red trotted back to his station, beside Cat. "Aaaaaaand ACTION."

Tommi Ann strode across the center of the parking lot toward the red sports car. Ron vaulted the wall neatly, timed his "Hey, Kate, whaddaya, mad?" to coincide with Tommi Ann hitting her mark. The sallow makeup, the floppy brown wig converted Ron to Jerry.

Tommi Ann did her half turn, raised her chin on her line with a tremulous bravado that triggered a sense of synthesis in Cat. *She knows how I felt that night, how much of my so-called courage was sheer stubbornness, determination not to let Jerry intimidate me. She's me.*

Almost over, Cat told herself. *Five more lines. Three more lines. She'll say "Drop dead" and it'll be over.* From the corner of her eye, she saw Harold raising the gun.

A cry, the unified ecstasy of the crowd behind her, rose and drowned out Tommi Ann's last line. The cry took on a cadence, volume.

"OOOOOooooouuuuuuuEEEEE! OOOOooooouuuuuuuEEEEE!"

Cat heard Ben Butler say, "Oh, no," turned in her chair and saw Gary Biggs emerge from the trailer. A chorus of "OOOOoooo-uuuuuuuEEEEE!" expanded, hung in the air, waned, rose again. The uniforms closed ranks as the crowd rushed the barricade, arms out-stretched, screaming, "Piggy! Pi*GGY! Over here!*"

Cat saw the *NewsLine90* cameraman muscle through the crowd, gripping his lens in one hand, saw the private security fill the gaps in uniform blue, forming an unbroken barrier of muscle and flesh between the rapper and the crowd.

Cat barely heard Red's "CUT!" She watched, fascinated as Biggs grinned his bashful, dimpled grin. He looked as amazed at their reaction as they were at his appearance. Butler's mouth was turned down into a frown, but the eyes were smiling; the effect Biggs had on the crowd made him amused, proud. He had taken this kid, this nobody with a talent for rhythm and rhyme and turned him into an object of frenzied devotion. "Hey!" he called to *CopWatch* security. "You wanna help corral him?"

Cat heard Tommi Ann at her shoulder, chuckling. "April's gonna have kittens."

"He said something about wanting to watch the scene shoot, I didn't think he meant that he was coming on to the lot." Dianne was unflappable. "Would you hold my coffee, Mrs. Austen? I'll have a word with his security," she assured Tommi Ann.

Cat saw Mark's head poke out of the trailer door, eyes wide. The kid had seen a lot in his fourteen years, but he hadn't seen anything like this.

"PiggyPi*GGYPIGGY!*"

Red Melendez, indifferent to the blown take, maneuvered himself in front of the *NewsLine90* lens, called up his ingratiating I'm-Somebody-Too smile, hoping to fan the ember of recognition in the crowd. Cat saw a woman some years older than her reach out to touch Melendez's sleeve, nod. *Probably remembers him from* The Advocates, Cat thought, watched as Dianne approached Biggs, spoke to him for a few moments. Biggs shrugged and offered the crowd a wave, allowed himself to be herded back into the trailer.

Cat saw Melendez hesitate at the curb, as if he would like to linger a bit until recognition of who he was kicked in. But with Biggs' appearance, the commotion lost its ballast. The sight of Tommi Ann, so close, so perfect, converted it to a hush that had the rhythm of worship, then settled into silence.

Red called for Take Two; the set up was rapid and the players moved into place.

Action.

Tommi Ann took off across the lot, Ron in pursuit. The lines went smoothly, the movements practiced, fluid, perfect.

They're going to get it in two takes, Cat thought with relief. *I won't have to watch this fifteen times. I'm going to make it.*

Out of the corner of her eye, she saw Harold move toward his mark, raise his hand, Red's bobbing head timing out the movements.

"—don't need you! 'Cause I can get what I want anywhere I want, all's I gotta do is drop a dime."

"Drop dead."

Crack!

Ron did his spin too early and the powder guy jumped the charge, fired the squib that spurted Karo-and-red-food-coloring movie blood all over Tommi Ann's sweater. Ron fell, toppling onto Tommi Ann, throwing both of them to the asphalt.

"Cut. *Cut!* Jesus, Spivak, can't you count? Somebody help Tommi Ann up!"

April turned a baleful eye on Wally, who was staring at his board with a baffled expression on his face. "There must be a short on my board—"

"If board was sword, I'd be Basil Rathbone! Spivak, get the hell off the ground," she screamed. "And June, get me Wardrobe!"

They'll have to do it again, Cat thought. *Thank heaven they've got a half dozen costumes in Wardrobe, what a mess.*

Then: *Why doesn't he get up?*

Then: *What's the matter with Tommi Ann! Why is she screaming after Red yelled cut?*

Then: *WHY DOESN'T HE GET UP?*

Then: *It's only a movie, it's only a movie, it's only a movie.*

Then: *It's not a movie. It's real!*

CHAPTER EIGHTEEN

EXT: BEACHFRONT PARKING LOT: NIGHT

GERRY

All's I gotta do to cut you outta the loop
is drop a dime!

KATE yanks herself free, backs off.

KATE

Drop dead.

*The gun fires twice. GERRY lunges against
KATE, hit. He falls, pulling her down.*

The freeze frame exploded into violent jump cuts. Tommi Ann
swallowed up by a mass of bodies. April shrieking. The sea of onlookers
surging at the dam of cops. Cast and crew, frozen in place. Melendez,
Butler, Mae, Danny. Screaming: "Get her out! Get her out! He's down!
He's down! Where's the paramedic?" Cameras firing off like heat-
seeking missiles, targeting the key players. Dianne's overturned chair,
overturned cup, sending a dark stream of coffee across the scattered
papers, files, notebooks that had spilled out of her tote and Cat's.

Cat felt the edge of a folder cutting into her cheek, felt papers lumped under her midsection, saw more papers strewn in a wide arc, eye level, realized that she was viewing the mob scene from a low angle.

This isn't happening.

I'll get trampled on the ground.

Get up. Sit. Get your papers. Move.

Cat contracted into a tight huddle, her hands darting out to snatch her papers, stuff them into her bag. She heard the snapping of paper overlap the commotion, saw that the folders were shuddering in her grip, saw her hand jerking in tiny spasms that transmitted no sense of contact, pain, motion to her numbed brain.

"Goddamn it, you keep them away from her!" Butler was hollering and Cat caught a glimpse of Tommi Ann's russet hair against his shoulder.

Had she been hit? Bodies rushing past her.

Stay awake. Stay conscious. Don't pass out.

Screams.

"Move them back! Back off from the site! SHUT DOWN!"

Try to stand. Button your coat. Move. Shoving. Running.

Was Ron dead?

Cat saw the whirling bodies part, heard Carlo, bellowing her name, bisecting the sea of flesh like a towering, profane Moses. She had an instant to snatch her tote before he hauled her into his arms. The lenses caught him; Cat heard the reporters shouting, "King! King! Over here! King, can you give us a comment!" She shielded her face with her tote, not so far gone that the irony didn't hit home. An Academy Award nominee, a multiple Grammy winner, but to the locals, it was Carlo who was The King, the only celebrity they could count on for a colorful show, an off-color quote. Cat allowed him to carry her across the street, into the club where a handful of the crew had collected in a horrified knot. Carlo sat her in a chair, looked into her face. "You okay? You gonna be sick, or what?"

"What ..?" *Happened.*

"Somebody fired a live one onto the set. Stay put, I gotta go make sure the kid's okay."

"Is Ron dead?" Cat asked. She didn't need for him to answer anymore than she had needed for him to tell her, on that Easter Saturday three years before, that she had seen Chris for the last time.

Through sleep, the ring fired Victor's neurons and he rolled, gripped the edge of the coffee table, the neurons alerting him to the fact that he was on the couch.

"*Madre de Dios.*" He got to his feet, stumbled toward the kitchen and grabbed the phone before it woke Remy, mumbled something that he hoped resembled a civil greeting, adrenaline trickling into his muscles.

It was Kurt Raab, the county DA. "Victor, look, I just got a call from someone on the scene, there's been a shooting. I need for you to go over and check it out."

"Where?" His gut told him where.

"Over by CV's, where they've been shooting that cop show. I don't have any details, don't know about casualties." Raab's exhale was shaky. "Jeez, this was a mistake, letting them shoot in AC."

Remy stumbled out of the bedroom, wearing a hip-length sheath. Her face was white, her dark eyes tense, as though she had been shaken from a troubled dream. "Victor, *que paso?*"

"*Nada.* Go back to bed." He spoke into the phone. "What kind of security have they got over there?"

"They got uniforms on OT for the crowd control, but the rest are rentals or Phoenix security they put on her, Tommi Ann. Victor, I don't need to tell you, I don't need for there to be a scratch on Tommi Ann Butler on my watch." Raab's voice was quaking with the prospect of having to appear at a press conference in front of the sort of media the star's arrival had attracted. "I mean, God, I'm seein' myself on *Entertainment Tonight* and it's not pretty."

"So far it's just a shots-fired?"

"So far."

"I'll take care of it." Victor hung up and dialed Adane's number. Mary Grace answered, sounded awake.

"Jeannie already got a call, she's on her way over there. I'll call Kurt." Mary Grace was one of Raab's ADAs.

Victor dialed the dispatcher, got her to fill him in. "Sorry, Lieutenant, I've got a call for the EMTs, but I don't have a status report. They were filming a scene on the corner of Belmont and Pacific, that parking lot? You know where I mean."

He knew. November. He had made it to the scene in minutes, the intersection was only a couple blocks from his apartment on Delancy. Not fast enough to beat the couple hundred clubgoers and two units, and not much before *NewsLine90*. Dudek cold and Cat already in the ER.

Cat.

EMTs.

He checked the clock on the kitchen wall: one fifty-five. She couldn't be there at this time of night. Morning.

Victor went into his bedroom, pulled clothes from the drawers in the dark, told Remy to go back to sleep. He dressed quickly in his living room, and stepped outside, checked his weapon under the porch light and shoved it in his waistband, jogged down the steps. Mrs. DiLorenzo, her brassy hair precisely partitioned and bound around curlers, hurried onto the sidewalk. "Lieutenant Victor, did you hear? Somebody shot at Tommi Ann Butler! Lina Ricci called me, her granddaughter was right there when it happened!"

"I don't know if anything's been determined yet," he said. "Please go inside, Mrs. DiLorenzo, it's cold."

"It's less than a week until the Oscars!" she fretted.

Victor walked her to her door, assured her that she would hear as soon as anything had been determined. He saw Mrs. Ricci's drapes yanked closed as he walked to his car.

His car phone rang immediately. Stan Rice. "You're not gonna believe this."

"I'm on my way over there. Fill me in. Anybody hurt?"

"Worse. Jackie just phoned me. It's that reporter, the one they got playin' Dudek? Didn't get outta the line of fire."

Spivak. *Madre de Dios.* "Anyone else?"

"Not that I heard, but it's nutso over there."

"I'll be there in five minutes."

It took more than that just to get the Jag past the turnoff onto Pacific, where bodies had flowed off the curb, backed up into the narrow street. He didn't carry a dashboard light, rolled down the window and held his shield out, honking his horn. The crowd parted reluctantly and he made it to a patch of yellow curb a block from the site, pulled over and strode toward Belmont, using the large white van as his beacon, picked out the paid muscle: Sterling's green jackets, privately contracted bodies in blue windbreakers, uniforms. The mob outnumbered them twenty to one, but they were keeping the lot and Belmont clear.

The crowd caught sight of the grim face, the dark indecipherable gaze, the mustache turned down in an involuntary scowl and shrank back. Victor picked up audible phrases from the hubbub. "Is it her? Is it her?," played in his brain as *Radio jock. Dudek, Jerry Dudek,* and it was November all over again.

"Lieutenant! Lieutenant!" He saw the *NewsLine90* anchor, a videographer at her shoulder approaching him, turned and vaulted a sawhorse, nodded to a uniform who recognized him.

"Stan Rice is already here," he said. "They hustled Tommi Ann and her posse into the club."

"Coroner arrive yet?"

"No."

He made his way toward the parking lot, his eyes panning the scene. A few cars, the ground thick with snaking cables, stacks of equipment, folding chairs scattered at the perimeter of what must have been the area where they were filming. He checked his watch, quickly established the cast of characters: local cops, private security, Phoenix security; the kids in ragged jeans, parkas, were production assistants or interns; the ones with the headsets hanging around their necks were upper level assistants or crew. Different set, different cast of characters, same plot. He thought of Sherlock Holmes lamenting the decline in criminal ingenuity: *There is nothing new under the sun. It has all been done before.*

Where was Cat?

"Lieutenant!"

Victor turned and allowed his glance to sweep above the woman with the mike, *NewsLine90*, past her to the others trotting toward the yellow tape, camera operators shouldering their equipment, lumbering in the wake of the anchors. April Steinmetz, her candy-apple-colored hair spilling onto her shoulders, alternated her instructions to the crew with the expletives she was shouting into her cell phone. "We gotta get her outta here. Go tell my unions make themselves useful, help keep some of those cameras off us."

A sullen guy in tattered jeans muttered, "It's not in our contract—"

"If a contract was a compact, I'd be Max Factor." She said into the cell, "No, Bennie, I don't want her near here and for God's sake, keep The Pig in a blanket."

Victor turned to the two uniforms in front of him. The younger of the two uniforms spoke up. "I was monitoring the crowd by the curb, I couldn't see the action. Looked like this guy was playing the shooter fired the prop he was holding and there were live rounds and it hit the vic."

"How many shots fired?"

"Two."

"Three."

"One."

Steinmetz snapped her phone shut. "Two. Look, are we gonna lose our permits? Are they gonna shut us down? Are you gonna arrest Harold?" Before he could answer, she turned, screamed into a knot of PAs, "Who's on the cell to Lou? Somebody get me Paragon!" Turned back. "Look, it was an accident, Harold flipped out when he realized what he did, I thought he was gonna have a seizure."

Victor turned to the second cop. "What'd you see?"

The second uniform spoke. "Not much. I was manning the trailer to make sure Pig wouldn't make another appearance." Victor gestured for him to explain. "They call sound off, which means everyone shut up. They're doin' this scene, the vic is followin' Tommi Ann across the lot, they have words, it looks to be good, then Bigg Phat P.I.G., he comes outta the trailer and the crowd goes berserk and that screwed up the take. They run it again, it looks to be goin' okay, then, bang. The vic goes down."

April was unconsciously tucking her hair back into the beehive at the top of her head. "Spivak knocked over Tommi Ann, she goes down and she's not supposed to do the fall. I'm in a twist because I thought the powder guy blew the caps too soon and it's another take gone south and Red tells them to cut, and then it gets quiet, you know what I mean? Like when a tornado scarfs up all the noise and then, bam, you're Hoovered over to Oz?" She jammed the last pin into her crown.

"Miss Steinmetz, you have a log of everyone scheduled to participate in tonight's shooting?"

"Yeah, June, she can give it to you." Her head whipped around, scanning the crowd. "Where's JUNE!"

"I think she went with Wally."

"WALLY TOOK OFF?"

"He went with Harold to the hospital."

"*IT TAKES TWO PEOPLE TO GET ONE GUY SIX BLOCKS TO THE E.R.! WHO DO THEY THINK THEY ARE, UNIONS?*"

"Victor! Yo!" Victor turned and saw the massive form of Carlo Fortunati, the sight producing the same subtle reassurance his towering form had ever since the night young Officer Fortunati had shown up at the site of Victor's father's murder twenty-six years before.

"Cat," Victor said.

"She's okay, I stuck her in the club."

"Did you see it?"

"No, we're in the trailer, me and the kid, Mark. Cat got us passes to watch the shoot. I'm in there with Biggs and one of his people, the girl who's Tommi Ann's stand in, she came in after she was done helping them set up the shot, couple people comin' in and out. We didn't even hear the shots. Biggs' shields come in, give us a run-down, hustle him into the club." His dark eyes scanned the crowd. "They took Tommi Ann over to the club. I heard they hustled Anderson over to the ER." He paused, rubbed his hand over his broad face.

"What?"

"Gino Forschetti okayed it. He was acting as some kinda observer." He paused. "Look, the condition Anderson was in, I prob'ly woulda okayed it, too."

"No you wouldn't, not unless he was injured. You would have kept all the witnesses on the scene."

"Yeah, well, I sent two of ours over to keep an eye on him." Two years into retirement and they were still "ours." "I heard one of the assistants and the guy in charge of the ammo took him to the ER. There's another situation."

"What?"

"The ammo guy, his name's Wally. Just now, the ki— Mark? He tells me he recognized him. Mark says this Wally's the guy sold him that tape. I wanna trust the kid, but he's off the streets, so I gotta take it slow, but he's swearin' up and down, it's the guy."

"Okay. I'm going to want to talk to him, but right now, I think you'd better take him home. Can you get out of here?"

"Yeah. I gotta check on Mom first."

"Tell Cat to wait for me."

Carlo lumbered off. Victor heard the media screaming, "King! King!"

Stan Rice piloted Jean Adane through the crowd. "Long's on his way. Jeez. 'King.' Sounds like we stashed Elvis here."

Victor's peripheral vision caught an approaching figure; a camera flashed. He turned, saw Melendez wrapped in a black trench coat, baseball cap turned backward, a ponytail hanging below the brim. Melendez turned profile for the photographer who was angling for a shot of Cardenas (the real Victor Calderone) and Red Melendez (the *CopWatch* Calderone).

He recognized the kid who'd staked out the bureau parking lot. Victor laid his palm lightly over the lens, said, "Disappear."

The kid locked eyes with Victor; fled.

April screamed, "Get me the unit publicist, what's her name?"

"Kathy!" someone shouted.

"Get Kathy over to the med center to keep the scavengers offa Harold. Mae, herd the players into the club. And you—" she turned to Melendez, "I see you on *Front Cover* giving an interview to Callie O'Connor with the caption actor-slash-activist under your mug, you're gonna be the late director, you got it?"

"April, in a situation like this, it's important to designate a spokesperson so that we can maintain a sense of cooperation and synergy with the media—"

"If synergy was symphony, I'd be George Gershwin—"

"Mr. Melendez," Victor interrupted.

Melendez gave him a put-upon, man-to-man smile.

"Go inside the club and stay there until you're questioned and released."

Melendez hesitated, shrugged. Detouring past the equipment, he managed a pass by the straining news crews.

Victor turned to Steinmetz. "How was security?"

"Overkill. The production's paying for private shields for the names, Sterling's put some of his guys on the talent staying at his hotel, the city's fronting our overtime."

"Miss Steinmetz, it would be helpful if you could take Sergeant Rice inside and give him a list of everyone on the scene. Rice, take as many uniforms as you need and start taking statements inside the club. Everyone goes in, nobody leaves without making a statement."

"Got it."

"Leave me your number," April told Rice as he walked off. "We might need a body double for Spivak's pick-ups."

Victor spoke to Adane. "The weapons manager's name is Wally, apparently he accompanied the actor who fired the gun over to the med center. Carlo Fortunati sent a couple uniforms over, call them and have them hold Anderson until I can get over there. They had someone from the city department observing him. Gino Forschetti."

"And you want me to find out if he's been drinking," Adane concluded, calmly.

Victor nodded, turned and walked to the center of the lot where three uniforms, some private security were huddled over the body. The impact and the fall had dislodged not only the wig, but the prosthetic nose, which was lying in a thin tributary of blood that trickled off from the larger pool under his skull. "Who saw what happened?"

One spoke up, a uniform barely past the rookie stage. "I was stationed over by the ramp, make sure no one tried to get onto the set under the boards. We got the boards cut off two blocks each way. I see them talking to the director, getting ready for the take, the big guy, with the braid down his back, he checked the chamber, hands the gun to the blonde actor, what's-his-name, Anderson? They roll, Tommi Ann and Spivak, they're in the middle of their scene and Bigg Phat P.I.G. comes out to watch and the crowd goes berserk. They shove him in the trailer, go for a second take, what's-his-name? Anderson? He fires the gun and Spivak goes down. I'm thinking it's whaddaya call, a wrap? But they start yelling 'Cut, Cut,' and Tommi Ann starts screaming and I see uniforms rush her."

"Give me some light."

One of the uniforms angled his flashlight directly onto the body. Victor saw the wound; precise, a good hit. This was an accident? How could such an accident have happened? Surely they didn't use live rounds on a movie location, did they? And even if they did, what were the chances an actor firing the gun would have hit the mark with such accuracy?

He looked up at the gelled lights, the movie moonlight, the real moonlight. Good illumination, maybe twenty feet from the shooter, give or take.

The ME was hustled up to the scene, his lanky assistant at his side. "What's the deal? Where's my lens jockey? If this isn't *déjà vu*, I don't know what is." He squatted down, snapping on Latex gloves. "Hey, I know this guy, he did a piece on my office last year, the bum. Made out like all's I got workin' for me is space cadets and slackers."

Victor looked at the assistant, ripped jeans, shaved head, small gold hoop in one ear.

"Hell, I thought of shootin' the bastard, but he got off a good picture of me." The ME prodded at the flesh, scoped out the wound with a pen light. "Button, button, who has the button. This ain't amateur night."

"It was an accident. Apparently a prop gun was loaded."

"You tellin' me some professional face with a stunt piece pulled off this shot?" He leaned over and eyed the wound. "I was six feet off, I couldn't hit this good. Did she get hurt? Tommi Ann Butler?"

"I understand she wasn't hurt."

"You see her in *Double Jeopardy*? Jeez. Why she didn't get herself the Oscar for that one, I'll never know. I guess we can bag him. Keith, you got a LifeSaver?"

Keith drew a role out of his pocket, thumbed one into the ME's open mouth, as if this were their usual ritual. "Uh, whaddawe do with the nose?"

The ME drew a pen out of his pocket protector, scratched his head, leaving a blue tracing below the thinning hair. "I guess we gotta take it with us, we'll give it over when the next of kin arranges a pickup. You think Tommi Ann needs someone to check her out?"

"I'm sure she's being taken care of," Victor said. "You think this wasn't an accident?"

The ME edged aside for the paramedics with the gurney. "I'm not sayin' that, I'm sayin' the guy fired the shot had good aim. I guess 'accident' depends on whether or not he knew it was loaded."

"I don't guess, Doctor."

"Lucky for her Mrs. Austen wasn't around. She got an eyeful of this, it'd be enough to put her on a slab."

Victor felt the weight of attention settle on him. His gaze panned the crowd being hustled off Pacific, the *NewsLine90* crew obstinately refusing to yield, the videographer, shivering in the cold, adjusting the weight on his shoulder, waiting for the anchor to cue him. His gaze moved toward the mounted cameras on the edge of the parking lot. "They were shooting," he said. "Where's the footage?"

"Still in the camera, I guess," a nearby blue replied.

Victor cleared his throat.

"I'll find out, Lieutenant."

Victor nodded. "Communicate to the officers that I'd like them to check the crowd, see if anyone happened to be carrying a camcorder. Get to them before *Front Cover* or *NewsLine90* takes out a checkbook."

One of the cops snorted, "May be too late for that," but they shuffled off to do Victor's bidding.

"Autopsy results by nine a.m., Doctor?"

"Jeezoo."

Victor took that for acquiescence. Phil Long approached and

Victor observed the frisson of interest at the sight of the lean black cop with the drooping mustache. Long's counterpart had been incorporated into the first draft as Victor Calderone's sidekick, the earnest, Harvard-educated requisite minority who had worked undercover as a female decoy. Word was, it was Ron Spivak who had heard about Long's exploits with AC Vice and passed them along to Harold, and that it was Butler who nixed the comic colleague. Not before word had passed, however, that he had been based on a real life detective in Victor's unit.

"Sorry to have to call you in."

"How come everyone's starin'?" Long asked.

"Perhaps they've never seen a real cop." Victor filled him in on what had happened. "There's been a call placed to Raab. Stan's got people taking statements inside. The guy in charge of the munitions left the scene, apparently he accompanied Anderson to the ER. Name's Wally. Find out if there's a sheet on him."

"What am I lookin' for?"

"Theft. Pirating merchandise. Weapons offenses."

Victor headed for the club. Inside, Stan had shoved tables into a line along the side of the dance floor, had recruited a handful of uniforms to take statements.

The club was as he remembered except for the cables on the floor, the boom mikes propped against the rear wall, a mounted camera with a viewer, mounted lights.

He passed along the corridor, saw a woman in a double-breasted jacket, short skirt, on the pay phone, saying, "... no I'm not kidding, if there are any more delays, I won't get back to LA for the *Bel Air Beat* auditions. Who the hell knows? Ask April ..." The girl looked him over, raked her fingers through her blond hair.

In the restaurant, the Daughters of Sicily were serving food to a queue of cast, techies. Victor went over to Jennie, who was running a knife through a pan of lasagna. She looked up, extended her cheek to be kissed.

"Cat, she's okay? Carlo said she was shook up."

"Carlo said she was in here."

"Maybe she's in the ladies' room, she didn't come through here. She"—the raised eyebrows identified the "she" as Tommi Ann—"they just took outta here."

Victor looked around. "When?"

Jennie shook her head. "Five minutes ago. Danny, he got her and that Mrs. King and the young girl, had a car brought right up the Boardwalk. That boy have family?"

Victor realized she was talking about Ron Spivak. "I don't know. How will you get home, Jennie?"

"Gary, he's got a car takes us wherever we want. But we'll be here awhile. It's gonna take some time to see what's what, and all these people can't go without something in their stomachs. You see Cat, you tell her come in here, she's gotta keep her strength up."

"And how do you keep your strength up?"

"I keep myself busy."

He headed toward the office, opened the door. Ben Butler was pacing by the window, looking through the slats in the blinds as he spoke into his cell phone. "No, Dianne, you just take the phone off the hook. Put Tommi Ann on once more."

A large black kid pushed himself off the sofa. Victor held up his shield. The kid nodded, genially, said, "I'm The Pig."

When you don't know what to say, then it's time to be silent, Victor's father had told him. Victor nodded, silently.

"Honey, you don't think about anything, you just let me see what's what." He turned, saw Victor. "Honey, I gotta go, the police are here. Don't you worry, that's my job, honey." He hung up the phone, held out his hand and Victor shook it. "That young fella's Gary Biggs, Lieutenant. You want him to stay or you need to talk to me alone?"

"Were you a witness to the shooting, Mr. Biggs?"

The kid shook his head. "I's in the trailer wit' Miz Austen's brother and his kid, some of my homes. Cici."

"You're staying at the Phoenix?"

"Yeah."

Victor handed him a card. "The number at the bureau. I'd like you to arrange to make a statement tomorrow."

"Have your people get you out of here, Gary, an' tell Tommi Ann I'll be over directly."

"I gotta make sure Mama Jen an' her posse's took care of." The kid offered Victor his hand once more and left.

Victor turned to Butler. "I was hoping to speak to Mrs. Butler."

"Lieutenant, I had them get Tommi Ann outta here, she's all worked up."

"She was also the primary witness to what occurred."

"Hell, but—" Butler shook his head. "It was an accident. A damned accident." He looked up, there was real emotion in his dark eyes. "That coulda been Tommi Ann lyin' on the ground. You wanna talk to someone, you talk to the guy loaded up that gun."

"Wally."

"Hell yes."

"Wally have a last name?"

"Reid. R-e-i-d."

"Your wife ever work with him before?"

Butler shook his head. "No. Now, Cici made a film last year, her an' Hal Anderson, I b'lieve Wally was weapons master on that shoot. Damned if that wasn't the same shoot Spivak was on."

"The one filmed in Philadelphia last year?"

"Yeah. Hard to believe he wasn't a pro. Spivak. Only had three, four scenes, just about hijacked every one."

"Did you know him at all? Personally?"

"No." He hesitated. "Hell, you're gonna hear about this, Lieutenant. Cici Bonaker, she's my wife's stand-in, her acting career's starting to take off, she met Spivak in Philadelphia. They were a couple for awhile, broke up. She and Harold are together now." He chuckled, wryly. "They call it 'bein' in a relationship.' Hell."

"In a relationship with the man who shot Spivak? Did Spivak seem jealous of this relationship?"

"Not as far as I could see."

"What about Anderson, was he jealous of Spivak?"

Butler shook his head.

"I understand Mr. Spivak had been out of town. You know what time he clocked in tonight?"

Butler shrugged. "Miz Austen told April or Dianne that he was driving here straight from the airport, they started rolling around eight, he was made up and ready to go." Butler leaned forward. "Look, Lieutenant, shoot straight. Your questions make out like Spivak was gunned down on purpose."

"I can't rule it out. He had quite a reputation around here for his investigative work and for his aggressiveness. People like that make enemies. What about the gun. Why was it loaded?"

"You'd have to ask Wally that. Live ammunition on the set, I been around, I've never seen it. Gun Harold was using fired blanks. The other one didn't have any powder."

"What other one? Another weapon?"

"Yeah, there were two props. One Red was usin' for close-ups, he wanted to aim the camera down the barrel, shoot into the chamber so you could see the dummy."

"Dummy?"

"An empty cartridge, sometimes just the metal tip. Like I said, no powder in it."

Victor nodded, slowly. "And this was similar to the gun that Anderson used when he was shooting at Spivak?"

"Identical."

"Blanks have powder, isn't that right? If a blank was inadvertently chambered in the close-up prop, behind this metal dummy, it would blast it out, fire it like a projectile. Like a live round."

"It might at that," Butler conceded.

CHAPTER NINETEEN

INT: EMERGENCY ROOM CUBICLE: NIGHT

KATE (obstinately)
I'm not staying overnight! I want to go home!

DOCTOR
I'm sorry, Miss Auletta—

KATE
Not as sorry as you will be if you don't let me
out of here!

Cat's brain began playing her past like the script, the scenes, the dialogue interchangeable. Only in her own mind was she the star, though. No one else in the club gave her a glance. They were more absorbed with processing and exploring their own responses to the event, estimating what effect it ought to have on them, if it had some promotional value they had not yet assessed.

Cat slipped upstairs to the loft. The makeup was strewn across the tables, a chair was overturned, clothing on the floor. She saw that Ron's old leather jacket had slipped off the peg on the wall, leaned down and picked it up. Her hands warmed the leather to body temperature. *Of course he's not dead. He's finished up his last shot and gone home.*

I gotta jet. I got some copy I gotta get down tonight.

Her hand closed over the zippered pouch at the shoulder, and she felt something hard, probed and came up with Ron's key ring. She caught a whiff of tobacco and salt worked into the old leather.

He left without his keys.

She would drop them off on her way home, then crawl in bed and get some sleep. Tomorrow, she would wake up and tell Ellice, *I had the weirdest dream, I dreamt that they were filming the shooting scene and Ron actually got shot, just like Jerry, what do you suppose that means?*

And Ellice would say, *It probably means you think art has sunk to imitating the lowest form of life,* or something like that and they would have a good laugh over it. And Cat would tell Jane how Bigg Phat P.I.G. had appeared and the crowd began to scream *OOOOuuuuuuueeeeEEEE,* and how the crew had to coax him into the trailer so they could continue filming because he was too much of a ... diversion.

Cat slipped down the narrow staircase that connected the loft to the pantry behind the kitchen, feeling her way in the dark. She heard the cadence of voices through the thin walls. The pantry had a service entrance that opened onto Albion, a small half street behind the club. Cat crept between a pair of Dumpsters, saw that the intersection of Albion and Pacific was lined with uniformed police, stationed to prevent the press or the crowd from sneaking onto the set through a back route. Cat swung under the railing and hopped to the ground, retreated to the dark shelter beneath the boards and, slowly treading sand, headed away from the scene. The sand was as cool and slick as water; the chill under her soles kept her conscious and conscious of her purpose. At each ramp, she looked toward Pacific, saw a couple uniforms or a black and white, pushed on until she came upon one that was unguarded, and turned toward the intersection.

Cat wasn't sure how she got to her car. Instinct, perhaps; after all, she had grown up in Atlantic City. She unlocked it and got behind the wheel and began to think about how easy it had been to just walk away from the scene with a few hundred people around, how it was so much easier to hide in a crowd, how easy it would have been to shoot someone out in the open, how the blindness of a few hundred star-struck eyes, and the shelter of a few hundred disparate angles was a more potent screen than the cover of silence, of darkness.

Victor looked toward the corner of Belmont and Pacific where the television stations had set up banks of mikes, shivering anchors standing several feet apart, each giving the hair one last pat-down before he cued the camera operator to hit the lights. Red Melendez had issued a hasty statement, slipped past April and gotten back outside, taken up his post at the bank of microphones. He began working his way down the line, answering questions, giving them a somber, Roberto Aguilar nod for the cutaways. Victor heard an angry voice in the vicinity of the crew, heard Adane's patient reply, strolled over to the camera operators dismantling their equipment. Adane was standing before them, clutching her billfolded shield in both hands.

"—'cause we got our city permits, so don't try to muscle me, bitch. You want to confiscate any of our property, you show me some paper."

Victor stepped up behind Adane.

"Your film is evidence in a police investigation," she explained, patiently.

"I don't give you squat without it goes through the DP and April. So you can take your little gold badge and your two brass—" The camera operator caught Victor's eye, fell silent.

Victor cleared his throat. "Please continue. You were going to tell my detective what she should do with her shield and her two most recent commendations."

The guy swallowed, hesitated.

Victor waited.

The guy glanced around at the crew who suddenly became very preoccupied.

Victor waited.

The guy handed over the circular tin he had tucked under his arm, made a show of taking down the information printed on the label. "Anything happens to this, April'll file suit with the city."

"Understood," Victor said. "And this is Detective Adane. If you prefer not to address her as 'Detective,' I expect you to come up with an epithet that takes into consideration the fact that she is a professional woman, that she is a lady and that she's acting under my direction. Will that be a problem?"

"Whatever," the guy said, turned back to his equipment.

Victor stepped between him and his gear. "Whatever what?"

"Whatever you say, *Lieutenant.*"

Victor nodded, turned to Adane. "They rarely have fewer than two or three cameras running, so we only have what they gave us, but it should be enough to get a take on what went down. And Adane? I apologize for interfering."

She hesitated. He wouldn't have intervened if it had been Stan or Phil. Perhaps chivalry was like any other chronic habit, impossible to overcome. "I suspect your reprimand was lost on him. He seems to be the sort of person who says 'epitaph' when he means 'epithet.' If it's part of his vocabulary at all."

Victor related what Butler had told him about the two props, his theory about how the gun had fired.

Adane nodded. "I spoke to Detective Forschetti. He seemed very distressed. He said that he assumed Mr. Reid would be watching the table, and it seemed that he might have been needed for crowd control—"

"How long were his eyes off the weapons?"

"He said two minutes, maybe three."

"Had he been drinking?"

"No, it didn't appear so. When Mr. Biggs went back into the trailer, he went back to his post. He said it appeared that Mr. Reid and Anderson were having words."

"About what?"

"He didn't hear. They set up for the next take very quickly. From his perspective everything seemed to be progressing normally—even after Mr. Spivak fell, it looked so much like the script that it took a few moments for people to realize that Mr. Spivak had been hit."

"And Anderson?"

"He said Anderson fell apart when he realized what happened. One of the production assistants offered to drive him to the ER, Wally Reid offered to give her a hand and Detective Forschetti okayed it, told him to stay at the ER, that there would be someone there to question him."

"The procedure was for the weapon to be checked before each take?"

"Yes. Mr. Reid loaded it, handed it to Mr. Anderson. When they concluded the scene, Mr. Anderson was to hand it back to him."

"Was the weapon checked again, before the second take?"

Adane shook her head. "Detective Forschetti stated that Mr. Anderson had already been handed the gun when the commotion started, and was still holding it when they resumed the filming."

"Go see if you can get some projection equipment, so that we can screen the film before they talk a judge into making us give it back."

He saw Red Melendez moving to the *NewsLine90* mike, adjusting his position for Whitney Rocap. Victor shook his head. The Rocap woman had been one of Dudek's "fiancées," a passable copywriter, promoted to marginally competent weathergirl, promoted to less-than-sterling anchor. She was filming for tomorrow's AM newsbreak, trying to fake that female morning TV personality perky/competent persona. She gave a "three-two-one," swung into anchor mode. "Early this morning, during the shooting of an episode of the popular television docudrama, *CopWatch*, being shot in Atlantic City, shots rang out during a critical scene which recreated the shooting of disk jockey Jerry Dudek at almost exactly the same location where he was shot."

Sending cast and crew shooting for cover, Victor thought, cynically.

"Here with me now is actor and activist Red Melendez, who was directing the scene outside Club Circolo Venerdi when the shots rang out. Mr. Melendez, you were on the scene. Can you tell us exactly what happened?"

He couldn't, but that didn't prevent him from spinning out a reply that had all of the adjectives to indicate substance without uttering anything more specific than his own respectful attitude toward fire-arms since he had been trained in their "utilization" when he had starred in *The Advocates*, and how he had been taking a refresher course on their utilization since he would have to handle firearms as co-star to Tommi Ann Butler in the *CopWatch* episode, *Death of a Shock Jock*.

Victor turned away. He didn't trust anyone who said utilization when he might easily have said use, didn't trust anyone who allowed himself to be referred to as an activist.

He headed toward the trailer, sensed the advancing heat of lights, kept walking, ignoring the: "He's the real one!" The: "Lieutenant! Lieutenant Calderone!"

Dios mio.

Cat huddled behind the wheel of her car, shivering. Her hands crawled into the pockets, seeking warmth, felt the cold metal of a key ring, the keys Ron had given her. She felt an unfamiliar texture, drew them out of her pocket. Not his spares, his own set, two keys identical to the ones he had given her and a third, narrow, rubber-tipped key that had to be his car key. She had taken them from Ron's pocket. She was going to drop them at his apartment. But that was absurd because Ron was ...

Car keys. Ron had come straight from the airport. *I hadda park all the way over on Fairmount!* His luggage, briefcase, would still be in the car.

Cat dug up her own keys and started her engine, felt the blast of cold air from the dormant heater. Fairmount ran parallel to Atlantic; unlike Pacific, it was away from the action. She turned on her car radio, caught a snatch of "... the death of the local journalist as a tragic accident—" snapped it off. Cat spotted Ron's brown sedan wedged between a couple of 4WDs, parked across the street, got out, and approached Ron's car with the confidence of ownership in case she was spotted by a passing cruiser. She unlocked the driver's side door. His apartment, his desk had been orderly, but his car was a mess; a stack of yellowing newspapers were on the floor of the back, a couple empty soda cans, fast food wrappers crumpled around hunks of long-expired edibles.

Cat checked the glove compartment, found nothing but the registration and a couple toll receipts, checked the side compartments inside the doors, nothing. She winced and slid her hands into the recesses of the seat cushions, came up with ninety-one cents in coin, a parkway token. She tossed them in the ashtray and wriggled down to prod underneath the seat. Her fingers hit on the trunk release and she popped it. A jack, a flashlight, a pair of well-worn insulated gloves, a small suitcase—heavy canvas with outside pockets, collapsible handle, scaled to be a carry-on. Carry-off, so that he could jump ship on that layover at Dallas. The zippers were locked with those mini-padlocks that could be opened with a bobby pin. Cat probed her hair for a bobby pin, pulled one free and set to work on the locks, popping them easily. She wondered if Kate Auletta would settle for something as sissy as a bobby pin, she'd probably have one of those oversized hatpins, ornate head, razor tip, the sort of femme/macho accessory Kate would go in for. Last January, Cat and Ellice had rented a movie where a woman killed her lovers with a hatpin like that right after—or during—sex. The movie was in Spanish, with subtitles; Cat had thought since she couldn't weasel out of the trip to San Juan she might as well buff up her Spanish, though she didn't find the point of the film to be so obscure that it required translation.

Nothing but a small toiletries pouch in the outer pocket, clothes stuffed in a mass. Cat prodded at the shirt, the pockets of the khaki trousers, felt nothing, but her fingers hit upon the slick manila of a folder, and shoving the clothes to one side, pulled it from the bottom of the compartment. Papers. A lot of photocopies of what appeared to be newspaper articles, faintly veined where they had been creased, folded. A legal pad with a list of names and addresses on the top sheet, the only one Cat recognized was David Wheeler's. The lower sheets were filled with Ron's scribblings, notes and what appeared to be quotes or dialogue. Cat wondered if—like the unpaid interns yearning to be PAs, the PAs longing to be crew, the crew looking to head up units, the background angling for the bit player's two lines, the bit players with stars in their eyes—he was just another ambitious small-time writer with a paper dream in the bottom drawer.

Cat grabbed the flashlight and snapped it on, angled it over the papers. The lines, the patches of blurred and faded type suggested that the articles had not been in the best of condition. The fact that Ron had taken the time to photocopy them meant that: a) he couldn't obtain the original articles, they were probably not from a recent publication; b) though not current, they were important enough to copy, yet c) had not been considered relevant enough for someone to put up on a webpage where Ron might simply have printed them out. Cat squinted at the truncated banner, was able to make out enough of a date to let her know that it was at least twenty years old.

The first article was written in the hyperbole of small-time journalism. Cat winced, recognized her own early errors in this vein echoing in the writer's rendition. *The mutilated, bloody and severely dismembered corpse of Thomas Roy Sontag, Senior, of Imogene, Texas, was discovered today by his horrorstruck ranch hand, Alden Hewitt, after Sontag did not show up for work and several attempts to reach him at his home went unanswered. "He was whacked up good," was Hewitt's comment to the police, and a later statement from the office of the state medical examiner stated that Sontag met with foul play and died as the result of blood loss from mutilations to his person.*

Sontag, former King County sheriff, was a widower, survived by his four children: three daughters, Mrs. Steven Lee Finney, Mrs. Pernell Knox, Mrs. Stuart Lee Roper; and one son, Thomas Roy Sontag, Junior.

The photocopy ended there. Cat took up the next one, read, MINORS SOUGHT FOR QUESTIONING IN BRUTAL MURDER. *Thomas Roy Sontag, Jr., and Annie Cox are being sought for questioning in the murder of former county sheriff Thomas Roy Sontag, Sr. The deceased was found dead in his home, having suffered multiple stab wounds. Young Sontag, known as "TJ," and Annie Cox are minors who already had one run-in with the law when they attempted to elope to Mexico. Miss Cox resided in Imogene with her sister and brother-in-law, Mr. and Mrs. Joe Turner, and attended school with Sontag. Suspicion is turning toward Cox as the possible perpetrator of the act. High school teacher, Mrs. Raquel Diaz, spoke up for the pair. "Annie Cox was just a sweet, talented girl and as for TJ Sontag, if all my pupils are as bright and good-natured as that boy, I'll have a happy career as a teacher. He was a joy to have in class." Mrs. Turner has not seen her sister for two days. She would not confirm that Miss Cox was in a family way—*

Cat checked the folder, saw that there were three or four more sheets like that one; one had the banner intact, displaying *Imogene Weekly Advisor* at the head. If Imogene was a ghost town, the *Advisor* was likewise deceased. Ron had to have dug up these articles in a library somewhere.

Poverty, illegitimate pregnancy, baby selling, murder. The more the past peeled away, the darker its core became. Sixty thousand dollars made sense now. It was not just the price of the Bonakers' desperation, it was what escape had cost a couple kids; it was the down payment on a goddess. Murder in a small town; repercussions that lasted for decades; the murderer's coming to terms with guilt, responsibility, consequences. The plot of *Redemption, Texas.* Davey Wheeler had tapped the only exciting event in his past for his bestseller. What had Tommi Ann done by taking on the role? Had that been her admission of guilt, her act of contrition?

CHAPTER TWENTY

EXT: BEACHFRONT PARKING LOT: NIGHT
The uniformed police listen attentively to
LIEUTENANT CALDERONE.

CALDERONE

Where's this witness?

COP #1

Out cold. They took her to the ER.

CALDERONE

She a hooker?

COP #1

Didn't look to be.

CALDERONE

Looks can be deceiving.

Victor left Rice in charge and drove to the medical center with Adane. The entrance was clogged with media; Victor took Adane's arm and wedged past them; the uniforms dispatched by Carlo ushered them to the ER.

Mary Grace Keller was standing outside a curtained cubicle, talking to a third uniform. The poor light seemed to leech color from her aquamarine eyes, filter it into her milky complexion.

"Raab assigned you?"

"I took pity on him and volunteered."

"He's called a lawyer," the uniform told Victor.

"Who?"

"I don't know. He's, 'Oh-my-God, how could it happen?' They're checking him out and one of the nurses says they got a call tellin' them not to ask him any questions, someone from the PD's office is on the way."

Victor parted the curtain a few inches, saw Harold Anderson sitting in a chair, his shoulders slumped, his hands dangling loosely between his legs. His body was heaving in deep, soundless sobs. He looked nothing like the prep-yet-roguish PI he had played in *South Street Shootout*. No, *Stakeout*.

"He doesn't look with it enough to answer questions," the officer observed.

"Looks can be deceiving," Adane replied, calmly, and a faint smile flitted across Mary Grace's delicate features.

"Where are the people who came in with him?" Victor asked. "A big guy, long blonde hair, a young girl?"

The officer shook his head. "Nobody like that when I got here."

They heard the staccato of pumps on the linoleum corridor. Lauren Robinson stalked down the hall wearing a sealskin coat over designer jeans, a white silk shirt. "Okay, whoever's making the call for the PD roster owes me a dozen roses. The clock has officially started. Who's my client?"

Victor nodded toward the cubicle. Lauren took a look at Harold, shook her head. "*CopWatch* shooting?"

"Yes."

"Somebody give me fifty or fewer, wordwise."

"Anderson's character is supposed to fire a gun at another actor. The prop gun apparently had a live round. The other actor was killed. Did I make the word count?" the officer asked.

"I think you came up short, dear," Lauren replied. "Anybody talk to him yet?"

Victor repressed a smile. "You mean did we question your client without the benefit of legal counsel? Lauren."

"That's exactly what I mean. Victor."

"Not yet."

"Then let's find a nice little room somewhere."

Adane secured the use of a doctor's lounge. There was a desk with a computer terminal, a couple cots, chairs, a bathroom. Victor pushed in a couple chairs from a waiting station, closed and locked the door.

Harold Anderson followed their instructions like a dumb animal, sank into a chair beside the monitor, the fluctuating images of the screen-saver throwing animated lights on his white profile.

"My name is Lauren Robinson, I'm your legal counsel. This is Lieutenant Cardenas, and his left brain, Detective Adane. That's assistant DA Mary Grace Keller. Now, Harold— I can call you Harold, right?"

"Yeah. Or Hal."

"Harold, who called me?"

Harold looked up, his blue eyes blurry. "I–I didn't."

"Okay, well, it seems you've got a friend in court."

Victor leaned toward Adane, whispered, "Steinmetz?"

Adane looked at him, shrugged.

"No whispering in class, children," Lauren counseled. "Now Harold, if we were in the interrogation cell over in Northfield, the efficient Detective Adane would be handing you a consent form, stating that you agree to be questioned. I would review it before you signed it. And I would ask to have a comprehensive private interview with you, but I'm hearing that this was an accident, so I'm going to let the lieutenant ask a few questions; if he gets out of line, I'll put him in his place. I tell you not to answer something, you keep it in the can, understood?"

Harold looked up at her, nodded mutely.

Lauren sat, crossed her legs. Victor noticed that she wore an anklet, tiny diamonds suspended on a fine gold chain.

"Stop looking at my legs, Lieutenant, and come up with a question."

Victor repressed a smile. "Mr. Anderson, where's Wally?"

"Who's Wally?" Lauren asked.

"Wally Reid," Harold replied, tonelessly. "He's the powder man. He and June got me over here."

"And who's June?"

"She's April's assistant."

Lauren looked up at Victor with an exaggerated sigh.

"April Steinmetz," Victor explained. "She's the producer of the television show."

"And where are they now?" Lauren asked.

"I don't know. I think I might've blacked out for a couple minutes. I think June got the cop to let her bring me here. I guess she asked Wally to help her, 'cause he was right there. Maybe they went back to the Marinea. That's where we're staying. Except for, well, Tommi Ann and Ben and Gary and Cici and Dianne King."

Adane excused herself. Victor knew she was going to phone the Marinea Towers, send a unit over there. "How long have you known Mr. Spivak?" he asked.

"I met him last year. He had been talking to my casting agent about getting onto the shoot of *South Street Stakeout*, said he wanted the inside story."

"A TV movie?"

Harold nodded. "Flora—my agent—she did a test on video, sent it to their casting director. It was okay." He paused, conceded, "Better than okay. He got a couple lines."

"You socialize?"

"A little. He was more into ... he and Cici Bonaker sort of hooked up. She was the co-star."

"I understand that if the *CopWatch* episode spins off to a series, she'll play the lead."

Harold nodded, a bit wistfully.

"So you were acquainted with Mr. Spivak and Miss Bonaker before the shoot. Anyone else involved in this production that you worked with before?"

Harold shook his head.

"What about Wally Reid, the powder man?" Victor asked.

"Oh, yeah. *South Street Stakeout.* Yeah."

"Between the time that shoot concluded in Philadelphia last year, and the time this show started shooting, did you see Mr. Spivak?"

Harold shifted in his chair. "I sent him a flyer on a one-act play I wrote. They did it down on Walnut Street, I thought if he came, maybe he'd give me a little press."

"Did he?"

"I don't know. If he did, he never told me. He did send me a copy of an article he did on the Philly shoot, mentioned me in that."

"But aside from that, from the time you worked together in Philly until the shooting here started, you had no communication."

"Yeah. I mean, no. I heard he got hurt last fall."

"Tell me your version of what happened tonight."

Harold ran his fingers through his hair. "It was, like, we were on track. Of course, everyone was on edge before Ron checked into the set. April was going out of her mind, because we already had his other scenes shot and if he didn't show and they had to replace him, it was time and money April doesn't have. I was in the restaurant when someone told me he showed up, was getting makeup."

"What was his mood? Was he stressed, apologetic?"

"He seemed upbeat. Ready to go. Had his scenes cold. We got derailed maybe once, he jumped right back on track."

"Give me an example of getting derailed," Victor said.

Harold shrugged, feebly. "When Cat almost passed out."

Victor felt the swift brush of Lauren's glance. "When was this?"

"Ron and Tommi Ann were into a take, Ben Butler yells for them to cut, he said it looked to him like Cat was gonna pass out, so he had one of the security guys take her outside. Second take, rest of the scenes, were fine."

"What happened then?"

Harold shifted in his chair. "We broke for dinner and they set up ... they set up to do the scene in the parking lot."

"The scene where the DJ is shot."

Harold swallowed, shuddered.

Victor paused, decided to back up, keep him a little off balance. "I understand that you were picked to rewrite the screenplay, that it's your screen credit."

"I'm SAG. Flora, she gets this distress call from April Steinmetz asking if I can get it in shape. Because of what happened with the guy they had writing it. Cusack."

"Why you?"

"I think maybe Cici might have said something to Tommi Ann or Butler. You know they get to green light everything."

"And your relationship with Miss Bonaker is such that she would have used her influence with them?"

Harold nodded.

Adane quietly stepped back into the room, caught Victor's eye, shook her head.

Victor ran his thumb across his mustache. "Did you write the parking lot scene, or was that Cusack's work?"

"I wrote it."

"Why'd you put yourself in the parking lot?"

"Huh?"

Lauren sat up, her back plank-straight.

"In the actual incident, the shooter was behind the lot on the beach. No possible way he could have been seen by either Mrs. Austen or Mr. Dudek. But I've been told that the script places you inside the perimeter of the parking lot and places your gun hand in the frame. Was that your idea?"

"I forget. When you're working with people like Tommi Ann and The Pig, you have to leave your options open, count on there being a lotta rewrites. I mean, like I said, she approves everything, then I can't make it too complicated for The Pig, because he's got this retention problem. I've tried to keep up with everything realistic but ... I mean, it's in the script we were working from, but I forget how it first got in there. Red liked the effect and Tommi Ann didn't nix it, so it stayed in."

Victor was silent for a moment. "What was your cue to fire?"

"Tommi Ann's line. Drop—um—dead. Then I fire the shots and Ron lunges toward Tommi Ann and then they were supposed to cut to have Cici come in and do Tommi Ann's fall. I mean, when Tommi Ann fell, that shoulda cued us that something was wrong, but ..." Harold shrugged.

"Put me on the set. From everything you did until the shots were fired."

"Well, Wally got the weapons out of lockup. There's a safe in the trailer, you gotta keep firing props and the rounds, even the dummies, locked up unless they're in use."

"Dummies. A round with no powder, is that right?"

"Sort of. Sometimes it's just the tip. But, yeah, it can be a whole bullet with the powder taken out. The gun we're using is a revolver. Red, he wanted an insert, a close-up of the head of the bullet in the chamber."

"And the chamber of a prop gun is scaled to accommodate these blanks and dummies?"

"Yeah. But it's not a prop."

"What?" Victor demanded.

"I mean, it is a prop in the sense of something we handle on the set, but it's not like a toy or anything."

"You were using a real firearm?"

"My client was *handed* a real firearm," Lauren corrected.

"You knew it was a real gun when you fired it?"

"Victor, dear." Lauren shook her finger at him.

"Did you check the chamber?"

Harold's blue eyes were hectic; the film of astonishment was starting to burn off, the panic setting in. "Look, I don't do that. Wally's in charge of firing props, ammo and powder, he loads the guns. I can't so much as pick them up, Wally's gotta hand them to me."

Victor scowled pensively. "Mr. Anderson, take me down the chain of possession, until the gun was handed to you."

"There were two guns. The hero prop, with a dummy head, for the close-up, and the firing prop with the blanks. Wally gets the weapons from lockup, sets up his board, loads the weapons. He can load them any time, but he's gotta keep 'em in his possession until he hands it over to me and when I'm done with it, after they cut, I hand it back to him. The city makes us put a cop on the scene to make sure Wally's not mishandling the firearms, make sure no one else gets to them during the shoot."

"And once it was handed over to you, you didn't set it down until after you fired?"

A flush crept from his open collar. "Oh, God."

"Do you need to speak to me alone, Harold?" Lauren asked.

Harold shook his head. "It was when they blew the first take. When The Pig came out of his trailer. God." Anderson's voice was awestruck. "You should've seen them go nuts. The Pig, he's what, twenty years old?"

"You were in the middle of a take, and Biggs came out from his trailer, and that started a commotion among the onlookers."

Harold nodded.

"And it took some time to get them settled down and set up for another take, and it was in the middle of this take that you fired and shot Mr. Spivak."

"Honey, honey, honey," Lauren said.

"I'm only stating what a few hundred people must have seen," Victor replied.

"Oh? Well, why don't I come by your office when we're all fresh and rested up and we'll read over all those statements our poor overworked boys"—she looked at Adane—"excuse me, *persons* in blue are taking and we'll see if we can find a consistent point of view in those couple hundred statements."

"And where was the gun when all this happened?"

"I was in position. Holding it. And then The Pig comes out of the trailer, to watch us shoot I guess, and the crowd in the street goes off the wall. The cops double up on the barricade, they're afraid the crowd's gonna jump The Pig and when it all settles down, we set up for the next take."

"And you were holding the gun the whole time?"

"Well, I'd been holding it, but I got—it was heavy, so I set it down on the table. It was just for a few seconds! I was two feet from it!"

"Could someone have picked it up?"

"We're not going to speculate on that," Lauren said.

"But you admit that you were not in physical possession the entire time between the first and second takes," Victor persisted. "That you put it down briefly. Is that what you and Wally Reid were arguing about before the second take?"

"I—" Harold paused, seemed to strain to recall the details. "I think—Wally was helping the cops shield The Pig and he comes back and sees the gun on the table and he grabs it and hands it to me. He, like, slaps it into my palm. He was ticked."

"Did Wally check the chamber when he picked it up and handed it to you?"

"I don't remember. Why?"

Victor pressed his fingertips together. "Well, the gun you were holding at that time was the one with the blanks, correct? Because the one with the dummy head, that was for a close-up that would be shot separately."

"Yeah. Yeah."

"It would seem logical that if there was no actual round involved, then the projectile would have to be this dummy, and that it fired when a blank was chambered behind it. It would be simple to determine whether the chamber would accommodate both. Quite likely, if the bullet was just a metal tip and the blank was not the length of an average round. Which means that the gun that was fired could not have been the one with two blanks in it. It would have been the one with the metal tip in it, with one of the blanks chambered behind it."

Harold's eyes were dazed. "They were i-identical ..."

"Is it possible you put down the prop with the blanks and picked up the one with the dummy?"

"Was handed," Lauren said, emphatically.

Harold swallowed. He got it now and it horrified him. "They ... Wally couldn't have handed me the wrong gun. He's a pro. He's ..."

"When he picked it up and handed it to you, did you check the chamber?" Victor asked again.

"It's not my client's job to check the chamber. He hits his mark, he's handed his prop, he does what he's told. He's an"— she lifted her straight brows, the amber eyes flashing a warning and Victor heard *Dummy*—" actor. Unless you have reason to believe that checking the condition of the props is his responsibility, I suggest we move on."

Victor rubbed his palms together, changed course. "When you fire a weapon during production, do you aim at the target?"

"Huh?"

"You hit Spivak. Is it your contention that you were pointing the gun in his general direction when you fired and it just happened to hit him? Or were you aiming directly at him?"

Harold began to sob. "Oh, God. Oh, God."

"I think we're going to bring this to a close," Lauren said. "Mr. Anderson, I'm taking you back to the Marinea Towers."

Harold looked up, wiped his eyes on his sleeve. "Do you think— can we get past the reporters outside?"

"Leave it to me."

"Excuse me," Adane said. "I—could I ask a question?"

Victor looked at Lauren. Lauren shrugged.

"How many years have you been acting, Mr. Anderson?"

Harold blinked. "I, uh, right out of high school. Seventeen years."

Victor had never seen him before last night, sitting through *South Street Stakeout. Seventeen years ago*, Victor thought, *I was a rookie*. What would it be like to be nearly forty-one and still a rookie?

"*South Street Stakeout*," Victor said.

Harold sniffed. "You saw that?"

"Have you worked steadily?"

"I had a couple good parts. Nothing big."

"Is this a good part, the *CopWatch* role?"

Harold nodded, mutely.

Lauren put her hand on Harold's sleeve. "Unless you're going to charge my client now, Mary Grace, I'm going to get him back to his hotel."

"I'm not going to make a call before I talk to Kurt," Mary Grace said evenly. "You won't make yourself difficult to find, will you Mr. Anderson?"

Harold shook his head.

Lauren tugged on Harold's sleeve. "And it goes without saying that if anyone attempts to speak to my client without representation, I'm gonna have to put his footage through the splicer." That, with an ominous glance at Victor.

She opened the door and summoned the uniformed officer. "Honey," she asked him, "you remember in *Les Misérables* how Jean Valjean escaped through the sewers?"

He shook his head.

Lauren sighed. "Okay, you remember *The Fugitive*, Harrison Ford sneaks outta the hospital through the basement?"

"Yeah. Great flick."

"We're gonna be doin' that."

"Do we got a basement like that?"

Lauren looked at Victor, rolled her eyes. "Let's try using our underworked imaginations, see what we can turn up."

Victor stood until they walked out, turned to Adane and Keller. "Ladies?"

Mary Grace sighed. "It's a tough call. I don't see intent. If Anderson handled the gun prior to this without incident, and if he was not responsible for maintaining or checking the weapons, I don't see that we can even make a charge of negligence stick. Even reckless disregard—" She shrugged, helplessly, shook her head. "This pair, Wally and June, why would they bring him all the way here, and drop him at the door?"

"Perhaps," Adane suggested, "they weren't as concerned with seeing that he got medical assistance as they were with getting him away from the scene."

"I want this guy Wally picked up," Mary Grace said. "What's your opinion, Lieutenant?"

Victor ran his thumb along his mustache, absently. "I agree that there's not much to hold Anderson, until we talk to Wally Reid, check the witness statements. Adane?"

Adane's blue eyes had the dreamy thoughtfulness that Cat's had when her mind was at work. "I was just thinking. If the incident was not an accident, if it was deliberately arranged, I wonder what the advantage might be in taking such a risk. A few hours later, Mr. Spivak might be killed in his apartment much less conspicuously."

Naked is the best disguise, Victor thought.

CHAPTER TWENTY-ONE

INT: KATE'S APARTMENT: MORNING
*KATE peers through the peephole of her apartment
door, backs up and unlocks it, quickly retrieves
the morning paper, opens it to check the headline.*

CUT TO:
*The headline reads: SHOCK JOCK SHOT IN HOT SPOT
LOT.*

Sleep had ambushed her; dreams wrapped a diaphanous screen in front of the incident as it played out, a curtain that obscured any detail that would have distinguished Ron's death from Jerry Dudek's death, so that the images she saw were barely discernible, so that she could not see whether the victim in her mind was Jerry or Ron, could not see whether the woman scanning the headlines was an actress playing her alter ego or was Cat herself.

Kate closes her eyes, horrified, and drops the paper, lets the sections scatter on the floor. Cat opened her eyes and saw immediately that something was wrong. Kate Auletta would never have chosen the conservative green plush, she would go for blood red. And the squares of white on the carpet were not newspaper now, but note paper, faxes, printed sheets with the *CopWatch* logo at the top. The dread that her exhaustion had muffled began to seep back, though it took Cat a moment to identify its source. Jerry Dudek was dead, she told herself. Not Jerry, *Ron. Ron was dead.*

Hearing hooked into the network of sensations stimulated by rising consciousness. Sound, a murmur more urgent, more imperative than the chronic rush of surf that was the underlying score to all other sound when one lived at the shore. It was discordant; human, too, coming from outside the house. Who could be outside her house? Year round, there was only her household, the Nixon ladies and the Ufflanders on Morningside Drive. The other homes were summer getaways, shut up, or visited for a brief weekend over the Christmas or Easter holidays.

Cat pushed the covers back. Her clothes, her sandy boots, her bag, papers spilled out on the carpet. A glistening rectangle caught her eye, a glossy purple and silver image protruding from her upturned tote bag. Cat dropped one arm over the side of the bed, made a swipe at the canvas strap of her tote, missed, tried a second swipe, netted the mess of folders, papers, notepads she had hastily stuffed in her bag after the shooting. She piled them on the bed, and began to shuffle through them to see if anything was missing, turned up the image that had caught her eye, one of Remy's postcards, creased and trampled, stained with coffee and grit. She flipped it over and saw an odd phrase written in black marker.

tommi ann butler is a maJor shootyng STaR.

Cat frowned, shook her head, puzzled. She had put Remy's cards on the bar last night, hoping to bait some of the cast and crew. Some bit player had been doodling fan notes to Tommi Ann, lost the card in the stampede following the shooting, perhaps. Then Cat remembered that June Mathis had handed Dianne King a postcard and something had been written on the back. Dianne had read it, slipped it into her bag. It had seemed to Cat at the time that a shade of tension had passed over Dianne's features. Had Dianne, the gatekeeper, taken the note to be threatening in some way? Had the phrase "shooting (shootyng?) star" been a hint that a shooting was going to take place?

Cat rolled out of bed, stumbled over clothes stale with last night's anxiety and headed into the shower. She stood and let the water beat down on her as if it could beat the events of the past hours back into the realm of fiction, fantasy. She closed her eyes and let the warm water bring up her pulse, felt the palpation in her temples, her palms. The dread wouldn't wash off; neither would the sense that the script was invading her life. Would the headline in the morning paper read MOCK JOCK SHOT ON COPWATCH LOT?

Cat stepped out of the shower and dried herself, the roughness of the terry cloth, the sweep of cool air, the chilly tile under her feet anchoring her to consciousness.

She pulled her old blue robe around her, heard a shuffling footstep outside her door. "Mats?"

He poked his head in. He was still in his pajamas, his hair sticking out at odd angles. Cat slipped the postcard into her tote, lifted him onto the bed. "Is my baby sleepy?"

Mats put his head on her shoulder, his thumb stealing toward his mouth. "I just woke up."

"Didn't you go to bed for Ellice?"

"I tried."

Cat checked the clock on her night table. Almost nine. An italicized exclamation caught her ear. "Is Jane home?"

"Uh-huh. 'Llice said she can't go to school 'cause there's all these people."

"What people?"

"Outside."

Cat picked up Mats and trotted down the stairs, found Ellice drawing Jane away from the front door, just as the phone began to ring.

"Let me get it," Ellice was dressed in jeans, a long-sleeved T-shirt, Jane in the khakis and red shirt she and Cat had picked out.

"Why aren't you in school?" Cat asked over Ellice's wary, uninviting "Hello?"

"Ellice wouldn't *let* me. There're all these *people*."

"What people?"

Ellice was saying, "No, not a chance" into the receiver, hung up, pointed toward the front sidewalk. "Every local reporter is on the curb. I already had the cops dislodge them from the porch, they've been cruising by every half hour or so to keep the trespassers at bay."

Cat walked into the dining room, crept up to the corner of the window, peeked out. There were about fifty or sixty people milling in the center of Morningside Drive, the *NewsLine90* van, Karen Friedlander, Morgan Wszybyk, someone from Philly 104, a few more she didn't recognize. Photographers.

Ellice tugged on her shoulder. "I didn't want to walk Jane to the bus through that gauntlet, I thought it would be okay if she stayed home. I called the school."

Cat nodded numbly. "Who was on the phone?"

"Somebody from the *Inquirer* wanting a statement from you."

"Mom, do they want to put us on TV?" Jane demanded.

"I guess." Victor's least favorite phrase.

"What time did you get in?"

Cat could see in Ellice's grave expression that she had heard the news, kept it from the kids.

"I don't know."

"I told Freddy you'd call him as soon as you got up."

Cat got a Pepsi out of the refrigerator, popped the lid. "Who else called?"

"*Famiglia* Fortunati. Jennie was a little concerned. Ritchie Landis called about a dozen times. April Steinmetz, a Cici Bonaker, and a woman named King. Press."

Cat kissed the top of Mats' hair and told the kids to go up and make their beds, waited for them to go before she spoke. "Ron's ... I don't know what happened. Someone fired onto the set. I don't know what happened."

Ellice took Cat's hands in hers, gave them a squeeze, then held up the morning paper so that Cat could see the headline, *Local Reporter Killed in Movie Mishap.* "The press is playing it like it was an accident. Somehow, the gun that some actor named Anderson was using in the shooting scene got a live round in it, and it went off."

The phone rang again. Ellice ran into the living room to pick up the extension. Cat pulled the paper in front of her, read: *A resourceful bid for the inside scoop on television production turned to disaster last night for a local reporter, Ron Spivak, who was shot and killed during the filming of an episode of* CopWatch. *The shooting, according to early reports, appears to be the result of negligence. A revolver, used by co-star Harold Anderson, was loaded with live ammunition. Anderson's role called for him to fire the weapon in the direction of Spivak in a re-creation of the shooting of popular local disk jockey, Jerry Dudek.*

Dudek was shot and killed last November while he and local reporter, Mrs. Cat Austen, were conversing in the parking lot at Pacific and Belmont Avenues in Atlantic City. Ironically, the accident very nearly replicates the shooting of Dudek. Mrs. Austen, who has been hired as a consultant for the episode, entitled Death of a Shock Jock, *was present when the shooting occurred.*

It has been learned that Mr. Anderson was interviewed by investigators from the Major Crimes Bureau shortly after the incident. Sources close to the investigation state that weapons protocol called for the gun to be loaded and kept in the custody of the weapons supervisor before it was handed to Anderson.

"A terrible tragedy. I can only hope that we can find it in ourselves to come together in crisis," was the statement released by director and co-star Eduardo "Red" Melendez who was interviewed shortly after the event. "My heartfelt sympathy goes out to Mr. Spivak's family and friends, and I would like to assure the public that this topical and relevant episode of CopWatch *will not be derailed by this unfortunate accident."*

When asked if Melendez's comments were an indication that the filming will continue, producer April Steinmetz offered no comment.

Ellice came into the room. "That was Victor. I think you should call him back right away."

Cat nodded, reached for the phone; it rang as her fingers closed over the receiver and she wedged it against her ear with her shoulder, turned the newspaper page and continued looking over the headline story.

It was Jennie. "So, you all right? Victor, he was looking for you last night."

"I'm fine, Mama. I'm sorry if I worried you."

"You don't all gotta tiptoe around me like I'm gonna have a heart attack. You get anything in your stomach?"

"I just got up."

"So how about I bring dinner tonight, that producer calls, she told me they're not gonna film tonight, so I don't gotta cook, you want me to bring dinner over?"

"Mama, maybe you better not come by."

"I can get some lamb chops."

"Mama. Lamb chops are up to nine-fifty a pound. But you can do something for me. Could I send the kids over to your place today?"

"Why isn't Jane in school?"

"There're all these reporters in front of the house—"

"You want me to send Carlo over, get rid of them?"

Cat sighed. "No, Mama. Just let me send the kids over for a few hours. I can have Ellice bring them."

"Will Jane eat lamb chops?"

"Mama, please don't go to any trouble."

"So whaddaya think about Tommi Ann? I got a look at her real close up, there's not a line on that face."

"Mama, she's the second most beautiful woman I've ever seen. Next to you."

"I'm almost seventy-one years old, and I don't forget it."

"But you don't look it."

"That's 'cause I eat right."

Cat promised Jennie that she would get something in her stomach, hung up and told the kids they were going over Nonna's. She dialed Victor's number, was not kept waiting.

"Where did you go last night?" he demanded.

Cat hesitated. Ron's car, the file came into focus. "I just had to get out of there. I just ... I just didn't think it was real."

His voice softened. "Are you all right?"

"As well as can be expected, under the circumstances."

"I want to see you today."

"Don't come here, Victor, unless you want to see your picture in tomorrow's paper. There are press from my front sidewalk out to the street. I'm going to be homebound, and I don't think you'd like to run that gauntlet."

"Well, I can't say I'm sorry about the homebound part. Is there someone staying with you today?"

"I'm fine, Victor, I'm not going to—" *lose my mind.*

"You don't sound fine."

"My mother attributes that to the fact that I don't have anything in my stomach." She sighed. "Except for gut instinct, perhaps. I don't suppose you believe in it. The sort of instinct that's in opposition to the testimony of your eyes."

"Well, when I see a magician saw his assistant in half, common sense tells me it isn't happening."

"How come it's 'common sense' when a man has it and 'instinct' when a woman has it?"

"And what does your common sense tell you?"

Cat pushed her hair behind her ear. "That if the woman who got sawed in half was about to leak some scandalous story about the magician, I wouldn't be so quick to chalk it up to an accident if she wound up dead."

"Spivak confirmed that Mrs. Butler was the Bonaker girl's mother? What makes that copy worth killing over?"

"Don't you think that everyone has one reason they would kill someone for?" Cat asked.

"Perhaps. But unwed motherhood isn't exactly taboo among film stars, is it? It appears to be more like a prerequisite from what I've observed."

"Have you questioned Wally Reid yet?"

"He took off."

"Off as in ... he's gone?"

"Correct. He and the Mathis girl volunteered to get Anderson to the med center. Reid disappeared in transit. Something else," Victor added, "that cell phone conversation you overheard at St. Agnes? Your instincts were good there. Mark got a glimpse of Reid last night, he told Carlo that Reid was the one who sold him the pirated tape."

"Do you think Wally set Ron up? I mean he was the one who coached Harold in how to position the shot."

"I won't know until Wally's picked up. I'll call you later."

Cat went upstairs and dressed in slacks and a sweater, peeked out her bedroom window. Karen Friedlander sipped from a Wawa coffee cup, checked her watch, talked on her cell phone.

Ellice rapped on the door, poked her head in. "I called Freddy, he's going to pick us up and bring us over to Jennie's."

Cat looked up. "Ellice, when you ran away from Ira, did you think about where you'd go? What you were going to do?"

Ellice smiled. Serene, at peace with whatever she'd had to do to survive. Tommi Ann smiled like that. "When you're running for your life, you're not thinking about what you're going to do. All I knew was, if I stayed, it would kill me. He had this image in his mind, and he wanted to bully me into it. And he knew I was never going to get there, that was part of the game. All the beating me down and raising the bar was really to get me so consumed in trying to get there that I wouldn't look around, look for a way out. You know, keep her so busy she won't have any fight left."

"But you made it, because you were older and smart—"

"And got lucky," Ellice reminded her. "*La fortuna.*"

"Well, there's an Italian saying that fortune is as brittle as glass. What if you weren't old enough, or skilled, or smart or lucky?"

"Then I guess I'd be dead. Or had myself turned into something else."

Cat went downstairs. Mats was sitting at the dining room table, his mouth pressed into a quivering pout. "What's the matter, don't you want to go over Nonna's? I'll tell Uncle Freddy to bring your bike over."

"I wanna stay here with you."

"I'll come by a little later. I have some work to do."

"I'll be good for you."

Cat sat beside him, kissed the top of his head. "What's the matter, baby boy?"

Mats' mouth quivered. "Is those people gonna get you?"

"No, honey. A lot of those people are friends of mine. They just want to talk to Mommy because Mommy's been hanging around that TV show. You know how much people like TV."

"And they're not bad people?"

"Of course not. If they were bad people, I'd just call the police."

"And you'll come over Nonna's?"

"Yes, honey, as soon as I get a little work done." She heard Freddy's quick footstep on the porch, hurried to open the door, hid behind it while he slipped through, slammed it closed.

Cat kissed him on the cheek. "I really owe you for this."

Freddy chucked her under the chin. "How you holdin' up?"

"Okay. I'm just going to shut my drapes and get some work done. They can't stand around in the street all day. Jane, where *are* you?"

"I'm *coming.*" Jane jogged down the stairs wearing her sunglasses with pink plastic frames, rhinestone stars at the corners.

Cat looked at Ellice, shook her head.

"Uncle Freddy, is those people gonna get us?" Mats trusted his mother, but a second opinion never hurt.

"Not a chance," Freddy assured him.

Cat watched as Freddy carried Mats down the porch steps, put him in the back seat of his Cherokee. The reporters kept a tenuous distance; they didn't recognize Freddy as anyone special, and going after kids didn't always play well with the audience.

Cat called her mother back and told her that Freddy was on his way, assured Jennie that they had eaten breakfast.

She poured herself some coffee and trudged up to her bedroom, turned on the computer and settled on the bed, her feet tucked under her. She began to put the papers on her bed in order, one-handed. Ron's folder from last night, the files she had gotten from his apartment, her own notes of the Tommi Ann interview, notes of last night's shoot. That odd postcard.

Cat flipped through Ron's *South Street Stakeout* articles. *What am I looking for?* They were lengthy articles, even the ones with trivial titles. Ron was a researcher; backstory had been his forte. Cat would never have gotten to the root of the Dudek murder if Ron hadn't shared the background material he'd dug up.

The phone rang. Cat balanced the coffee mug in one palm and reached for it. It was April Steinmetz. "Look, I can't find his sheets, did Spivak have family?"

"No, I don't think so. Why?"

"I been on the phone all morning with Paragon, they're putting their shysters on standby in case anyone files against the production. God, I haven't been handed a mess like this since we were shooting an episode of *Bayou Blues* and one of the trained crocodiles—or maybe it was a 'gator—snaps his lead and gets the wrangler's butt in a vise and the star—you remember Johnny Crocker? He grabs this machete, which you ordinarily wouldn't just have lying around, except in a couple of your swamp states like Florida and Louisiana, and *Bayou Blues* was doin' almost all of its shooting on location. Run of the show, real estate in Saint Bernard Parish went through the roof. So he—"

"The crocodile?"

"Crocker. God, he'd bed anything with a heartbeat. I tell you, that croc' was female and willing, he woulda thought twice before he hacks off a hunk of its tail—"

"The crocodile's tail?" Cat forgot why April had called.

April chuckled. "Yeah. Except the croc' or 'gator or whatever doesn't let go, I think it's something with the way their jaws are constructed, something like that, he's really got a lock on the wrangler's butt and Crocker, he's hackin' and whackin', which doesn't do a damn thing because them being so primitive?"

"Actors?"

"Crocodiles. But actors, too. You can practically hack them down to a stump and they still figure, what the hell, a set of decent head shots and a bit part with a few good lines to get a foot in some casting director's door—"

"Of course, if they're down to a stump, there's no longer a foot to wedge into the door," Cat reminded her.

April emitted her one-syllable laugh. "HAW! So finally one of the non-unions gets a chain saw, because the unions, they're all in a huddle tryin' to figure out where's the clause in their contract says it's their job to pry a swamp creature off the hired help's heinie, and well, you know."

Cat didn't know and was not going to ask.

"PETA, the ASPCA, they tried to shut us down."

"What did you do?"

April chuckled. "I squared it with state endangered and ASPCA, had a few belts made up outta the hide and sent it to PETA's chapter president."

"How's Harold doing?"

"He's pretty shaken up, keeps saying he shoulda checked the gun, he shoulda checked the gun. Damn Wally— The cops pick him up yet? You should see how they got the Marinea Towers staked out."

"The police?"

"Media. Trying to get Hal." April snorted. "He's not at the Towers. Ben moved him over to the Phoenix, he's on the twenty-fifth floor with Pig. Poor ki— Gee, I almost said 'kid.' The 'kid's' thirty-five years old. I heard Ben or Dianne dimed in to Legal Aid, came up golden."

"Have you talked to him?"

"No, I got lunch with him and Tommi Ann and Ben."

"What will this do to Harold's career?"

April snorted. "Ben's released a statement says Hal's gonna cooperate completely with the investigation and work on getting past his own trauma to finish out the shoot for the sake of everyone who put so much work into the project. I think it was Dianne's copy. Trust me, she knows how to work the press. By noon he'll have a dozen interviews lined up where he comes off like some poor schmo who's the fall guy in some techie's negligence, and this time tomorrow there'll be two dozen scripts on Flora Durkin's desk, except this time tomorrow he'll probably be signed with Butler. Me, I don't go for your puppy-dog types, I like something hunkier, like your lieutenant, but I guess Cici's had all she can take of hustlers, after Spivak."

"And what happens with the show?"

"Hal can pull himself together I think I can still pull it off. I'll know better after I see last night's footage. We may have to wrap the shoot in LA. That'll nix the elephant. Damn shame, be a great place to have Kate and Tim slug it out."

"But I mean, how will you reshoot Ron's scene?"

"May not have to. Let's face it, it went down just about like it was scripted; Spivak didn't drop until after the shots. As soon as we get it back from the cops, I'll check it out, see how much we can use."

"Use ..?"

"And if we gotta can it, we might still recoup. June's been on the phone all morning with *America's Deadliest Disasters*, they're up to half a mil for the footage."

Cat swallowed hard. "Of the ..?"

"Shooting. Yeah."

"Of someone who got ..?" Cat was certain that she misunderstood.

But April reiterated, "Shot. Yeah. It's no worse than what you see on *Hot Pursuit, Crime's Craziest Capers, Code Four-Fifteen*."

"I—I guess not." Cat supposed they were television programs, had never seen them.

"They all use amateur footage, accident videos, outtakes. There's a pretty hot market for what's left on the cutting room floor. Of course, this all depends on whether Paragon's shysters can get the footage back from the cops."

"They confiscated it?"

"Yeah, but I think the Third Amendment's on our side. Or maybe it's the Fourth or the Sixth, I get 'em mixed up. Look, Cat," April got down to the purpose of her call. "What I said the other day, about Spivak, it was just words."

Cat tried to recall what April had said.

I have half a mind to shove a live round in the gun and let that jerk take a shot to the head.

"Everybody had it in for that jerk, it wasn't just me. Besides, it was an accident. At least I think it was an accident. Unless someone really had it in for Spivak big time and used Harold to off him."

Cat thought about Jerry Dudek, keeper of dirty secrets, the guy everyone loved to hate.

"Be some plot, though, wouldn't it? You think it'd be too tacky to ask Hal if he could work up a treatment? Maybe wait a day or two, whaddaya think?"

CHAPTER TWENTY-TWO

INT: CALDERONE'S OFFICE: MORNING
VICTOR is sitting behind his desk. SERGEANT JOHN NESTOR enters.

NESTOR

What can I get you?

CALDERONE

The phone number of the Auletta woman. I want to see her in my office this morning.

NESTOR

Hey, lemme tell you, I know Kate Auletta.
She wants to talk to you, she'll call you.
And it'll be on her turf.

CUT TO:
KATE AULETTA knocks on the open door, steps into the office.

KATE

I had a feeling you'd want to talk to me, Lieutenant.

CALDERONE (to NESTOR)

You were saying?

Victor's unit detected nothing in his implacable demeanor to suggest that this day was more than any other. He motioned them into his office, closed the door. "Anything that takes precedence over last night?"

"Are you kiddin'?" Rice asked. "You seen the papers? I heard they got Cat's house staked out."

Victor settled into his chair, nodded. "What time is Anderson coming in to make his statement?"

"I haven't gotten through to him yet. Lauren Robinson called this morning, she said he got moved to the Phoenix."

Victor cocked an eyebrow. "How'd that come about?"

"Don't know. Sounded like it was a surprise to Lauren, and she doesn't surprise easy."

Adane settled three blue canvas binders on her lap. Her pale face was set with exhaustion; there were faint blue crescents under her eyes. "Sir, I've divided the statements into the crew who were present on the set; the officers and security who were present; and the onlookers, the ones who didn't vacate the scene."

"How many in all?"

"One hundred eighty-nine. There are no statements recorded from either of the Butlers, Mr. Biggs or—or Mrs. Austen. Or Miss Steinmetz's assistant, Miss Mathis."

"The one who accompanied Anderson to the med center?"

"Along with Reid," Long added. "Who's still AWOL."

Victor's phone rang. It was Raab. "I talked to Mary Grace, I'm gonna be pushed to call the toss on this one. Right now, my thinking is we're not gonna be charging Anderson if there's enough backup on his story that he doesn't check the weapons. I'm looking at criminal negligence on the weapons guy. How'd Mary Grace do?"

"Fine."

"We charge the prop guy, there'll be a plea, I figure Mary Grace can handle that, no problem." He sighed, heavily. "I don't gotta tell you, Tommi Ann Butler got shot on my watch, Patsy'd have my head. You schedule time with her? Tommi Ann?"

"I plan to do that this morning. Rice said that Anderson's been moved to the Phoenix."

"Who engineered that, the producer?"

"Or the Butlers."

"That's got a weird feel to it. How's Cat Austen?"

"She's okay, considering."

"Must be like a nightmare she can't wake up from. Call me after you talk to Tommi Ann. I'll be here late. Patsy says I don't get her a picture of Tommi Ann from *Black Orchid,* there's no point in me goin' home."

Victor hung up, sat back in his chair, nodded for Stan to close the door. "Raab's looking at a possible charge of criminal negligence against the firearms manager."

Long shifted in his chair. "Still a lotta damn 'ifs.' If someone could get a round, if they can chamber it without anyone noticing, if Anderson doesn't check the chamber, if Reid doesn't check it, if Anderson'll hit Spivak and not Tommi Ann, not miss."

"How can we start to eliminate them?"

Adane slid a folder onto his desk. "The preliminary autopsy shows a single injury. The projectile entered behind the right ear, penetrated the carotid and a cervical artery. There was no exit wound, and the ME recovered a metal slug, what I believe was what Mr. Anderson referred to as a dummy. With a blank chambered behind it, it could be expelled like an ordinary round and be capable of inflicting serious injury, depending upon the point of impact, the accuracy of the weapon, distance and the skill of the shooter. So, as to whether it would be possible for someone to obtain a blank, and chamber it behind the weapon that had a dummy in the chamber, the answer is obviously yes, because it was done."

"When?"

Adane shrugged. "Well, the obvious time would have been when Mr. Biggs inadvertently caused a distraction."

"Let's back up," Victor suggested. "The props are on the table. They'd been using one for close-ups that they had shot, or were going to shoot. Some time before they start filming, the weapons are loaded. They call for a take and the weapon with the blanks is handed to Anderson. Now Anderson had been coached to aim and fire the weapon in a certain manner. So, there would be little doubt that he'd aim at Spivak or hit him if he was aiming at him."

"Coached by Reid," Stan added. "Anderson good with a firearm?"

Victor shrugged. "I saw that TV movie he made last year, he appeared completely adept, quite skilled."

"As an actor using a prop," Stan replied.

"Well, there're props and there're props," Long interjected. "I talked to a couple crew. There're what they call your hero props, the ones the stars use. They can be real guns. Like what they used for the close-ups. The stunt guns, they're the ones the rest of the cast uses, and then they got cheap, mass-produced background props for the extras. Like say you need a hundred weapons for an army or something? They're usually made of plastic painted over."

Victor nodded, slowly. "Biggs incites a diversion. In the commotion that follows, Anderson sets the gun down. A blank—or blanks—is removed from the firing prop and chambered in the close-up model. Order is restored and Reid chews out Anderson for relinquishing custody of the weapon, hands it back to him. Once that loaded gun is in Anderson's hand, there's no question that he'll hit the mark."

"Real convenient diversion," Long muttered.

Victor nodded, grimly, traced an imaginary line on his blotter with his index finger. "So, we have the ability to load the gun, a convenient diversion, a standard weapon and a reasonably skilled shooter. For it to be murder, we'd need to add intent to the mix. Motive?"

"One could be you wanna whack Spivak, set it up to look like an accident. Another is you're out to shake up Tommi Ann or throw the show off track," Stan proposed.

"So, who would benefit from one scenario or the other?"

"From nixing the shoot? Nobody," Stan asserted. "You got locals makin' money off the shoot, you got people like the producer, the director, the Bonaker girl, even Anderson figuring this is the project's gonna revive a career or make their bones."

"Plus, they already got advertisers lined up," Long interjected. "Had sponsors beat down the door when they heard the name Tommi Ann Butler and sweeps month in the same sentence, signed blind."

"What kind of money are we talking about?"

"Three million per slot."

"For a *minute*?" Stan asked.

"Thirty seconds."

"That's six million dollars for sixty seconds."

"Einstein," Long chuckled.

Victor stroked his chin, thoughtfully. "So advertising revenue and career advancement are powerful motivations to keep this production on course. Who might profit if it's shelved?"

"Hopper or his family?" Phil hazarded.

Stan shook his head. "Nope. I heard from Cat and from Jackie both that Hopper—he's 'Harper' in the script, the one Anderson's playin'—comes off looking real sympathetic. You know those Left Coast types love their sensitive perps, plus natch Anderson's gonna write himself a nice, fat Emmy contender. Hopper's team probably figures the better he looks to the jury pool, the better chance their boy's got to walk." He shook his head. "What went down last night makes everyone a loser."

"I think we can only infer that if we're convinced that the shooting was accidental. If it was intentional, then we have to infer that there was some benefit, real or imagined, and decide if that benefit was realized," Victor proposed.

"I don't get it," Stan said.

"If we conclude that there was no motive to derail the production, then perhaps the motive was to keep it on track."

"Like somehow Spivak was a threat to it." Stan smacked his palm to his forehead. "Lieutenant, I forgot something. I'm driving Jackie back to her place last night, she told how she's hanging out with Sherrie Fortunati, the two of them, they're like kids in a candy store last night. Sherrie's tellin' Jackie and Cat how she was scopin' out the crew on the Boards, heard two people talking, a woman's sayin' something about she doesn't know how much *he* knows, but how she's worried it could kill the shoot. She said she thought the woman sounded like the Bonaker girl."

Victor sat upright. "Who was she talking to?"

Stan shrugged, shook his head. "Wasn't Spivak, it was before he got there." He paused, ran his fingers through his curls. "Coulda been talking *about* Spivak."

"But," Long protested, "say Spivak does have something could shelve the show. You're gonna do him on camera? You tellin' me *that's* not gonna can the shoot?"

"Not necessarily," Adane said. "I spoke to Ms. Steinmetz early this morning. The scene that was shot last night was the last of Mr. Spivak's principal photography. The morning papers reported—and Miss Steinmetz confirmed—that there has been no determination made as to whether they will use the footage shot last night."

"Jeannie, the guy got himself whacked."

"Yes, Stanley," Adane replied. "But the fact that he was whacked, as you put it, in the manner and at the moment called for in the script did allow them to commit the completed scene to film. Whether they choose to shelve it or not would seem to be a matter of discretion, not utility."

"Jeannie, that's too gross to even think about." Stan was not cut out for homicide; he continued to view killing with something like wonder, incomprehension.

"Yes, but not impossible. I thought of it, Stanley. It's not a matter of what one can conceive, it's a matter of how willing one is to act on what one conceives, and whether one has the means to execute it. What you've decided is worth killing for."

"That's cold, Jeannie," Long said.

"I think it's the world that's cold, Phil."

"How much longer were they supposed to shoot in this area?" Victor asked.

"Three more days," Stan said. "Tommi Ann's scheduled to leave for LA Saturday night or early Sunday morning. The rest of the principal photography shoots there. Second unit might stick around a few more days, but Sunday, she's gone."

Victor nodded to the binders on Adane's lap. "What Miss Wing told you, is that in her statement?"

"I didn't get to hers yet," Stan admitted.

"How many of the statements have you gone over?"

"Half," Long said.

Rice added, "About that."

Adane looked down at her lap.

All, Victor thought. "Any inconsistencies?"

"Not so far," Stan replied. "Spivak makes it to the set just in the nick, they run through it once, got it down cold. They're doin' a take inside the club, it gets blown when Cat started to fade—"

"The scene when Butler called for them to cut."

"Yeah. Jackie said Butler made out like Spivak blew his lines, called Furina to take Cat out for some air."

Victor turned to Adane. "We have that footage?"

"Yes, sir."

"Have you viewed it yet?"

"Not yet, sir."

"I want to view it, right after I get back from the Phoenix. Call the Butlers' suite, tell them I'll be over within the hour, and imply as politely as you can that the DA can arrange for them to stay around as long as it takes to get to the bottom of this. Rice, see if you can arrange to have a word with the Bonaker girl, get her version of this argument, and with the assistant, June Mathis. I want to know how she came to be Anderson's paramedic, if she overheard anything that might indicate where Wally Reid disappeared to." He turned to Long. "He have a sheet?"

"Juvie high jinks. No felonies."

Victor nodded. "Long, find out how much red tape we have to hack through to arrange an interview with Biggs." He rose and dismissed them, reached for the phone to call the city department, find out if any disciplinary charges had been lodged against Gino. He felt the receiver tremble under his palm, heard the glass in his wall vibrate, ceased dialing.

Long opened the door, poked his head in. "Red tape just snapped. Biggs is outside with his posse. And his lawyer."

CHAPTER TWENTY-THREE

INT: HARPER'S AND DONNER'S OFFICE: MORNING

KATE

Who hated Gerry that much? Who wanted
him dead?

TIM

Who didn't? You wanna see his freak mail?
Dear Gerry, Would you be the main course
at our Donner party. Get it? Donner party?
And that one came today.

She was using her machine to screen her calls, but when she
heard Harold Anderson's, "Cat, it's me, I was just wondering how
you were making out," she grabbed the receiver. "Harold?"

"I see that you're surrounded, too," he said.

"Unfortunately, I can see them from my bedroom window. I
hardly think that's the case at the Phoenix."

"You heard?"

"April told me. She the one who found Lauren Robinson?"

"I think it was Cici, or maybe Dianne."

"Did they pick up Wally Reid yet?"

"I don't know."

"You know if he's ever been cited for negligence, anything like that?" Cat reached for a pencil, ready to scribble anything relevant.

"I don't know. I mean, the only time I ever met him before this was on *South Street Stakeout*. He always seemed so professional, like he knew what he was doing. And now ..." his voice broke. "Jesus, this is such a mess."

"How's Cici holding up?"

"She's wiped out. She's got some idea that Ron had something on Tommi Ann he was gonna print. I know that she had words with him last—" He broke off. "Everyone was mad at him, April, the crew, everyone, the way he just took off."

"What was April yelling about when they were setting up for the parking lot scene? Telling you to wait until after the scene before you crossed swords with that"—*schmuck*—"person."

"Cici asked me to tell Ron to lay off, maybe just for a few days. I go to talk to him, I guess June overheard us arguing and rats to April. What is it Cici thinks he had on Tommi Ann, anyway?"

"Didn't she tell you?"

"No. And I don't know if I should say something to Dianne or Ben or—" Cat heard one bitter syllable, an aborted laugh. "Jesus, you were right, be careful what you wish for? I wanted a part would give me maximum exposure. Well, I sure got it. God, you asked me a week ago, I woulda told you how I'da killed for some PR."

And Ron was dying to get the big story.

"Anyway, you wanna cancel for tomorrow, that's fine, I understand."

Tomorrow. She had set up interviews with Red and Harold tomorrow, worked it so she could make each the excuse for getting rid of the other. "Let's not cancel yet, let's see how the next twenty-four hours play out," Cat suggested. "Unless of course Ben Butler's handling your PR now, doesn't want you talking to me."

"He and Dianne've already got me lined up, but I guess I owe you an interview more than I owe one to Callie O'Connor."

Callie O'Connor! He was being interviewed by FRONT COVER? Fortunately, the shriek was confined to her head. Her voice was quite normal when she asked, "You have an interview with Callie O'Connor?"

"Yeah." Another short laugh, cynical. "I been watching *Front Cover* for fifteen years, rehearsing what I'd say if I ever found myself sitting on the couch, and now I don't have any idea what I'm supposed to talk about."

"I'm sure Dianne King can prep you." Cat wondered if Dianne was going to expect Cat to submit her questions, promise a cover for an interview with Harold now. "You still want to do this at my place?"

"Anyplace outta the spotlight."

Cat told him she'd keep in touch and fell back on her bed, thinking. Either Ron had died because of something he knew about Tommi Ann, or because of something he knew about Wally Reid. Did she lean toward the Tommi Ann story because it was darker, juicier? (More lucrative?) After all, Reid was the one who had controlled the firearms, Reid was the one who had fled.

She took up the folder she had gotten from Ron's apartment, the *South Street Stakeout* articles he had offered to let her review. Wally had worked on *South Street Stakeout* with Ron. A frail link, but a link all the same.

She dropped onto the bed and checked out the headers: *Cops Prove Tough Critics on "Stakeout" Shoot.*

Esprit de Corpse: Playing Dead Is Harder Than It Looks.

Don't Call Them "Extras": Screen Lingo 101.

Take Two, They're Free.

Cheesesteaks and Tasty Cakes: Stars Feed on Philly Fare.

Local Actor Stakes Out Lead in Area Shoot.

She primed her eyes to seek out familiar names. Harold was the Local Actor, a good write-up. The rest appeared to be entertaining observations on *South Street Stakeout*'s location shoot. She turned her attention to *Take Two, They're Free*, because the header conveyed so little about the subject. *As the old saying goes, "It's funny how you miss the little things, 'cause little things mean a lot." Well, when a TV shoot has finally wrapped, you find that you do miss the little things, and little things add up. Choice props, accessories, wardrobe items, memos, press kits have a way of disappearing by the end of a shoot, often to become the object of desire in the high stakes, black market trafficking in film memorabilia. These are not your every-day giveaways we're talking about, but property underwritten in the production budget. Unit Production Manager Sidney Olcott discloses that a smart line pro-ducer will budget for these "losses," and estimates that the* South Street Stake-out *shoot has already written off ten thousand dollars in purloined clothing, hand props, wigs, not to mention the bootlegged copies of outtakes and unused footage. "Right now, Cici Bonaker and Harold Anderson aren't names," Olcott states, "but if their stars rise, someone with early footage of them could turn a handsome profit." Weapons master Wally Reid agrees, though the controls on his items are considerably tighter—*

Mark's pirated video. She had seen a cassette labeled *South Street Stakeout Outtakes* in Ron's apartment. If Ron had done a piece on trafficking in film set trophies, perhaps he had fingered Wally as a sort of kingpin of contraband, was doing a follow-up article.

Cat wished she had taken the cassette of outtakes when she had gone to Ron's apartment. Of course, there was no reason why she couldn't go over there now and get it. After all, she had a key, there might even be some mail to take in. Her promise to look after his place hadn't contained a contingency clause that required he be alive, had it?

She rose up on her knees, saw the clutch of die-hard reporters still camped on her front walk. She flopped back on the bed, felt some-thing slick under her arm, groped and came up with the postcard with the clumsy, misspelled tribute (or threat) to Tommi Ann inked on the back of the announcement promoting Remy's trunk show.

Cat snapped her fingers, did her Lucille Ball, "I've got an idea!",

rooted around for the numbers of *NewsLine90, Philly5Live!*, the *Press*.
She did *NewsLine90* first, got a timid, "Hello, *NewsLineNinety*, KRZI?"
realized she was talking to Sondra DuBois, the station manager's secretary. Jerry's "fiancée." *Dejerry vu*, Cat thought, and forced her voice
down half an octave, tried out a weak British accent. "Yes, I'm the
camera operator for *Front Cover*, I'm a bit lost, where on the mezzanine
at the Phoenix were we supposed to set up for the press conference,
do you know? Was it in front of CapriOH!?"

"Uh ... press conference?"

"Tommi Ann Butler's supposed to come down and speak to the
press here, but I don't know where she was gonna do the speakin'."

"At the Phoenix?"

"Righto." *Oh, Lord.*

"I, uh, I'll have to see ..."

Cat heard a frantic shuffling of paper. "Perhaps I'd better give
Channel Five a ring. Thanks awfully for your time."

She got the pressroom of a local affiliate next, ran pretty much the
same routine, changed the accent for *Philly5Live*. She crept over to the
window and saw Karen Friedlander, her Olympian stride breaking her
away from the pack. Saw cell phones whipped out. The dismantling
of equipment.

Her phone rang immediately, and Ritchie started in as soon as she
picked up. "Austen, Austen, what's with this press conference, my
moles didn't pick up a tremor!"

"Press conference?"

"Yeah, it's just been called over the Phoenix."

"Who called a press conference?"

"Tommi Ann Butler, she's maybe gonna say something about what
went down last night! Get over there!"

"That's funny," Cat drawled. "I didn't hear anything about the press
conference. Are you sure it's not some prank?"

"Sure I'm sure! Who would pull a prank like that? I think Cherry
said she heard it was called for eleven."

"I'll check it out, Ritchie, but I've already got my material on the interview I did with Tommi Ann."

"Yeah, but that was before Spivak got shot. Jeez, remember how he was always saying how he'd kill for a hot story? Never thought he'd *get* himself killed for one."

"It's amazing what people will do for a story," Cat agreed, hung up.

Four hours staked-out in front of her apartment and they were gone in under fifteen minutes. Not only had she got rid of them, but she had managed to deposit them squarely in front of CapriOH!. Cat pulled on an old pair of running shoes, grabbed her keys and a jacket and hurried to her car.

She allowed herself one leisurely pass by Ron's parking lot to make sure no stray media had staked it out to shoot cutaways of the victim's apartment before she parked and got out. She approached Ron's place with an aloof, I-live-here stroll, took out Ron's keys, unlocked his mailbox. There were a couple bills, one large manila envelope with the return address Zeda A. Banks, a librarian from King County, Texas, written in the sort of penmanship they didn't teach you anymore.

I told that fella Spivak Miss Zeda might be able to dig up a few copies of the old Advisor.

Cat mentally put "Miss Zeda" on her list of people to be called, walked up the stairs, unlocked the door with Ron's keys, let herself in, dredged her pocket for her own key chain, held the keys in her palm, the heavy metal tab loose the way Marco instructed in his self-defense classes. Everything was the same as the day Cici had walked in on her. She closed the door quietly and headed toward the bookcase, her eyes seeing it several seconds before the brain registered. Too many seconds.

A plate and the crust of a sandwich.

Even then, the rationalizing cells tried to tell her that maybe Ron had run home last night for a quick sandwich; then the rational ones, a step behind as always, reminded her that he had gone straight to the set from the airport, reminded her a scant second before she was thrown down on the carpet.

CHAPTER TWENTY-FOUR

INT: MAJOR CRIMES BUREAU: AFTERNOON
CALDERONE is pacing, addressing his unit.

CALDERONE
Miss Auletta claims that Donner's sister showed
up in the club that night, then ran off. As if
she didn't want to be seen.

JOHN NESTOR
Something spooked her.

CALDERONE
Perhaps. But if you're easily spooked, if you
don't want to be seen, a crowded nightclub is
the last place you show yourself, *verdad?*

Victor saw a cluster of guys from Arson and Narcotics hanging
in the doorway, getting autographs signed. Biggs nodded and chatted
diffidently, no posturing, no phony homeboy arrogance. His smile
was congenial, the voice that asked for the correct spelling of each
name before he wrote it out was polite. "When he's finished, show
him into interrogation. Who's his attorney? Robinson?"
"Steve Delareto."

Long didn't often have the opportunity to surprise his commander, see the surprise register. But Victor merely said, "Okay," shook his head. Steve Delareto was an old schoolmate of Cat's and Freddy's; he regarded Cat's relationship with Victor with extreme skepticism, and a touch of envy.

Victor nodded, walked to the interrogation room. He plugged in the audiotape, walked into the room on the other side of the two-way glass and got rid of the detectives who wanted a peek at the show.

Delareto entered, nodded to Victor.

"Counselor," Victor said.

"Lieutenant." Delareto was good-looking in a dapper sort of way, and an efficient lawyer.

"Your client sign a consent to be questioned?"

"He's going over it with Adane, so that he understands the deal."

"Who put you together? Cat?"

Delareto shook his head, smiled. "Jennie. She thinks a nice boy who appreciates good home cooking ought not to be questioned without counsel. And arrest him at your peril, because she's expecting him for supper."

There was a knock on the door and Biggs poked his head in, looked around, a bit shyly. Victor reminded himself that the kid was an actor, that deception was his occupation.

"Take a chair, Mr. Biggs." Victor explained that the questioning was being taped, that Biggs didn't have to answer any questions and could terminate the interview.

Biggs gave the straight oak chair a once-over, sat gingerly, testing his weight on the four slender legs. "You go ahead ax me what you want, I don't know what I can tell you, I was in my trailer all night, mostly."

"Why were you on the set, Mr. Biggs?"

"I's in the background for some of the interior shoot, then they's gonna shoot the next scene, where the cop— Hey, that's you, man."

The kid chuckled. "Where the cop comes scopes the d.b.? I got a couple lines. After the hit, you know the crowd comes outta the club and the cops gotta hold them off? I say, 'It ain't Gerry! Gerry ain't dead! He can't be!' So after the dinner break, I go in the trailer."

"Alone?"

Biggs shook his head. "It's me, a couple of my homes, Mama Jen's boy, Carlo an' his boy, Mark. Dianne come in to get some coffee. Cici in there awhile. Wally goes in to get in the safe. I leave the door open so's people can run in get outta the cold, it's real cold."

"But you went out into the cold."

"Jus' to watch Tommi Ann. It's a treat to watch Tommi Ann. I forget ..." He shook his head. "I keep forgettin'—it's like ..." he shook his head, decided not to wrack his brains for a simile, simply said, "I don't always remember how I can't just walk down a street no more."

Victor nodded, slowly. "Mr. Biggs, how well did you know Ron Spivak?"

"I seen him on the set."

"He didn't approach you, try to set up an interview, anything like that?"

Biggs shook his head.

Delareto turned to him. "They're tape recording this, Mr. Biggs, so you'll have to give a verbal reply."

"Oh, yeah. No, he didn't talk to me about nothin' like that. Unless he axed Dianne. Stuff like that anyway goes through Ben's office for Dianne to set up."

"Mr. Biggs, how did Ben Butler come to represent you?"

"I's between hauls and me an' some homes hook up an' we're rappin' down by Fortieth and Broadway. Tommi Ann comes by one day, I don't recognize her at first, she's got dark glasses on and her hair all tied back and she walks right up to us and she stands there and listens for five and she coughs up a C. Cops come give us the boost, an' they're axin' our names, I'm thinkin' we gonna get arrested, but Tommi Ann comes over,

she says somethin' to the cop an' they just lemme go an' I see the way
they lookin' at her, she somebody. An' she goes, 'Biggs, is it? I know
di'lects, I think I hear West Texas in those vowels of yours' and I say
'uh-huh,' 'cause that's where I from. She says 'I'm Tommi Ann Butler'
and do I got a demo tape, and do I wanna come meet her husband and
I'm like, I must be on somethin'. I mean, I don't got a lotta spare cash,
but even I get to the movies, I know who Tommi Ann Butler is. I do a
few raps for Ben and he says where'm I from, do I got family and stuff,
and he says he wants to sign me. Puts me together with music people
and dance people, whaddaya call them, choreographers? An' he got me
a place in the city and he got some lawyer get Jonah and Charlene outta
foster care and move them to New York wit' me."

"Who are Jonah and Charlene?"

"My brother an' sister. My folks, they's never married, they both run
out, my grammpop, my mom's dad? He took us in, raised us up good
enough, but he was old. He's a trucker, hauled liquor and pop down
Tijuana an' back. So I gotta be in charge a lot at home, look after 'em."

"Where's home?"

"Finery, Texas." He chuckled. "Town not much bigger than this
office but all the space in the world around it. Anyway, gramps died,
I tried to hold it together, but they put my brother an' sister in foster
care. All I know how to do to make me some money was drive a
truck. Guy gimme work on a vendin' machine route. He hooks me
up with a carrier hauls produce 'round the country. I don't wanna
go off an' leave the kids, but money's a lot better an' I figure I put
enough by, I be able to go to court and get Charlene and Jonah back.
I mean, where they put 'em wasn't bad or nothin', but they's blood,
you know what I'm sayin'?"

Victor remembered what it had been like at fourteen, his father
killed, and everyone telling him he was the man of the family now. As
if, at fourteen, devastated, he was man enough for anything. Thought
of how he still worried about his mother, who was working and self-

sufficient, about Milly, who had a husband and two children, about Remy. "Yes," Victor said, quietly. "I know exactly what you're saying." He paused. "Didn't you think that was an odd coincidence, though? Mrs. Butler just happens by?"

Biggs looked at him. "Man, you ever read the Book?"

"Book?"

"The Bible, man. My grammpop, he read it day and night. Angel of the Lord come by the 'hood, go out to the fields to tell folks the way it's gonna go down, nobody goes, 'Angel, how come you stoppin' by here, this ain't your usual stomp.' Angel say, 'Son of God gonna be born right under that star there,' they don't go 'Right here where we at? Well, ain't' that a coincidence.' They just go by what the angel got to say."

Victor stroked his mustache thoughtfully, saw Delareto rein in a smile. "And Tommi Ann Butler was your angel?"

Biggs looked at him earnestly. "I's drivin' a truck. I's on the corner, rappin' for change. Tommi Ann walks by an' my whole life turn around, you see what I'm sayin? That don't make someone a angel, I don't know what does."

"So, I guess there's not much you wouldn't do for the Butlers."

"Let's not go there, Victor," Delareto interjected.

"Hey, I don't care who knows. There's nothin' I wouldn't do for them, man. Tommi Ann, Ben, Dianne, Cici, they's my family. They want me to do for them, they don't gotta ax twice."

"Let's move on to last night. You said you wanted to watch Tommi Ann work. You have a lot of opportunities to do that, don't you? What was so special about this time?"

Biggs grinned, sheepishly. "Spivak, I don't think he treated Cici right, she real upset wit' him, I figure it'd be a kick watch him get shot."

"Let's delete that," Delareto said.

The weight on top of her shifted, trying to pin her arm in back of her. Cat raised her neck and wedged her free hand behind her head, grabbed a handful of the face behind her shoulder, felt her fingers dig into a soft, fleshy cheek, her thumb compress the bridge of a nose; enough to startle the assailant and loosen up his grip. Cat rolled back onto her right side and snapped her left leg; her foot connected with a beefy thigh and she saw, through the hair in her eyes, the face of the powder man, Wally. She rotated her wrist, yanked it free from his grasp and grabbed for the key ring she had dropped, shoved her car key toward his face, bracing her fist on his forehead, holding the sharp, narrow metal tip of the key a half an inch from his left eye. "You even inhale the wrong way, I'll shove this clear through to the ceiling light fixture in the downstairs apartment."

She was lying, of course, but it seemed like a Kate Auletta way to handle the situation, since he was the one who attacked her, a fugitive from the law, and all.

He raised his hands to either side of his head, palms up. "Look, I didn't know who the hell you were, I thought you were the cops."

"The cops are on their way," she lied.

"When'd you call 'em?"

"Just now. From my car phone."

"You don't have a car phone. You got a navy Maxima and you don't got a car phone."

Cat told herself she had to get a car phone. A cell. Marco had been after her forever about driving around without one. "How do you know what I drive?"

"I checked out *NewsLineNinety* this morning, they got a shot of your place. You had a lotta company outside. I was gonna wait awhile, see if they took off, pay you a visit."

Cat angled the key closer to his eye, the point against his pale lashes. "I got kids in that house. You're lucky you didn't come by my house." She didn't need a Kate Auletta spin for that line; this, she said with feeling.

"Look, I know that guy was a pal of yours."

"Ron Spivak."

"Lemme up."

Cat hesitated. Then she sprang back, got on her feet and sprinted toward the door, ready to scream, expecting him on her heels. Her hand on the knob, she heard, "Look, I thought he was a real hustler, I didn't like him, but I know how to do my job and I never loaded the damn gun. I'm not gonna take the fall for whoever it was screwed up and got your pal whacked."

Cat turned. He hadn't moved from the spot, except to shift to a sitting position, his back against the coffee table. "If it wasn't loaded, how could it fire?" she asked.

"Hero model we used for the close-ups had a head in it. Metal tip, so Red could shoot a close-up of the chamber, it would look like there was a round in it. Red's a pain, pan here, pan there, move in on the hand, back to the gun, down the barrel, to the chamber so you can see the head."

Cat nodded to show she was following.

"Second weapon had two blanks. For the shots. They were both on the table. Pig does his little meet and greet, Anderson puts down his piece while we're on crowd control. He shouldn'ta let go of it. I pick it up, slap it into his hand, give him hell for putting it down."

"You handed him the wrong gun."

"Don't you get it? There *was* no wrong gun. He fires the one with the head, it goes 'click.' He fires the one with the blanks, it goes 'bang.' Someone hadda put the two together, chamber a blank in back of the head."

"Which would turn a metal capsule into a projectile?"

"What, you never hocked spitballs outta a straw?"

"Not recently."

"Same principle. Don't need to be a fuckin' Isaac Newman—"

"Newton."

"—to know that if you got a hard object and you back it up with powder, it's gonna blow. Any SAG deadbeat got two lines playin' a blue in *Just In Crime* knows that."

"Why were both guns out? Why didn't you keep the one with the blanks locked up until right before you needed it?"

"You ever been on a television shoot?"

Cat shook her head. "This is my first." *Last.*

"All you see from your POV is how slow everything goes, but lemme tell you, the meter's runnin'. You wanna bet that little stunt of Pig's cost a few hundred? Kid's such a jerk, it's like he hasn't figured out how a gander at him sets 'em off. I mean, what planet's he livin' on? Doesn't he ever read *Billboard*, f'Crissakes?"

He can't read, Cat thought. "And in the confusion, that's when someone could have put a blank in the chamber behind the metal tip? I don't see how that lets you off the hook."

His mouth twisted and he emitted a dry laugh. "Kate—"

"Cat."

"There's no way I'm off the hook, I won't be working again anytime soon, not on a film crew. I'm done. But somebody's tryin' to make me the patsy and I don't like it."

"Who? And why?"

"You didn't see how high Spivak was last night? He had some red hot copy and someone was about to get torched."

Cat closed her hand tightly over the doorknob, gave it a stealthy turn. "Like what? Take two, they're free?"

Wally looked at her. His blue eyes were red-rimmed, weary, but not particularly guileful. "What, that piece he ran last year? That's old news. Look. An actress, she sees a costume she likes, she helps herself to a piece of jewelry, it's just a 'gotta keep 'em happy' write-off. Hell, I knew one actress had it in her contract end of every week of the shoot, she hadda get a little cake and a present that hadda cost five bills, minimum. Like it's her fuckin' birthday every week. By the end of the shoot, she's had more birthdays than she'd admit to on her bio sheet. She don't get her cake and her goodies, she's gonna get herself a case of those creative differences and we're in limbo until she snaps to. Limbo? We're in hell. But me, I run off some outtakes, make ten bucks a cut, I'm a thief."

"So you're saying Ron wasn't going to blow the whistle on your pirating operation?"

"How would I know? I didn't exchange two words with the guy."

"You didn't want him dead?"

"I won't say I didn't wanna smack him over, but I want my whack at him, I'm gonna have to get in line behind just about everyone else."

"Who, specifically?"

"April, for one. I had a dime for every time she said she was gonna shoot him, I could retire. I got the feeling Anderson wasn't too crazy about him, but I'm thinking he was snapping outta that since things were looking up for him. With Cici Bonaker and all. Now Cici, she was really turned off to him. And you know what they say when Cici ain't happy, ain't nobody happy. She's the only one I know did have words with him that night."

"How do you know that?"

"June Mathis told me. June says she's cutting through the kitchen to Makeup, up in the loft? She's on the back stairs and she can hear them real clear. June says Cici's goin' 'Whatever you have, can't it wait, at least until after the Oscars?' He goes, 'Baby, it's five days to the Oscars. I'm gonna sweat it out five days and hope somebody else doesn't jump me?' And she goes, 'How can they if nobody else knows,' and he goes, 'Don't bet on it, somebody figures out where I been puts two and two together, by the weekend it could be all over the Internet.'"

"Did you mention this to anyone?"

"Anderson, when we were workin' out his moves. I don't know if Dianne or one of the cops heard me, I just said, like, 'Cici, she's really worked up, I think she and Spivak had words' and Harold, he goes, 'Cici's just worked up about the show goin' series.'"

"So what're you going to do?"

"I'm thinking the cops won't believe me. And it goes down I was responsible for a loaded firearm on the set, I'll never pack heat in H-wood again. Unless," he studied her. "Unless you can help me."

"Help you what?"

"Find out who turned me into the fall guy."

"What makes you think I can?"

"Hell, you're Kate Auletta."

"No I'm not."

"C'mon, they couldn'ta made all that up, trust me, I worked with screenwriters, they're not that bright."

"What do I get in exchange?" Bartering with a possible felon; at least she was thinking like Kate Auletta.

"A story. Hell, that's all you want anyway, isn't it, a good story? It's all Spivak wanted."

"And end up like Ron? I'd have to be nuts."

"You're not nuts. I read the Dudek piece. They shoulda got you to write the damn script, insteada that hack Anderson. Hack writer, I should say, he's a damn good actor."

"Was he a good shot?" Cat asked.

"What, you mean could Hal handle a gun? Yeah. You didn't see *South Street Stakeout?*"

Cat shrugged. "So, if he was aiming toward Ron, or *at* Ron, it's almost certain he'd *hit* Ron."

"Not 'almost.' Dead certain. Spivak was half the distance, he might still be alive," Wally added.

"How so?"

"At close range, with a blank? There could be some blowout, so you cheat the shot. But Spivak was far enough away so none of the wadding would hit him. Plus Red was real particular about the angle."

"So everyone within earshot knew that Harold was reasonably comfortable with a firearm, took direction faithfully and was told to aim directly at Ron."

Wally got to his feet, rubbed the back of his hand over his chin, shook his head. "Well, it's been nice chattin' with you. I don't see those cops you said you called, but I figure you'll dime me out five minutes after you split, so I may as well hit the road myself." He looked at her earnestly. "My mistake was not checking the piece when I handed it back to Anderson. But I didn't load it, Mrs. Austen."

Cat turned the knob, opened the door an inch.

A click, a hollow, whirring ring coming from the bedroom.

Cat froze. The fax machine in the bedroom.

"What the hell ..?" Wally demanded.

"It's the fax machine." Someone faxing Ron, or communicating with Wally? How had he gotten in the apartment, anyway? She had Ron's keys, Ron's spares.

Wally stalked into the bedroom. Cat heard him muttering, "Where does the damn sheet come out?"

She took a few tenuous steps toward a short hallway between the living room and the bedroom. Who else could have given Wally a key? Who else had a key?

Cici.

Her peripheral vision caught a fleeting shadow passing behind the translucent curtains drawn across the sliding glass doors. Had someone overheard them, called the police?

"There's no damn fax— Hey! *HEY!*"

Wally made a lateral dive into the hallway. Cat heard a crystalline explosion, and it took a few seconds for her to realize that it had come in the wake of a shot.

Wally shoved her into the tiny powder room, backed out, yanked the door closed.

Another shot.

Don't move, don't move, don't move.
Don't breathe, don't breathe, don't breathe.
Breathe, breathe, breathe.

Absurdly, she thought of *South Street Stakeout*, heard Ron's lines in her head, "He's got a gun! He's got a *gun*!"

She heard her own panting, in and out, echoing in the small, tiled chamber.

Move? Freeze? Scream? Hush? Hide? Run?

She heard the front door open, close.

Weapon? Weapon? She realized she didn't even have the key ring she had used against Wally. She crawled along the tiles, pulled herself up, opened the medicine cabinet. A bottle of isopropyl alcohol, half full. A fine-toothed comb. Nail scissors.

She sat there for half an hour, armed for combat.

CHAPTER TWENTY-FIVE

INT: KATE'S APARTMENT: AFTERNOON
*Camera follows KATE as she surveys her trashed
apartment. Dazed, she picks up the phone and
dials 911.*

DISPATCHER'S VOICE
Nine-one-one police emergency. What's your
location?

KATE
My apartment. Somebody broke into my apartment
and trashed it.

DISPATCHER'S VOICE
Is the intruder still inside, ma'am?

CUT TO: CLOSE UP
*KATE clearly has not considered the fact
that the intruder might be in her apartment.*

Victor heard the short rap on the two-way glass, excused himself.
Stan Rice met him in the corridor. "Look, I don't mean to interrupt,
and everything's probably okay, they've already got a couple units on
the way to the scene and they said she's not hurt."

Victor sighed. "I think proper nouns would be more accurate than pronouns, Sergeant, although I believe I can safely transpose Mrs. Austen's name for the 'she.'"

"She's—Cat—she's over Spivak's apartment, there was some kind of run-in, some guy jumped her, they think it might have been Reid. There were shots fired. She's okay."

"Where's the assailant?"

"He split."

Victor felt the iron in his jaw. "I was just finishing in there, get Adane to transcribe his statement and have him sign it. Don't say anything to Delareto about Mrs. Austen, and call Mrs. Butler's suite and tell her I'll be delayed."

"Gotcha."

Victor signed out, strode out of the building, felt their eyes in his wake, wondered what the hell she was doing snooping around Spivak's apartment like the headstrong heroine in some damned TV show.

The dispatcher seemed coolly indifferent to Cat's declaration that her car had been stolen by a man wanted for questioning in Atlantic County, only marginally more impressed when Cat added that shots had been fired at the Bayside Condos, but livened up considerably when Cat added that the suspect had been attached to the *CopWatch* production.

Within two minutes, Cat heard the whine of a mobile unit, the crunch of tires on the gravelly surface of the parking lot, the tramp of footsteps on the thin metal stairs. She had left the door open, was sitting on the arm of the couch when two uniformed officers approached, the point man with his weapon drawn, the other with one hand on his hip, walking a cautious, sidling gait.

"Ma'am, can you step over where we can see you?"

Cat rose, stepped into the shaft of light thrown by the open door.

The cop who brought up the rear said, "Mrs. Austen?"

"Yes." Cat was surprised at how normal her voice sounded, how businesslike while she was thinking that Most Likely To Be Found In Proximity To A Crime Scene should have been her yearbook category.

"I gotta ask what you were doing here, Mrs. Austen."

"I'd been watching this apartment for Mr. Spivak—"

"Guy got shot over AC last night?"

Cat nodded. "He had asked me to take in his mail, said I could borrow one of his videotapes. I came by to borrow—" she swallowed. "Can you borrow from someone who died?"

"Why'n'cha sit back down, ma'am."

Cat sank back onto the arm of the couch. "I forgot to pick up the tape last time I was here, I came by, I took in his mail, and was coming in to get the tape and he—jumped me. I— He said he thought I might be a cop. He let up when he recognized me."

"You knew him?"

Cat pushed a strand of hair behind her ear. "His name's Wally Reid. The Atlantic City DA's got a warrant out for him, I think."

"The guy who was handling the guns for *CopWatch*?"

"Yes."

The other officer associated her name with a previous event. "Spivak got himself roughed up last fall, you were the one to come in here, find him, as I recall. You think that's odd?"

"Officer—" she squinted to read the nameplate clipped to his breast pocket, "Rieck—am I pronouncing that right? For the past week, I've been watching a television crew film their version of something that I lived through, distorting the facts so thoroughly I don't even recognize events I was part of, not to mention having Tommi Ann Butler playing someone who's supposed to be me, the fact that I was in that parking lot last night when Ron Spivak was shot just like I was there when Jerry Dudek got shot. I'm watching a bad movie of my own life being"—she was losing it, she could hear it in her voice—"being committed to celluloid or whatever they use today and I walk in here, get jumped, get shot at and have my car stolen and *you want to know if I think something's ODD?*"

"Ma'am, just calm down, please."

"I've got the rest of my *life* to calm down!"

Cat heard the approach of another car, heard the car door open, slam. A plainclothes detective entered the room, with a cop's purposeful, I'm-in-charge gait, the pan-and-scan survey of the scene.

"Mrs. Austen, Detective Sergeant Booker."

Cat tried a smile, failed.

"I know your brothers, Mrs. Austen. You've been drumming up quite a bit of business for the profession lately, you think maybe you can lay off a month or so, until the book gets closed on a couple of them?"

"I'll give it my best ..." *Shot.*

The first officer recited, "She says she came in to drop the owner's mail, pick up a tape he said she could have, the guy jumped her when she walked in, they talked a few minutes, then someone fired shots through the bedroom window, the guy took off with her wheels."

"How'd he get in here?"

Cat shook her head.

"He say anything to you?"

"He said he'd been set up. That he didn't load the gun that shot Ron Spivak, but because the firearms were his responsibility, he was going to take the fall."

There was a firm, steady footstep on the metal stairs outside the open door. Cat realized, even through her distress, that she recognized it, and the realization rattled her. She had come to know Chris' footstep on the porch steps that way, knew the rhythm of him. How was it she had come to identify Victor's so soon?

Victor stepped into the room, his eyes directed at her, revealing nothing, only fixing on her a few seconds before he produced his ID for Booker.

Booker nodded, turned back to Cat. "And you were having this chat in the bedroom?"

Cat winced. "No, out here. Then the fax machine kicked in and he went in to check it out, he was having trouble finding the fax, and I—" she turned and looked at the sliding door. "I thought I saw someone, out of the corner of my eye, someone walking along the deck outside. And then I heard him yell, and he came flying out of the room and there were shots and he pushed me into the powder room there." Cat twisted a strand of hair with shaking fingers, pushed it behind her ear. "I heard the shots, the glass breaking, but—" *Everything happened so fast.* That's what Kate would say, but she'd respond fast, too, wouldn't have let herself get trapped in a bathroom with half a bottle of alcohol, a comb and nail scissors.

"You touch anything in the bedroom?"

"I didn't go in there. I waited about half an hour and then I came out and called you."

"Let's have a look." The detective put a hand under her elbow. Cat felt Victor's gaze, steady, unreadable.

They walked into Ron's bedroom. The shots had punched holes in the drapes. There was a dark indentation beside the closet where the round had embedded itself in the wall. A spray of glass lay over the bedspread and carpet.

Booker examined the fax tray. "Nothing here. Drapes open or shut?"

"When I was here before, the sheers were closed, the others were tied back. Like they are now."

"I was hidin' out in here, I woulda shut the drapes," remarked one of the uniforms.

"Maybe not," Cat suggested. "Not if you thought one of Ron's neighbors might have noticed a change, gotten the manager or the police to check it out. The off-season isolation in a place like this? It cuts both ways. Fewer people to observe something that's out of place, but what's out of place is more conspicuous. If I were a fugitive, I'd leave as much as possible as it was."

Victor walked back into the living room, let himself out the sliding glass doors in the living room onto the long narrow deck that ran along the bay side of the building. He examined the shattered sliding door of the bedroom. Through the translucent curtains, he could see the silhouettes of Cat and the officers clearly enough. The shooter had seen Wally Reid. *Dialed the fax number to line him up for the kill shot?*

He looked around the deck. It was weather-worn, the wooden planks faded to a dull gray-brown by salt air, sun, time. It was scuffed and scored with the marks of dozens of shoes, deck chairs, portable grills, the paraphernalia people crammed onto their tiny bayfront turf. A small overhang above; the floor he stood on was the roof for the first-floor deck below.

He walked back in. One of the uniforms was on the way out. "Gonna knock on a few doors. Prob'ly not more than two, three occupied, but it's worth a shot."

Cat was sitting on the arm of the couch, her hands clasped in her lap. Victor lowered himself onto the padded arm of a chair, faced her. "Well, Mrs. Austen."

Cat looked at him. Belladonna pupils, the eyes of a cat making its way in the dark. "I knew your footstep," she said softly, her tone slightly amazed. "I knew it wasn't another cop, or the building manager coming up. I knew it was you"—she fluttered her index finger past her ear—"just by the sound."

Booker came out of the bedroom. "Look, you two don't have to stick around. You come down later for a statement, file a report on your car, okay? How'd he get the keys, anyway?"

"I had them in my hand. I dropped them when he pushed me into the powder room."

"I meant keys to this place? Doesn't look like there's any sign of forced entry."

Cat hesitated. "I don't know. I've got both sets of Ron's keys."

"There's a third," Victor said. "Miss Bonaker, one of the actresses. She and Spivak had been close for a while last year, she had a key."

"Can I go now?" Cat asked.

"Yeah. You good to drive?"

"All I need is the car."

"We'll get it back," Booker said, confidently. "One more question, Mrs. Austen."

Cat sighed.

"Tommi Ann Butler. What's she really like?"

Victor drove Cat home, walked her in. "Are you going to be all right by yourself?"

"I'm not going to be by myself. There are hundreds of people over at the Phoenix."

"And how do you propose to get to the Phoenix?"

"You're taking me."

"And what makes you think I'm going to the Phoenix?"

"Because you haven't interviewed Tommi Ann yet."

"How do you know that?"

"Have you?"

"No."

"See? But you'll have to wait until I get changed, I'm a mess. And there's something I want to show you."

"That sounds inviting."

"Wait here."

"That sounds less inviting."

Cat sprinted up to her bedroom, pried off her shoes, wriggled out of her jeans. The struggle with Wally had pulled large looping threads from the weave in her sweater. She shucked it off and threw it on the floor, pulled on a long, loose denim skirt, a white tunic sweater, rooted around under the bed for her white leather sneakers with one hand, while she reached for the phone with the other, made a quick call to her mother's to talk to the kids.

She grabbed the photocopied articles she had gotten from Ron's car. Articles he had obtained with the assistance of Zeda Banks. Why hadn't she brought Ron's mail with her? No matter, it was probably nothing more than additional photocopies from the *Advisor*, stringing out the saga of Sheriff Sontag's murder. Cat dialed Information, got the number of the county library and asked for either head librarian or Miss Banks, got both in one. Miss Zeda Banks informed Cat that she was not only head librarian, but the only librarian, "Except for the Guild Ladies who volunteer now and again and the boys from the high school class who come in to show us how to use the new computers."

"I'm calling from New Jersey," Cat explained. "I'm a friend of Ron Spivak's."

"Such a mannerly young man." Miss Banks had the sweet, ageless voice of a woman bred to civility from the cradle. "You don't often find that in folks"—*from the East*—"today."

"You helped him find some articles from an old newspaper."

"Yes, we had to go over to the Historical Society to hunt up copies of the *Advisor.* I finally turned up the obituaries and put them in the mail."

"Couldn't you just fax them to him?"

"Fax it? Oh, my, no." She sounded as if Cat had asked her to do something indecent. "I can't fax anything unless one of the high school boys comes in to show me how."

"I don't suppose you heard what happened to him. Mr. Spivak."

"Happened to him?"

"He was, well, he was killed in an accidental shooting while they were filming a television show around here."

"The show with Tommi Ann Butler? Oh, my."

"Miss Banks, I had been collaborating with Ron, but I'm not sure what he wanted this material for."

"I believe he said he was doing a story on Gloria Ramirez. You know she's a King County girl."

"Yes, I've heard."

"I believe he said he wanted to look up the folks in her high school class. He spoke to Davey Wheeler. My, my, that boy has gone places."

"Professionally, you mean."

"I beg your pardon?"

"I mean, he's still living in King County."

"Oh, yes. My. Do you know what he did when he got the money for that book? Why, he bought computers to put here in the public library. Think of it."

Cat couldn't help herself, said, "My."

"Computers. My, my."

"So Ron was asking about Gloria Ramirez's high school class?"

"What became of them. They did all right by themselves, except for the one."

"The Sontag boy."

"My, and wasn't that a scandal. You'd reckon *CopWatch* would want to do a story on that, wouldn't you, for all it's been, Lord. More than twenty-five years now."

"He ran away with a girl named Annie Cox. They hitched a ride to Mexico to get married."

"I expect they figured the folks wouldn't be too p'ticular down there about matters. I believe they gave that fella a hard time, the one gave them a ride across the border. Why, the story was, he actually stood as witness when they got themselves married."

"You wouldn't remember his name, would you? The man who helped the Sontag boy and the Cox girl run away to Mexico?"

"Why Mr. Spivak asked the same thing. I do believe it was Briggs, or Riggs or something like that. I wouldn't even remember that much, except the police brought the poor fella in for questioning when Big Tom Sontag got himself killed."

"Did they ever find out who did it?"

"No. But," Miss Banks lowered her voice, though Cat suspected eavesdroppers were few, unless the Guild Ladies were listening in. "I asked that poor Spivak boy not to print this. If there was ever a man needed killin', it was Big Tom. Handsome as the devil and ten times as wicked. He just bullied his poor wife to death. She put herself between plenty of blows meant for poor TJ, that boy was her baby, but once she was gone, Big Tom—" She sighed. "The girls got themselves married and left Imogene behind, left that poor sweet boy with that old monster. You woulda thought at least one of them woulda taken poor TJ in, he wouldna been a lick of trouble. And that little Cox girl didn't have it much better over to her sister's. One of TJ's teachers actually tried to talk the Sheriff and the Coxes into letting her raise those children, but I guess there's some folks just need themselves a whipping boy, or worse. Two lost souls didn't fit in anywhere; it's no wonder they found their way to each other. Today, children like that, they go shoot up a school." She sighed again. "What are we doing to our children? I used to ask the Lord why he didn't see fit to find me a husband, give me children of my own, now I figure, maybe it was a blessing."

"You said one of the high school teachers wanted to adopt them?"

"Mrs. Diaz. And her with five children of her own. And Annie getting herself in the family way. But she didn't care, Raquel Diaz was one of those folks whose heart's like to bust what with all the love they have to give. She taught English. Still does, though I hear her granddaughter'd be more than willing to make her comfortable enough to retire."

Grandmother? "She must be terribly proud of Teresa D."

"My, yes. We've got quite a few folks around here did all right by themselves."

Or had a bit of help, Cat thought. "And this is what Ron Spivak was asking about?"

"Mostly, yes. He seemed mighty interested in Annie Cox, what became of her, and her baby. After she and TJ run off, nobody ever heard from them again. Oh, the law made a show of hunting them up when they found Big Tom, but I don't believe anyone looked all that hard." She sighed for the third time. "There wasn't much to either one of them. Why little Annie didn't weigh more than a ten-year-old. The voice of an angel, though. I don't believe I ever heard a sweeter voice. Nothin' to her at all but that voice and those eyes of hers, eyes like moonlight. I don't know why, but I can still see those staring eyes of hers, for all it's been a good twenty-five years since she and the Sontag boy disappeared."

Perhaps, Cat thought, *you can still see those eyes of hers because you have seen them, looking down from a thirty-foot screen into the dark.*

CHAPTER TWENTY-SIX

INT: KATE'S APARTMENT: AFTERNOON
KATE is scrutinizing her apartment; CALDERONE

CALDERONE
You look like someone whose thoughts are
ripe with mischief.

KATE (surprised)
Twelfth Night?

CALDERONE
What? You never met a cop who reads Shakespeare?

KATE
I've never met a cop who reads, period.

"What kept you? I was starting to wonder what sort of mischief
you were up to."

Cat handed him the photocopies. "Don't be silly, Victor. I'm
limiting myself to one skirmish per day; I've had my quota."

"Pencil me in for tomorrow." He glanced over the papers. "What
are these?"

"They're copies of an article that appeared in a small-town Texas
paper, twenty-five years ago."

Victor scanned them, one eyebrow peaked. "'Severely dismembered'? Hmm ... 'mutilations to his person ...'" He looked up. "Where'd you get them?"

"From the long-defunct Imogene *Weekly Advisor*, Imogene, Texas. Ron had to go to a lot of trouble to find these articles; he had to think they were relevant."

"Spivak gave these to you?"

"Well ... technically, yes."

Victor sighed. "Define 'technically.'"

"Before Ron left on Saturday, when he asked me to check on his place? He said I could look over his files, that I might find some material I might use for features on Cici or Harold."

"I don't see anything that relates to Cici Bonaker or Anderson here."

"There isn't."

Victor looked at his watch, sank into a chair with an exaggerated sigh.

"Okay, I found these in an overnight bag in his car. Apparently, he photocopied them on his Texas trip."

"And how did you get in his car?"

"It's *not* breaking and entering if you have a key, don't tell me it is." Cat settled onto the arm of one of the overstuffed chairs, pushed her hair behind her ear.

"Why don't we just keep this on a hypothetical plane? Just tell it to me like you're writing a script."

"Interior, nightclub, night. Kate Auletta, smart, sassy ace reporter slinks up—"

"Cut. 'Slinks'?"

Cat nodded. "It's one of Harold's favorite verbs. I think his electrons slink around his nuclei. Slinks up to the loft where slimy DJ Gerry Donner—"

"Ron."

"Right. —Is touching up his makeup, remarking about a recent skirmish, probably with Harold."

"Are you saying Anderson roughed Spivak up shortly before he was killed?"

"He didn't look very roughed up, but he made some crack about going a couple rounds and I know that Cici asked Harold to talk to Ron."

"How do you know this?"

"From Cici. And Harold mentioned it this morning."

"You talked to Anderson this morning?"

Cat nodded. "He called to ask how I was doing. I'd seen April yelling at him about waiting until after the shoot to cross swords with someone; he said he just asked Ron to hold off on whatever it was Cici was concerned about."

"He doesn't know what it is? Bonaker didn't tell him about the adoption, or Spivak's suspicions?"

"Apparently not. He said Ron brushed him off and then he got called over to do a run-through and then they started, well, shooting."

"How'd Anderson sound?"

"A little dazed. The Butlers moved him over to the Phoenix."

"Spin control?"

Cat shrugged. "April seems to think so."

"So tell me what Wally Reid said to you."

Cat repeated the conversation, told him about the article *Take Two, They're Free*. "That's why I went over to Ron's. After I'd read the article, I remembered a video I'd seen at Ron's place, some outtakes from *South Street Stakeout*. I wanted to check it out."

"Reid come off as credible?"

Cat lifted her brows, nodded.

"Is Spivak's car still parked on Fairmount?"

"I guess."

"And this folder is all that you took?"

"Yes. And that makes me think Wally might be telling the truth. I mean, Ron went to Texas, talked to Davey Wheeler, went to the trouble of getting these articles copied. I think he was on to something a lot deeper than prop pilfering."

"Then why did Wally run?"

Cat's gaze was patronizing. "Victor, who had custody of the weapons, the powder? Wally's the perfect fall guy, and he seemed very determined not to take the fall."

Victor rose, cupped her chin in his hand, tilted her face toward his. "I don't want you to find yourself alone with a very determined suspect again, you understand?"

Cat looked at him, saw something in his gaze. "You hate this, don't you? Not Ron's death, that's routine for you. But the shoot. I knew you didn't like it, but you hate it."

"I do hate it. I hate seeing what was real, even the corrupt reality of the Dudek case, twisted to put a bump in the overnights and launch the pilot for *Auletta*. Exclamation point."

"I know ..." She shook her head. "I keep seeing last November in my head. But the words I hear are lines from the script. I feel like I can't remember what I know happened." *Reality is what you make it.* "And you're talking to someone. Jerry Dudek, Ron." *Kevin. Kevin.* "And they imprint on your life and then they're gone. And it's like ... And it's like ... it doesn't sink in. I still turn on the radio in the morning, and half expect to hear the Six A.M. Circus, hear Jerry Dudek. I still ..."

"Expect to hear Chris' footstep on the porch."

Cat shook her head. "Not anymore."

Victor took her shoulders, more gently now. "It's all right." He kissed her hair. "Sometimes, not often, I see a woman in a crowd, I see a certain texture of the hair, a certain rhythm in the step and I expect her to turn, to be Marisol. And I was there when she died. I imagine that sensation is even more profound when the last you saw someone, he was alive."

"I wonder if Tommi Ann provokes that? I wonder if there's anyone left who looks at her and says, 'I knew you when you were Annie Cox'? You'd think there'd be something that would survive, that couldn't be transformed, wouldn't you? You'd think that someone would see it in her eyes ..."

"Wheeler didn't."

"Neither does Miss Banks, apparently."

"Who's Miss Banks?"

"These were old articles, from a town that's been wiped off the map. I figured Ron had to get them from a library or historical society. Miss Banks is the local librarian. I called her."

"When?"

"Just now. Goodness, what did you think I was doing up there? How long do you think it takes me to throw on a skirt and sweater?"

Victor arched an eyebrow. "And what did you and Miss Banks talk about?"

"Let's head over to the Phoenix, I'll tell you in the car."

Cat settled in the passenger seat, recited her conversation with Zeda Banks. "Tommi Ann's bio is pretty sketchy, says she's from somewhere in Kansas. But the geography that she's linked to most strongly is an area of West Texas that most of Butler's clients come from. Wheeler and Ramirez—that's why I suspected that Ron might be doing something on Butler's clients. The teacher who tried to help the Cox and Sontag kids is Teresa D.'s grandmother. And Biggs," Cat added, significantly, "was the name of the man who gave those kids a lift to Mexico." *He's a trucker, hauled liquor and pop down Tijuana an' back.* "I suppose I can't come with you when you interview Tommi Ann."

"You suppose correctly."

The Phoenix lobby throbbed like a hive, jangled with the cadence of idleness and waste, buzzers, bells, whistles mingling with the rattle of change, the murmurs and shouts. It was alive with scandal and celebrity and the cash that followed in their wake. Sterling's hubris had failed to generate what a few days' worth of contact with Hollywood had done. Of course, how much of the take had to do with the prospect of a glimpse of Tommi Ann Butler or Bigg Phat P.I.G., the *CopWatch* shoot or last night's scandal was irrelevant as far as receipts were concerned. Cat was certain Sterling didn't care why his slot machine lounges, restaurants, shopping mezzanine were filled, as long as the wallets emptied, as long as he could take credit for it when the quarterly revenues were tallied.

They ascended the escalators to the mezzanine level, a broad avenue of upscale shops. Cat saw the news crews marking time in front of CapriOH!, saw Karen Friedlander pacing irritably, her eyes flicking to her watch, waiting for a Tommi Ann Butler press conference to materialize. Media presence seemed to stimulate the flow of traffic in the direction of the boutique where Remy was holding her show.

Victor glanced at the crowd milling in front of Remy's chiffon and gemstone treasure chest. "I had no idea that a couple postcards and flyers were that effective," he said.

Cat felt a wave of hilarity mixed with a trace of guilt. She kept Victor between her and the roving eyes of the press.

"Where will you be?" he asked her.

"I'm going up to Twenty-five. Harold told me that he'd been set up with a *Front Cover* interview."

Victor turned to her. "Damage control?"

"Or image control," Cat shrugged. "Or both."

"That's impressive control over an image the media hasn't had time to damage," Victor commented. "And if the media's marking time down in the mezzanine, Anderson's interview may be off limits to you," he warned her.

"To the real-life Kate Auletta? Don't be silly."

"Meet me down here in an hour."

***

Victor took the elevator to the floor above, found Danny Furina stationed in the hallway outside the penthouses. Furina's dark eyes were wicked. "Hey, Lieutenant, I heard you guys had Wally Reid, he gave you the slip."

"He a friend of yours, Furina?"

Danny shook his head. "I try to make friends, it's not gonna be with the peons."

"You see Reid during the shoot?"

"Before. I was watching while he worked Anderson."

"How'd he do?" Victor asked.

"What, Anderson? Let's just say that I'm glad I was standing behind the piece rather than in front of it."

"That bad?"

Danny shook his head. "That good. I seen cops who aren't as comfortable with a piece as this guy was. Of course, to him it's just a hand prop. He probably doesn't even think of it like a gun."

"What's a hand prop?"

"Hand prop's anything the actor's got in his hand, an umbrella, a book, a gun, whatever. Two kinds. The background props are cheapo replicas. Look good enough to pass, but they're plastic or tin painted over. The heroes, that's what the stars get or what they use for close-ups. When they fire, they're called 'firing props.'"

"And these can be the real thing?"

Danny nodded. "Were, too. Looked to be forty-one mags. Nice piece of work, but damn hard on the wrist. Heavy."

Victor nodded toward the suite. "Who's around?"

Danny pushed the doorbell to the Butlers' suite. "Anderson, Steinmetz, the Mathis gal were here earlier. Anderson's downstairs, Butler hooked him up with *Front Cover*, they agreed not to run the tape until Raab's made the call on whether he's bringing charges. There's a dressmaker and Mrs. King in there with her now. Butler's out."

"What about the Bonaker girl?"

"Haven't seen her all morning."

Dianne King opened the door to the Butlers' suite. She seemed unperturbed despite an obvious lack of sleep. Her skin was ashen; her rust-colored hair, severely pinned back, revealed the framework of her prominent cheekbones, angular jaw, like a bust in bronze, seamless and immutable.

Tommi Ann Butler was standing on a footstool, her profile outlined against the dull gold sheers at the window, her form framed by the deep gold valance and drapes bordering the broad window. The window overlooked the city; the gold sheers gave a shimmer to the landscape and the twenty-six stories were more than enough to camouflage the unsightly details of the street.

She turned to look at him, her face a work of symmetry, the level cheekbones, the contouring of the jaw, the slightest squaring of the chin. Last night's tragedy had etched no shadows, made no inroads on the lovely face. The camera had not lied to him. Tommi Ann Butler was the most beautiful woman he had ever seen.

"You're staring, Lieutenant."

He smiled, faintly. "My father used to say that there's nothing wrong in staring at a beautiful woman, and something very wrong with you if you don't."

"Was your father an artist?"

"He owned a bodega. You can see where it was from your window with a sharp eye and a bit of imagination."

"And your family lived in a flat above the store."

"That's right."

Remy would kill to be where he was at this moment; Tommi Ann was wearing The Dress, standing on a wooden footstool while a seamstress tugged and squinted at the hem. The gown was strapless and unadorned, no more than a length of thin satin, coated with matching silk chiffon that clung like a cloud to the actress' slender form, shimmered like a living thing when she moved. Its ice blue shade converted her eyes to azure, contrasted perfectly with her warm complexion, the ruddy hair that fell loosely to her shoulders.

"And does he live there still? Your father."

"He was murdered there twenty-six years ago."

The warm complexion cooled and the generous lower lip wavered. Was she thinking of Sheriff Sontag, he wondered?

But she only asked, "Did they find the person who did it?"

"People. Two kids. About my age at the time."

"Tommi, Callie O'Connor's assistant called up and asked if she could have a few minutes when she's finished taping," Dianne said.

It was smooth, very professionally done, and very deliberate, Victor thought. *She doesn't like the subject of the conversation*, he decided. *Why not?*

Tommi Ann addressed the seamstress. "Tell Mrs. Sterling the length is perfect. I'll have Dianne call her this evening." The voice was a low and lovely contralto. Victor heard the practiced enunciation, rhythm, of one who had worn smooth any imperfections of speech that might have bound her to some era, some region. She turned to Victor. "My husband is attending to business, so perhaps you would give us a man's opinion." Tommi Ann smiled and extended a willowy arm.

Victor took her hand and helped her down from the footstool. "It suits you," he said.

The smile shifted, a shadow of melancholy lowered the corners of the eyes. "Perhaps it only serves to 'conceal me what I am and be my aid, for such disguise has haply become the form of my intent.'"

It was a line from *Twelfth Night.* He knew that her film debut had been a modern-dress rendition of the play. "Well, I might reply that 'it is the first quality of a criminal investigator that he should see through a disguise.'"

Her arched brows lifted.

It was Mrs. King who spoke. "Sherlock Holmes. *The Hound of the Baskervilles.*"

"And do you see through mine, Lieutenant?"

"Do you want to be seen, Mrs. Butler?"

The smile relaxed. "Of course not. Disguise is my career. Dianne, you'll have to make some excuse to Ms. O'Connor, I wouldn't want to consent to an interview unless I discussed it with Ben first. Excuse me just for a minute, Lieutenant? And please sit down."

Victor waited for the women to leave the room before he sat, studied the surroundings. The carpet was coppery with a gold border, the furniture earthy velvets, gilt and smoke glass, more to his taste than the anemic Orchid Suite the Sterlings occupied. The walls were covered in an ecru fabric with a border at the top of gilt (or gelded, Victor thought) cherubs. Books that didn't match the surroundings, looked like they had been read, a lamp pushed between the pair of brocade chairs that flanked a small square table with a half-finished game of Scrabble. Victor arched his neck, saw that "lingam" had been intersected by "gonidium" which begat "mutagen." High stakes. A library table against a wall with a stack of books, a copy of *MENSA Mindbenders* lying on top of a vinyl-bound copy of *Death of a Shock Jock*.

He heard the penthouse door open, close, heard a deep voice call out, "Tommi Ann? Tommi Ann, honey?"

Ben Butler walked into the room. He was dressed in jeans and a shearling jacket over a pale blue shirt, a brown plaid muffler hanging loosely around his neck, and carried a sheaf of long-stemmed roses in his fist as casually as if it were a rolled-up newspaper. He looked nothing at all like a talent agent. Perhaps the garb was also intended to conceal what he was, disguise his intent. "Lieutenant? Tommi Ann all right?"

The concern was genuine; so was the adoration when Tommi Ann re-entered the room. She was wearing a green silk robe wrapped around her thin form, stockings but no shoes. Victor watched him as his wife took the flowers, gave him a kiss on the cheek. "I just went down to see that Hal got off to a good start."

"And are they peddling roses on the twenty-fifth floor?"

Butler grinned. "I told Callie to go easy on him. His lawyer's off to the side, to make sure Callie keeps to the straight and narrow." Butler sat on the couch and Tommi Ann nestled beside him, tucking her feet under her. Victor saw her hand steal into his, almost unconsciously.

"There's a hell of a lotta press downstairs," Butler commented. "What's this Furina's tellin' me about Wally Reid?"

"This morning Mrs. Austen went to collect Mr. Spivak's mail and check his apartment as she had been doing this week, it seems that Mr. Reid had been hiding out there."

"No lie?" Butler said.

"I didn't realize he knew Ron Spivak," Tommi Ann commented. "Why would Wally think to go there?"

"I'm more curious to know how he got in there. There was no sign of forced entry."

"Is he under arrest?"

"No. He got away. Took Mrs. Austen's car." He deliberately withheld information of the shooting.

"How awful. Is Mrs. Austen all right?"

"She's fine."

Mrs. King drew a chair beside the couch, sat. "Lieutenant, if he's at large, you don't think that Tommi Ann might be in danger, do you? That he would try to come after her?"

Tommi Ann reached over and patted the woman's arm. Victor thought there was something more than reassurance in the touch, wasn't sure.

"When I asked if Mrs. Austen was all right, I meant last night, too. It must have been horrible for her, watching that. Unimaginable."

Moving right to the subject at hand. *Bold*, he thought. Telling him she had nothing to hide. "Is there anything that's unimaginable to an actress, Mrs. Butler?"

Her nod inclined her head toward Butler's shoulder, rested there.

"Perhaps there shouldn't be. But I've always thought the real talent came not in feeling, but in convincing people that you feel."

"Sherlock Holmes said 'what you do is not as important as what you can make people believe you have done.'"

Tommi Ann nodded. "I think our last hold on decency is the tenet that some horrors ought to be unimaginable, completely out of the range of human understanding." She drew her knees up, tucked her shins under the skirt of her robe. On screen, she moved with the bold grace of a panther, but in repose, her posture was quietly defensive. Victor imagined many celebrities held themselves so; their bodies had gone public, so to speak, and the public could be greedy, and threatening. "Don't you think so?" she asked him.

"I would like to think so. Mrs. Butler, in your scenes with Mr. Spivak last night, I imagine you had to run through them a few times, film them more than once?"

"We did a few run-throughs, yes. Just to make sure he was up to speed. His work had taken him out of town for a few days and he just made it to the set for the call."

"Did you converse with him at all?"

Tommi Ann shook her head, shrugged. "A few words about how the scene would be played, nothing important."

"Had you met him before the show?"

"No."

"But Miss Bonaker had."

"Yes."

"Was it Miss Bonaker who recommended him for the part?"

"No." Butler answered this time. "Spivak had an agent. She sent some tape on him over to the casting director."

"Wasn't that unusual? He wasn't a professional, after all."

"He was damn close," Butler replied. "Besides, the script, sure it's based on the Dudek murder, so I guess you'd assume Spivak had a starring role. Fact is, he only had two, three scenes. Good scenes, showy, but not close to Red or Harold or even Kelli."

"What was his relationship with the rest of the cast? Did they resent the fact that an amateur had been handed those good scenes? After all," Victor added, "he may not have had much screen time, but those scenes put him on camera with Mrs. Butler."

Tommi Ann looked at him. Her chameleon eyes had converted from azure to emerald with the change of clothing. "Lieutenant, your questions imply that this isn't an accident investigation."

"Mrs. Butler, a man is dead. I have to determine whether his death was accidental or deliberate. If it was accidental, I have to investigate the possibility of negligence and if it was deliberate, I'm faced with the question of motive."

"I don't understand. How could it have been anything other than a horrible accident?"

"If someone deliberately sabotaged the weapon, knowing that Mr. Anderson had been coached to direct his shot at Mr. Spivak, the relationship Mr. Spivak had to the people in the cast and crew becomes very important. The possibility also exists that the incident was intended to have some effect on the progress of the production."

"What effect?" Butler demanded.

"I was hoping that you could tell me. Is there anyone you can think of who would want to disrupt this production?"

Butler shook his head.

"Or take your wife out?"

Butler disengaged himself from Tommi Ann, leaned forward. "What do you mean, take her out?"

"Has she received any threats that you're aware of?"

"No. I know about threat assessment." Butler's tone was cold, very assured. "All of Tommi Ann's mail comes through my agency, the packages are scanned and opened there. She doesn't pick up a phone before the call's been screened."

"How many people involved in the production had you known or worked with before?"

"Nobody. Except Cici and Gary, of course."

"You gave Biggs his start."

"He told you that story?" Tommi Ann asked.

"Yes. What about Miss Bonaker?"

Tommi Ann's fingers laced through Butler's. "Ben and I saw her during a college film festival. She was a theatre major, wanted a career on the screen. Of course we noticed the resemblance, so we used her as my stand-in. When she worked with me, she lived with us in New York, and after she graduated, she moved there permanently."

"And the career in film?"

"She had a few scenes in *Redemption* and co-starred in a television movie last year. She has a small part in this show."

"And she still lives with you?"

"She and Dianne share a townhouse. On our block."

"What about her personal life? She met both Spivak and Harold Anderson on the set of that TV movie. There's a romantic relationship with Anderson, I understand."

"She's fond of Harold, yes."

"She was fond of Spivak at one time."

"She was charmed by him," Tommi Ann rephrased. "He's very bright, very amusing. But I believe Cici came to think that he had attached himself to her in order to secure access to me."

"Did Mr. Spivak ever attempt to contact you?"

"Not that I'm aware, though it would have gone through Ben's office or Dianne."

Victor looked at Dianne. She shook her head.

"I don't do lengthy interviews, as a rule. You see—I don't expect you to understand this—when your"—she swept her hand over the aura that enveloped her—"when your shell is imprinted upon the popular consciousness, and everyone comes to believe that seeing you is knowing you, the desire for a bit of privacy becomes almost obsession."

"Then you had something in common with Spivak. Obsessiveness. He's been called a pit bull. He sinks his teeth into a subject and doesn't let go." Victor's beeper went off. He checked the number, asked if he might use the phone. Tommi Ann gestured to the phone on the library table.

Victor dialed his office. His gaze dropped to the unfinished game of Scrabble. *MENSA level, or damn close.*

Adane picked up. "I'm sorry, Lieutenant, this could have waited, but I—well—it might be something you would want to ask the Butlers about one of them."

"No problem. What is it?"

"The first concerns Mr. Spivak's car. It was found parked on Fairmount. Officers unlocked the car and found his luggage."

"Yes, I'm aware of that. Did Ocean City contact you?"

"About Mr. Reid? Yes."

"Anything else?"

"Two things. The first is that someone, apparently with the DA's office, leaked that Mr. Raab was not inclined to file charges against Mr. Anderson."

"Is Raab going to issue a clarification?"

"I don't know, I haven't been able to reach him. The other matter involves Mr. Biggs. I invited him to wait while I transcribed his statement, and asked him to read it over and sign it so that I could provide a copy to Mr. Delareto. And he asked me if there was somewhere he could read it in private, which I didn't think was unusual. I mean, even the clerks and the custodial people have been dropping by the unit when they heard he was here. So I let him sit in Interrogation, and I went into the next room to wait. It wasn't my intention to spy on him, and anyway the mike wasn't turned on, but I was just sort of watching them, and it appeared that Mr. Biggs was taking an unusually long time to read the statement and finally one of his bodyguards took the paper and started reading it to him, and showed him where he should sign. And it's just that ... I don't suppose it's relevant in any way, and I didn't want to ask him, but I was wondering if Mr. Biggs was able to read."

"Thank you. I'll be back soon." He hung up. "I beg your pardon," he said to Tommi Ann.

"You were saying that Mr. Spivak was a pit bull," Tommi Ann reminded him.

The phone rang. Dianne King picked it up, signaled to Butler. Butler excused himself and left the room.

"Of course, my only acquaintance with him was that of one performer to another. If being a 'pit bull' means that he was well-prepared, competent and professional, then I agree, at least as far as his acting was concerned."

"I heard that he was responsible for blowing one of the takes. Inside the club."

"No, Lieutenant," Dianne King spoke up. "It was Mrs. Austen. I suspect something about the dialogue hit a little too close to home, she looked like she might faint. Ben just didn't want Mrs. Austen to think she was at fault for ruining the take."

Butler returned and took his place beside Tommi Ann. "Report outta the DA's office they're not gonna charge Harold. Dianne, phone downstairs, tell Callie's people she can run the interview on tomorrow's show."

Victor rose, waited until Mrs. King left the room before he resumed his seat.

"Just a few more questions. Why do you think Mr. Biggs came out of his trailer when filming began on the parking lot?"

"Look, Lieutenant," Butler explained, "Gary gets a kick out of watching Tommi Ann work. This whole movie-making, it's like a big picnic to him. He's twenty years old, he's gone from makin' ends meet by haulin' produce, to makin' twenty million a year. It hasn't sunk in yet."

"That he's not in Kansas anymore." Victor didn't know why he uttered that particular phrase; perhaps because Tommi Ann's bio claimed she was from Kansas, he was going for a reaction.

He got none, persisted. "His story is that Mrs. Butler found him singing in the street, heard West Texas in his vowels. Do you have a particular affinity for that part of the country, Mrs. Butler?"

"I have no geographical allegiances, Lieutenant," Tommi Ann replied, coolly. "Only personal ones."

"So you read nothing into Mr. Biggs' appearance other than his desire to watch a movie being made."

"Of course not. Do you?"

"I don't want to be accused of coming to conclusions too rapidly," Victor paraphrased Holmes. "But logic would indicate that if the weapons had been previously checked, and yet had been altered before the second take, the disruption that Mr. Biggs caused provided an excellent diversion."

"Lieutenant, if you think that Gary—"

"I'm merely posing a hypothesis, Mr. Butler. After all, Mr. Biggs also seems to have strong allegiances. He told me that there was nothing he wouldn't do for you, your wife, Mrs. King or Miss Bonaker, that you were his family."

"Gary has the kindest, most uncorrupted heart I've ever encountered," Tommi Ann said with feeling.

Victor thought of Adane's observation. "Did Mr. Spivak ever try to get an interview with Mr. Biggs?"

"Dianne never mentioned it, if he did. Why?"

An exposé on Biggs' illiteracy? If it was true, that Biggs couldn't read, these two had to know. "It would be helpful to know any prior contact that Spivak had with anyone involved in the production, that's all." Victor paused. "Mrs. Butler, there is one more question, but I would like to ask it privately?"

Tommi Ann arched her neck, looked up at him. "Lieutenant Cardenas, I have no secrets from my husband."

Victor hesitated. *Ask it*, he told himself. *The worst they can do is throw you out, file a complaint with Raab.* "Very well. Ron Spivak believed that your allegiance to Cici Bonaker is very personal, and that the resemblance is no matter of chance. He believed that you're Miss Bonaker's mother. Are you?"

He saw nothing in her face. It was the simple and perfect composition of flesh overlying bone, of the fine arrangement of the features, of symmetry. "No," she said quietly.

It is a sin for a woman to be that beautiful, his father had said once. *God does not give such beauty without demanding some sacrifice in return.* He had been watching Garbo's *Queen Christina,* his gaze fixed on the mesmerizing final shot.

"No," she repeated, but as consummate an actress as she was, Victor didn't believe her.

CHAPTER TWENTY-SEVEN

INT: MAJOR CRIMES BUREAU INTERROGATION ROOM: DAY
CALDERONE, WANDA and WANDA'S attorney are in the room. WANDA is seated next to her lawyer.

CALDERONE
How well did you know the deceased?

WANDA
How well does anybody know anybody?

CALDERONE
You knew him well enough to be intimate. You were engaged to him.

WANDA
I knew what he wanted me to know. And most of that was a lie.

Dianne King returned, told Butler that Paragon Studios was on the line, and reminded Tommi Ann that a call from Los Angeles was expected shortly, of her luncheon meeting with April and Paragon's attorney. Victor wondered whether there were calls, meetings, or whether he was just being shown the door.

"I'm sorry that I couldn't be more help," Tommi Ann said, so sincerely that Victor found himself wanting to believe her.

He asked Dianne King to walk him to the elevator, stopped in the corridor, well away from Danny Furina, who looked as though he would love an excuse to cruise within earshot. "Mrs. King, I understand you're sharing a suite with Miss Bonaker."

"Yes."

"How was she last night?"

"Upset, of course."

"And before the incident?"

"I don't understand."

"How did she seem before the incident? Wasn't it uncomfortable for her, working with Spivak?"

"Do you like everyone you work with, Lieutenant? Cici is a professional. Her relationship with Mr. Spivak had no effect on her work."

"But it must have affected her attitude toward Spivak."

"Not seriously enough to want him dead, if that's what you are implying, Lieutenant."

He wished he could see the expression behind those tinted lenses, wondered about a mind that quoted Conan Doyle, played MENSA-level Scrabble. "Mrs. King, how long have you been with Mrs. Butler?"

"Twenty years. I'm really employed by Butler Talent Management; I oversee public relations. But I personally handle all of Tommi Ann's interviews and releases."

"Did you know her before her marriage to Butler?"

"May I ask the purpose of these questions, Lieutenant?"

"Mrs. King, I know that Mr. Spivak initiated a relationship with Miss Bonaker last year, and with all due respect to Miss Bonaker's attractions, it was most likely an attempt to get close to Mrs. Butler. An attempt that he abandoned. Now, I know Mr. Spivak's reputation for tenacity, and I have to wonder whether he abandoned his relationship with Miss Bonaker because he got what he was after somewhere else, and whether what he was after was something someone would kill him for."

"Lieutenant. Killing for nasty secrets is the stuff of screenwriters. *Death of a Shock Jock.*"

"The script is based on fact, isn't it, Mrs. King? The Dudek murder was a reality."

"Reality is what we make it," she replied, and left him at the elevator.

The elevator descended one floor, stopped. A pair of Phoenix security held the door and Victor saw a clutch of Phoenix suits surrounding someone.

"Excuse me, sir, would you step out of the elevator?"

Victor hesitated. "Is there an emergency?"

"No, step out please for Miss O'Connor."

It was Victor's nature to be courteous, even chivalrous, but not to the exclusion of common sense. "If there is no emergency, I see no reason that Miss O'Connor should be unwilling to cede me my small portion of the elevator."

Standoff. Victor waited patiently. Finally, a female voice snapped, "Oh, the hell with this," emerged from the wall of green jackets and stalked into the elevator, was immediately swallowed up in entourage. Victor kept his gaze trained calmly on the elevator doors, ignoring the stares of "Miss O'Connor" and her posse.

The door opened and media swarmed as the woman emerged. Victor realized he had seen her face from some morning show Remy had been watching. The one who had locked in an interview with Harold Anderson. Casey or Cassie O'Connor. The woman sailed across the mezzanine, waving at the dribbling of applause from the people who spotted her. Victor saw Red Melendez, clinging to the inner orbit; he was cut loose at the escalators as her escort closed at the flank, cut off the wake. He was drawn back toward the nucleus of the mezzanine, the mass of remaining media exerting too much of a gratificational pull. The reporters looked fool's-errand weary, impatient, and Victor sensed that there was something other than a glimpse of Casey or Cassie—no, Callie—O'Connor that had drawn them to the mezzanine, hadn't materialized. A few of them decided to make do with the actor-activist-director.

"The scene in question ended with the shooting, and we were working with sound, so when we heard the shots, it didn't register at first that anything had gone wrong. I think I was the first one to notice it, because you know from a director's perspective, you will get a little signal that something is off, your instincts are developed to the point that you establish a sort of synchronicity with your talent that will keep you attuned to anything that goes off the mark—"
A tall, blond woman, Cat's sometime nemesis Karen Friedlander, cut him off. "But this synchronicity didn't kick in until after Mr. Spivak had been shot, did it?"

Melendez's ferret face contracted, he wasted precious air seconds assimilating that. "Well ..."

Victor had read Melendez's statement that morning; in eighteen years of police work, he'd never seen the phrase "appreciate the cultural texture of the diverse viewpoints that supersede the literal reality." Adane hadn't even amended it, which suggested that she was developing either a sense of humor or a sense of futility, he wasn't sure which. He had an uncomfortable sensation that in Melendez's hands, "Calderone" was going to turn out to be one of those damned New Age cops, weepy and conflicted, quoting verses about finding one's inner oasis. *Madre de Dios.*

Mischief seized him. He cut a visible course toward CapriOH!, was still a good six feet from the clutch of media when he heard the first, "Lieutenant! Lieutenant Calderone!"

Calderone. *Dios mio.* But it was something to see, the shift of bodies from the TV Calderone to the real one, the mikes arcing from Melendez to Victor.

"I have no comment regarding the incident with Mr. Reid this morning in Ocean City." He paused, a faint smile visible beneath the downturned mustache. "I was just going to stop in on my sister. Excuse me."

"What incident! What incident, Lieutenant! Was there an encounter with Mr. Reid? Was he armed?"

Victor opened the door to CapriOH!, entered. Remy was standing behind a stout woman, draping two necklaces over the shawl the woman had suspended from one shoulder. The woman looked up, her glance clearly recognizing Victor from that picture in the paper. "Aren't you ..?" she whispered, "The one who's directing *CopWatch?*"

Victor's smile was wicked. Remy gave him a look.

He glanced through CapriOH!'s beveled glass windows, saw those who had cell phones yank them out, the rest fled to the pay phones, leaving Melendez abandoned.

Victor turned to the customer. "The opal," he suggested. "It goes with your eyes."

Remy shot him a glance, exasperation colliding with mirth.

"Excuse me, ladies," Victor said, made his exit. He saw Melendez standing alone, checking his watch, trying to look preoccupied, felt a nudge of guilt.

Melendez approached. "What you said about Wally, it's true? He was spotted today?"

Victor nodded. Melendez looked a bit alarmed, but guiltless; the consternation of someone who feels the cooling of the limelight, Victor assessed. There were times that Victor thought it was the worst job in the world, being a homicide cop, but not today. He had wanted to erase himself after Marisol's death, but in the three years of undercover work, the erosion of identity had become merciless. How could someone choose it?

Victor sighed, inwardly. He had conducted his share of reluctant interviews, none of them could be characterized as an act of charity. But it had been mean, siphoning off the limelight like that.

"Mr. Melendez, could I ask you a few questions?"

Melendez put the grave/weary/long-suffering smile he had presented on *Good Morning, Delaware Valley* earlier that day, ACTOR/ACTIVIST captioned under his name, the one he wore as a "spokesperson for the *CopWatch* production."

"Anything I can do."

"How many people on this shoot have you worked with before?"

"There was some talk about The Pig and me both doing the *Para Los Niños* concert, but nothing's been signed. Kelli Connaughton did a guest shot on *The Advocates* in her ingenue days."

"Tommi Ann? The Bonaker girl? Anderson?"

Melendez shook his head, frowned. Victor wasn't sure if the frown was genuine sobriety or if he was flexing his Calderone moves. "He's tough to work with."

"Anderson?"

"Anderson's a breeze. Biggs."

"Really? My impression is that he's quite cooperative."

"Oh, he's real cooperative, that's not it. Maybe it's just nerves, *quien sabe?* Maybe it's just that you see an amateur like Spivak, getting it in one take and The Pig, it's ten, twelve, twenty. I guess it's one thing to shoot a music video, you're pretty much in your element, major television gig, that's something else. Back when I was doing *The Advo—*"

Victor noticed that some shoppers slowed as they passed, noticed Melendez straighten up when he felt their eyes on him, elevate his jawline to lift off the hint of a second chin. "Did you get cast approval?"

"You kidding? Butler dangles Tommi Ann in front of April and then writes the deal memo that says they gotta take The Pig and use *Killadilla*, and they gotta cast Cici and they gotta test Harold for the part of Tim and they gotta give him the script."

"He a good writer?"

"He's okay. He's not gonna win any awards. He's better in front of the camera."

Victor glanced toward the elevator, wondered what was keeping Cat. "What about Bonaker? She any good?"

"Very. Butler doesn't back losers."

"Tell me—professional opinion"—Melendez inflated—"how does he do it?"

"Huh?"

"He doesn't back losers, but he doesn't back winners, either. He creates them. What do you think he sees in them?"

"What do any of us see in anybody?"

Victor thought of Cat, that first shaky encounter in the emergency room, the follow-up interview the next day, some instinct that overruled his canon of never-a-witness/never-a-suspect/never-a-coworker, discovering and continuing to discover that his instinct had been correct. How had he known? "I don't know," he said. "But I know the odds are against picking winners with the consistency Butler seems to exhibit."

"Maybe he's rigged the system," Melendez proposed.

"One more question. Last night, Biggs came out of his trailer and caused a stir. Why do you think he did that?"

He shrugged. "Between you and me, he's not too bright. Somebody should have stopped him."

"Like who?"

Melendez shrugged. "I guess his posse doesn't know the drill, but I saw Cici and Dianne run into his trailer and they're pros, they know what 'sound off' means."

The second person in fifteen minutes to mention what a pro the Bonaker girl was. "Meaning," Victor concluded, "that if he'd let on he wanted to watch Tommi Ann work, one of them would have stopped him?"

"Unless they thought it'd be a kick to see us go haywire."

CHAPTER TWENTY-EIGHT

INT: MAJOR CRIMES BUREAU INTERROGATION ROOM: DAY

WANDA

I knew what he wanted me to know. And most of
that was a lie.

CALDERONE

And you were prepared to marry him? Live with
a man you didn't know?

WANDA

The lies were easy to live with. It was the
reality I couldn't have handled.

When Cat stepped out on Twenty-five, she found four Sterling
security guards stationed between her and the action at the end of
the hall.

"Ma'am, can I see some ID?"

Cat took out her ID. One of Biggs' bodyguards was making his
pass down the hall as she handed it over, said, "She's okay. She c'n
come through."

Cat smiled a "thank you," followed the network of cables coiled
like serpents around the phoenixes on the carpet. Midway along the

corridor, bodies were jammed around the open door of a suite. Cat felt the guard's broad hand on her elbow, felt herself navigated through a sea of bodies that backed off for Biggs' massive protector. He parked Cat a few feet from the open doorway, angled her so that Cat could see Callie O'Connor, the girlish, percolating host of the morning news show *Front Cover* sitting in one of a pair of upholstered armchairs. Cat saw the thin form of June Mathis at the threshold, her eyes fixed on Harold Anderson, who looked ghoulish, his face thickly pancaked and rouged, his hair gelled in place. He was dressed in gray slacks, white shirt, navy cardigan, looked more frozen in place than relaxed. Off camera, Lauren Robinson was sitting, monitoring the conversation.

"—because I have to think," Harold was saying, "that whoever is responsible for what happened intended for someone to get hurt or did it to sabotage the *CopWatch* production." Earnest, controlled; Lauren Robinson had probably rehearsed him.

Callie, on the other hand, sounded like she was swapping recipes, even when she asked, "Do you mean that you believe someone deliberately loaded the gun, not that it was an act of negligence, an oversight?"

"I don't know. That's for the police to decide."

"And what role do you believe Wally Reid, powder man—for our audience, that's the prop manager who's in charge of the weapons and explosives"—she wiggled two fingers of each hand to signify a quote for "powder"—"played in this act? Did someone manage to sabotage the weapon without his detecting it? And was he acquainted with the victim?"

Harold shook his head, baffled. "I just don't know. There may have been some sort of relationship, some dealings between them that predated this shoot. After all, Ron was a reporter first, the acting, well ..."

"Now, I'm sure the notification we've just received is a relief to you and your attorney—"

"What notification?" Cat whispered.

"Shhh!"

"But there have to be emotional repercussions."

"She's gonna ask how does he *feel*," grunted a crew member.

"SHHH!"

"How do you feel?"

Harold sighed. Cat saw the camera roll in for a close-up, saw Harold arch his chin the way Melendez would have done it, giving tomorrow's *Front Cover* viewers his noblest angle.

"I feel like"—Harold cupped his hands—"a weight was lifted, but the burden is still there, you know? Like I know I wasn't responsible but the gun was in my hand? Like up here"—he tapped his forehead—"I know I'm not guilty, but here"—he patted his breastbone—"I feel at fault."

Callie nodded, sympathetically. Cat glanced at the women watching from the doorway, their faces glowing with reflected light. *Like cave creatures around flame,* Cat thought. Clinging to the fire because fire was light and warmth and shelter, it was what kept them alive. It was, Cat recalled April's phrase, what made them real. Except this fire was false, the light reflected, the reality whatever they chose to make it.

Callie's "poor baby" nod, and pursed lips, were her seals of sympathy, would coach sympathy out of tomorrow's morning audience.

Cat hopped up on tiptoe, whispered, "Is Gary around?" in the ear of the massive bodyguard. The guy nodded, used his broad body to plow a path through the crowd. There was a guy with a walkie-talkie standing outside Biggs' room, though the door was open. Cat knocked on the doorjamb, poked her head inside.

"Hey, Ms Austen, c'mon in." Biggs was dressed in an enormous black nylon running suit. "I's on my way down to the gym, work out before I go over your mom's for supper. Ben says I gotta lose a couple pounds."

"I won't keep you," Cat said. She was surprised to see that the room, though large, was no more than a double room in a luxury hotel.

Beautifully furnished with its emerald carpets, its phoenix wallpaper, quilted satin spreads on the two king-size beds. A basket of towering fruit, higher than the tree she and Chris had on their first Christmas together. "I wanted to ask you something." She glanced around at the guard outside the door, moved out of earshot. The guard eyed her as she approached Biggs, slipping one hand into her tote bag, took a half step over the threshold.

"Did you write this?" Cat held up the postcard with the crude accolade, calling Tommi Ann a "maJor shootyng STaR."

Biggs was guileless. "Even I know you don't spell shooting wit' a Y."

"Then'd be yooting," commented the guard at the door.

"No, insteada where the 'i' goes." Biggs smiled, a little sadly. "I guess someone like you, got all those books, it wa'n't too hard to figure me out."

"That you can't read and write."

"Not real good. Cici, she been like my big sister, she comes, helps me out so I read good enough to get a tutor. You know, like when you got a house cleaner coming, you tidy up first, so they won't think you a slob? I gotta learn just enough so won't no teacher think I'm dumb."

"You're not dumb. You just can't read."

Biggs looked at Cat. "You gonna write about it?"

It hit her, when he said it, what a coup it would be, what a story. What it would do for her reputation to break that caliber of story in *South Jersey Magazine. Rapper Can't Read.*

"Just if you are, lemme have a chance to tell Charlene and Jonah, so's they don't read it first in *Teen Talk.*"

"It must be awful, to have kept it from them."

"You know how hard it is to keep a secret from family?"

Cat thought of Ted Cusack. "Yes I do. And no, I'm not going to write anything. What about Ron Spivak, Gary? Did he ever talk to you about this, suggest he was going to write about it?"

Biggs shook his head. "I hardly ever talked to him. Didn't like

him, he don't treat Cici right. I thought it'd be a kick see him get shot."
He shook his head, ashamed of his callousness. "It's not like in the
movies, man." He sounded truly surprised.

"And that's why you went out? Because you thought it would be a
kick to see him get shot?"

"Cici come in, said if I wanted to check out the scene, they were
gonna roll in a couple minutes."

Cat felt a slow tension tightening up her stomach. "You mean it
was Cici's suggestion? That you should go watch?"

Biggs nodded.

Cat excused herself, winnowed back down the hall to watch the
rest of Harold's shoot, saw Cici Bonaker hanging back against the
wall, her height allowing her to see past the bodies layered between
her and the open door.

Cat approached, laid a hand lightly on her arm. Cici turned; her
face was drawn, weary, too exhausted to greet Cat with more than a
faint flicker of acknowledgment.

"—because," Callie was waving a fax toward the camera, "we've
just obtained a copy of a deal memo that was sent to Butler Talent
Management this week, stipulating the terms of their agreement to
represent you."

Harold looked like he'd been jumped in an alley. "I—I didn't
know anything about this ... Ben never ... Boy, you got me good."

Callie laughed; the camera crew laughed. Tomorrow, when this
aired, they'd leave the background laughter in, look what great sports
we are, all one big showbiz clan.

"Hi," Cat mouthed to Cici. She winnowed between bodies, whispered, "Are you okay? You look sick."

"I'm fine."

There was a rustle of movement from the room; after a moment,
Callie O'Connor emerged to a flurry of faint applause as she nodded
her I'm-a-working-mother-just-like-you smile and turned to the as-

sistant on her right, asked what time the limo had been ordered to pick her up.

Harold squeezed through; hands reached out to pat him on the back, a little eddy of applause followed him. The deal memo cinched it, he was the anointed, someone they had to know. Red Melendez materialized and grabbed his hand, shook it, his radar picking out the Instamatic, grinning into a barely visible lens. Melendez took on the role of usher, working Harold through the crowd, up to Callie O'Connor. Callie grabbed Harold around the waist, posed, posed, posed; her lens-seeking capability far surpassed Red's, though he did manage to wedge into the frame of the last shot. (Callie would later have him cropped out.)

Harold waved toward Cici. She offered a faint wave that barely carried over the bodies between her and the actor. She turned to Cat. "I was upstairs, Dianne came in, said the lieutenant had been there. He said Wally Reid was in Ron's apartment, that he escaped right before the police could seize him."

Cat nodded.

"I don't understand," Cici frowned. "What could he have been doing there?"

"I think the question is how he got in. There was no sign of forced entry and I had both sets of Ron's keys."

Cici realized what Cat was saying. "He can't have gotten mine ..."

"Are you certain?"

Harold came up, kissed Cici on the cheek. "Whew, I'm glad that's over. Dianne had Callie run off a tape so that I could go over it, see how godawful I looked. That Callie's an ambush artist if there ever was one."

"I thought I told you that Ben had sent a deal memo to New York. You acted like it was a surprise," Cici said.

Harold shook his head. "Cici, I thought ..." he took her by the shoulders, looked into her eyes. "Look, I thought you were just saying that. You know, trying to make me feel better because things were looking so bad."

"Why would I make something like that up?"

"In this profession, everything's made up. Everything's hustle and hype and hope. I'm sorry. I'm not used to having important things happen to me."

"It looks like you'd better get used to it," Cat said.

Harold gave Cici a squeeze. "Are you up for lunch? A few of us are going to the coffee shop. You too, Cat."

"I'll come down in a couple minutes," Cici told him. "I just need to run upstairs for a few minutes, I left something in the suite."

"What?"

"My keys to Ron's place."

"What do you need them for?" Someone called Harold's name, he waved a one-fingered "Wait-a-minute."

Cici looked at Cat. Cat spoke. "They found out Wally Reid was holed up in Ron's apartment, and he didn't break in. The cops are asking around, they want to know how he got in there."

"You're kidding me!"

Cici shook her head. "I just want to make sure I still have my set. Besides, I'm not in a very public mood right now."

"Want me to wait?"

"No, you go on ahead."

Cici held back, waited for the crowd to ebb. "Let's go up the service stairs," she suggested.

Cat wondered if Cici was afraid of running into the police, but agreed, followed Cici up the one flight to the penthouse level. Hotel security was stationed inside the door. He nodded amiably to Cici.

Cat saw Danny Furina's surprised expression as they approached the suite from the far end of the hallway. Cici paid no attention, unlocked the door to the suite she shared with Dianne King, pushed it open. "Dianne?" she called softly.

Cat followed her down a long corridor that opened into an elegant living area, the mirror image of Tommi Ann's suite in layout, but decorated in mint and candy pink.

"Sit down. They were in the pocket of the coat I was wearing last night, I think." Cici opened a mirrored closet door. Cat glanced around, saw an open laptop on the coffee table, a stack of call sheets with Revised shooting schedule scribbled on a Post-it stuck to the top sheet. There were books on the library table, Dianne's crosswords and anagrams. The small desk had been converted to a workstation with a fax, Rollodex, a stack of folders. She wondered if Victor was still interviewing Tommi Ann.

Cat looked up and saw confusion, then consternation cloud Cici's features. She began running her hands through the other coats in the closet. "I put it right back in my pocket, I never took it out after that day ..."

"Were you wearing that coat on the set last night?"

"Not after I changed into my costume. I left it in the club."

"Hanging up in the loft? Where they had Makeup?"

"Yes."

Cat recalled the disarray, the coats on the floor. Had someone fled to the club, rifled through them quickly, taken Cici's key? He—or she—would have to know that Cici possessed the key, recognize her coat. Another thought occurred to her. "Cici," she asked, "can you check the fax log on Dianne's machine?"

"Sure, why?" Cici walked over to the library table, running her eyes over the carpet as she walked. She sat at the keyboard, began typing. "Several to New York. A couple to LA, Paragon Studios, I think."

"None local?"

Cici continued scrolling, shook her head.

"Can I use the phone?"

Cici nodded. Cat dialed Victor's beeper, hung up. In a moment, the phone rang. "Can I get it? I beeped Victor."

Cici nodded, a bit apprehensively.

"Where are you?" Victor demanded.

Cat looked at Cici. The girl was truly frightened. Common sense told Cat that whoever had set Ron up to be killed was a lot colder, a lot more conniving than Cici appeared to be. *Appearances are deceiving,* she reminded her common sense.

"Look, I have a shot at an interview myself, I can get a cab to my mother's or have someone over there pick me up when I'm done here."

"Have you seen Harold Anderson or June Mathis or Cici Bonaker?"

"Yes." Cat crossed her fingers behind her back. "I just ran into Harold on his way down to the coffee shop with some people, I think June was with him. Why?"

"They owe me a statement. You're going directly to your mother's from here, and then straight to Ocean City?"

"Absolutely."

"You're not in any trouble, are you?"

"Why would you ask that?"

"Just a feeling I get."

"You see? You're exactly like Victor Calderone. He's sopping with empathy. I think he even sheds a tear or two."

"Extracted when Kate Auletta wrings his neck?"

"I don't think it was his neck. I can probably talk Harold into *changing* it to his neck, if that would make you happy."

"I suspect Calderone would be happier if he left it as is. I'll pick you up at your mother's, we'll take the kids out to eat."

"Victor, do you seriously believe that you can walk into my mother's house and take anyone *out* to eat?"

"What can I have been thinking? Call me when you get over there."

"Okay." Cat hung up.

Cici smiled, faintly. "You're in love with him, aren't you?"

"Why do you ask?"

"You talk to him like you've known him forever. Like you can tell him anything. Tommi Ann and Ben talk to each other like that." Cici got up and dropped back onto one of the wintergreen couches with the peppermint throws. Cat felt like she was in an ice cream parlor. "Is it true that they're not going to charge Harold?"

"I don't know."

"Because they suspect someone else?"

Cat looked at her. Was Cici wondering if she was a suspect?

"Cici, if I didn't believe that Ron was on to some exclusive, I would write off the shooting as some horrendous accident or negligence. But it's just too much of a coincidence. That Ron would get killed when it looks like he was about to go to press with something on Tommi Ann."

"I admit I'm not the best judge of character, but it just doesn't seem like she could do something like that."

Cat's heart gave a little jolt. Then she realized that Cici was talking about Ron's killing, that she knew nothing about Sheriff Sontag and the "mutilations to his person." "Look Cici, when a crime is committed, you look to three things: motive, means, opportunity."

"You really are her," Cici's smile was more open than Tommi Ann's; the configuration of the lips was similar but there were fewer secrets concealed behind them. "Kate Auletta. If ..."

Cat lifted her brows, inquisitively.

The wider her smile became, the more distance it put between hers and Tommi Ann's. "I was going to say that if the show goes series, they should sign you as a technical consultant."

"I don't think I could stand the excitement. Motive? I can think of two. To deliberately get rid of Ron, or to sabotage the shoot. In which case, Ron's just a casualty." Cici pursed her lips. "I guess it would be best to reason backward. Sherlock Holmes saw the advantage of that once."

"I don't understand."

"Instead of compiling the clues and forming your conclusion, you *start* with one possible conclusion. For example, your conclusion is: the shooting was intended to sabotage the show, which would lead you to ask—"

"Whether the show *has* been sabotaged?" Cici shook her head, slowly. "I think, from something Dianne said this morning, that Paragon hasn't pulled the plug. April has enough footage; if they can get the parking lot scene shot, all that's left is principal photography with Tommi Ann, Harold and Red."

"And what if Ron hadn't been killed?" Cat hypothesized. "What would be the status of the shoot today?"

Cici raked her slender fingers through her hair. "I never thought about it like that. You mean if Ron went to press with something that shook up Tommi Ann? Might it upset her so badly that she wasn't able to continue the project?"

Cat nodded. "Sweeps month, timely story, fast-tracked production, none of that sets this apart from any other episode of *CopWatch*. It's Tommi Ann's participation that a lot of people are hitching their own careers to, you said so yourself. Not the crew, they're journeymen, they go where the work goes, their union sees to it they're taken care of. But what about what they call the talent? Who was riding the current of this show? If it sinks, who sinks with it?"

"I guess we all just go on to the next job, too."

"No, Cici, *you* just go on to the next job because you've got Ben Butler to lock you into a next job. What about people like April, Red, Harold, Kelli Connaughton, June Mathis who depended on having this on their résumés?"

Cici blinked. "You're right. Even if the series fell through, I'm the only one who's certain of a second shot."

A simple comment, but it touched off an echo, a bit too distant, the reverberation a bit too indistinct. Cat's instincts prickled with adrenaline, but she couldn't determine what had set them off. "Okay, look. The gun fired. Reason backward to when someone would have the opportunity to rig it." Cat paused. "That's not hard, Cici. It had to be when Gary came out to watch them shoot the scene."

Cici looked puzzled, then a knowing flush crept over her features. "It's not what you think. I was going in to get out of the cold. June said as long as I was going in, would I give Gary a message, that they'd be rolling in a few minutes if he still wanted to watch Tommi Ann."

"June? That doesn't make sense. She wouldn't do something like that on her own authority, and April never would have sanctioned it; she had a fit when Gary got the crowd riled up."

"But it only took a few minutes to talk him back inside," Cici protested.

"You know how long it takes to shove a round into a chamber?" Cici shook her head.

Cat snapped her fingers. "And almost everyone knew that Red was coaching Harold to aim directly at Ron."

"Red said he didn't have to cheat the shot because of the distance."

"Well, that was stupid. You never point and shoot unless you intend to hit."

"But they were just supposed to be blanks."

"But they weren't." *And they weren't blanks that someone was shooting into Ron's apartment a couple hours ago.*

The trilling sound cut her off. Cat realized in the backwash of adrenaline that the sound had made her start.

Cici got up and took the fax that slid into the tray, scribbled something on a Post-it and laid it on the stack of folders. "Why did you ask me to check the fax log?" Cici asked.

"When I ran into Wally over at Ron's place? We were talking and Ron's fax machine went off. I don't think the cops found a fax."

"I don't get it."

"When Wally went in there to check it out, someone fired shots through the window, almost hit him. The police suspect that someone used the fax to lure Wally into position."

"You mean someone tried to kill him? But who knew he was there?"

Who knew Ron's fax number? Who had a key? "I was too busy at the time staying out of the line of fire to give it a lot of thought. You don't know anyone who owns a gun, do you?"

"Are you kidding?" Cici asked.

It was worth a shot.

"Practically everyone around Tommi Ann has a carry permit."

CHAPTER TWENTY-NINE

INT: CALDERONE'S OFFICE: AFTERNOON
CALDERONE is discussing his interview with
SERGEANT NESTOR.

NESTOR
So, you don't think the girlfriend did it?
I mean, if she knew he had other women ...

CALDERONE (shaking his head)
She's not that bright. Donner's killing
was opportunistic. The shooter got off a
good shot and got away clean. That takes a
quicker mind than she has. No ... this goes
deeper than a love triangle.

Victor settled behind the wheel and called his office from his car, negotiating his way out of the Phoenix garage one-handed. "Adane, I'd like you to see if you can get in touch with a Mr. David Wheeler, he's the editor of a local weekly in King County, Texas. *The Western Counties Gazette*, something like that. I want you to ask him about the murder of a man named Thomas Sontag"—he spelled it—"Senior. This would be about twenty-five years ago, but I believe he discussed this with Spivak earlier this week, he should have the facts in the case at hand. Rice talk to Bonaker and Mathis?"

"No, sir. He hasn't been able to get in touch with Miss Bonaker and he kept missing Miss Mathis."

Victor had missed her, too, missed Anderson and Bonaker. Hadn't turned either her or Anderson up at the Phoenix. "Leave a message at their production offices—"

"I already have, sir," Adane interrupted. "We received a call from an attorney for Paragon Studios, he said he was faxing us an order for the return of the film we confiscated last night. Apparently, it went before Judge Harkness and she stated that the seizure was a—"

"Fourth Amendment violation."

"Yes, sir. So I retrieved Miss Steinmetz's cell phone number from her statement and suggested that she send Miss Mathis to come over and sign for the film, and we would release it."

"And she fell for that?"

"They're television people, sir. I'm sure they take it to be standard operating procedure."

"Quite. Speaking of faxes, did Ocean City come up with one in Spivak's apartment? Mrs. Austen said Spivak's fax machine went off right before someone fired into the room."

"Nothing. I wonder whether someone dialed Mr. Spivak's fax number deliberately in order to lure Mr. Reid into the bedroom."

"See if they can check the—"

"Fax log. Yes, sir, I've already requested it."

When Victor entered the day room, Adane was sitting at her desk, showing some paper to June Mathis, indicating where she should sign. Victor looked the girl over. Somewhere in her twenties, thin, anemically pale. He had gotten a glimpse of her at St. Agnes earlier in the week. She had worn jeans that she seemed likely to float out of when she moved, a baggy sweatshirt with CopWatch Productions on the front, the lank hair stuffed under a baseball cap, no makeup. To-day, the dull flaxen hair was swept into an intricate braid, and she had attempted to relieve the pallor with a touch of blush, lipstick. *Who's she fixing herself up for?*

"Miss Mathis," he greeted. "Since you're here, would you mind if I spoke to you for a few minutes?"

She tensed. "I have to get this film back to April."

"Of course. I just have a few routine questions. I didn't have the opportunity to speak to you last night."

"I don't know if I should talk to you."

"You don't have to, of course. Not right now. I simply wanted to caution you about Wally Reid."

"Wally?" The pale eyes darted away from his. She clutched the round canister in both hands.

Victor put a hand under her elbow. "Why don't you come into my office, I think it would be better if we discussed this privately."

June rose. He could feel her arm trembling in his grip, but she allowed herself to be led into the office.

Victor eased her into a chair, left the door open. He noticed the soft cotton dress, tiny hoop earrings. She had made herself as close to pretty as she was going to get today, and she wasn't the type who did that for the face in the mirror.

"It was pretty chaotic last night."

June's head bobbed.

"Mr. Anderson was understandably upset. It was good of you to see him to the hospital."

"It's my job."

Victor nodded, slowly. "You and Wally Reid. I imagine he was upset, too. After all, the nature of the accident, responsibility for that would fall on him, wouldn't it?"

"I don't know. I guess. I was thinking more about—"

"About?"

"Well, Harold looked like he was going to pass out."

"You and Reid went with him to the ER."

"I asked the officer, Forschetti, if it was all right, and he said to go ahead."

"And told you to remain there, isn't that right?"

She began to gnaw on her lower lip. "Harold said we could go, it would be all right, and they would know where to find us if we were wanted for questioning or anything. And Wally was starting to get nervous, too."

"So you took off."

The head bobbed.

"Did you use an ambulance?"

"No, Harold was parked on the street behind the club."

"He had his own car?"

The head bobbed again. "He's from Philadelphia. He drove down."

"Who drove him to the hospital?"

"I did."

"He say anything on the way to the hospital?" Victor kept his tone to an impersonal, keep-them-talking level.

"He just kept saying, 'What went wrong?'; 'How could it happen?'; 'Wally told me the guns had been checked out.' That started to get Wally freaked and that's when Harold said we didn't have to worry about him, we could take off, and maybe I should get Wally back to the Marinea."

"And that's where you went?"

June's head bobbed, but this time stayed down on the decline, her eyes fixed on the metal canister on her lap.

"Wally didn't indicate that he might take off?"

She shook her head; the eyes stayed down.

"Have you heard from him since last night?"

She shook her head again.

"Miss Mathis?"

She looked up. The eyes had the fire of a trapped animal.

She knows something. Overheard something. Or promised something and extracting that promise could take a lot more pressure than he was willing to exert. "Miss Mathis, did you speak to Ron Spivak at all last night?"

She nodded, looked a bit relieved that he had backed away from the subject of Wally Reid. "A little."

"What did you talk about?"

"He just— Well, he asked me to give this card to Dianne, and then afterward, he was asking what she said when I gave it to her, stuff like that."

"One of his business cards? Like he was trying to set up an interview?"

"No, just— There were these postcards, something about a jewelry show at the Phoenix."

"Why did he think Mrs. King would be interested in it?"

"I don't think he did. It was just something to write on."

"And what did he write on it?"

June blushed scarlet, ashamed to admit she had read it. "Just like a fan letter. That he thought Tommi Ann was a major star. A major shooting star."

Victor stroked his chin, thoughtfully. "Like he was trying to ingratiate himself with Mrs. King?"

June blinked.

Victor repressed a sigh. "As though he were trying to get in good with Mrs. King?"

"Oh. I don't know."

"Did you mention this to anyone else?"

She shook her head.

"Not with Anderson or Mrs. Butler or Miss Bonaker, anyone like that?"

Another shake of the head.

"Did you hear that Spivak had words with Anderson?"

She began to work on the lower lip again. The teeth were small, uniform, like first teeth. "I did hear he had some kind of argument with Cici. Some of the background people were talking about it."

"You don't know what it was about?"

She shook her head again. "Can I go now?"

Victor rose. "Yes, of course. How will you get back to Atlantic City? Anderson's car?"

"I signed out one of the rentals. The transportation coordinator usually hires them out on a location shoot."

He walked her out of the office. She kept the canister clasped to her breast like a shield. "Detective Adane will show you out. Thank you for your time, Miss Mathis."

Victor went back to his office, shaking his head. That one was hiding something. Push her and she'd either crumble or clam up. When Adane returned, he rapped on the two-way glass, waved her into his office. "Call this transportation coordinator—"

"To see who's been checking out the rentals. Yes, sir, I just did."

"Did you manage to get a look at the film?"

"No, sir."

Victor frowned. "Call Mary Grace, see if she can work on getting us a screening, at least."

"I'm not sure that will be necessary, sir. The court order only specified the return of the confiscated footage. I read it very carefully. It said nothing about the video."

"What video?"

"I suspected that you wouldn't have time to screen it before they got an order for its return so I found a twenty-four-hour lab and took the liberty of having the film transferred to video. I hope I didn't overstep my authority."

"If you have, I hope you'll make a habit of it. Ask Rice to see who's got the monitor, and roll it in here."

"Yes, sir." Adane went out to give the order, returned and took the chair Victor held out for her. "I called Mr. Wheeler's office and spoke to someone in the pressroom. Mr. Spivak did visit Mr. Wheeler earlier this week, but I wasn't able to speak to Mr. Wheeler. He's left for Los Angeles to attend the Oscar Awards ceremony."

"That's still a couple days off, isn't it?"

"Yes, sir. The man in the pressroom referred me to a Mrs. Diaz. She's taught in the local school system for more than thirty years, she recalls the incident quite well. Apparently this Sheriff Sontag was something of a tyrant. A monster, that's what Mrs. Diaz called him. His son was the youngest of four, the only boy. The boy fell in love—I suppose it was love, although he wasn't much more than sixteen—with a young girl named Annie Cox."

"I know about how they ran off, tried to get married."

"They did get married, apparently, although since they were so young, and used an alias, it's unlikely the marriage would be considered legal. However brutal this Sontag was to his son before the elopement, it was much worse after the boy was brought home. Apparently, this Mrs. Diaz tried to persuade both families to give her custody of the children."

Victor nodded, stroked his mustache absently. "There was a pregnancy."

"Yes, sir. Mrs. Diaz said that the rumor was the Sheriff paid off Miss Cox's sister and brother-in-law to send her someplace East, to put some distance between her and his boy. The two young people disappeared and shortly after, the father's body was discovered. Several people were questioned, a man named Biggs who gave the children a lift to Mexico, David Wheeler and Gloria Ramirez, too."

"Why were they questioned?"

"Well, it was thought that it was because they were in the same class with the boy. But the other classmates weren't questioned. Mrs. Diaz told me that Mr. Wheeler confessed something to her afterward that he never told the police. I don't know if he mentioned it to Mr. Spivak. I suspect not."

"What was that?"

"He and the Sontag boy were close. Apparently the Sontag boy and the Cox girl came to him when they were planning to run away, asked for money. Wheeler gave them the money he had saved from his part-time job. Gloria Ramirez was present and she gave them money she had been saving for a graduation dress. This was the night before the Sontag boy and the Cox girl disappeared. Mrs. Diaz said she never told anyone this, and she's certain that neither Mr. Wheeler nor Ms. Ramirez did, although she does recall that Ms. Ramirez wore her *quince* gown to her graduation party."

Victor recalled Remy's *quince*, the battles over the configuration of the sleeves, the altitude of the neckline, the volume of the skirt.

"Mrs. Diaz is the grandmother of Teresa D., the singer? And wasn't Mr. Wheeler's novel the book that Mrs. Butler's latest movie was based on?"

"*Redemption,*" Victor said, thoughtfully.

Stan Rice shuffled in, Phil Long at his heels. Stan was pushing a television monitor on a wheeled cart with one hand; the other arm was wrapped around two tubs of popcorn, a six-pack of soda dangling from one index finger.

"Sergeant."

"What's a movie without snacks?" He plopped one container on the desk, a few kernels bobbling over the side, hauled in a folding chair and sat, settling the other tub of popcorn on his lap. Phil hit the lights.

"The lab got all the footage on one tape, but there may be blank spaces, and the sound may be iffy."

"Let's run it," Victor said.

The tape began a few seconds into the first take shot inside the club, Harold flubbing his entrance, Tommi Ann telling him to relax.

"Jeez, he looks like Hopper, you think?" Stan mumbled through a mouthful of popcorn.

Victor could see the shadow he threw over Tommi Ann, missing his mark.

The cuts between the takes were rude breaks, a few seconds of black screen before the following attempt.

"She does look a little like Cat," Stan observed. "Way she moves. Like she's got her pegged"—he tapped his temple—"up here."

Harold finally nailed his entrance, got his lines off smoothly. Victor was impressed. *He's not bad.*

Ron Spivak made his entrance.

Wanna dance?

I've used up all my good moves, thanks.

C'mon, we'll make it a threesome, I'll get Timmy. You seen him by the way? He went looking for some girl. Tall, very pretty, auburn hair ...

Nadine. Then it's you an' me.

No, it's just you.

Want a preview of tomorrow's headline, Tommi? Want a family secret to end all family secrets?

Cut! Cut, damn it—

Victor grabbed the remote and stopped the tape.

"He blew his line," Adane said. "He said, 'Do you want a preview of tomorrow's headline, *Tommi.*' He called her by name."

"I don't get it," Stan said through a mouthful of popcorn. "The word Jackie got was that Butler called 'cut' 'cause Cat was startin' to fade. Just made out like Spivak was at fault so Cat wouldn't feel guilty."

Victor frowned, thoughtfully. "Or to divert attention from what was going on in front of the camera."

"I don't get it," Stan repeated.

"Spivak was a quick study," Victor remarked. "Mrs. Butler said he had the scene down, Butler said he was as good as a pro, so did Melendez. Spivak blew his lines, he might have done it deliberately. Play it back. We were focusing on him. This time I want to watch her."

Want a preview of tomorrow's headline, Tommi? Want a family secret to end all family secrets?

Tommi Ann snapped into a posture of frozen fright, not the surprise of a fellow actor handed the wrong cue, not the congenial "Relax, Hal" when Harold had blown his line. Dread.

"He did that deliberately to shake her up," Victor declared. "He wasn't Gerry Donner telling Kate Auletta he had gotten hold of a scandal, he was Ron Spivak telling Tommi Ann Butler he had gotten to the bottom of *her* scandal." He filled Stan in on what he knew about the Sontag boy and Annie Cox, the unsolved murder of Sontag's father.

"Murder?" Stan pronounced the word as though it was foreign to him.

"No statute of limitations," Long stated. "Spivak ties her to killing the boyfriend's dad, she could be hauled back to Texas and prosecuted."

"I wonder if that was it. Just murder," Adane murmured.

"Jeannie. Murder's as deep as it gets."

"Phil, think about it," she replied. "Celebrity with millions of dollars is accused of murdering a man who everyone refers to as a monster. If, with all the forensic evidence and circumstantial evidence, the LA prosecutors couldn't get a conviction in the Brentwood case, what makes you think they have the evidence they could need, the means or even the desire to open up a twenty-five-year-old murder case and attempt a prosecution of Tommi Ann Butler?"

"Because," Phil shot back, "it's something they can put on TV."

Practical Jean shook her head. "Without witnesses, without the boyfriend and apparently without anyone alive who really cares one way or the other that the Sheriff is dead? That's hardly something worth air time."

"Jeannie," Phil's tone was exasperated. "Last night, prime time, they put on a home video of some folks out in Oregon had a whale carcass wash up, and they dynamited it."

"You're kiddin' me," Stan interjected. "What channel?"

"Boom!" Long splayed his spindly fingers. "Two tons of whale blubber all up an' down the beach, some guy's half a block off, walkin' down the street, five-pound hunk of mammal meat—" Long smacked the top of his head. "They interview him from hospital. Jeannie," he concluded, emphatically, "you gotta start watchin' television, I'm tellin' you."

Victor cleared his throat. "I think we're digressing just a bit. The subject was whether Spivak was able to tie Mrs. Butler to a twenty-five-year-old murder."

"Wait," Stan muttered. "This Wheeler, he wrote that book *Redemption*, right? If he knows the Cox girl from back in the day, you're tellin' me he doesn't recognize Tommi Ann?"

"You're old enough to have reached your twentieth high school reunion, Stan. Did you go?" Adane asked him.

"You kiddin' me? It was a freakin' nightmare."

"Did you wear the little 'Hello-my-name-is' on your lapel?"

"Yeah."

"How many of your former classmates would you have recognized without it?"

"Four and a half."

"So you're saying it's unlikely Wheeler would recognize Tommi Ann Butler?" Victor asked.

"He never knew Tommi Ann Butler," Adane replied. "He knew Annie Cox. She vanishes. A few years later, Tommi Ann Butler appears in *Illyria*. It's said that when Mr. Butler went looking for the actress, he didn't recognize her in person. And that was shortly after he'd seen the film. Would Mr. Wheeler have recognized her twenty years after she ran away from home?"

Victor stroked his chin. "The girl Butler looked up. She wasn't Tommi Ann Butler."

"Sir?"

"She was Tommi Ann Somebody, isn't that the bio? She became Butler when he married her. The story is that he bought up the prints of that film and had the credits altered. Adane, I'd like you and Phil to go through the Web, see if you can dig up some film archives, something like that, something that would tell us how she was credited when *Illyria* was first released."

Victor's phone rang. It was Cat. She got right to the point. "Cici Bonaker can't find her key to Ron's place."

"What? When did you learn this?"

"When I was over her place."

"When were you over her place?"

"When I talked to you earlier."

Victor allowed himself a moment. "You didn't mention it at the time."

"You didn't ask. You just asked if I'd *seen* her. You know, I've got this wonderful investigative technique for getting the answers you want."

"And what is that?"

"Ask the right questions."

His unit saw nothing in his demeanor, except for a slight softening in the dark gaze perhaps, to indicate that he was speaking to Cat.

"Tell me about the key."

"I ran into her at Harold's interview, and asked her about it. She said it was in her coat pocket. We went up to her place to check and it was gone. She said her coat had been up in Makeup, anyone could have gotten to it."

"Or she could have used it and then misplaced it. Or given it to Wally."

"Guess what else I found out?"

"Cat."

"Sorry. Gary Biggs told me that Cici was the one who suggested he watch Tommi Ann shoot. I asked Cici about it. She told me that she was only passing along a message, and that June Mathis was the messenger. But June Mathis doesn't give orders, she takes them."

"From whom?"

"From anyone higher up on the food chain. Do you have a ballistics report on the rounds that were fired into Ron's place?"

"No. That'll go to Ocean City before it comes here, anyway. Why?"

"Guess who's got a carry permit?"

"Cici Bonaker."

"Yup. And everyone else around Tommi Ann: Butler, Mrs. King, the people in Butler's agency. So I'll bet if you get the report and match the rounds with the type of gun and get copies of the permits to see what they're all licensed to carry, you'll find that the gun may have belonged to someone very close to Tommi Ann."

CHAPTER THIRTY

INT: KATE'S APARTMENT: NIGHT

KATE

Donner's got a gun. It's in his glove
compartment.

CALDERONE

How do you know that?

KATE

You don't want to know. But if I got
to it, anyone could.

Cat leaned over the railing of the long elliptical opening in the
center of the mezzanine, looked down at the casino floor below,
watched the scores of little dramas: the guy in the wheelchair smoothly
coasting the slot aisles, one hand sweeping the trays for uncollected
change; the two women depositing quarters, yanking handles in syn-
chronized motion; the weary waitress in the dark green shorts and
mustard-colored cutaway holding a tray of juice and soft drinks
above her head as she made her way down the aisles; the woman
trotting toward the cashier's cage, clutching an overflowing plastic
tub of quarters to her breast; the guard at the perimeter of the casino;

the women behind the information booth wearing flat, weary stares and locked-in-place smiles.

Cat closed her eyes and called up scenes from *South Street Stakeout*, shifted the focus from Harold's performance to Cici's. Cici had handled a gun, too, come off as convincing as Harold. How much of that had been an act? How much of any of them was real?

The clash of make-believe with memory was shorting out her instincts; those that had insisted Cici could not kill anyone were losing ground. Had she worked up enough hatred or fear to kill Ron? Cat recalled Stan Rice saying, "I don't get why anybody kills anybody. I mean I hear what they tell me, but down deep, I just don't get it."

I don't get it, either, Cat thought. *I don't get Tom and Cookie Amis and—and Kevin.*

"You lookin' to get picked up? Me, I'd be trollin' the baccarat lounge." Remy looked up, waved flirtatiously to the smoked glass bulb of the eye-in-the-sky.

"I was just thinking."

"You sound like Victor. He's always thinking. He comes in the store and this woman, she thinks he's Red Melendez and he plays along. He's crazy, don't you think? Victor?"

"No, I've never met anyone saner."

Remy laughed as though Cat had said something hugely funny. "You on your way home?"

Cat nodded. "I thought we could share a cab. My car got stolen today."

"Stolen?"

"Long story. I have to make a stop at my mother's. Would you like to come along? They'd love to meet Victor's sister."

"No kidding? It'd be a kick. Victor hardly tells us anything about your family except, you know, how your husband died, and that you got a couple kids."

They cut through the casino to the broad corridor that ran along its outer perimeter. Cat glanced in the Golden Dragon Coffee Shop, saw that Harold was sitting with a half-dozen people from the show, his food untouched, talking into a cell phone. He looked up and their eyes locked.

"Those people from the TV show?" Remy whispered.

Cat nodded. She saw Harold gesture toward her, excuse himself from the table.

"Cat, I just talked to Cici, she told me what happened to you. Over at Ron's place? God, are you all right? Why didn't you say something up there?"

Cat introduced Remy. Harold shook hands. "How'd it happen that Wally turned up in Ron's apartment?"

"I don't know. We didn't have a lot of time for conversation. Cici tell you that someone took a shot at us?"

A young woman appeared at Harold's side. "Excuse me, aren't you Harold Anderson?"

Harold blushed a little, nodded.

The woman produced a notebook and pen.

Harold looked baffled for a minute, then it kicked in. "Oh, oh yeah, sure." He signed his name and handed it back to her. "God," he whispered. "I shoulda asked her name. You know, like when people frame the first dollar they make?" He returned to the subject. "Yeah, Cici said you said that. You guys wanna come sit with us?"

"No, I have to go get my kids."

"We're still on for tomorrow, right?" Harold asked.

"Unless you get too famous before then," Cat said.

"He's cute," Remy hissed, as they headed out toward the street entrance. "He with anyone?"

"One of his co-stars."

"Anyone else straight and single?"

Cat signaled the cab at the curb. "Red Melendez."

Remy made a face.

They settled in the cab and Cat gave the driver her mother's Richmond Avenue address.

"We used to live there." Remy pointed out the back window toward Euclid Avenue as the cab headed in the other direction. "God, nothing looks like it did, you know? It's like it's not even the same town. Look at that ugly thing, supposed to be a lighthouse? Everything here now, it's like it's got a shape and an outside all dressed up with lights, but in here"—Remy patted her fist against her heart—"it's twisted metal and rust. You know what I mean?"

"'Nature with a beauteous wall doth oft close in pollution,'" Cat murmured.

"Huh?"

"It's Shakespeare. From *Twelfth Night*."

The cab turned down Richmond Avenue. Cat saw Carlo's Volvo parked behind her mother's red Buick.

Cat let herself in, called out, "I'm here! Who wants to give Mommy a kiss!"

Mats came running from the kitchen in his stocking feet, a smear of chocolate on his chin. "Nonna let us make cupcakes and lick the bowl. Who's that?"

"Cat, what the fuck happened to your car, I'm—" Carlo stopped in the doorway, looked at Remy.

"This is my brother," Cat introduced. "I know you probably don't remember—"

Amazement flowed into Remy's gaze, darkening the irises, dilating the pupils. "It's not Officer Carlo! It's not Officer Carlo!" she shrieked and ran toward him like a little girl, threw her arms around his neck.

Carlo grinned, sheepishly. "You're the younger one, right? I guess I changed from back when you knew me."

Cat saw Mark glance out from the kitchen, curiosity overwhelming his hostility.

"Oh, no." She actually reached up and tousled his hair. "You got gray, you know, but on you it looks good."

"I put on a couple pounds."

Remy giggled, threw her arms around him. "But I can reach all the way around you now. Remember when I was so little, how I tried to make my arms ..." It dawned on her. She looked at Cat. "He's your brother?"

Cat nodded.

"Officer Carlo is your brother? The King is your brother?"

"Yes."

"I'll kill Victor for not telling me!" She looked at Mark. "Is this your boy?"

"Yeah. Mark, say hi to Victor's sister."

Mark's eyes crept up Carlo's massive form in awe. Asked if he was Carlo's kid and Carlo said "Yeah" right off, didn't blink. "Hi."

"Oh, you don't know. You don't know how your dad is my hero!" she laughed. "I was this high—" she lowered her palm to the top of Mats' head. "And I thought he was a giant, you know." She turned to Cat. "Oh," she cried. "You will have to marry him now, *si*? *Mami* will never let you hear the end of it if you don't! Oh, she'll just drop dead when I tell her!"

Drop dead.

The focus shifted to the gloved hand rising in the foreground, adjusted for the depth of field so that Tommi Ann and Ron could be seen clearly. She was at a diagonal, about three feet from Ron, his face visible.

Crack!

Spivak lurched forward, the camera with him, cutting the shooter's hand out of the frame. Tommi Ann toppled into the foreground, out of the frame; the camera kept rolling, someone shouted, "Cut. *Cut.* Jesus, Spivak, can't you count—" and the screen went black. Victor fast-forwarded a little; there was nothing more on the tape.

Something not right. Something he wasn't seeing, hearing. In front of his eyes, but not connecting with his brain. He scowled at the flat blue screen, wondered if Cat could stand to watch it. Perhaps she would get whatever it was he was missing.

He got up and pushed the television monitor into a corner, went into the day room. Adane and Long were sitting at the computer terminal; he knew from the perplexed look on her face that her search had been fruitless.

"Nothing?"

Adane shook her head, a faint flush tinting her pale features. She took defeat as a personal failure. "I can't come up with anything. The most comprehensive database lists her as Tommi Ann Butler, and gives her birthplace as Kingman, Kansas, so I've put in a call to their Records Bureau. It's difficult without a birth name."

"Try—"

"Cox. I have. They promised to get back to me today."

"Where were they married?"

"Outside the country. In the Caribbean, I believe."

"What about film archives?"

"I have calls in to Dayton, Rochester and New York."

"You have a sheet on the evidence logged in after the incident?"

Adane handed him a sheet from a folder on her desk.

"They were using forty-one Magnums, you ever fire one?"

"Yeah," Long said. "I can see why Anderson put it down, they're heavy mothers. I don't see 'em around much."

"One was clean. The other had one blank intact, one had been fired ..."

"So both blanks had been transferred to the gun with the metal head," Adane said.

"What's the matter, Lieutenant?" Long asked.

Victor shook his head. "Something doesn't jell. Something's not right. I'm signing out. Long, take one more look at that tape, see if anything fires up gut instinct."

"How come it's instinct when I got it and common sense when Jeannie's got it?" Long inquired.

Victor sensed the hush when he walked into Bud-N-Lou's, detected something more than the hush that his presence seemed to provoke. His reputation made him untrustworthy to many of them. If it came down to the blue or the truth, Cardenas was the type who would bust the wall, tell the truth, no question. No question that's why he was here now.

The bar gleamed. Lou was polishing it anyway, his creased face fixed in a resolute frown. He looked up, jerked his head to a booth at the very back of the dim room, went back to his task. Victor walked calmly to the booth, saw the broad back hunched over a mug on the table, the too-long arms folded around it, awkwardly.

Victor sat. In the years he had known Gino Forschetti, Gino had not changed one hair, one line, had remained immutable, ageless as only the very beautiful or very ugly could be. Gino was ugly. The low forehead, the black brows, the elongated arms, broad shoulders, loping gait gave him a simian appearance. Yet somewhere on that hirsute body there was the small, shiny indentation left by a bullet meant for Victor, and deeper still was a heart that must put a strain on his massive chest. Gino was still ugly, still ungainly, but he had changed.

He looked up at Victor, jerked his chin toward the beer. "It's my first today."

"You need to get some help, Gino."

The beady eyes looked at him from beneath the protruding brow. "I'm not gonna make it without her, Victor."

"Do you want to make it?"

"No."

"Then you won't. Because you don't want to. Don't put it on Sheila."

"She was so full of— I mean, everything about her was so alive. God, she was ... God ..."

Victor said nothing. He didn't need Gino to tell him what Sheila had been. He wondered if she had ever told Gino about their brief relationship. It didn't matter now. "Talk to me about Wednesday night."

Gino rolled the mug between his palms. "I been on leave for almost a month, I guess they figured this was a cake job, ease me back into the rhythm. I go with the guy—"

"Wally?"

"Right. Wally. Go with him when he gets the round out of the safe. I watch him load the guns. Head in the hero model, two blanks in the firing model. See? I got the lingo down."

Victor nodded, silently.

"Then I just gotta watch. They shoot some close-ups, down the chamber of the dummy? They coach what's-his-name, Anderson?"

"He any good?"

Gino's massive head bobbed. "Yeah. Takes direction well, does what he's told, good grip, doesn't play the show-off. They're gonna go for a take. Wally checks the chamber, hands the piece to Harold. It's a forty-one Mag, heavy sonofabitch. Everything's cool, then I hear people screaming, they're goin' Ooooouuuuuuweeee. I look, there's Biggs standing outside his trailer, watching, and the crowd gets a gander and they go berserk. They start pushin' at the barricade, I'm afraid they're gonna kill him, someone might take a potshot, this location stuff, I'm with Raab on this one, it's bad news. So I go get on his flank while his team hustles him inside."

Ready to take a potshot for some kid he doesn't even know. "Go on."

"I'm talking to The King, he says he'll keep the kid in the trailer, I go back. Wally and Anderson are having words about something, the gun being too heavy, something like that. I didn't hear what they said."

"When you went back to where the props were, Anderson had the gun in his possession?"

"Yeah."

"Who else was around the table?"

"Everyone. That lady, Mrs. King, she came by earlier to see if she could get us some coffee. The young girl, Bonaker, she's around. The director. The Steinmetz woman and her assistant. Hair and makeup on standby." Gino shook his head. "Everyone. So they roll, Anderson does exactly what he's supposed to do, fires the shot, and it looks like Spivak takes his fall too soon. That's what they think happened. Then he doesn't get up. I think Tommi Ann was the first one to notice. She starts screaming. Butler's on her in a New York minute. The King woman hustles the girl outta the way, Anderson starts flippin' out. The assistant, June Something, she says she's afraid he's gonna have an attack, can she run him to the med center, I okayed it. I turn around, I see that Wally's gone. Someone told me he went to the ER with Anderson. I tell one of the uniforms to bag the guns on the table, then Biggs' team asks me to help move him into the club. When I came out, you all were there."

"How much did you have to drink Wednesday night, Gino?"

Gino looked at him. "I never took a drink on the job. You know me, I never ... just don't ask me how much I had to drink since."

Victor rose, signaled the waitress, paid Gino's tab. "Come with me."

CHAPTER THIRTY-ONE

INT: KATE'S APARTMENT: NIGHT

KATE

There's a point where white hot copy
turns into cold hard blackmail.

CALDERONE

And Donner was killed because he crossed
over?

KATE

Or because he was about to.

Jennie hit him with the bad news as soon as she opened the door.
"Your sister, she's too much. The stories she's tellin', she's got the
kids in stitches."

"Jennie, do you know Gino Forschetti?"

"Who don't I know?" Jennie actually pinched Gino's cheek.

"I ran into him. He was about"—Victor lowered his voice con-
spiratorially—"to pick up a burger at McDonald's for dinner."

Jennie looked as though he had uttered a blasphemy. "They
oughta close all those places," she declared. "Fast this and fast that,
you know what's gonna happen next? They're gonna put your dinner in a little pill."

Victor baited her. "It would save time."

"Whaddaya savin' all this time for? What do any of you do with all this saved-up time, anyway?"

Carlo lumbered into Jennie's small foyer. "Your sister, she's a pistol," Carlo chuckled. He shook hands with Gino, led him into Jennie's kitchen, never asked what he was doing there. Remy was sitting in the center of the crowded kitchen table, Jane and Mats bracketing the slight figure, saying "—and so Victor, he's convinced that he can pass off this goldfish to Milly as the one that died, but he's gotta make it back to the house before Milly gets home from cheerleading, you know, and all he's got is that old rusty bike, my *Papi*"—she made the sign of the cross over her lips—"he brought over from San Juan, an' poor Victor, he's pedalin' down Atlantic Ave—"

"Remy, what are you telling them?" he demanded.

"About when you killed Milly's goldfish, an' then you're gonna buy her another one before—"

"I didn't kill it, it died."

Remy's shrug clearly stated that the distinction was an arguable one, and paper-thin.

"Man, I couldn't keep a goldfish alive to save my own life," Biggs shook his head. "It's like the Kleenex of the fish world, you know what I'm sayin', like they set out to be disposable." He recognized Gino, half rose from his chair, extended his hand. "How you doin', man?"

Lorraine looked at Remy's spare figure. "How do you stay so thin?" She picked a celery stick from the antipasto tray in the center of the table.

Remy put her palms lightly over Mats' ears. "Sex, sex and more sex."

"Remedios, *los ninos, por Dios*," Victor commanded.

"You should eat more," Jennie said and Cat doubled over with laughter and even Gino cracked a smile.

"Grammom, you want me to help you?" Mark asked.

Cat gave Carlo a wink. Vinnie turned to his boys, "Get up help your Nonna, what're you sittin' there for?"

"Tell another story 'bout when Vi'tor was little," Mats urged.

"Don't you dare," Victor demanded. His beeper trilled; he asked Jennie if there was a phone he could use.

"You go around the dining room down the hall to my bedroom." She spooned sausage from a vat into a serving dish that Mark held for her. "You tell whoever it is you gotta eat. Johnnie, you go get me another chair for Victor. Gino," she threatened, "you better be hungry."

Jennie's room was as spare as a nun's cell save for the wall of family pictures in mismatched frames. All of the boys when they graduated from the academy; Dominic with his seminary class; Cat and Chris holding a blanketed bundle; a blow-up of Cat's high school graduation picture; all the grandchildren; Vinnie's boys, stiff and uncomfortable in a formal portrait; Marco, Jr., and Andrea against a Sears background; Sherrie and Joey with Meryl standing between them.

Victor studied the pictures. There wasn't a speck of dust on the frames, none of them were crooked by so much as a millimeter. *Family*, Victor's father had told him, *is the only thing that's worth anything. Tu no tienes una familia, tu no tienes nada.*

There was a heavy crucifix, dark wood, hanging over the bed, a rosary and a water glass on the night table next to the phone. Victor picked up the receiver and dialed Rice's cell phone.

"I checked up on it, called the Bonaker girl and asked her to turn over the key she had to Spivak's apartment. And get this: she's got it. No problem, she says."

"She told Mrs. Austen she couldn't find it."

"Yeah. She and Butler and Anderson and the King woman went through her stuff, it turned up in her jeans pocket. Want me to pick it up and run over to OC and make sure it's the real thing?"

"Sounds like a real team effort."

"Yeah, they look to be the Musketeers all right. Adane says she's comin' up dry with the Bureau of Records in Kansas, she's got Phil contacting SAG to see if they can locate any of the people were in that movie *Illyria*."

"Try King County. That's where Wheeler was from. Try Imogene. Try King. Annie, or Tommi Ann or Imogene King."

Victor hung up, went back to the kitchen. Remy was still regaling the kids with stories, "—so it's the first dance Victor ever went to in his life, he's twelve years old and—"

"Remy, enough. I'd like to leave here with my reputation intact."

Remy pursed her mouth. "That's your problem, always worrying about what's intact—"

That prompted a shout of laughter from Cat's brothers, a command from Jennie, "Is everyone getting enough to eat?"

Gino was swapping war stories with Vinnie, drinking club soda. Victor took the chair that had been wedged next to Cat, gave Remy a look. She made a face, pushed her fork across her plate.

"Vi'tor," Mats asked, "does you think men have two brain cells to rub together?"

Victor's scowling mustache twitched. "I'm reasonably certain I've got at least two," he assured Mats.

Mats looked at Remy triumphantly.

Remy winked at him. "Opinions vary," she said, ran her hands through his curls. "But I make exceptions for handsome five-year-old boys."

"All three my boys made honor roll," Vinnie grunted. "Got brains comin' out their—"

"Ears," Cat said. "Let them go a couple rounds with Dianne King, that'll challenge the IQ."

"You not kiddin'," Biggs concurred. "I tell her, Dianne your brain gonna catch fire you keep doin' those puzzles, figure out where this word's hid, where that word's hid, how she can get somethin' with a Q in it over the triple word square in Scrabble."

His words sent something tingling along some neural perimeter, trying to work its way to the core, the same sensation Cat had when she and Cici had talked about what would become of the cast and crew if the show folded, who would and would not get a second shot.

Figure it out, Cat thought. *You figure it out.*

After dinner, Victor dropped Remy at his apartment, drove Cat and the kids home. She had gotten quiet after dinner, fallen into that dreamy silence that veiled a racing mind. "What's circulating through your brain cells?" he asked as he helped her lift the kids out of the car.

Cat held Mats, squirmed her key out of her pocket and unlocked the door. "I like Aunt Remy," Jane yawned as she shuffled slowly to her room.

Aunt Remy? Victor mouthed.

Cat smiled and carried Mats up the stairs, got him into his pajamas, stood him up at the sink and helped him brush his teeth. She tucked him in beside his plush rabbit, went downstairs.

"I don't know if I should keep them home from school tomorrow or let them go." Checked the machine for messages.

"Let them sleep in."

"Aunt Remy was quite a hit. You want something to drink?"

"No. Just some company."

Cat got a Pepsi from the refrigerator, kicked off her shoes and tucked herself into the corner of the couch. "How did your interview go with Tommi Ann?"

"Tell me again what happened when you asked Cici Bonaker about her key to Ron's place."

"I already told you."

"Just one more time, and I'll give you something in exchange."

"What?"

Victor was elaborately casual. "Oh ... the dress."

"What dress?" She paused. "You mean you saw *the* dress?"

"I did."

Cat pounced, landed straddled on his lap, her hands gripping the collar of his shirt. "All right, start talking. Black? White?"

"No."

"Silver, gold, copper, pewter?"

"Hardly."

Cat slipped one hand under the knot of his tie, gave it a twist. "Red, pink, green, yellow, mauve?"

"Mauve? I don't think I'd say that."

"So it's not mauve."

"No, it may well be. It would just be out of character for me to have that particular hue in my vocabulary."

Cat pursed her lips, thoughtfully. "That's true. I don't think I ever heard my brothers refer to anything as mauve."

Victor pressed his lips to hers, felt her grip loosen, her arms slide around his neck.

"Mint? Mocha? Saffron?"

"Blue."

"Azure, cobalt, indigo, midnight, turquoise?"

He locked his arms around her waist. "A nice, light, non-mauve-like blue. Now, tell me, what did you talk to Bonaker about?"

"We were reasoning backward. Like Sherlock Holmes."

"And what did you come up with?"

"Quite a *mauvais livre*, actually."

"I love it when you talk like Anouk Aimee."

"You're dating yourself."

"Lately, it has seemed so."

Cat looked at him. "Anouk Aimee was born Francoise Dreyfus, did you know that? Now, there was nothing wrong with Francoise, of course, it's classy. But 'Anouk' has allure, you know? It's a movie star name. 'Tommi Ann' definitely isn't. When she rocketed to star-dom— Wait, delete that, no clichés, here. When she achieved fame or had it thrust upon her, Butler gave her his surname. But I can't think that he came up with 'Tommi Ann,' or she changed it from something else to that. You remember how Jerry Dudek's murder, the motive for it, reached way back into his past?"

Victor nodded.

Cat nodded. "Jerry changed his last name, too, but he'd been 'Jerry' and stayed 'Jerry.' Some parts of our identity, we just can't let go of. She couldn't let go of 'Annie' and she couldn't let go of her lover, who everyone called 'TJ,' but whose name was Thomas. Tom. As scared and desperate and determined to disappear as she was, she couldn't let go of the only thing, the only relationship that had meant anything to her. And yet ..."

"Yet?"

Cat's mouth puckered, absently. "She held out for that sixty thousand. Sixty thousand was a small fortune back then. I suspect it was well above the going rate for an outlaw adoption. You wouldn't think she would have bargained when a fifth of that would have done as well. Unless she needed to fund something more than fugitive expenses. Fast forward a few years and Tommi Ann is living in a walk-up, getting by God-knows-how and winding up in *Illyria*. Fast forward again and she's Tommi Ann Butler, rising star."

"That's a lot of fast-forwarding. You think Spivak turned up the lost episodes?"

Cat nodded. "And then there are Butler's clients. Eric Obermeyer, who gave Tommi Ann her break in films; he was *the* director to work with until he became ill. Gloria Ramirez, Wheeler, Mrs. Diaz, even Gary Biggs' grandfather. And who knows how many other debts they paid off over the years in the way of referrals and jobs and money?"

"My father used to say that the people you truly owe you can count on the fingers of one hand. But for those people, you cut off your hand if necessary to pay them back."

Cat shifted, uneasily. "I don't know. I think that Ron was killed by someone who owed Tommi Ann, and then I think, no, there had to be something more at stake. I just have this gut feeling that whatever Ron had, someone other than Tommi Ann stood to lose by it."

"Lose what?"

"Well, suppose Ron planned to run his exposé this week. Today. Tomorrow. Tommi Ann Butler, pregnant teenage murderer. Dredge up all those gory details about Sheriff Sontag's mutilations. Even Cici doubts whether Tommi Ann, the consummate pro, would continue with the *CopWatch* shoot if Ron trashed her image, and Cici only thinks Ron was looking into the adoption, she doesn't know anything about the murder, the money that changed hands with the Bonakers." Cat's mouth puckered, thoughtfully. "My theory is that Ron was killed to keep the shoot on track—keep Tommi Ann from walking away. Because, as awful as it is to think about it—"

"*Death of a Shock Jock* is still on track."

"Not only that, murder probably helps promote it. I've talked to April and her opinion seems to be that there's too much footage and too much money invested for the network to write it off. Just re-schedule the principal photography and wring a few more rewrites out of Harold, and they're a go."

"The show must go on?" Victor shook his head, scowling. "I'm not sure if that's indecent or courageous."

"Sometimes it's neither. Sometimes, it's just what you do to get through the moment." The morning after Chris had been killed, Easter morning, three AM, she had gotten out of bed and scrubbed the kitchen floor, scrubbed away all the pastel splashes of dye that the kids had dripped on the linoleum. They had been dying eggs, preparing for Easter when Carlo had come through the door, and the next hours had faded, dissolved, and memory fast-forwarded to three AM and Cat had looked at the bowl of colored eggs on the counter, took them in the living room and began to hide them, tucking them inside chair legs, on top of books, behind cushions, the first joint undertaking she had performed alone after his death, her body putting itself through the drill that her mind hadn't accepted, that it wasn't Cat and Chris any-more, it was just Cat, that what she had to do on her own had reached down even to these trifling rituals.

Victor watched the dark eyes flickering, walking through some corridor of her past, wondered what she was thinking. "So," he said, "if the motive was to keep the show on track, who would be most likely to be derailed by the cancellation of the project?"

Cat came back to the present. "That's why I can't think it was Cici. Because she's the only one who's got Butler's agency behind her, the only one who's certain to get another shot if the show, even the series, doesn't pan out. But it's got to be someone who has access to her stuff."

"Because it had to be her key they used."

Cat eased off his lap, paced, her arms crossed over her chest. "When I asked her about the key and she couldn't find it, she seemed genu-inely upset. What if someone took it to let Wally into Ron's place? That means it was someone who could get it from her pocket when her coat was hanging in Wardrobe—that could be anyone."

"But not anyone could put it back." He repeated his phone conversation with Stan Rice.

Cat twisted a strand of hair, absently. "Why put it back? And why not just give it to Wally?"

"Because," Victor theorized, "if Wally had it, he could come and go. Without it, he was more or less obligated to stay put. A sitting duck."

"How would Harold write this?" Cat speculated. "Killer: 'I can stash you for a couple days, if I need to get in touch, I'll phone you. Ring once, hang up, call right back.'"

"Or send a message through the fax," Victor suggested. "Which would program Wally to expect a call, or a fax."

"Why not put the key back right after Wally's stashed away?"

Victor shrugged. "No opportunity."

"Set up a shooting so it looks like a production accident. Isolate

Wally until you can arrange to get rid of him, because once he'd had time to think he's going to figure out who could have loaded the weapon." Cat threw her hands up in the air. "Why does Harold stress over this? I could write a *CopWatch* script in a couple days."

"Then slink back here, and whisper the villain's name in my ear."

Cat did a slow sashay toward the couch, leaned down to his ear. "Someone with talent and wanton desperation," she whispered.

CHAPTER THIRTY-TWO

EXT: BOARDWALK: MORNING
   KATE sprints along the Boardwalk, the early
   morning joggers no match for her brisk,
   long-legged gait.

Cat felt up to resuming her morning run until she took off
around Beach, felt all the resistance of muscles on furlough. A week.
CopWatch and Co. had been around for a week. It seemed like an
instant, and like an eternity. The wet ocean breeze nosed through the
gaps in her sweats, sending a chill along her throat, into her sleeves.
The air was heavy with salt, mist coated her like sweat and collected
on her lashes, condensed and dropped like tears.
   What am I going to do?
   The discovery hovering on the periphery of her brain would come
together, she was certain of that much. It would fall into place, and she
would figure out what Ron had known, what he had been killed for,
what a rigged prop, a misspelled fan note, a key lost and then found, a
fugitive prop manager meant. That's not what troubled her. What if it
was truly a million-dollar story? What would she do then?
   A million-dollar story meant no more fretting over the bills, no
more listening to commercials for tuition aid and equity loans more
carefully than she had a year before, no more looking over Jane's
outgrown sweats and pullovers, wondering if they were androgynous
enough to pass along to Mats.

She looked at the gulls, swooping down and battling each other for scraps of something picked out of the ocean, bullying off the timid wrens, the pigeons bobbling toward some crumb left behind by the insatiable gulls. Grab, or be satisfied with the crumbs. Who had said that?

Ron.

She trotted down the ramp and headed along Beach toward the intersection. Dunes on one side and headless parking meters, silence everywhere, large homes, some beautiful, closed up. Like gulls, the money-eyed swooped to the sea, snapped up the choice beachfront property. Few working families could afford a single-family home so close to the shore. Aunt Cat, trafficking in real estate with her compelling mix of inspiration and Sicilian common sense, had picked up the fixer-upper and turned it into a "2 story, 5 BR house w/ground floor apt"; when she had died, it had been bequeathed to Cat and Chris, who, moving from Chris' one-bedroom apartment had wandered the five bedrooms, the two-and-a-half baths, the long rectangle of a kitchen in awe.

Cat rounded the corner of Beach to Morningside, ran around the back of the house and up the rear steps to the back door landing, let herself in, pried off her shoes and kicked them into the little pantry that had been her office once. Now she worked in her bedroom.

Mats was kneeling at the kitchen booth, stirring chocolate into a glass of milk.

"How's my sweetie?"

"Are we goin' over Nonna's again today?"

"No, honey. You can stay home or you can go to school, what would you like?"

Ellice turned away from the counter, held up the morning paper. Cat glanced at the headline, CopWatch Crew Member Sought: No Charges Filed Against Actor/Screenwriter. "What time are your interviews with Melendez and Anderson?"

Cat smacked her forehead. "I forgot."

"Melendez didn't." Ellice nodded toward the radio that she had tuned to *Sonny At Sunrise*. "He's reiterating his profound shock at the"— she did a quote wiggle with the first two fingers of each hand—"'death' of Ron Spivak. 'I didn't know him that well, but on a location shoot you all become like family.' And Sonny's doing his thing, saying 'ekcetera' every third sentence and 'infer' when he means 'imply' and 'scrupules' for 'scruples.'" She snapped her fingers. "I've got it, grammar tutorials for local radio hosts, you think there's money in it?"

"I think there's a potential fortune. Where's Jane?"

"Getting dressed. Dress up? Dress down? Until Biggs leaves town, there's always the possibility of an encounter, so she wants to be appropriately attired."

Jane bounded into the kitchen, her hair in a high ponytail, dressed in khakis and a long-sleeved black T. Black Converse high-tops.

"We're going for the minimalist look," Ellice murmured.

"What can you tell us about Wally Reid?" Sonny asked. "According to the paper, I imply that he's likely to be charged with negligence."

Cat laughed aloud, poured out Cheerios for Mats and went up to take her shower. She decided to follow Jane's example, go for the minimalist look, pulled on khakis and a V-necked black sweater. She bounded down the stairs and grabbed Jane's insulated lunch box from the counter.

"Can I buy lunch today? It's pizza."

Cat hunted up her purse and got her wallet. She had exactly two dollars and fifty-six cents, had meant to get to the bank to cash a check before her car had been stolen. She gave Jane the two dollars without blinking, but her brain was mapping out a last-ditch cash hunt through pockets, old purses and drawers.

A million-dollar story.

She watched Jane get on the bus and went back to the kitchen to have breakfast with Mats. "So what's it gonna be, honey? School or no school?"

"So," Sonny at Sunrise was asking, "on a shoot like this when you have that many of these kinds of setbacks, when do you fold up your tents and throw in the towel?"

Cat looked up at Ellice. Ellice's eyes were dancing as she slid into the booth. "Lesson one," she said, "Similes and Metaphors: When they're a gold mine, when they're as deadly as the plague. I tell you, this is an idea whose time has came and went."

The phone rang. It was Victor.

"I thought you might be April," Cat said. "They were supposed to shoot the interviews today, in a conference suite over at the Phoenix." *CopWatch* topped off its "dramatic recreations of actual events" by filming interviews with "the actual people involved." Mats was squirming up against her, whispering that he had to talk to Victor. Cat handed him the receiver.

"Vi'tor, you're not asposed to hit people."

"No, it's not very nice."

"So how come Aunt Remy says when you was my age you was already beating off girls with a stick?"

"I'm sure you misunderstood Aunt Remy. I'll make sure I straighten Aunt Remy out."

"Can she come over today?"

"Don't you have preschool?"

"Mom says I can stay home."

"Well, I envy you. I'll make sure Aunt Remy visits you again before she goes back home. Can I talk to Mom again?"

Mats handed the phone back to Cat.

"You're not going to be wandering around today, are you?"

"I can't. I've got afternoon interviews here with Red Melendez and Harold. Are you listening to Red on the radio?"

"Now? No. Is he compassionate, inclusive, acutely aware of our diversities?"

"Absolutely."

"Can't think why I'm missing it. Ellice will be there, won't she?"

"Yes, why?"

"Your car's at large and that means your registration with your address on it is, too. I don't want Wally to decide that his only way out of this mess would be to take you hostage."

"Don't be silly, Victor. You'll start sounding like Harold's script."

"I have it on very good authority that Harold's script is based on 'actual fact.'"

"Victor, do you still have that tape of the footage they shot at the club?"

"Yes, why?"

"Can I have a look at it sometime?"

"Cat, even though you don't get a clear view of the shooting, it's pretty grim. And you can't see who's in back of the prop cart."

"If I can't take it, I'll hit the stop button. There's something about it that's nagging at me, and I can't figure out what it is."

Something had nagged him, too, about it. "I'll think it over," he promised.

Cat laid a bagel on top of her coffee mug, nodded to Ellice; they went into the den and turned on the television to catch the last couple minutes of Callie O'Connor's pre-taped interview with Harold Anderson. Cat munched and watched Callie draw Harold out of his shell-shocked demeanor, ease him into a chummy informality, coax forth a bit of winsome charm that would play well to at-home middle-aged moms, who were drinking coffee, trying to remember the name of that sweet boy they had known in college whose memory Harold Anderson's boyish face called up.

"He doesn't look riddled with insecurity," Ellice said.

"The insecurities only riddle the writing," Cat told her. "His acting's quite good, actually."

The phone rang. Cat padded into the living room to pick it up.

"So, you watchin' Anderson? You hear when he goes how part of him died Wednesday night when Spivak went down? Jeez. No wonder TV's so crappy, he can't come up with better material than that."

"I expect he was still in shock, Ritchie."

"You and him still on?"

"Yes, as far as I know. Although I keep expecting Dianne King to call me any minute and cancel or send me one of those drain-a-vein-and-sign-on-the-line releases. If she wants a cover, can I promise it?"

"Hell, I'll bump the Bonaker gal for him. I heard he's got offers to write three more MOWs, not to mention the head writing gig on *Auletta!* Whaddaya think that pays?"

"More than you pay me."

"So cozy up. Is it true he's signed with Butler?"

"That's what I heard."

"They're shooting tonight, the other half of the crowd scene. Just Melendez doing his cop routine and the background. Y'think they need a stand-in for the d.b.?"

Cat hung up; the phone rang again, almost immediately.

"Mrs. Austen?" It was Dianne King.

"Yes?"

"I'm afraid we're going to have to cancel the interview Harold Anderson promised you earlier this week. Mr. Butler thinks it best that we suspend interviews for the remainder of the shoot; a lot needs to be done to reschedule the work we're committed to here. They really only need to film Red's scene in the parking lot, that will be one a.m. if you'd like to observe, you're welcome to, of course. April is revising the roundtable shoot, I'm sure she'll fax you."

"Then I don't suppose I'll be seeing you again, or Tommi Ann or Cici."

"No."

Something needled her, some impulse that she obeyed blindly. "I still have your card. The note Ron delivered to you Wednesday night? It wound up in my tote bag."

The length of the silence told her that she had plucked a nerve. "Card?"

"The postcard with the note. Tommi Ann Butler, major shooting star? I didn't know if I should give it to the police, if it was evidence. And then there's my set pass, should I turn that in or—"

"I'd like it back."

"The set pass?"

"The note, Mrs. Austen." There was a pause. "You know exactly what we're talking about, don't you?"

Cat paused, too, did a "one Mississippi, two Mississippi" and said, "Yes," though she had no idea what she was talking about.

"This is probably something we should handle face to face, isn't it?"

Why? "When?"

"And privately, of course."

When? "Where?" *WHY?*

"I can come to Ocean City."

No way. "No, I'll come to the Phoenix."

Something told her not to meet her alone, away from public and familiar turf. "I don't think that would do. What about that monument we passed the day we came into Ocean City?"

Cat thought for a minute. Daylight, standing under a sixty-five-foot elephant wouldn't expose her to risk, would it? "All right, I'll meet you under the left"—she swallowed a laugh—"under the left rear leg."

"How soon?"

"Half an hour."

"I have to run into Margate," she told Ellice. "If I'm running late, I'll just have to cancel my one o'clock with Red," she added with mock disappointment.

Mats withdrew his concerns about Mom going out when Ellice came through with an offer of a couple games of Candy Land and a walk to the bookstore, a place for which, Cat suspected, Ellice was developing as much of a fascination as Mats. Ellice could be counted on to buy him a book even when he didn't *ask* for it, and one for Jane, too.

Cat had the cabbie run past the bank so that she could cash a check, forced herself to look squarely at the balance. *You're getting warmer,* she told herself. *Closer to Ron's million-dollar story. What will I do when I know the truth?*

It was different from the Dudek case. That had been about finding out how far her courage would take her, how much she was willing to risk for the truth. This was coming down to what she would do with that truth once it was in her possession, how much of herself she would have to trade off for the million-dollar story.

The cab driver had seen *Redemption* eight times. Cat believed that she looked like a person who could discern the number eight when she heard it, but he, too, felt compelled to reinforce it digitally, which required him to lift both hands from the wheel as the cab crossed the narrow Ocean City-Longport bridge, sent them coasting, briefly, into the opposite lane.

"She goes down to that graveyard which is nothing but desert now and she's brushing the sand away from the marker in the ground and it's got the name of her father on it and she, it's like she's tryin' to cry but she can't? You know, it's like on her face, you see it? Like everything he done to her is still in her head but she can't make it come out?" He picked up Cat's nod in the rearview, "You get what I'm talking about?" Cat nodded again.

Approaching from the downbeach end, the initial sighting was of Lucy's behind, a large elephant *derrière* rising more than sixty feet in the air, two narrow rectangular windows tucked under the sideways tail. The drizzle that had set in camouflaged the gray beast from a distance, until one could pick out the dark red of the blanket, the arcs of the howdah.

There were a few cars parked on Atlantic. Margate was considered upscale, with a commercial stretch that had the usual complement of boutiques, cafés, ice cream parlors. The elephant was on a small pavilion with a detached gift shop off to the side. There were doors tucked into the rear legs, a narrow stair that led up to the top, where one could visit a tiny museum, watch a video about the history of this hunk of Jersey-shore kitsch.

Cat paid the cabbie, pulled her black blazer tightly around her. She approached slowly, the sound of light traffic mingling with the surf. She stopped at the curb, began walking along the sidewalk rounding the area, felt the sting of mist-encrusted wind on her left cheek, wind coming off the water. It would carry sound to her ear, if there was any sound, but it was quiet.

Something fluttered, something Cat's left eye took for a swooping gull, but the gulls were canny, efficient, didn't descend unless there was promise of a feed. Cat turned, saw the flapping of a pale wing at the enormous rear foot of the statue. It wasn't a gull, it was a cloth, a scarf perhaps, snagged on the rough metal structure, flapping with the rhythm of a metronome at the base of the stump-like leg.

Cat began to approach the beast, slowly, her eyes doing a continuous pan, her gait forward, then sideways. She approached the massive gray stump, allowed her eyes to adjust for mist and light, saw that the cloth was a length of coat, a loose, light coat, beige.

Cat began to move faster, pressed her palms to the rough metal of the elephant to steady herself, rounded it. Dianne King was lying on the ground inside the rear right leg. Her tightly bound hair had been pulled loose in a struggle, the coat flung open. Cat heard a moan, and the moan cut through her trance; she sprinted the last few feet to the body and dropped to her knees.

Dianne's bag was lying beside her, the white blouse had been pulled free from her waistband and her palm was pressed to a dark wound under her left breast.

"Dianne! Dianne!" Cat pressed the hand down with both of hers, looked around and began to scream for help. She flicked her hair away from her face, saw Dianne's eyes roam, felt some slight pulsation under her hands. On the ground beside her throat, the chain she had worn had broken loose, the letters scattered into an odd and ominous pattern.

d i e

a   n n

Cat started screaming, screaming; a passing cruiser stopped, two patrol officers came at a sprint.

Cat felt the rawness in her throat, felt the narrowness of the ribs under her palms, was afraid that she would crush the woman with her pressure.

"I—found her. Like this," she gasped. How frail Dianne was; Cat had not realized it. She was so composed, so decisive that she gave the impression of weight. But there was nothing to her, Cat realized. And another piece clicked into place.

"Looks like a struggle." One of the officers shot a skeptical glance at Cat. "What were you doing here, ma'am?"

The whine of the ambulance cut off her answer. Cat felt something tug her sleeve, saw Dianne's smooth forehead furrow with effort. She leaned down, heard Dianne whisper, "It was ... help ... help Cici ... help my ... Cici ..."

It came together, then. The cliché winnowed through her muddled gray matter, *Better late than never.*

Better never, she thought.

CHAPTER THIRTY-THREE

INT: HOSPITAL EMERGENCY ROOM
*KATE is pacing, her long legs straining
against the confines of her short, narrow
skirt. She checks her watch, whispers
CALDERONE'S name a few times. A pair of
orderlies rush by with NADINE on a gurney.*

Cat sat in a vinyl chair in the waiting area of the emergency
room, the officer who had accompanied her leaning at the sign-in
desk, chatting with the young girl who was counting the names on
the clipboard. She looked around at the people: a kid with tear tracks
on his face, nursing his elbow; a man with a blood-tinged square of
gauze wadded at his temple; another who had an icepack balanced
on his dishtowel-wrapped right hand, his left hand holding something wrapped in another towel.

Cat wondered wildly if Ron had sat like that after the Nucci
business, holding his ice-wrapped appendage on his lap. Of course
not, Nucci had swallowed it. She felt a wild shudder scurry up her
throat, the pressure of a repressed laugh forcing tears from her eyes.

The door whooshed open. The security guard looked up and she
saw Victor, tall, unsmiling, flash his shield to the uniform. He looked
at Cat, huddled in her chair, his gaze resting on her for a moment,
assessing her condition, assuring himself that she was okay.

Cat watched him exchange a few brief words with the uniform who brought her in; heard "gunshot," "surgery," saw the cop's indifference dissolve when Victor uttered a certain phrase. Probably "Tommi Ann Butler," Cat surmised.

He walked over to Cat, hunkered down beside her chair. "Do I want to know what you were doing in Margate?"

Cat wiped her eyes on her sleeve, shook her head.

"Where was she shot?"

"Under Lucy the Elephant." Cat swallowed a shuddery laugh, swiped at another tear. "It's where we arranged to meet."

Victor took a white handkerchief from his breast pocket, pressed it into her fist, noticed that she was clutching a fine gold chain, gold letters.

"Dianne's necklace," she sniffed. "It must have broken in the struggle."

"She was wearing her ring, too, her wallet wasn't touched. There was a struggle, but it wasn't a mugging." He glanced at the cop and the nurse, watching them, the patients waiting in the lounge. He helped her up, walked her outside the hospital, away from the wide rotating doors.

His roving gaze was on yellow alert, scanning for eavesdroppers, press. "If memory serves you were going to be close to home today. Had interviews lined up with Melendez and Anderson."

Cat nodded. "Dianne called. To cancel Harold's interview. She said Butler's holding off on more coverage."

"Then why did she arrange to meet with you?"

"I let on that I knew something about Ron's murder, something I didn't really know. I mean, there were bits of it lodged way back in my cluttered brain. And then I remembered the postcard—"

"One Spivak asked the Mathis girl to deliver?"

Cat nodded. "And I remembered what you said Sherlock Holmes said about circumstantial evidence."

Victor knew better than to rein her back on course. "That it's a very tricky thing. That it seems to point straight to one thing, but if you shift your point of view a little you may find it pointing in an equally uncompromising manner to something entirely different. As I recall, Holmes was investigating a murder that had its roots in the criminal history of the murderer."

Cat pushed her hair behind her ear. The breeze quickly dislodged it, blew it across her face. She saw a young guy walk into the emergency entrance. She recognized him from the reporters who had hung around her front yard, probably had the ER beat, the police blotter.

"What about this note? What'd it say?"

Cat drew it out of her pocket, handed it to him.

Victor glanced past her, saw a young reporter watching them through the glass panel next to the revolving door, watched him slide out of view, one hand slipping into his pocket for his cell phone or change. Turned his eyes to the card. "This was important enough for her to retrieve?"

"What is Dianne always doing?"

"Running interference for Mrs. Butler. And Butler and the Bonaker girl."

"What else?"

"I give up. You tell me."

Cat laid her hand against his cheek; her fingers were very cold. "I know what Ron knew," she said, simply. "And Tommi Ann has a right to know that I've figured her out."

"Meaning what?"

"Meaning you can take me over to the Phoenix with you right now, or I'll go over there myself. You'll want to notify them before the press picks it up on a scanner."

Victor dispatched Long to the ER from his car, told him it was "No comment" on the King woman's shooting. He swung down to Pacific; Cat allowed herself to take in the eye-level shabbiness, then looked up to the gold pagoda lights of the Phoenix hovering above, beckoning. Beautiful from a distance; closer, one could make out the configuration of the bulbs, the ubiquitous coating of sand, the sporadic burnouts, the litter that scudded around the corners, the fast food vendors thirty feet from the velveteen-uniformed doormen at the entrance. Anything—anyone—can be beautiful, be something other than what it truly is if enough distance is put between image and memory.

Victor pulled into the self-park, helped Cat out of the car. Cat felt her heart floundering when they approached the narrow cubicle of the elevator that serviced the parking garage. She could never enter it without feeling the rise of hyperventilation, seeing the crumpled, blanketed figure she had discovered last December. A whiff of the salt, grime, mildew kept at bay was endemic to any space exposed to the elements at the shore, but Cat smelled death along with it.

I'd love to hear the story.

Which would you prefer, their fiction or my reality?

Is there a difference? In the end, reality's whatever we have to do to survive the day. Reality's what we make it.

It was Cici Bonaker who answered the ring at the suite. Her russet hair was drawn away from her pale face, her expression mildly puzzled.

"We're here to speak to Mr. and Mrs. Butler."

Victor's grave expression fanned a spark of apprehension in her gaze; she turned her eyes to Cat. "What's wrong? Has something happened to Harold?"

"No. Are the Butlers in?"

Victor felt Cat grip his arm above the elbow as they followed Cici into the living room. Tommi Ann was sitting by the window, outlined against the curtains. She looked like a portrait. Cat recalled how ancient artists would work some little imperfection into their art, so as not to taunt the gods. No imperfection had been worked into Tommi Ann. Or perhaps it was too deep to see with the naked eye.

Butler was sitting beside the coffee table, his fingers playing the laptop keyboard with the dexterity of a virtuoso.

He looked up, over the rims of narrow spectacles, rose. "What is it now, Lieutenant?"

"Dianne King has been shot," Victor said.

Cici gave a little cry. The vinyl-bound script Tommi Ann had been reading fell from her hands, the loose pages of the rewrites spilling onto the carpet.

"She's in surgery right now."

Tommi Ann rose, tried a step, wavered. "I have to see her."

Butler eased her back into her chair. "You can't, now, honey. The lieutenant said she's in surgery. That means she's still alive, isn't that right, Lieutenant?"

"Yes. As far as I know."

"Ben, call the hospital—"

"Honey, I'll call them in a minute, let's just hear what happened."

"I'll go," Cici declared. "I can get one of the security people to take me over there."

"Now, Cici, there might be reporters—"

"I don't care!"

Ben took her by the shoulders. "Cici," he said, firmly, "Let me take care of this." He turned to Victor. "Where did this happen?"

"In Margate, in a public park."

"The hell— Cici, you know she was goin' out this morning?"

Cici shook her head, dropped onto the arm of the sofa.

"She was there to meet me," Cat said.

"Can't we answer your questions on the way to the hospital, Lieutenant?" Tommi Ann begged.

Ben put his arm around her. "When did this happen?"

"An hour ago." Victor looked at them. "I'll have to ask you where you all were an hour ago."

"We were here. We had breakfast together, the five of us, and then Dianne and Harold went over to her suite to get some copy for a call-in show he's doing this morning, touch base with April about tonight. Cici's been here with us the whole time."

Victor was silent a moment. "Mrs. King's jewelry, her money weren't taken. But she was shot in a struggle. Someone didn't want her to meet with Mrs. Austen. Was afraid, perhaps, of something she was going to reveal."

Cat bit her lip. She could not look at Tommi Ann.

"I don't like to think about what might have occurred if Mrs. Austen had arrived five minutes earlier."

There was no emotion, no anger; in fact, his voice was barely audible. But Cat saw Tommi Ann freeze, saw Cici shudder.

Cat laid a hand on Victor's sleeve. "Dianne owns a gun, doesn't she?"

"Hell yes. So do I. Most people who travel with Tommi Ann do. And we're all licensed, if that's the question."

"Does Mrs. King generally carry hers when she goes out?" Victor asked.

"Around here? Hell, I don't think Dianne's gone out on her own around here, an' we've had plenty of security for Tommi Ann. Dianne's been workin' and readin'."

"Where does she keep it?" Victor asked.

"Cici oughta know. She got her gun case in your suite?"

Cici nodded, mutely.

"Is it locked?"

"I think so."

Victor strode to the door, summoned Danny Furina into the room. "I want you to go with Miss Bonaker to her suite, see if you can open Dianne King's gun case. What sort of gun was it?"

"Thirty-eight. Revolver."

Victor jerked his head toward the door. Danny shot Cat a "What's up?" look. She just shook her head, looked away.

When the door closed, Cat looked at Tommi Ann. Allowed herself one indulgence, one long look at the last great face. "This was broken in the struggle." She reached into her pocket and took out the necklace, spilled the broken strand, the six letters onto the table in front of her. "Funny, when they broke free, they got rearranged, like this." Cat pushed them with the tip of her index finger to spell out "die ann." "I think I knew before that, but sometimes you see something and it shakes the last piece of the puzzle into place. Confirms it."

"Confirms what?" Butler demanded.

Tommi Ann laid a hand on his arm. "It's all right, Ben. It's very clear that she knows."

The suite door opened and shut. Cici's face was dead white. "It's not there," she whispered.

"You want me to check the place out?" Danny asked Victor. "Report a theft?"

"No. Go back outside. Don't let anyone into the suite."

"Not even Mrs. King when she comes back?"

Cici choked on a sob, covered her mouth.

Cat waited until she heard the door close, took the postcard out of her pocket, laid it on the table beside the letters. "Ron wrote this Wednesday night, to taunt Dianne. Gave it to June Mathis to hand to Dianne, told her that Dianne would figure out what it meant. It got mixed up with my things. When I told Mrs. King I had it, she insisted we meet, to retrieve it."

Butler reached out, snatched the postcard from Cat, looked it over. "What is this, some kid's scribble, what is this?"

Tommi Ann took it; her eyes rested on it for a long time, not reading it, Cat thought, just giving herself time to accept how completely she had been revealed, to try to draw the mask back into place. The eyes looked up at Cat; she wore a maroon sweater that altered the color of her eyes, today they were the color of blood.

"I don't understand," Cici said. "Is this all because Ron thought you were my mother? Is that what people are dying for?"

"Cici, please—"

"I want to see Dianne."

"Cici—" Ben's voice was firm. "When she gets out of surgery, they're not gonna let anyone see her right off—"

"They'll let her in," Cat said, looked at Tommi Ann. "Won't they?"

Tommi Ann nodded.

"She was just barely conscious, she could have told me who shot her. But she only had time enough, breath enough for a few words. And those few words were to look out for Cici. Her Cici. It wasn't nearly as important to her to name the person who shot her as it was to make sure Cici wasn't a suspect, that Cici was in the clear."

"I don't understand." Cici's voice was high, rising toward hysteria.

Tommi Ann flicked the postcard against her fingertips, looked at Cat.

"Dianne told me to wait, to wait until you were ready to talk about whatever you were hiding," Cici said. "I shouldn't have listened to her, I should have asked you as soon as Ron started hinting that it might be true. Well, I'm asking now, are you my mother or not?"

Tommi Ann laid the card down, took Cici's shaking hands between hers. "The Bonakers were good people. I think they did a wonderful job. You wouldn't have thought, would you, that two desperate kids could have chosen so wisely in such hopeless straits."

Cici blinked; her hands dropped free of Tommi Ann's. "My mom and dad," she whispered. "Didn't they know who you were?"

Tommi Ann shook her head. "They wouldn't have recognized me in any case. It was more than twenty years ago." She looked up at Cat and Victor. "Please sit down."

Victor waited for Cat to sit, stood until Cici slumped onto the sofa.

"I'm sure you have been through my bio, what there is of it. There is a Kingman, Kansas, but I wasn't born there, I was born in a town small enough to fit in the palm of your hand. Imogene, Texas. It's the stuff of imagination now, or nightmares. Dreams of flight, that's what I lived on. What we lived on, the two of us, because there wasn't much else to keep us going from one breath to the next."

"Who's we?" Cici asked.

"Two kids. Annie and TJ. Annie Cox and Thomas Sontag, Junior. Two kids who were withering away for want of love. My God, there were times I thought we'd have every ounce of love sucked clean out of us, like the Texas heat desiccates anything with a drop of moisture to it. That we'd crumble into dust and blow away." She paused. "TJ was almost sixteen and Annie was fourteen. They ran off to Mexico. They wanted to get married before their baby was born."

"Got a lift from a trucker named Biggs," Cat added.

Tommi Ann smiled. "He let us sleep in the back of his truck. He gave us lime soda from the pop he was hauling and a few dollars. He knew the way it worked down there, knew where to go to change our names, get papers, find someone to perform the ceremony. A sweet man. Gary is just like him."

"Gary's ... grandfather?" Cici asked.

"Sheriff Sontag had them picked up and brought back. Annie was sent back to her sister's place. The boy was ... beaten. One of his teachers tried to get custody of them. TJ's sisters didn't want him and his mother was dead. Annie was something her sister and her sister's husband could use. They refused to give the kids up. The teacher said that if she saw another scratch on those kids, she would go to the law. But Sontag was the law, you see, and people turned their heads. So they ran away again and this time Sontag didn't come after them."

"Why not?" Cici asked.

"He was murdered."

The room fell into a dead silence for a moment; only Cici Bonaker's breathing could be heard.

"You read Sherlock Holmes, Lieutenant."

Victor nodded slowly.

"So do we. There's a passage in one of the stories, Holmes and Watson are on a train, traveling through the countryside. Watson extols the panorama of rolling hills and peaceful farmhouses, but Holmes

..." her ice eyes drifted, and she began to recite, "'... look at these lonely houses, each in its own field, filled for the most part with poor ignorant folk who know little of the law. Think of the deeds of hellish cruelty, the hidden wickedness which may go on, year in, year out, in such places and none the wiser.'" She looked toward the window. The drapes had been drawn open, the sky was clouding over and a translucent reflection of Tommi Ann looked back at her. "But they couldn't disappear with a baby."

"How did you find the Bonakers?" Victor asked.

"'Loving, financially secure couple seeks discreet infant adoption, sex, race unimportant.' All we needed was a newspaper, change for a pay phone, and we had our pick. And we chose well. Didn't we, Cici?"

Cici's gray-gold eyes were fixed, mesmerized.

"All Annie and TJ had to promise to do was walk away, never come back, never claim the child, disappear. And the baby was born. A girl. Annie and TJ got one look, got one kiss each, took the money and then they disappeared." She paused. "That was twenty-five years ago." The reflection looked at Cici over Tommi Ann's shoulder. "When you were born, you had hair past your ears. The texture of cornsilk. But it was red."

Victor saw Butler's hand tighten over hers.

"The Sherlock Holmes story is about a girl who is hired to step into someone else's life and play her part. She agrees to it because she has no other option, no benefactor, no friends, no family, only one choice between survival and starvation: become someone else."

"How did you manage?" Victor asked. His voice didn't make them shudder now.

"We headed East. I did the things people do to get by, waited tables, worked for a dry cleaner, walked people's dogs. I amused myself by getting work in student films. No money, but it was fun and free and sometimes they would give you a box lunch, and sometimes that lunch was all we ate for a day. Or two. And then one of those film students graduated and got the funds together to make *Illyria,* and it wasn't much money, but it was lunch every day." She smiled. "And like Viola, I would never have met Ben if disaster hadn't blown me to some distant shore and left me to fend among strangers. And Ben loved me as I was, and took on all the baggage that washed up with me."

"And what had happened to Sontag?" Victor asked.

Tommi Ann looked at Cat. "He disappeared."

"And," Victor said to Butler, "your clients. The director of *Illyria* was the first. And those clients are everyone your wife was beholden to."

"Everyone Tommi Ann owed, I owed."

Victor nodded, slowly. "And a television series, with all its wealth and celebrity, that's what you owe Miss Bonaker."

"I owe her a great deal more, Lieutenant," Tommi Ann said, quietly. "But this is what's in my power to give."

It was the gesture—for Cat couldn't bring herself to look Tommi Ann in the face—the hands, the slender fingers curved, cradling the air. She had lain in her bed, her own hands coiled in that identical gesture, the night she had lost the baby she had been carrying when Chris had been murdered, feeling the phantom weight of the little head in her palm, too grief-stricken to cry.

"Tommi Ann, you know I would never have asked you for anything. I never would have taken advantage of the truth," Cici sobbed, softly. "Why couldn't you just tell me you were my mother?"

Tommi Ann laid her hand on Cici's cheek. "Dianne is your mother, Cici. I'm your father."

CHAPTER THIRTY-FOUR

INT: HOSPITAL EMERGENCY ROOM: DAY

CALDERONE

Did Nadine say anything to you? Did she
tell you why she did it?

KATE

She just begged me not to tell Tim.

CALDERONE

Tell him what?

KATE

Whatever secret Gerry must have revealed to
her.

Cici's horrified gaze fell away from Tommi Ann's eyes, slipped
downward toward the form, the female form. She pressed her palms
over her eyes. "You're lying."

Cat glanced at Victor. He was looking at the Tommi Ann in the
glass, the reflection. Night sky, stars glowed through the translucent
image that wavered like a ghost against the glass.

The image spoke. "There's nothing I can say to anyone to explain what I was as a teenager. Or before. I don't see any point in looking to the root of it, trying to map it out for someone, or in my own mind. All I know is that nature committed the transgression and left me to serve the sentence. It was ... hiding it was torment. I think my mother knew, and perhaps betrayed that she knew in the way she pampered me, which didn't help the situation with my father. I would have been a disappointment to him in any case. I'll let you come to your own conclusions about what it means for the only son of a West Texas sheriff to be less than the man he'd hung all his hopes on. There was only one person I didn't have to hide it from."

"Dianne ..." Cici whispered.

Tommi Ann nodded. "She hated to be called 'Annie.' I always called her 'Dianne.' The rest?" Tommi Ann shrugged. "It's not much different from the bio Ben invented: Kid from a small town, has a knack for play acting and a liking for literature gets her big break, finds herself in the hands of a benevolent Svengali—" she looked at Ben. "A star is born." She looked at Victor. "So, Lieutenant, what happens now?"

Victor looked at Cici. "June Mathis told you that Gary was free to come out and watch Tommi Ann work—did she mention that it was Dianne's idea?"

Cici's hands slipped to her cheeks. She nodded.

There was a pounding on the door. Ben strode down the hallway. They heard an urgent exchange, male. Harold rushed into the room. "I just heard them reporting on the news—" he looked from Tommi Ann to Cat and Victor. "Cici." He put his arms around her, "What's going on? They said a female associate of Tommi Ann was rushed to the ER, my God, I thought it might be—" he looked at Cici.

"Dianne King was shot, she's at the medical center in surgery. Mr. Anderson, could you get Mr. Furina in here, I'd like to arrange to get the Butlers and Miss Bonaker to the hospital."

"Yeah ... yeah ... Cici, I'm sorry I wasn't here."

"It's all right, Harold." Her voice was dead. "How did your interview go?"

"That's not important." He hurried down the hall.

Victor waited until he heard the door close. "I'm going to have a uniformed officer come. I can assign a female officer if you prefer, Miss Bonaker, who will have to be present in your suite until a search warrant is issued for Mrs. King's weapon." He turned to Tommi Ann. *Nothing will surprise me ever again*, he resolved. *Nothing*. "Tell me, Mrs. Butler, what would have been the effect, if your story had made the headlines yesterday, today?"

Ben Butler answered for her. "I knew someone got hired onto this production was gonna do Tommi Ann like this, I'da pulled her out, whether she wanted to finish the project or not, that's what woulda happened."

"And if she didn't finish the project, what would have been the repercussions?"

Tommi Ann looked at him.

"As far as this project is concerned, you're the Titanic, Mrs. Butler. If you go down, who sinks with you, who stays afloat?"

"I never gave it a thought."

"Give it one on your way over to the ER."

Danny had a knack for shuttling celebrities. He secured a limo and six armed security guards so swiftly there was only a lone reporter at the *porte cochere* when they were whisked out of the Phoenix. He trotted after Cat and Victor as they headed back to the self-park. "Lieutenant Cardenas, you gonna give me something?" the reporter asked.

"What would you like?"

"A quote."

"'When you have eliminated the impossible, whatever remains, however improbable, must be the truth,'" Victor told him, got Cat into the car. "I'll take you over to Northfield, I have to check my desk. I can have Stan run you home. And when you get home, you stay there."

They drove in silence for a few minutes.

"How did you know?"

"You know how it is when you're putting a jigsaw puzzle together, and you're overwhelmed with these pieces, and then all of a sudden you get the outline in place, and then a few adjacent pieces, and then you start to see images, shapes, and pretty soon the whole picture's laid out in front of you? The postcard was the final piece. Tell Dianne to figure it out, that's what Ron said to June. All Dianne did was figure things out, crossword puzzles, brain teasers, word searches. Anagrams. Major with an upper case J, shootyng with a y, star with upper case S, T and R. It's an anagram for Thomas Roy Sontag, Jr."

"What else?"

Cat shifted, uneasily. "Something Miss Zeda said. About when the kids ran away, they might not have been too particular about 'matters,' down in Mexico. What she meant to say, in her genteel way, was that they might not be too particular about the fact that the boy was white and the girl was black. And she mentioned how frail Annie was, how there was nothing to her. Tommi Ann is slender, but she's tall. Dianne's so competent that you don't think about it, looking at her, but I'll bet she doesn't weight much more than Jane."

Victor pulled into his parking slot at the bureau, turned in his seat. He cupped his hand under her chin, leaned over, kissed her. He felt Cat's arms squirm awkwardly around the seatbelt, circle his neck. He kissed the angle of her jaw, the hollow of her throat, murmured, "This may not be the appropriate time to ask, but is there anything you need to tell me? Any anatomical revisions you might have undergone somewhere along the line?"

Cat pulled back, her mouth curving with amusement.

"Because the Fortunatis did seem to run to boys, you know, after six of them—"

"You got lucky," Cat told him.

Victor got out, helped Cat out of the car. Cat was conscious of the stares as he walked her toward his second-floor office. If Victor was, he was inured to them, didn't care.

Adane jumped up when he entered, said "Good morning" to Cat. "Lieutenant, I've had Ernestine Moore sent to guard the suite at the Phoenix. And I was finally able to locate someone who knew about Mrs. Butler in *Illyria*. Of all people, it was a man who worked in the box office at a theatre in downtown Manhattan when it was playing. He kept one of the original film posters when it was first distributed."

"What's his name?" Cat asked.

Victor looked at her.

"Well, there might be a story, Victor."

"His name is Harold Lockwood. He lives in a senior citizen residence in north Jersey. And Mrs. Butler was first billed as Tommi Ann—"

"King." Victor completed her sentence.

Adane stared. "That's right."

Victor seated Cat in his office, dialed Raab, filled him in on Dianne King's shooting. "She had called Cat, arranged to meet. There was something she wanted to discuss."

"About Spivak? It was a hit?"

"Apparently. It looks like King set up the diversion; she was responsible for getting Biggs to come out of his trailer."

"She load the gun?"

"I don't know. But she knows firearms, and she had access. So did Anderson, Reid, the director, anyone who was hanging around the table when Biggs caused the distraction." Victor paused. "There's something more."

"Uh-oh. It's not like, go check your doorstep, *NewsLineNinety*'s on the stoop, is it?"

"Not unless they're after details about the King woman."

"How is she?"

"In surgery."

"Okay, I'm sitting down."

"It goes to motive."

"Hit me."

Victor told him. In his calm monotone, he recited the story Tommi Ann had delivered to him and Cat and Cici, spoke as evenly as though he were discussing his quarterly evaluations, the recital punctuated by Raab's "Aw, Jeez," "You *are* kiddin' me, right?" and something Victor could not comprehend.

"Victor. Just between the two of us and I will kill you if you ever let on to Patsy, but I had some serious dreams about Tommi Ann Butler after I saw *Black Orchid*, dreams of a very low caliber if you get my meaning."

"I suspect that puts you in considerable and disparate company."

"I am never gonna be able to watch that—well, her—in a movie again without, you know."

"I know. Apparently Spivak dug up this information, and Mrs. Austen is convinced he would have gone to press. Whether it goes to motive? Not directly, but indirectly I believe someone was convinced that Spivak had copy that would sink the *CopWatch* production and sink the killer with it."

"Then she had an accomplice."

"Yes. Mrs. King would have done anything to protect Tommi Ann Butler. But I'm thinking there was someone else who had less to fear from an exposé—probably didn't even know what the information was—as he or she was by the information appearing in the press at this time."

"So who gets made by *CopWatch*? Steinmetz? She's got a lot riding on it," Raab theorized.

"Maybe. But so does Melendez. So does Anderson."

"Look, Victor, I don't mean to say I don't trust your people, but for now, this doesn't go anywhere. Jeez, this means I don't wanna pass it on to the ADAs, I gotta talk to Tommi Ann Butler myself. What about Mrs. Austen, do I gotta worry about her?"

"If you like. It's been my experience it doesn't alter her course of action, but if you're asking whether you can count on her silence, yes, I think so."

"What about Butler. He kill for his, er, wife?"

"I suspect wringing Spivak's neck would have been more his fashion."

"And he"—Raab's voice dropped to a whisper, although it was unlikely that anyone was within earshot—"he knew ... before they got married ... about—there hadda be some kinda surgery, right? That she'd been ... Jeez, Victor, I'm sittin' here with my legs crossed. This is not good."

"Well, he wasn't shocked, if that's what you mean. I don't know how long he's known, but it was no secret to him."

"Okay. I'll send Mary Grace over to the med center."

Adane appeared at his threshold. "Excuse me, Lieutenant?"

Victor rose, turned the receiver to his shoulder.

"Stan's on line two, he said it's very important."

"Thanks. Wait here."

Victor signed off with Raab, punched the second line.

"We caught a break," Rice told him. "Mrs. Austen's car was spotted in a motel lot out the Black Horse right past the circle. Cardiff Court Motel. Reid was holed up there, we picked him up not five minutes ago."

"You've got him?"

"Yup."

"Was he armed?"

"Nope. No shots fired. Why?"

"How long had he been there?"

"Desk clerk said he checked in yesterday. He's askin' for a lawyer."

"See if he had a weapon in his possession. After they've checked out Mrs. Austen's car, have them bring it down here." He hung up, filled Adane in. "Ask Mrs. Austen to step in here, will you?"

"They found your car," he said to Cat.

She squinted, peeked at him through pressed lids. "Is it in one piece?"

"Apparently. Stan's going to see if they can have it brought over here."

Cat remembered how her car had been confiscated after the Dudek shooting, how Steve Delareto had gotten it thoroughly washed before he brought it back. Everything was coming back to her, every event echoing a sister-happening in her past.

"Did they find Wally Reid anywhere near my car?"

Victor nodded. "They're bringing him here for questioning."

"Can I–"

"No." Victor's mouth set in a resolved frown. "Adane will notify you when your car's ready to be released. Then you get in it and drive straight home, *me entiendes?*"

"*Yo no hablo ingles.* Was he armed?"

"*No hablo ingles tambien.* Sit here until your car's brought in."

"Can I use your phone? I want to try to cancel Red, and let Ellice know where I am."

"Make yourself comfortable."

Cat settled behind Victor's desk. There was an almost carnal luxuriance about the unmarked, buttery leather, the high back, that contrasted with the secondhand furnishings in the room. Cat called the Marinea Towers, got Mae on the phone. "Red said he was going right from his radio interview to the club to check on the setup for tonight, then he had a conference with Tommi Ann and April and Harold."

She hadn't heard. "If he checks in, tell him I've had to cancel our interview for this afternoon, okay? I'll call him later and reschedule."

"Is something wrong?" Mae had the keen instincts of a good right arm.

"Dianne King was shot this morning. They don't know if it was a mugging or a drive-by or what, but she's in the hospital. Tommi Ann and Ben have been notified and they're over the hospital right now."

"My God." That was all the shock Mae allowed herself. "I won't tell Red until he gets back. Otherwise, he'll be scouting out the nearest lens to do his 'production spokesperson' show. Is there anything I can do?"

"No, just give Red my message." Cat hung up and called April's cell phone.

"Did you talk to Tommi Ann?" April demanded. "Did she say whether she's going to go ahead with tonight's shoot? I got the permits and June's rounding up my background, we can go ahead with the investigation scene, push the interviews back to tomorrow, it's gonna mean OT for the unions. Can you shoot your interview tomorrow?"

"I don't know. April, do you know where Red is?"

"I haven't seen him all morning." Cat heard a muffled howl. "JUNE! You know where Red was going after that radio gig?" Heard, "If CBS was PBS, I'd be Alastair Cooke." April came back on the line. "Media hopping. He hasn't gotten this much exposure since those love scenes in *The Advocates* the censors weren't gonna run because of his butt?"

Conversations with April tended to stray off course and Cat, unaccountably, found the detours oddly fascinating, found herself asking, "What was the matter with his butt?"

"Don't ask me. But this was before you had the full moon rising in prime time four times a week, so it was a big deal. Actually, I heard it wasn't even his butt."

"You don't mean they got away with, well, frontal exposure?"

"No. That's a scary thought, isn't it? Red? It was *a* butt, just not *his* butt."

"You mean they had a—a *derrière* double?"

"Yup. You weren't gonna tell Red about Dianne King, were you? I don't wanna see him runnin' his act in front of the med center."

"No. We were supposed to meet at my place today, I was going to interview him."

"I'll put June on it. Keep her mind off thinkin' about Harold over the hospital, giving aid and comfort to Cici."

Cat hung up, her eyes settling on the television monitor, VCR. She noticed a cassette in a generic jacket laying on top of the console. She glanced through the glass, saw that the day room was quiet, Adane at the keyboard of the lone computer terminal beside her desk. Cat surveyed the objects on it, impersonal, arranged with such mathematical precision that everything was accessible, with space to spare, a direct contrast to the haphazard workspace opposite.

Cat picked up the phone once more, called home.

"Ritchie Landis called here three times," Ellice told her. "What's this about someone from *CopWatch* getting shot?"

"It was Ben Butler's publicist. Mrs. King?" Cat looked at the palm lying in her lap as if she could still see the bloodstains on her hands. "Is Mats okay?"

"A little bored."

Cat lifted the remote from the desk and clicked it on. Several seconds of blue screen and then the tape jumped right into the first take of the nightclub scene, the one Harold had screwed up. "I'm canceling my interviews for this afternoon, so if he wants to go out for a walk, it's okay with me. They found my car, so I'll be home as soon as they release it to me."

"Is she going to be okay? The woman who got shot?"

"I don't know. Give Mats a kiss for me and tell him I'll be home soon."

Cat hung up, watched Harold Anderson's second take, third, fourth. Jitters, then perfection.

Better late than never.

A few seconds of snow, then Ron's scene with Tommi Ann. Cat hit the stop button, watched the two images waver slowly, marking time. Restarted it.

Want a preview of tomorrow's show, Tommi? Want a family secret to end all family secrets?

Tommi. Not Katie. She had been certain that she heard him say Katie, but she was listening to the words in the script, the scene playing out in her head.

Want a preview of tomorrow's show, Tommi? Goading her. In front of Dianne, then sending the card with the anagram to Dianne.

Mean. And fearless and deadly. Perhaps he had thought that if he could survive the assault last November, he could survive anything.

She fast-forwarded to the parking lot scene. Cat felt a slow tightening in her gut, felt something cut into her palms, saw that it was her own nails, her hands drawn into fists. Ron and Tommi Ann were in the background, getting off their lines, hitting their marks in perfect synchronicity. What a pro Tommi Ann was, Cat marveled; even after Ron threw her with his calculated flub, she pulled herself together, got back into the rhythm.

Cat rewound the tape, began running the segment again. How quickly she recovered, suspecting what Ron knew, how professional she was. Would Ron's exposé have caused Tommi Ann to walk away from the shoot? Maybe not. Most likely not. She had no more location scenes, after all, only interiors with the other principals; she would ride it out. Of course, the *CopWatch* episode would take on all the fascination, garner all the ratings of a freak show, and Tommi Ann would never win back what she had been in the public eye. But the show would go on.

Why did the killer think it wouldn't?

Because Dianne King had impressed it upon him or her, that Ron was close to scaring Tommi Ann away from the project. Had watched Ron blow his line on purpose, deciphered his brazen ana-

gram and targeted her accomplice. Or perhaps, she had started formu-
lating a plan earlier in the day, when Cat mentioned that Ron had gone
to Texas, not to LA, maybe that put Dianne's brain to work: "I can set
up a diversion. It will look like an accident. And the people in charge
of the weapons will take the heat."

Cat refocused her eyes on the screen. *How beautiful Tommi Ann is!*
How perfectly attuned to everything I felt that night. Cat felt the slow appre-
ciation for Tommi Ann's gift; everything she knew, and yet the woman
on the screen was Kate Auletta, ace reporter, gutsy amateur sleuth.
The arm, hand, gun rose in the foreground, and the camera drifted
back. Cat squeezed her eyes shut. Heard the shot, a shot, a dead silence and then the swell of noise, Tommi Ann's screams threading
through it, someone yelling at Ron, someone yelling "Cut!" and then
the rasp of snow, dead tape.

Something was wrong.

She called up the night Jerry Dudek had been killed. He had
promised her something. Something sensational. Collaring her as
she was fleeing to her car, urging her to let him put his secret in
someone's head, for safekeeping. And then the shot.

Shots.

The day after, Victor questioning her right here, she told him
about the shots.

Shots? More than one?

*Yes. Everything happened so fast, but when I play it back in my head, I
keep hearing two shots.*

She rewound the tape, took a deep breath and thumbed the
PLAY button. *Watch it like it's playing in your head,* she told herself.
Watch it like it's not real.

She got through it, a keen light in her dark eyes, scrutinizing it
like a filmmaker, scanning for continuity flaws.

Once more. This time with her eyes closed, playing the visuals out
in her head. Then she sighed, rewound it again, and put it in the
jacket, laid it on top of the monitor.

Detective Adane was typing rapidly, her eyes on the screen.

"Excuse me," Cat said. Adane looked up. "I was wondering, the statements taken by the police? Are they public record?"

"Did you want to see one of them?"

"If it's not too much trouble."

"There are three binders, is there a particular statement you'd like to see?"

"Let's just start at the beginning," Cat said.

CHAPTER THIRTY-FIVE

INT: TIM HARPER'S BUILDING: AFTERNOON
CALDERONE is interrogating the doorman.

DOORMAN

I don't have to talk to you.

CALDERONE

No. But when you consider the alternative,
you'll want to.

DOORMAN

I don't know anything about Donner. He came
here just that once, he and Harper's lady
had a big fight. She's beggin' him, "You
don't know what this'll do to him if it
gets out! Don't do it."

CALDERONE

What did Donner say to that?

DOORMAN

He just laughed. Just laughed like he was
gonna live forever.

***

Five men filed into the room beyond the glass. Bob Ginelli from Narcotics; Rudy Santuso from Arson; Marco Fortunati sent up one of the rookies from the Performance and Procedures class he was teaching down in the basement; Stan Rice and Wally Reid.

Victor met Carlo at the Dolphin Street entrance, ushered him and Mark through, noticed that the sharks had gotten a whiff of ink, were starting to cruise for copy.

The young Public Defender squeezed into the cubicle behind the one-way glass next to Carlo, Mark and Victor. "You don't have to say anything but a number," Victor counseled the kid, who slouched against the wall, his flat stare running swiftly down the line.

"Whaddaya think, I'm a dope? First guy's Narco, Two and Four are suits, Number Three's a rookie. It's Five."

"Hey," the PD interjected, "if the kid knows these people—"

"I never seen any of 'em. I got a nose for—"

Carlo cleared his throat. The kid shut up.

"That's the man who sold you the tape?" Victor asked. "You're positive?"

"Yeah. That was him."

Victor rapped on the glass, stepped outside. "Take Number Five upstairs," he said to the uniform outside the door, turned to Mark and Carlo. "Okay, thanks. You can go."

Stan Rice came out, adjusting his lapels. "Did he think it mighta been me?"

"Whaddaya, nuts?" Mark said.

"C'mon, kid, I thought I looked pretty skitzy in there—"

"Yeah, you're scarin' me."

"C'mon," Carlo said. Victor watched as he walked the kid down the hall. His arm rose at the kid's back, his hand settling on the boy's shoulder. Mark gave a little twitch, not quite enough to knock the hand away. It stayed. Mark didn't make another attempt to dislodge it.

Reid had the lines down cold. "I'm telling you, I loaded the dummy in the hero, so's Red could get his close-ups; I load the blanks in the other weapon right before we shoot and I hand the gun to Anderson."

"You couldn't have loaded a blank behind the head in the hero model, there's no possibility of error?"

"You ask the cop checked me out."

"He checked you out when you first handed the gun to Anderson, not before the retake." Victor did not add that the cop in question had handed in his resignation. He knew that the PD, Kenny Levine, knew it, the smug bastard. "Once more, is there any possibility that you might have accidentally shoved a blank into the—"

"No!"

"That's it, Lieutenant, unless you got something else."

"Okay, you were outside, the prop cart, the sound cart, who else was close enough to have gotten hold of the gun?"

"Who wasn't?" Wally frowned. "Red's coaching Anderson through the moves, so he was there until right before we started rolling. Bonaker finished her run-throughs, she hangs around, I'm thinkin' she's gettin' a kick outta seein' Spivak get whacked. Mrs. King came by, asked if we wanted some coffee. April, Mae and Junie Swooney. Sound guy, the peons. Sound off, it's just the cop, me and Anderson."

"'Junie?" Victor asked.

"She's got a thing for Anderson."

"How'd you get access to Spivak's apartment?"

"Hell, I didn't know it was Spivak's apartment until I was inside, I see his stuff. It was someplace to hole up a day or two until I could see which way it was blowin'."

"Access?" Victor repeated, patiently.

"When it happened, everyone's running to the vic, to Tommi Ann. Except Junie, she's, like, 'Harold's gonna pass out, somebody help me with him' and me, I'm figuring I wanna be elsewhere myself. Harold's got his own wheels, I mean he drove down from Philly,

Junie takes his car keys, we practically carry him to the car, he's freakin' out. 'How did it happen?' he goes. 'How did the gun get loaded?' he goes, which gets me thinkin' how the hell *did* it get loaded, thinkin' I am in for some serious heat. Hal goes, 'Wally, I know it wasn't you, man, but maybe you better go chill somewhere twenny-four hours—'"

"It was Anderson's idea that you take off?"

"Let's just say we were two minds with a single thought; he was just the one said it first. And I go, 'Where, man?' and he goes, 'Take off and wait by that big elephant statue downbeach.' So I split. Three hours later, Junie comes by, drives me over to Spivak's place, lets me into the apartment, tells me to stick by the phone."

"Where'd she get the key?"

"I dunno. I thought maybe she went through Spivak's stuff at the club."

"So the only people who knew you were at Spivak's were June Mathis and Harold Anderson?"

"I guess."

Victor rubbed his palm against his chin. "Let's go back to the gun," he said. "Guns. The hero model's got the head loaded in the chamber, the firing prop has a couple blanks."

"Two," Wally said, wearily. "I log out two for the shots. You check my sheet, you'll see it there. You go into the safe and do a shell count, you'll see that nothing's missing. And I loaded those two blanks into the firing prop and I didn't take any out, I didn't switch any to the other gun. And I handed the firing prop to Anderson."

"And Anderson picked it up, and then put it down. And when he set it down, someone evidently removed the blanks and chambered them in the other weapon. And there were no more than two blanks on the table, or in your possession?"

"That's right, like I said fifty times already, two. One, two. Bang, bang, just like it called for. Read the script."

"And a metal head in the—" Victor stopped. Froze. Abruptly, he turned and swung open the door, strode down the narrow corridor to the day room. "Adane, get me the Steinmetz woman on the phone."

"Yes, sir."

"Where's Mrs. Austen?"

"She left about twenty minutes ago. Her car was turned in here, and she said she had an interview."

Victor checked his watch. She might be home by now. He went into his office, began to dial Cat's number, saw the tape and the remote laid neatly on top of the monitor. He hung up the phone, went back to Adane. "Was she watching that tape?"

"I don't know, sir. She sat in your office for awhile, and then came out and asked if she could review some of the witness statements that were taken Wednesday night."

"Whose, specifically?"

"She didn't say, she just looked through the first binder, the A's through G's and then her car arrived, so she left."

Victor nodded, grabbed the last of the binders, flipped through to April's statement while he waited for the call to be put through. The square button on his phone began to flash and he picked up the receiver. "Ms. Steinmetz, when you were on the set Wednesday night, you witnessed the shooting, correct?"

"From where I was standing, why?"

"You remember how many times Anderson fired?"

"Twice. It's what's in the script."

"I have your statement here and it says, quote 'Harold fired and that'"—Victor cleared his throat—"'schmuck Spivak goes down and I'm thinking that's the second take blown, and this time Tommi Ann is gonna have to change because Wally fired the squib and the stuff got on her sweater.' Unquote. Now, Miss Steinmetz, you said 'Harold fired' and you said the take was blown because Wally discharged the squib too soon. Let me ask you again, how many shots were fired?"

"Two ... Or wait. Maybe it was just once. Yeah, I think it was just once because I thought Wally fired off the squib too soon, you know, after the first shot instead of the second."

He thanked her, hung up and dialed Cat's number again. The line was busy. He got the emergency operator and identified himself, asked her to cut into the connection. She informed him that the phone was off the hook. It was on the tape, and she had seen it, checked out the statements to back up what she knew.

Dread, anger, he had felt them last November, was feeling them now, except now they merged with a sense of absurdity, a sense that he was playing a scene in a film, a scene that he had flubbed, that would require a second take.

Cat drove slowly. Kate Auletta would be racing, and not to the safety of her home, instead arranging a confrontation with the killer, some deserted warehouse. By the water. There would be a foghorn, and even though it was not even noon, somehow she would arrange for it to take place at night.

Cat parked at the house, dragged her tote out. She saw Ellice wave from the dining room window, a moment later yank the door. "Thank God. I ran outta small talk fifteen minutes ago."

Cat checked her watch. "Sorry, I couldn't get in touch with him to cancel." She leaned down to kiss Mats.

"'Llice says we can go to the bookstore and I won't ask her to buy me anything," Mats informed his mother.

Cat buttoned him into a bulky cardigan. "I'll be right with you!" she called into the kitchen.

"Jackie just called from the med center. She said that Dianne King was out of surgery and she's stable."

"I guess every cop and every camera are around there. Better there than here." She handed over her car keys. "Take the car. That way you can speed up your trip, get back here in about twenty minutes with a 'Cat, did you forget about our lunch thing' routine."

"Are we still going to the playground?" Mats asked her.

"We're going to the playground *and* to see the fire trucks," Cat promised. "Just let Mommy listen to that man's humanistic perspective on the film industry and then we'll even get ourselves some ice cream."

"There were a few other calls, I left a sheet on the kitchen table."

Cat watched them go down the stairs, waved to Mats when he turned back to look. She hip-butted the door closed, glanced in the foyer mirror, pressed on a polite face, gave it a few seconds to set. "I'm sorry, Red, I thought you would cancel after this morning," she said, dropped her tote on a dining room chair, swung into the kitchen.

It wasn't Red, of course.

You should have read the script, she told herself.

CHAPTER THIRTY-SIX

INT: KATE'S APARTMENT: AFTERNOON
*TIM is holding KATE at gunpoint. Her phone begins
to ring.*

KATE
If I don't answer that, it'll look suspicious.

*TIM reaches for the wall phone, and with one
violent gesture, rips it out of the wall.*

The phone started to ring.

"If I don't answer that, it'll look suspicious," Cat said.

Harold grabbed the receiver, raised it and slammed it down. He slid out of the booth, Dianne's revolver in his right hand. He shoved her toward the living room, picked up the receiver on the end table phone, dropped it onto the chair.

He nodded toward the kitchen and Cat walked back there. "Maybe we'd better take this someplace else."

Cat thought of Lucy the Elephant, wondered how Harold would have rewritten this scene if April had insisted they shoot the climax there. "Harold," Cat said. "You've played cops. Don't you know that a smart hostage never goes to the secondary location?"

"I've got the gun, remember."

Cat leaned against the kitchen counter, her hands gripping the edge to keep them from shaking. "I figured it out, Harold. I figured it out when I was over at Major Crimes just now, and I left a note for them. You don't think there's going to be a unit over here in five minutes?"

Harold's blue eyes wavered, precariously. "You're a liar."

"No, you're the liar, Harold. It wasn't an accident. You shot Ron on purpose. I'm thinking it wasn't your idea, it was probably Dianne's. She wanted Tommi Ann protected from something that Ron was going to print. You didn't know what it was, but you did know that Cici was strung out. She told you if someone didn't talk Ron out of his exposé, it could kill the shoot. And who had the most to lose if they pulled the plug? You tell Red I canceled?"

Harold snorted. "Didn't have to. He knows where all the lenses are right now, and it's not here."

"When did Dianne recruit you?"

Harold said nothing.

"Doesn't matter," Cat continued. "It could have been after I let it slip that Ron was in Texas. Maybe it wasn't until that night, when he sent Dianne a note, hinting that he was going to press. She knew he was serious, and that you were desperate."

"I don't—"

"Harold, for heaven's sake, if you really say 'I don't know what you're talking about,' I'm going to make the WGA give you a refund on those dues."

"But I *don't* know what you're talking about."

"If you don't know what I'm talking about, why would you be here trying to silence me?"

He had to think about that one.

"You want to know how to script this, Harold, I'll tell you. First, you have to think plotting." Cat held up her thumb—"Character"—her index finger—"motivation"—her middle finger—"execution. After her fling with Ron, you grab Cici Bonaker on the rebound. Maybe you're really in love with her, maybe you aren't. The truth is, I think it's gonna be awhile before Cici figures out who really loves her for who she is and who's just trying to get close to Tommi Ann Butler." She paused. "With a couple exceptions maybe. Personally, I'd rather be a nobody all my life than never know who to trust."

"So, I hook up with Cici, and ..?"

"And *CopWatch*. The best part you've ever had, a showcase, an Emmy contender. And Cici tells you that Ron's gotten hold of something that's so hot it could shatter the enchantment of Tommi Ann Butler like a high note shatters glass."

"'Like a high note shatters glass.' I like that."

You told Ellice to be back in twenty minutes! Cat leaned against the counter, her hands in back of her, surreptitiously probing the drain board for a knife, a ... fork. "Cici didn't know what Ron had, not Wednesday night, all she knew was that it was dynamite and Ron was going to light the fuse. She begged him not to—a couple of the extras overheard them fighting. And begged you to talk to him. No deal. He was on an adrenaline high when I talked to him in Makeup, he told me he had to get right home and turn out some copy after the scene was shot."

Harold's blue eyes were hot, restless, but the gun in his hand was steady. "Go on."

"Dianne King'd probably been working on you before then but Ron has the effrontery—"

"The what?"

Actors. "The gall to send Dianne a note, taunting her with what he knew. So she goes to you and says something like—" Cat dredged up her store of B-movie dialogue. "'If he leaves here alive, we're done for. We've got to silence him. If you've got the guts for it, I can set up the diversion. And in return, I'll talk to Butler, kid, we'll make you a star.' And you say okay. Or maybe you don't say okay right off.

Maybe you don't seriously consider it until Gary's appearance does cause a diversion. A diversion that gives you a prime example of the kind of Butler's star-making ability. How am I doing?"

It looked to her as if he nodded, faintly; perhaps not.

"And you do it. Unload, chamber a couple rounds. I can do it in ten seconds. And still maybe you're not thinking you're seriously going to do it, still you're thinking Wally's gonna check the guns before the second take. Maybe, subconsciously that's why you put it down. So that Wally would see that the chain of possession had been broken, be sure to check it. One brief eddy of remorse." Cat shook her head. "Take notes, Harold, you may need to use this stuff in your defense."

"Keep goin'."

"He didn't check it. Has he ever, between takes? Probably not, and Dianne probably knew it. But maybe you didn't. Maybe you were just thinking, if you took it this far, it was meant to be."

"Okay, that covers character and execution. What about motive?"

"How about a part a guy like you would kill for? A sweeps-month special, starring an Oscar winner and a major recording star, when would you get that many eyes on you again? How long have you been pounding away, Harold?"

"Seventeen years." His voice choked, and the gun in his hand wavered a minute.

"You're handed an opportunity a thirty-five-year-old actor—"

"I'm thirty-four. Just thirty-four."

"Excuse me. A thirty-*four*-year-old actor isn't going to see again for some time. Ever."

Harold said the sort of nothing that said everything. *Ominous pause,* Cat thought, *close-up of Harold, and his line, "How did you figure it out?" Cut to commercial.*

"How did you figure it out?"

"*South Street Stakeout,* you played this yuppie undercover cop."

"They don't say 'yuppie' anymore."

Cat made a "May I?" gesture toward her tote bag on the dining room chair. Harold jerked the gun toward it and Cat picked it up, gave a listen. If anyone was on her porch, they were darned quiet.

She pulled out a folder. "Ron loaned me this. Some background material I could use for features on you and Cici." She strolled back to the kitchen, her eyes surveying the counter, the drain board, the drawers, leaned against it, began to read, "'Playing cops and robbers for pay is a breeze for actors like Harold Anderson—Caleb 'Cal' McKay—who took on the firearms instructors of Philadelphia's police force in his down time. Anderson's scenes have won praise from these streetwise cops who are quick to spot an amateur gun handler—' and so on, and so forth, 'the genuine article,' and dah dah dah, and 'perfect shot,' and 'only actor I've seen who handles his piece like a pro,' and you get the idea."

"I'm from Philly. Everyone knows how to use firearms. So did Wally, so does Ben, Dianne, all The Pig's bodyguards. Butler says he's always got people licensed to carry around Tommi Ann. That doesn't mean I loaded the gun or knew it was loaded. You need better proof than a magazine article."

"The footage they shot is the proof. I remember the first time Lieutenant Cardenas interviewed me after Jerry's murder. I told him there were shots. More than one. He was very insistent upon my recollection being accurate on that point. Because they assumed there had been one shot, but there had been two. In this case, when there should have been two, there was only one."

"I—"

"Don't know what I'm talking about. I know." Cat shook her head. Was Victor here yet? She set the article on the counter in back of her, left her hand resting there, near the drainboard. Keep talking, keep talking. Anyone with sense would have shot her ten minutes ago, been off the island, but Harold was a hack writer, he stuck to the stale script, talk, talk, talk.

"Bang, bang. That's what it said in the script, you were to fire twice, quickly. Red said it to you when he was running down the scene. You did it every time in rehearsal. You did it in the run-throughs. You did it when you were working with Wally. You had conditioned Tim Harper to fire twice, and that's what Tim Harper should have done. That's what everyone else thought he did, because everything else looked like the script. It was just one shot too soon."

I'll get a second shot, Cici had said.

"It didn't even sink in when April started yelling at Ron for falling too soon, shouting 'Can't you count?' And it looked so much like what was in the script that afterward everyone referred to your 'shots,' plural, when it was really *a* shot. Watch the footage. You fire once, because that's all you needed to do to get the job done, and you saw him fall and then you fell apart. Was that real, or staged, by the way?"

"You're so smart—"

"Don't tell me. 'You figure it out.' Dialogue's a breeze, Harold, I can't think why you have such a problem with it. So what happened this morning? I'm thinking you were with Dianne when I called. She told you about our meet. Was she going to come clean, try to buy me off, what? You were getting a taste of celebrity now, and you didn't want her to risk it so you either agreed to take her there or followed her. Argued some more. Her gun got into the mix and she was shot. Why didn't you wait around to do me in?"

"I had a radio call-in. Interview."

"And you were the one who replaced Cici's key?"

"Yeah. It woulda slipped my mind if you didn't ask her about it, get her panicked. Thanks, Kate."

"Cat."

"Right. Cat. Sorry, but this can't end with Kate Auletta getting rescued by Victor Calderone or disarming me with some fancy karate moves." He raised the gun level with her heart, and Cat noticed that his grip was assured, skilled.

"You'll never get away with that. This. You'll never get away with this," Cat said.

"Huh?"

Her hands were behind her back, gripping the only object in reach, the weighty handle of the skillet in the drainboard.

"It's what they say in the movies, Harold. You'll never get away with this."

"I know my line." He raised the gun. "Try me." Fired.

Cat didn't think she could outdraw him, but she had started her move while he was still raising the weapon. He would have nailed her if he hadn't gone for that last line, but they always had to go for that one last comeback. Make my day. I'll be back. Try me. Good Lord. If people were paid on the basis of originality, screenwriters would be poor as dirt.

PANG!

She whipped the cast-iron skillet in front of her breast and the bullet hit, ricocheted right back into Harold's left shoulder. Cat didn't wait for his reaction, she sprang, gave his forearm a swift uppercut with the base of the pan, whacking the weapon out of Harold's hand. It soared up in a neat arc and Cat backed up, righted the pan and caught it, dead center, just as Victor and three uniforms came through her back door.

The bullet had aligned the second indentation a few inches from the one Tom Hopper's gun had created. The revolver rested at the edge, angled like a crooked smile. Cat held out the frying pan, was feeling quite giddy, quite trite, quite Kate Auletta, said, "Have a nice day," and collapsed.

CHAPTER THIRTY-SEVEN

INT: HOSPITAL EMERGENCY ROOM: AFTERNOON
*KATE is rushed in on a gurney; CALDERONE is
hurrying beside.*

CALDERONE (to the paramedic)
Is she gonna make it?

PARAMEDIC
I don't know.

*Kate grabs him by the shirt front, yanks him
toward her.*

KATE
What do you mean, *you don't know?*

Harold figured he'd go noble, see how that played. Spivak had
been bugging Cici, Harold didn't like it. He'd been fooling around
with the guns in rehearsal, thought he'd throw a scare into Spivak. It
was an accident. That took June, Wally, Gino, Cici off the hook.
Called Ron's fax from his cell phone when he was on the deck, only
meant to throw a scare into Wally. He and Dianne were arguing, he
got hold of her gun; he only meant to throw a scare into her.

Raab sat across from Victor's desk, threw Harold's statement onto the blotter. "You wanna know what throws a scare into me? Bad TV. Guy can't plot worth squat." He yanked the rolled-up morning paper from his pocket, held it up so that Victor could read the headline: COPWATCH CURSE? SECOND SCRIPTER ARRESTED IN TWO MONTHS. "Thing is, I settle for his statement, holes and all, he cops to involuntary manslaughter. I get picky, it goes to trial and then I gotta call in the Butlers and Wally and everyone."

"What happens to Wally, and to June Mathis?"

"Reid, what can I do worse than what the industry's gonna do? Mathis is an accessory after the fact. I'm okay to deal, but she'd probably cop to it just to be doin' time concurrently with Anderson."

"And Mrs. King?"

"If I charge her with conspiracy, the press is gonna wanna know why, conspiracy doesn't jibe with Anderson's story. And then what happens? It all comes out? Right now, Anderson, all he knows is that Mrs. King told him the show was goin' down the tubes if Spivak went to press with something. I let Anderson take the rap, it all goes away." Raab sighed. "Anderson does time, Spivak's life is bein' paid for. Is it enough? Do I need to charge Mrs. King, too? Do I need to air the dirt? When is it enough? When is the debt paid? How do you take a pound of flesh without making someone bleed?"

"I don't know."

"I don't know either. But let me tell you, I'd take the guy with the space aliens over this any day of the week."

You still gotta eat.

Cat was not quite sure why Oscar night had called for a five-course meal. She listened to the commotion from too many people crammed into her small den, scrubbed the pots, ran through the week in her brain, decided she couldn't plot a week like that, sell it to television, no one would believe it. Maybe they would. She wasn't sure anymore.

She scoured the black skillet that had nearly taken her life when Tom Hopper's gun went off, had saved it when Harold Anderson's weapon discharged. She squirted a little crescent of liquid soap under the side-by-side indentations made by the bullets, two dents staring up at her like two little eyes. "Have a nice day," she murmured, heard the kids shout, "Victor's here! With *Aunt Remy!*"

They had been calling for three days, the *Inquirer, Entertainment Weekly, People, Front Cover,* even Callie O'Connor herself affecting a backyard fence intimacy. Harold Anderson pleaded to involuntary manslaughter, but what was the real story? Taking Cat's reticence for haggling, hinting at sums that got larger, larger, and Cat saw college paid for, a new car paid for, private school tuition paid for.

What was the real story?

tommi ann butler is a maJor shootyng STaR.

Dianne was helicoptered to New York; Cici, who had not left her side, went with her. Tommi Ann and Ben flew to LA.

"Mom! MOM! You're missing it!"

Cat rinsed the skillet, set it in the drainboard, dried her hands.

Victor came in, gave her a quick kiss. "Can't watch it?"

"Sometimes I feel like I can do anything. That nothing will shock me anymore." She looked up at him. "April called me from LA this morning, asked if I wanted to field a couple treatments she'd get them to the 'right eyes.' And you know what the worst of it is? After everything that's happened, as sick as I am of all of this, as stupid and shallow as most of these TV people turned out to be, I still felt this little thrill, you know? This little Hollywood thrill, like it was worth considering, like the glamour meant something. Like it would make me real."

Enough distance, and anything was beautiful. She hadn't meant to go, but she couldn't resist, had dressed and slipped out right before midnight, drove to Atlantic City. She'd parked on Victor's street, walked the several blocks to Belmont, followed the glow that rose above the parking lot. She stood in a huddle, watched like a spectator

as Red Melendez strode authoritatively through the background players to whoever was lying on the ground in a pool of Karo syrup and
red food coloring. She couldn't hear the lines, only saw, from the distance, in the dark, that it did look real, that Red looked like a real
detective surveying a real crime scene, that the eyes of the crowd
glowed like the eyes of predators, minds glazed with the craving to
make it real. And it had been real, for that moment between sound off
and cut; all of reality could be packed into a moment, like the kiss
that Chris had given her before he got into his car and had driven
away for good, like Kevin's grasp the moment before it disengaged
and he fell to his death in the dark.

"*Mom*! You're missing *everything*!"

Cat smiled, led Victor into the den. They wedged themselves into
a corner on the floor. Mats crawled in her lap.

"There's Biggs!" Carlo said. "That's not— Is that Gino Forschetti
with him, the sonofabitch?"

"He got a security gig with Biggs and his outfit," Marco said.
"Pay's five times what he made on the force."

"How'd he hook up with that, the sonofabitch?"

Jennie, seated on the sofa behind him, gave him a swat on the
back of his head. Mark laughed.

Cat looked up at Victor, who was watching the screen, his expression unreadable.

You gotta pass it on. That's what Tommi Ann always says.

"Shhhhh! He's gonna say something."

Biggs hunkered up to the mike, towering over the *Entertainment
Tonight* emcee. "Like to say hi back there to Jersey," he grinned into
the camera, raised one fist, his thumb, index finger, pinkie extended.
"Yo, Mama Jen!"

"Hey," Carlo demanded. "*Pirch' fari cornu?*"

"For heaven's sake, Carlo, he's not giving Mama the horns, it
means 'I love you' in sign language."

"You're kiddin'."

"Translation?" Victor murmured in her ear.

"I'll explain later."

"Oh, oh, oh!" Remy clapped her hands. "*Mira!* Look!"

Tommi Ann Butler floated along the red carpet, Butler at her side. Her russet hair was swept away from her neck in a French twist, revealing the necklace of silver filigree and aquamarine.

The hostess for *All About Oscar* snagged her, oohed over Tommi Ann's gown. "It's a CapriOH!," Tommi Ann said, graciously, her slender fingers brushing the necklace. "And the jewelry is by a talented new designer, Remy Cardenas."

Remy shrieked. "She said my name! She said my name on national television!" Jane and Remy clasped hands, wriggled like giddy children. Remy got to her feet. "Can I use your phone, I gotta call my mother!"

Cat waved her off, watched Tommi Ann float to the next mike. Too beautiful to be real. *Reality is what you make it.*

She won. There was never any question. The camera closed on the two of them, Butler took her face in his hands and kissed her lips lightly. She walked up to the microphone and waited for the cheering to settle, blew a brief kiss in the direction of her husband.

"Of course I acknowledge the kindness of everyone who saw something in this performance worth honoring, but I have to particularly thank the people who were there when there were no honors. Ben. And two other people who wouldn't want me to name them, but who know that I'm thinking of them now. And I thank David Wheeler for his wonderful book—"

"That's a novelty," Freddy muttered.

"—the director, Alice Guy. And I want to remind Cat that the message of *Redemption* is that whatever you have to do to survive, the people who love you will understand."

If you need my story to get by on, it's yours. If it's what you have to do to pay the bills, I'll understand.

Cat realized she wasn't going to write a Tommi Ann exposé, that she had never really considered it.

"How'd you think Forschetti got a gig like that?" Danny Furina asked. "I bet he's gonna pull in two, three grand a week. Did I tell you? Before she leaves for the airport, she thanks us all for our service, she says she wants to especially thank me and gives me one."

"One what?" Freddy asked.

Danny puckered his lips, made a loud kissing sound. "Frenched me. God, that woman can kiss! Hey!" he insisted. "It's true. Word of honor. It's *true*," he insisted to Cat. "What's so damn funny?"

Tuesday morning, Victor was glancing over the Missing Persons reports Long had left on his desk when he heard the quiet. He remembered April Steinmetz's description, "when the sound gets sucked up and you're Hoovered over to Oz," and looked up. Through the glass, he saw Tommi Ann Butler standing in the day room. He rose, stepped outside; the detectives were stunned. Speechless.

"It's not very flattering to imply that I'm one of the Gorgons," she said gently, and Adane—the only one who got the reference—smiled.

"Could I speak to you for a minute, Lieutenant?"

Victor nodded, invited her into his office. He closed the door, shut the blinds in the window that separated his quarters from the day room. "Please sit down, Mrs. Butler."

Tommi Ann sat. She was wearing a dark blue shirtwaist dress, canvas espadrilles, her hair was loose. She looked like nobody else on earth. "Mr. Raab says that the only charges are going to be against Harold, that even the charges against Wally and June probably won't mean jail time."

Victor nodded. "How is Miss Bonaker?"

"Cici's a pretty strong girl. I think none of us gave her the credit she deserves in that area."

"And Mrs. King?"

"She's going to recover. Mr. Raab said he's not going to charge her."

"Raab knows the game. When it's winnable and when you cut your losses." Victor leaned back in his chair. "Why are you here, Mrs. Butler?"

"Because there's one more question you wanted to ask me, Lieutenant."

"I know the answer."

A smile flitted across her features like a ghost from her past. "Do you?"

Victor nodded.

"By the time I was fifteen, I had pretty much reached the end of my rope. My mother had been the one frail barrier between me and my father's violence. Her death removed the veil that mitigated what I was. Didn't Sherlock Holmes say that human nature was a strange mixture?"

Victor nodded.

"I was an alien in my own flesh. I didn't recognize what I saw in the mirror, when I could stand to look. What my father thought—the obvious conclusion—disgusted him. I became a genius of disguise, masking every impulse I had, every sensation, playing the part as well as I could. How did I come to be the actress that I am? I've never been anything else."

"Except with Dianne King."

"Dianne was an outcast, too. Her sister's husband wanted to turn her out. On the streets. You know what I mean."

"Yes."

Tommi Ann laughed. "The flaw in the scheme was that there weren't all that many streets in Imogene. I think when I heard her sing once, that was when I noticed her. She has the most beautiful voice in the world. And no one to hear it. I heard it. We found each other. She told me everything she dreamed of, education, style, independence, and I didn't laugh, and I told her everything I was, and she wasn't disgusted. What happened—when she became pregnant? It was loneliness, that's all. An act of desperate loneliness and a terrible attempt, on my part, to be what I knew I was not. We married. She still wears the ring. I never thought that it was going to be possible for me to make myself whole, and Dianne and I cared for one another. But Dianne did believe. She was willing to exchange Cici for the chance. I never expected to be able to initiate treatment, to pass the psychological tests, but it wasn't hard to figure out what they wanted to hear and deliver it. It's all I ever did with most of the world, give them what they believe they want."

"And *Illyria?*"

"Started out as a lark. And then Ben appeared on my doorstep. And he loved me. What I had been, what I was, what I would become, loved me completely and without reservation. And the rest," she smiled, "is mystery."

"What happened to your father?"

The face settled into a mask. She didn't speak for a minute or two. "Even if I had tried to explain what I was to him, he would never have understood. He wanted a son and got a freak, or so he regarded me. I don't do nude scenes, Lieutenant, and it's not vanity. It's because there are still scars." She sighed. "When we came back from Mexico, he gave the Turners money to send Dianne away. I threatened to run away with her. He became enraged. He had abused me in every way imaginable, because of course, some abuses are unimaginable between parents and children. Father and son. And then he did the unimaginable." She paused. "Some outrages are better left in the past."

Is there anything that's unimaginable to an actress? "Who killed him, you or Dianne?"

"I did."

Dianne, he thought. Both perhaps. Did it matter now?

"Tell me something, Lieutenant. Those two boys who were about your age, the boys who killed your father. Do you still hate them?"

"I don't even think about them."

"Your mother?"

"My mother was devastated, and that lasted a long time. She was only thirty-three. She didn't deserve that." The corner of the mustache twitched. "Now she says rosaries for the salvation of their souls."

"Ask her to say one for mine."

At first she thought the knocking was the sound of Freddy and Ellice putting up drapery rods in the apartment's bedroom. She looked past the stove, down the little corridor to the back door, saw Ben Butler's face looking through the glass. She lifted Mats down from the counter, where they had been rolling cookie dough, hurried to the door.

"I should've called, Mrs. Austen."

"I heard you were arranging for Dianne to be moved." She waved him into the kitchen. "I'm happy for Tommi Ann. Is she here?"

"No, she wanted to have a talk with the Lieutenant."

"Sit down." Cat poured coffee into white porcelain mugs, sat across from him.

Butler looked around. "Gary said you had a nice place. Couldn't stop talking about it." He shook his head. "He's a hell of a nice kid. I don't think he gets it, that he was used as a blind to set up Spivak."

"I won't tell him. What he did for Gino, that was really nice."

"Yeah, well Gary's got this expression. 'Nice don't cost you nothin'.'" Butler laughed.

"What's going to happen with the show?"

"I don't know. I'm holding the network to the series, forty weeks. The deal wasn't contingent on *CopWatch*."

"And Cici?"

"Cici's gonna come out of this all right. It was bad for her when the Bonakers died, they were fine folks, and I guess that's what made her fodder for someone like Spivak. Tommi Ann, well, she wanted to tell Cici the truth, she woulda come to it, but she didn't want to make it seem like she was violating the promise she made to the Bonakers, not to jump their claim, you know."

"But it must have broken Dianne's heart to give her up."

"I b'lieve it did. Tommi Ann always promised she'd figure out some way to get them back together."

Cat nodded. "And the sixty thousand dollars was ..."

"You know what's involved?"

Cat shook her head.

"Presurgical work can take awhile, even after you pass the psychological tests, get hooked into the system. Just about impossible if the patient is a minor. Thing is, that's when you get the best results. Physically speaking."

Cat swallowed. "I understand." She paused. "Is that when you met her, when she was recovering?"

"You read her bio?"

Cat nodded. "How much of it is the truth?"

Butler snorted. "Truth. Reality's what we make it. That was the motto of the guy I worked for. His name doesn't matter, he was the president of Aspira Talent. He'd been gettin' threatening phone calls, letters. I had a PI license, working for a security firm, personal protection and threat assessment. I got hired on as this guy's bodyguard. Every day, go to work, check his mail, arrange coverage for his schedule. Spent a lot of time inside his agency." Butler shrugged. "For me, the transition was a natural. What I did was evaluate communication, the type of person who wrote it, was he serious, what would he do in any given situation, how would he respond, how should we respond, anticipating his move so we could map out our strategy. You watch enough stalkers, you know how they think, what they want, what they go in for, how to get their attention." He chuckled. "What are fans, but a bunch of stalkers? The mistake a lot of talent managers make is to give them what they say they want. Wrong. The public doesn't know what it wants from one minute to the next. You create something and then you tell them why they can't have it. Or can have only as much as you give 'em."

Butler took a sip of his coffee. "Anyway, week after week of twenty-four seven, we nail the creep. All of a sudden, I've got my first night off and I'm trolling around, and I walk into some art theatre, someone told me they saw this incredible young gal in this movie *Illyria*, I figure what the hell. I didn't like movie folks much, but I liked movies. What the hell ..." he repeated, softly, still surprised at the effect that impulse had had on his life. "Anyway, most of the time I spent at Aspira, I spent hanging around, watching, soaking up the way it worked. I knew I could work it better. To start me off, I needed to get the movie and get the girl. Gettin' the movie was easy. Eric Obermeyer owned the film, the distribution rights. I bought *Illyria*, pulled all the prints from the exhibitors—hell, there were only a handful—got a buzz goin'. 'You hear about *Illyria*,' 'What's with this movie *Illyria*?'" He shook his head, grinning. "Suckers."

"And then you had to find the girl."

Butler's eyes were dark, direct. "And then I had to find the girl. Wasn't easy, she was ..." he sighed. "She was pretty washed-out, thin, not eating right, darned near the bottom. But up here—" he tapped his forehead, "I still had that picture in my mind, that angel in *Illyria*, and I knew it was only a matter of time before they saw it too, came for her. And I knew I was the one who could give some shape to that shadow on the screen, so that everyone who looked at her would have this—this notion of perfection in their minds that crystallized every time they saw Tommi Ann. If they got to her, she'd just be a fluke, or a freak. I could make her a goddess. I promised to look after her, look after Dianne, and she agreed to marry me."

"She was living with Mrs. King?"

"Yes."

"And when was their marriage dissolved?"

"It never was. Of course, they were minors when they ran off to Mexico, it wasn't legal, but they went through the ceremony. I didn't care about anything. I was in love."

"With the girl on the screen."

"The girl in the flesh, what flesh she had on her bones, had the most beautiful spirit I ever saw in a human being. You know what it's like to be in love so bad that nothing else matters? Hell, it happened to me, I hadda throw out everything I thought I knew about myself and start fresh."

"And she fell in love with you?"

"She agreed to marry me. I thought it was just because I was strong enough for all of us, and she was grateful. I put *Illyria* back into distribution and got a six-picture deal for Eric Obermeyer right off."

"The first of all those debts you repaid for Tommi Ann."

"Gloria, Davey Wheeler, Gary, they deserved it."

"We don't always get what we deserve," Cat told him.

"Tommi Ann, Dianne, they didn't get what they deserved. Life has nothing to do with what we deserve or don't deserve. It's what we make outta what's handed to us."

"And you went to the Caribbean to get married and then went abroad to start making her a goddess?"

His mouth twisted in an odd smile. "You could put it like that."

"And that's not true?"

"It's half of the truth. The other half was that Tommi Ann had been putting herself through the preparation, that's what took up the couple years she was in the city, that's what took up the money. I decided it would be better if she had her surgery abroad, and then she had to recuperate."

"But I don't understand," Cat said. "I thought ... you mean when she made *Illyria* ..?"

Butler nodded.

"And when you married her she was still ..?"

"Sometimes," Butler sighed. "You dream of seeing your soul in someone else, and then you find them and it's not what you expected to find, but damned if it isn't your soul you're lookin' at all the same, and aren't you the most surprised person on God's green earth."

That evening was mild. After dinner, Cat and Victor took Mats onto the Boardwalk, strolled behind him as he pedaled a wobbling course down the planks. "Ben Butler came to see me today." *How much should she tell him?*

Victor's gaze was fixed on Mats. "Yes, I know. Mrs. Butler dropped in on me." He was thinking of Sontag, what he had done to his boy; was there anything that should be beyond the realm of imagination? Was there some zone of decency that should not be bridged, could not be bridged if one was to survive? He was not afraid that Cat would use the information, if he told her; he knew that she had tucked Tommi Ann's secret into some recess of her mind, where the other horrible things kept company. But some horrors ought not to be shared.

"What did Butler have to say?"

Cat had played the scene out in her mind all afternoon, Butler climbing those oppressive flights, knocking on the door, that first look at the shadow that his spirit had recognized, his mind had made real. Married what she had not yet become. What must it be like to love like that?

And Cat knew she was not going to tell Victor, not today, that she was not going to kill what was left of Tommi Ann's image. "Nothing," she replied. "Just thanks, you know. Nothing important. What about Tommi Ann?"

Victor looked at the ocean, the low rollers rising and falling like the quiet respiration of a buried secret. He knew he wasn't going to tell her, not today.